BLOSSOMING PATH

BOOK THREE

BLOSSOMING PATH

BOOK THREE

Carlos Calma

Podium

Copyright © 2025 by Carlos Calma

Cover design by Kongsi

ISBN: 978-1-0394-8858-8

Published in 2025 by Podium Publishing
www.podiumentertainment.com

Podium

BLOSSOMING PATH

BOOK THREE

CHAPTER ONE

The Agony of Almost

I blinked, the familiar lighting of my room at the Jade Harmony Inn slowly coming into focus. The warm golden glow from the lantern on the nightstand cast gentle shadows across the walls.

For a moment, I wondered if it had all been a dream. If the intense battle, the desperate struggle, and the crushing loss were just figments of my imagination, conjured by my anxieties.

A fleeting hope stirred within me. Maybe I hadn't lost. Maybe the final round was a hallucination, a product of my restless mind. I sat up slowly, the bed creaking beneath me. But as I moved, a sharp pain flared in my chest, drawing a wince from my lips.

I glanced down, pulling aside the loose fabric of my robe. There it was—bruising on my sternum, dark and harsh against my skin. The exact spot where Jingyu Lian's needle had struck me. Reality hit with a cold, unyielding certainty.

It was real. The final round had happened, and I lost.

I moved to sit up, each muscle protesting with a dull ache. The bruising on my chest sent a fresh wave of nausea through me. It wasn't just the physical pain; it was the sting of failure, the bitter taste of *what if.*

What if I had reacted faster?

What if I had anticipated her last move?

What if I had simply been better?

The memories of the battle swirled in my mind, each detail etched with painful clarity: the searing heat of the fire zone, the acrid scent of the paralyzing poison, the chilling finality of Jingyu Lian's gaze, tinged with guilt. I could still feel the poison's tendrils coursing through my veins, leaving a trail of weakness and regret in their wake.

A heavy sigh escaped my lips, the sound echoing in the quiet room. I had come so far, fought so hard, only to be cut down in the final moments.

The door creaked open, and Feng Wu's concerned face appeared. His eyes immediately fell on me, and his brow furrowed with worry. He stepped inside, the soft *click* of the door closing behind him the only sound.

"Kai," he began with gentle concern as he approached the bedside. He reached out, hesitating for a moment before resting a comforting hand on my shoulder. "How are you feeling?"

I mustered a lopsided grin, the effort tugging at the corners of my mouth like a rusty hinge. "Eh, could be worse," I quipped with false cheeriness. "At least I didn't get flattened by a runaway pill furnace like Tian Zhu."

Feng Wu's lips quirked into a half smile, but his eyes remained troubled. "That's one way to look at it," he acknowledged. He paused, studying my face intently. "But honestly, Kai, how are you *really* holding up?"

I shrugged, the movement sending pain through my bruised chest. My words caught in my throat, and I had to clear it before I could speak. "Oh, you know, just contemplating a career change," I said, the joke tasting bitter on my tongue. "Maybe a professional pillow tester? I've had plenty of practice in the last few hours."

His expression softened, the hint of amusement replaced by empathy. "Kai—"

"It's fine, Feng Wu," I interrupted, forcing a laugh that sounded more like a choked sob. "I'm just kidding. It's just a competition, right? No big deal."

I couldn't fool him. He knew me too well.

But he didn't say anything, just nodded slowly, his eyes filled with understanding. "I know it's hard. You gave it everything you had. Sometimes that's all we can do."

As he spoke, he gently set down Tianyi, who fluttered her blue wings and settled on the edge of the bed, sending waves of concern through our link. From his sleeve, Windy slithered out, the pure-white serpent curling around Feng Wu's arm before making his way toward me.

"Spend some time with them," Feng Wu urged. "They've been worried about you too."

Silence hung between us for a moment, heavy and oppressive. I could see the sympathy in Feng Wu's eyes, his desire to say something that would make it all better.

But there were no words that could erase the sting of defeat.

"I'll give you some space to work it out," he said finally. "Take the time you need. Process this. You'll come back stronger, I know it."

"Thank you."

He gave me a small encouraging smile before turning to leave. As the door closed behind him, the room fell into silence once more. I leaned back into the pillows, staring at the ceiling, my mind a tumult of thoughts and emotions.

Tianyi nuzzled my cheek, and Windy tightened his coil slightly, as if to offer comfort. I had lost. There was no denying that. But how I chose to move forward from this moment would define me more than the defeat itself.

I took a deep breath, trying to shift my focus away from the sting of loss. "Well," I murmured, forcing a smile, "looks like we have some free time. Maybe it's a good thing. I can finally catch up on sleep. Maybe even read a book that isn't about alchemy or combat for once."

The two Spirit Beasts looked at me, listening.

"Yeah, maybe losing isn't so bad. I mean, I don't have to deal with the pressure of being the Grand Alchemy Gauntlet Champion. No more expectations, no more eyes watching my every move."

I chuckled, but it was a brittle sound that cracked in the quiet. "I can just . . . relax. Take it easy for a while. Go back to the village and expand the garden. I'm able to build that greenhouse now."

But as I spoke, my words started to blur together, my forced positivity crumbling under the weight of reality. My vision wavered, and I blinked rapidly, trying to clear my sudden haze. A single tear slipped down my cheek, followed by another, and then more, until they were streaming freely.

I brushed them with the back of my hand, frustration bubbling up. "Dammit," I whispered, my voice breaking. "I was so close. So damn close."

The pain in my chest wasn't just from the bruising anymore. It was deeper, a hollow ache that gnawed at my heart. The image of Jingyu Lian standing victorious and the cheers of the crowd ringing in my ears played over and over in my mind.

I tried to tell myself it was just a setback, that I'd come back stronger, like Feng Wu had said. But the rationalizations felt empty, mere echoes in the vast chasm of my disappointment. The fight, the effort, the dreams—all felt shattered, scattered like ashes in the wind.

For the first time in a long while, I allowed myself to simply feel. To mourn the loss, to acknowledge the pain. The path to healing, I knew, would be long and arduous. But it was a path I had to walk one step at a time.

"I'll get through this. Somehow. But right now . . . it just hurts."

In that moment, I allowed the grief to wash over me, knowing that only by facing it head-on could I ever hope to overcome it.

I stared dumbly at the pile of gifts and letters on my table. It was a mountain of silk, parchment, and gleaming metal.

"This . . . It's all for me?"

Feng Wu chuckled. "There's been a veritable flood since the final round, Kai. I've spent most of my time fending off well-wishers and merchants eager to shower you with their wares." He gestured at the teetering stacks. "I barely managed to keep them from turning our room into a bazaar."

I reached for one of the letters, my fingers trembling slightly. The envelope was made of fine parchment. With a careful hand, I broke the seal and unfolded the letter inside.

"'Dear Kai Liu,'" I read aloud. "'Congratulations on your remarkable performance in the Grand Alchemy Gauntlet. We are in awe of your skills and potential. Enclosed is a gift—a robe crafted from the finest silks. We hope you will keep us in mind for your future clothing needs. With admiration, the Golden Thread Textile Company.'"

I set the letter down and unfolded the robe. It was beautiful, made of rich, deep blue silk that shimmered in the light. The embroidery was intricate, depicting scenes of nature in silver and gold thread. I ran my fingers over the fabric, feeling the quality and craftsmanship.

"Why?" I asked, looking up at Feng Wu. "Why would they send me something like this? I lost!"

Feng Wu smiled, a knowing look in his eyes. "You've made quite an impression, Kai. Companies, sects, clans, they all see your potential, and know you'll likely be a significant figure in the years to come. These gifts and favors are investments in your future."

I nodded slowly, absorbing his words. It made sense in a way. My performance in the Gauntlet had put me on the map, so to speak. These companies were betting on my future success.

I opened more letters, each one offering congratulations and gifts. There were high-grade herbs from a renowned apothecary, a set of alchemical tools from a prominent merchant family, and even a small box of precious stones from a mining consortium. Each gift came with a letter expressing admiration and extending offers of future collaboration.

As I sorted through the gifts and letters, one particular envelope caught my eye. It was sealed with blue wax in the shape of a crescent moon. My heart sank. I carefully broke the seal and unfolded the letter inside.

"'Dear Kai Liu,'" I read quietly, the words dripping with subtle venom. "'Congratulations on your impressive performance in the Grand Alchemy Gauntlet. Despite your *unfortunate* defeat, your skills and determination were truly remarkable. It is with great admiration that I present to you a token of my respect. May it serve you well in your future endeavors.'"

I stared at the small Beast Core nestled in the envelope. My hands trembled with confusion and shock as I read the signature at the bottom.

"'All the best . . . Sect Leader Jun of the Silent Moon Sect'?"

Feng Wu's expression darkened as he took the letter from my hands and scanned it. "That man is playing mind games," he muttered.

I stared at the letter, trying to make sense of it. "Sect Leader? How is he calling himself a sect leader now?"

He shook his head, a deep frown etched on his face. "I don't know all the details, but he interrupted the announcement of Jingyu Lian's victory, declaring himself the new Sect Leader of the Silent Moon Sect. He introduced four new elders—powerful figures who we've never seen or heard of before. It's likely they're from the mainland."

The mainland? But . . . hadn't the route there been lost decades ago?

A knot of unease tightened in my stomach. "What does this mean for us, Feng Wu?"

The second-class disciple sighed, the worry lines on his face deepening. "I'm not sure, Kai. It's unsettling, to say the least. I've already sent a letter back to the sect informing them of the news, but I'll likely have to head back soon to relay the information myself."

He looked at me, his expression softening. "Time is of essence. Before we leave, do you have any loose ends to tie up? Anyone you'd like to say farewell to?"

I took a deep breath, my mind racing through the possibilities. There were people I needed to see, gifts to buy, and farewells to make. But the thought of facing everyone, especially after my defeat, was daunting.

But I couldn't lounge about here forever.

"Yeah," I finally said, my voice steadying. "I'll spend today doing what I need to do."

Feng Wu nodded. "Take your time, Kai. I'll prepare for our departure in the meantime."

Determined, I gathered my resolve and left the inn with Tianyi perched on my shoulder and Windy coiled around my arm. The bustling streets of the city greeted me, a stark contrast to the quiet solitude of my room.

As I stepped into the crowded streets, whispers and stares followed me like shadows. People recognized me with curiosity and admiration. It was an odd feeling, being acknowledged and even revered by strangers. But beneath their gazes, I felt a creeping sense of embarrassment. I had lost the Gauntlet. How could I face them with pride?

Swallowing my nerves, I walked quickly to the market, my heart pounding with each step. The lively atmosphere was a welcome distraction, with vendors shouting out their wares and children laughing as they played. I needed to focus on something other than my turmoil.

My first stop was the Azure Silk Trading Company. The building stood tall and imposing. I stepped inside, the cool air and rich aroma of exotic goods enveloping me.

CHAPTER TWO

From Ashes to Azure Silk

Decadent desserts, delicate pastries, and fragrant teas adorned every inch of the table before me. A servant carefully placed a cup of fruit wine and roasted quail skewers before me.

Tianyi fluttered her blue wings softly as she perched on the cup, while Windy slithered out of my sleeve and began his feast on the roasted quails.

I cleared my throat and addressed the man seated across from me. "Thank you for taking the time to meet with me, Patriarch Wei Yong. Your hospitality is truly generous."

The man inclined his head slightly, a small smile playing at the corners of his mouth. His black hair, streaked with silver, flowed down to his shoulders, and a long, well-groomed beard framed his stern yet dignified face. He exuded an aura of dependability, every bit the leader of the Azure Silk Trading Company. My two companions didn't seem to care, however, as they gleefully dug into the lavish meal before them.

"It is my pleasure, Kai Liu," he replied, his voice deep and measured. The man's gaze lingered over Tianyi and Windy for a moment. "Your performance in the Gauntlet was nothing short of extraordinary. You have earned this meeting and more. To command two Spirit Beasts is a rare blessing, a sign of heaven's favor."

I nodded, still getting acclimated to the opulence I was surrounded by. "They have been invaluable partners in my journey. I must also thank Lady Xiao Yun for giving me this opportunity. Without her initial support, I wouldn't be here today."

Wei Yong's eyes twinkled with a hint of pride. "My daughter has a keen eye for talent. She spoke highly of you even before the Gauntlet. But your near victory was . . . *unexpected*, to say the least."

In my mind, I couldn't help but marvel at how quickly my fortunes had changed. Lady Xiao Yun probably thought I'd make it one or two rounds into the Gauntlet, but certainly not a hair's breadth from winning it all. It was no wonder the patriarch himself was now involved; I was no longer just a promising alchemist—I was a high-profile one with potential for years to come.

"I appreciate her belief in me. I hope to continue proving myself worthy of that trust."

"Precisely why we're here today," Wei Yong said, his tone shifting to a more businesslike manner. With a subtle gesture, two attendants stepped forward, unrolling a scroll upon the table. "We are interested in extending our contract with you, Kai Liu. In light of your recent achievements, we propose a revised agreement with significantly improved terms."

I leaned forward, feigning interest while my mind raced. "Improved terms, you say? I'm intrigued. But before we delve into specifics, I'd like to discuss the potential value of my new concoctions. I believe they could significantly enhance your company's offerings."

The Celestial Mind Illuminating Elixir and Ambrosia of Radiant Dawn were potent products, and I couldn't let those recipes sit around collecting dust when there was gold to be made!

Wei Yong's eyes narrowed slightly, a flicker of calculation passing over his face. "Your new concoctions, you say? We are always open to innovation, but their value must be demonstrated."

"Of course," I replied smoothly, reaching for a skewer and taking a bite of the succulent quail. Mmm, glazed with honey and just a hint of fire spice. "But I believe a demonstration would be premature. After all, their true worth lies in their exclusivity."

A tense silence hung in the air as we assessed each other, a subtle battle of wills playing out beneath the veneer of pleasantries. These Azure Silk folks are used to getting what they want. I need to play this carefully, make them sweat a little. Being the sole distributor of my products was an undeniable advantage for the Azure Silk Trading Company, and I needed to ensure they recognized the opportunity.

"Exclusivity has its price, Kai Liu. We are willing to negotiate."

"Speaking of exclusivity," I added casually, "I've recently established a close relationship with Bai Hua, the heir to Summer Sun Cosmetics. He's expressed great interest in my work and has even suggested a potential collaboration."

Hopefully Bai didn't mind me dropping his name in negotiations. Though, knowing him, he'd probably be flattered.

Wei Yong's eyebrows rose slightly, his composure briefly faltering.

Hah, got him! I thought, suppressing a smirk.

He recovered quickly, however, his smile returning, though a touch strained. "Summer Sun Cosmetics is a respected establishment. Their interest in you is a testament to your talent."

"Indeed," I replied, my tone light yet pointed. "But I value loyalty and long-term partnerships. The Azure Silk Trading Company has been my first supporter, and I am inclined to honor that."

He nodded thoughtfully, a hint of respect in his eyes. "Loyalty is a valuable commodity, Kai Liu. And one we are willing to reward."

Things went smoothly after that. It looked like mentioning Bai Hua really lit a fire under them. Clearly eager to prevent me from considering other offers, he agreed to even more favorable terms. By the end of our discussion, I had secured a steady supply of high-quality ingredients, ensuring I wouldn't need to worry about growing my own to fulfill the contract.

Not bad. Not bad at all.

Additionally, I managed to negotiate an advance on my first shipment, providing me with the resources to start production immediately.

With the ink barely dry on my lucrative new contract, I found myself at my next destination: Summer Sun Cosmetics.

The sun shone brightly over the city as I approached the grand entrance of Bai Hua's flagship store. The elegant building was adorned with vibrant banners displaying their latest products. Inside, the scent of exotic flowers and essential oils wafted through the air, creating an atmosphere of luxury and refinement. I could see two familiar figures talking animatedly from afar.

"Tao Ren! Bai Hua!"

Ever the gracious host, Bai Hua greeted me with a flourish. "Kai, my dear friend! It's a pleasure to see you again."

He then noticed Windy slithering around my arm, his eyes lighting up. "Ah! I finally get to see *you* in all your glory," he said with a flourish, bowing slightly to the serpent. "Your scales are even more magnificent than I imagined. What a treat to have you all grace this humble establishment!"

Windy flicked his tongue out in what seemed like a pleased gesture, while Tianyi fluttered her wings excitedly. My friends gathered closely to admire them. It had taken so long for them to meet, despite me having talked their ears off about them whenever we shared drinks.

Tao Ren, standing beside him in his usual soot-stained attire, let out a hearty laugh. "Humble? This place is anything but humble, Bai Hua. I'm just here for the free samples. A blacksmith's got no need for such frivolities."

The perfumer chuckled, playfully swatting the larger man's arm. "Nonsense! Even a master of metal deserves a touch of luxury. Besides, I'll give you both generous discounts."

I raised a hand and smiled. "A discount? How generous of you, Bai Hua," I drawled, pulling out a stack of money slips bearing the prestigious Azure Silk Trading Company seal. "But fear not, my friend, for this young master's coffers overflow with riches. A mere discount would be an insult to my wealth!"

Tao Ren's eyes widened as he let out a low whistle. "Looks like someone's been busy," he remarked, eyeing the stack of money slips with a mix of awe and amusement.

"Very well, Kai," Bai Hua said, his smile genuine. "If you insist. But allow me to offer you our most exclusive line of products."

He gestured to a display of shimmering bottles and jars. I couldn't help but feel a surge of pride. I had come a long way from the humble village herbalist, and my success in the Gauntlet had opened doors I had never dreamed of.

As we made our way through the shelves overflowing with luxurious cosmetics and skin-care products, we chatted about our future plans. Tao Ren spoke animatedly about his recently acquired permit to open a smithing shop in Crescent Bay City, his eyes alight with excitement as he described his plans for the forge and the weapons he would create.

"I've always dreamed of having my own shop," he said, brimming with enthusiasm. "This city is the perfect place to start."

Bai Hua nodded in agreement, subtly applying perfume around his neck and wrists. "And Summer Sun Cosmetics is expanding as well. It's a lot of work, but I'm excited for what's to come."

I listened, nodding along, but my thoughts drifted to the recent negotiations. "I've secured a new contract with the Azure Silk Trading Company, and I'll be expanding my shop back home to include a greenhouse. It's going to be an expensive project, but one I'll be able to afford now."

Tao Ren clapped me on the back. "That's fantastic news, Kai! You've earned it."

As we continued our shopping spree, I couldn't help but think about a certain librarian. "Where is Zhi Ruo?"

"Last I heard, he's in negotiations to join Whispering Wind Sect's Alchemy Pavilion. He's likely discussing the terms right now," Bai Hua explained.

A pang of sadness hit me. "I doubt I'll catch him before I leave the city. Still, I'm sure our paths will cross again."

After tallying up my purchases, I handed over a money slip from the Azure Silk Trading Company, its value far exceeding the total cost. The perfumer accepted it with a flourish, presenting me with a small bag of gold as change.

"Is that everything, then?" His voice was laced with amusement as he pointed at the several boxes of luxurious goods. I placed them in the storage ring, alongside my pill furnace.

I glanced at the ring, a silent thank-you to Guowei Wang for the invaluable gift. "One last stop," I replied and smiled. "But thank you both for the excellent company and your—ahem—*generous* discounts."

With warm farewells and promises of future revelry exchanged, I made my way toward the towering edifice of the Alchemy Association.

Inside, the atmosphere was as I remembered—serious and focused, with alchemists of various ranks going about their business. I made my way to the front desk, where a young clerk looked up, her eyes widening slightly as they took in the serpent coiled around my arm and the butterfly fluttering above my head.

"Good day," I greeted her, holding out the talisman Guowei Wang had given me. "I'm here to see the vault-keeper."

Her surprise quickly turned to deference. "Of course. Please follow me."

She led me through a labyrinth of dimly lit corridors, the air growing cooler with each step. We passed several guarded doors, the stoic cultivators posted outside each one giving me curious glances. Finally, we reached a familiar ornate door, guarded by the person I wanted to see.

Guowei Wang stood in the doorway, his face breaking into a warm smile as he recognized me. "Kai Liu!" he exclaimed in genuine delight. "It's good to see you again. Tell me, did you win the Gauntlet?"

I shook my head, my disappointment returning. "No, I didn't. But I came here to say goodbye before I return home and to thank you for all your help." I touched the storage ring on my finger, a gesture of gratitude for his invaluable gift.

Guowei Wang waved away my thanks with amusement. "Think nothing of it, young friend. A mere trinket for a rising star. But tell me"—he leaned in, his curiosity piqued—"what are these two delightful creatures accompanying you?"

As if on cue, Tianyi flitted down from my shoulder, executing a graceful loop around the vault before landing on Guowei Wang's outstretched hand. Windy, not to be outdone, uncoiled from my arm and slithered onto the old man's desk, his iridescent scales shimmering in the dim light.

The two chased each other around the vault, their playful antics echoing through the otherwise silent chamber, I regaled the vault-keeper with tales of their adventures and unique abilities.

The conversation lulled for a moment as Tianyi and Windy's games filled the silence. I took another sip of the fragrant tea, appreciating the warmth it spread through my chilled limbs.

"Guowei," I began, my curiosity sparking, "what do you do to pass the time here? Surely guarding a vault can't be all that exciting outside of the Grand Alchemy Gauntlet."

A chuckle rumbled in his chest. "Ah, you underestimate the allure of solitude. Besides, who says guarding a vault can't be interesting?"

He gestured to a stack of worn books tucked neatly beneath his desk. "These old friends keep me company. Philosophy, history, poetry—they offer endless worlds to explore."

I leaned forward, intrigued. "Philosophy, huh?"

"The mind is as vast and valuable as any treasure, young alchemist. And just like any treasure, it needs to be nurtured and expanded."

I nodded in agreement. "Speaking of books, I've been looking for a gift for Elder Ming. He's my mentor from back home. He's an avid reader, and I thought a few new novels might be a nice surprise."

"What kind of novels?" Guowei Wang inquired.

"He's quite fond of Liang Feng's work," I replied. "Stories of cultivators embarking on epic quests, facing mythical beasts, and uncovering ancient secrets. I've been searching high and low, but I haven't had any luck finding them."

I had been passively searching this entire time. But it was surprisingly difficult to find the genre. Most bookshops only offered nonfiction. And the ones who did offer fiction, they tended to be . . . *unique.*

The Peasant Who Stole the Demonic Senior Disciple's Heart—*I'll never forget it*, I thought, feeling a chill go down my spine.

A flicker of recognition crossed his face. "Liang Feng, you say? That's quite a specific request."

"Yeah! I've been looking everywhere! I even went to this place called the Scroll and Tome, and it *definitely* wasn't—"

He began coughing into his fist. "Perhaps I can be of assistance. There's a small publishing house in the Old Pine District, about four li west of here, called Wandering Wind Press. They specialize in Liang Feng's works."

"Really? Thank you for letting me know, Guowei! I'm curious, though . . . do you read Liang Feng's novels yourself?"

Guowei Wang's smile turned enigmatic. "Let's just say," he replied, leaning back in his chair, "I have a unique perspective on the author's work."

CHAPTER THREE

Seeing Beyond Sight

Well, this is the place."

My destination was a small, unassuming building at the end of the street. Its wooden facade showed signs of wear, the paint peeling, and the signboard above the door swayed gently in the breeze.

Wandering Wind Press, it read, the letters faded and chipped, giving it a look of quiet dignity. Despite its disrepair, there was something inviting about the place.

I pushed open the creaky door, the bell above jingling softly to announce my arrival. The scent of old paper and ink greeted me, wrapping around me like a familiar embrace. The interior was dimly lit, casting long shadows that danced on the walls. Shelves filled with books lined the walls, their spines displaying titles in elegant calligraphy. The smell of ink and old paper was strong, mingling with the faint scent of incense burning in a corner. A small window allowed a beam of sunlight to filter through, illuminating motes of dust floating in the air.

An old man with ink-stained sleeves and closed eyes stood behind the counter. His movements were slow but precise, each action deliberate and careful.

"Good day," he greeted me, his voice soft yet clear. "How may I assist you?"

"I'm looking for Liang Feng's novels. I was told this was where I could acquire them."

"Ah, Liang Feng," the old man said, a hint of a smile playing on his lips. "A popular request. You'll find his works on the second shelf to your left. Please, take your time."

I nodded and moved toward the indicated section, examining the spines of the books. Familiar titles caught my eye, bringing back memories of late-night reading sessions: Storm Sage Chronicles, *A Journey to the North, Beware of*

Rooster . . . But there were also new titles, ones I hadn't seen before. As I held the books in my hands, a wave of nostalgia washed over me. These stories had been my companions during countless lonely nights, their characters my mentors and friends. Now, as I stood on the brink of a new chapter in my own story, I felt a mix of excitement and uncertainty.

Renegade Insanity? *That sounds fun—I'll give it a try!*

"You have quite the collection here," I remarked, pulling a few books off the shelf to examine them more closely. The other shelves were laden with cultivator tales and similar works of fiction but under different author names.

"Thank you," he replied, inclining his head slightly. "We strive to offer the best selection for our patrons. Liang Feng's works are among our most cherished. His tales have a way of capturing the imagination, don't they?"

I nodded, smiling. "They do indeed. His stories have been a source of inspiration for me. I grew up on the Storm Sage Chronicles."

"Really? What'd you like about them?"

"Mostly how he portrays the wanderer's lifestyle," I said, scanning the shelves. "The way cultivators are written so colorfully; their journeys filled with both adventure and hardship. It's like you can feel the wind in your hair and the dust under your feet."

The old man nodded, a soft smile on his lips. "Liang Feng does have a talent for bringing his characters to life."

I pulled another book from the shelf, its cover depicting a lone figure standing atop a mountain peak. "Though, I do wish some aspects were more accurate to real life," I added with a slight shrug.

"Oh? Do elaborate."

"Well, for one thing," I said, turning to face him, "I'm an alchemist, and in the series, alchemy is portrayed as this ritualistic, almost mystical practice. In reality, it's much closer to cooking. Precise measurements, careful timing, and knowing your ingredients. It was quite a shock when I entered my first alchemy class expecting grand incantations and found myself chopping herbs and stirring cauldrons instead."

The old man let out a slight chuckle. "Ah, but a good storyteller must capture the essence of a craft, not merely its mundane details. Perhaps Liang Feng sought to convey the transformative power of alchemy, not its precise methodology."

That's true. Capturing every nuance would be quite the task.

"And then there are the characters," I continued, my tone lightening. "These are great stories, but sometimes the characters make really dumb decisions. In the second book, when Elder Xiaochun got tricked by the Storm Sage—why would a cultivator who's lived for centuries fall for such an obvious trap?"

The old man paused, surprise and amusement on his face. "Perhaps it's a reminder that wisdom doesn't always guarantee good judgment."

I chuckled. "You have a point there. Wisdom and judgment don't always go hand in hand."

I remembered Elder—*Sect Leader*—Jun. It was hard calling him by his actual title now. Even though he was a ruthless man, I still managed to one-up him in our wager. Nobody was invincible.

With a pile of new books, I carried it over to the counter. Windy poked out of my sleeve, flicking his tongue out curiously. Tianyi fluttered in circles over the man's head, our emotional bond flowing with waves of curiosity. The shopkeeper didn't react.

"I'll take these."

The old man carefully accepted the stack of books, his fingers moving deftly over the covers and spines, as if reading the titles through touch. It was then that I noticed the precision in his movements, the way he placed each book down with exacting care.

"Ah, a fine selection," he remarked, his tone appreciative. "You have good taste."

I watched him, and my suspicions were confirmed—he was blind. The old man's eyes remained closed as he worked, his other senses seemingly heightened to compensate.

How can he run a bookshop . . . ?

He named the total, which was surprisingly reasonable considering the number of books I had chosen. I reached into my pocket and pulled out a gold piece, handing it to him.

"Here, this should cover it. Keep the change as a token of appreciation for continuing to produce Liang Feng's works."

The old man accepted the gold piece with a gracious nod. "Thank you, young master. Your generosity is much appreciated. Enjoy your reading, and do come by again. We update our catalog frequently."

As I turned to leave, I couldn't help but wonder.

How could a blind man read and know the characters from Liang Feng's novels so well when he was unable to see? I shook my head. That was a mystery for another time, I supposed.

Once outside, I took a deep breath, the fresh air a welcome contrast to the musty interior of the shop. I looked down at the books in my arms, feeling a sense of excitement and nostalgia. Liang Feng's tales had been a part of my life for so long, and now I had new stories to dive in to.

"Elder Ming's going to be excited!"

The sky was beginning to darken, and soon, I'd have to meet up with Feng Wu. There was no telling what would happen if I was caught on my lonesome again.

As I walked, I checked over my mental list. *I've gotten gifts for everybody back home, said my farewells to my new friends and acquaintances.*

I've handled all my loose ends.

My mind flashed back to a certain blue-eyed alchemist, and I shook my head quickly. "There's no need. We don't know each other like that anyway."

I ignored the weird fluttery feeling in my stomach as I continued to the inn. There, I saw Feng Wu waiting outside with the cart and horses. He noticed me approaching and smiled.

"Did you get everything you needed?"

I nodded, pointing to the ring on my finger. "All here. At least it won't be too heavy of a load on the horses."

"Make sure to check the weight it can carry. It's usually marked on the inner diameter. It'll refuse to work past that."

I took off the ring and saw it clearly marked. *Five shi, huh?* About the weight of five people. The pill furnace alone was likely more than half the ring's capacity, so it was fortunate I finished my shopping within the designed limit. The thought of lugging that thing around without this was daunting.

We entered the inn for one last time, making sure we didn't leave anything before handing the keys to the front desk.

I lingered at the inn's entrance, my gaze sweeping over the familiar surroundings one last time. The bustling streets, the vibrant market stalls—Crescent Bay City had been my home for the past few weeks, a place of trials and tribulations, of triumphs and defeats. A mere moment in time, but it was here that I had forged friendships, honed my skills, and faced challenges that pushed me to my limits.

A bittersweet pang tugged at my heart as I thought of the friends I was leaving behind.

A gentle hand on my shoulder pulled me from my reverie. "Ready to go, Kai?" Feng Wu's voice, warm and reassuring, broke through the silence.

"Yes," I replied, sounding a bit husky. "I'm ready."

We climbed onto the cart, Tianyi settling comfortably on my shoulder while Windy coiled himself on my lap. As the horses pulled us away from the inn, I couldn't help but take one last look at the city that had become a part of me.

White flakes landed on my nose as we departed.

"Hey, it's snowing! I suppose this is our first official winter together, eh?"

I looked down at the two Spirit Beasts. Windy poked out my sleeve, looking upward with his large, blue eyes to observe the snowflakes, before retreating back into the warmth of my robes. Tianyi seemed to stave off the cold with her bluish aura, unaffected by the chill.

The cart continued to move forward amid the snowfall. The crisp air was filled with the fresh scent of winter, each breath invigorating and clear.

It took a few hours to make our way back to the Verdant Lotus Sect. The blanket of snow that surrounded the area stopped just at the perimeter of the compound.

It was nearing midnight when we finally arrived. We passed through the entrance, where the disciples guarding it greeted us warmly.

"You must be tired," Feng Wu said. "Go rest. I'll put the cart away and report to the mission chamber."

With that, I bade him good night and walked toward the guest quarters. My room, untouched since my departure, greeted me with a chaotic jumble of books and alchemical notes. A reminder of the whirlwind of the past few weeks, and the relentless pursuit of knowledge and skill that had consumed me.

I set down Tianyi and let Windy slither out of my sleeve. I looked out the window and sighed. *What now?* The question echoed in the hollow chambers of my heart.

The Gauntlet was over. The fire that had fueled my every move, the relentless drive to prove myself, had dwindled to a mere ember. A sense of emptiness gnawed at me, a void where ambition and purpose once resided.

I closed my eyes, the image of Jingyu Lian's triumphant smile flashing before me. The sting of defeat, the bitterness of falling short, still lingered, a persistent ache that refused to fade.

If you remain as weak as you are, it's only a matter of time before this Wind Serpent, and that butterfly, are taken away from you.

Xu Ziqing's words, once dismissed as mere provocation, now rang with chilling clarity. I had been so focused on the Gauntlet, on proving my worth as an alchemist, that I had neglected the other aspects of my cultivation.

He was right. Even though I had grown immensely since I first stepped foot into the Jianghu, it still wasn't enough.

I reached into my pocket, closing around the smooth, cool surface of the Beast Core. It was time to harness its power, to push my cultivation to new heights.

"Hopefully Elder Zhu doesn't mind helping me with this."

The recipe to refine the Beast Core wasn't complex, but it was resource-intensive. It was etched into my memory, and would require meticulous precision and unwavering focus. But I was no longer the hesitant novice I once was. I had the Refinement Simulation Technique, the Two-Star Pagoda Pill Furnace, and a burning desire to prove myself.

With a newfound sense of purpose, I settled into bed, eager to embrace the restorative power of sleep. But as I closed my eyes, my mind buzzed with restless energy. The thrill of the Gauntlet, the adrenaline rush of the battle, still coursed through my veins.

My body and mind, rewired from countless late nights of study and work, couldn't find solace going to sleep without doing anything of note.

Sleep, it seemed, was a luxury I couldn't afford. Not yet.

I sat up and crossed my legs on the bed, deciding to meditate. I closed my eyes and took a deep breath, centering myself. The Crimson Lotus Purification Technique had always been a reliable method to calm my mind and focus my energies.

Time seemed to lose meaning as I continued to cultivate. The rhythmic flow of qi through my meridians was like a gentle river, washing away the remnants of doubt and fatigue.

Your Qi has reached Qi Initiation Stage—Rank 2.

CHAPTER FOUR

Shared Strength, Shared Destiny

Kai, have you been waiting here this entire time?"

The predawn chill clung to my bones as Elder Zhu's concerned gaze met mine.

I pulled my robe tighter, a futile attempt to ward off the cold. "Just wanted to catch you early, Elder," I replied, trying to sound casual despite the shiver in my voice. "Before the pavilion opens. I have a favor to ask."

His weathered face softened into a warm smile. "Come in, come in. We can't have you freezing out here. Favors can wait until you've thawed a bit."

He ushered me into the pavilion, the warmth inside a stark contrast to the biting wind outside. Within minutes, we were seated in his office, steaming cups of tea cradled in our hands. The familiar scent of herbs and parchment filled the air, a comforting reminder of the countless hours I'd spent here.

"Now, then," Elder Zhu began, taking a sip of his tea, "what brings you here at such an early hour? And don't tell me it's just for a friendly chat. I've heard about your performance in the Gauntlet."

I smiled, trying my best to hide the rising sense of embarrassment. "Yes, Elder Zhu," I replied, a bit hesitant. "I made it to the finals, but . . . I fell short."

The warmth from the teacup radiated into my hands, offering a small comfort against the chill that lingered from outside.

"I apologize," I continued, my gaze falling to the floor. "I know you had high hopes for me. I . . . I'm sorry I couldn't bring back a victory with me."

Elder Zhu chuckled, his eyes crinkling at the corners. "Kai," he said, warm and reassuring, "there's no need to apologize for giving your all. You made it further than any of us could have imagined. You represented the Verdant Lotus Sect with honor and skill, and that is something to be proud of."

He leaned forward, his gaze piercing through my facade of forced cheerfulness. "I know the loss stings, but it's in these moments of defeat that we truly learn and grow. Remember, Kai, the Gauntlet is just one step on your journey. There are countless more challenges ahead, and I have no doubt that you will overcome them all."

His words, filled with unwavering belief in my abilities . . . It was all too much.

Sometimes, my heart wavered. I wondered if rejecting the opportunity to join the sect as his apprentice was the wrong choice.

I clasped my hands together and bowed deeply.

"Thank you, Elder."

"Now, what was it you'd like to talk about?"

My eyes sharpened. I brought out the two Beast Cores in my pocket, each brimming with latent power. One earned through grit and wit, the other a gilded insult. Together, they represented a turning point, a crossroads.

"I need your help in refining these into an elixir."

The ingredients were laid out, a small fortune in herbs and essence: two Wind Serpent cores, a Breezesong Fruit, ginseng, and white peony root.

I took a deep breath, recalling the guide for refining Beast Cores into elixirs. There was a general rule of thumb to follow, a method honed over centuries of trial and error by countless alchemists. The first step was to pair the Beast Core with a compatible qi ingredient. In this case, the Breezesong Fruit, of the same element, was the perfect match for the Wind Serpent core.

"Beast Core first, paired with its elemental twin," I muttered, selecting the Breezesong Fruit. A bittersweet reminder of my reward, used so soon.

Next came the ginseng, a stabilizing force in the concoction. With its ability to ground and support the body's energies, it'd provide a stable base for the powerful qi released during the refining process.

Finally, the white peony root. This ingredient would make the elixir easier to assimilate into my dantian, ensuring that the refined qi could be smoothly integrated into my cultivation. The white peony root's gentle properties were essential for creating a seamless blend, allowing the qi to flow effortlessly within me.

"The white peony root is added last," I said, feeling a sense of calm wash over me. I knew the theory well, and now it was time to put it into practice.

"Are you ready?" Elder Zhu asked.

"Yes, Elder. Let's begin."

I activated my Refinement Simulation Technique, overlaying a vision of the process before me. In my mind's eye, I saw the steps unfold, the ingredients interacting, the heat rising. I immediately noticed that the two Beast Cores, being of different sizes, could make the concoction more volatile. I'd have to be vigilant during the process.

My hands became more confident, steadier, and I began prepping the ingredients.

I started with the Breezesong Fruit, carefully slicing it and laying the pieces out. The ginseng came next, its roots twisted and strong, a grounding presence amid the volatile energy. Last, the white peony root, its pale color a stark contrast to the other ingredients.

Elder Zhu's watchful eyes followed my every move. "Your hands are steady, Kai. You've grown."

I allowed a smile to appear on my face as I worked. "Thank you, Elder. The Gauntlet has made working under pressure quite easy."

With the ingredients prepared, it was time to start the refining process.

As I placed the first Wind Serpent core into the furnace, Elder Zhu calmly walked toward a nearby wall. With a gentle press of his palm against a specific point on the wall, faint lines of light began to emanate outward, like glowing veins spreading across the surface. The air thrummed with a subtle energy, and I could feel a sense of stability settle over the furnace.

Arrays. The one aspect of alchemy still out of my reach, but within Elder Zhu's capabilities. But with these in place, I have a bit more room to maneuver.

With the two Beast Cores into the large pill furnace, their power resonated within the chamber. Elder Zhu added a piece of Qinglian Jadeite, its green fire casting an ethereal glow.

The cores slowly began to dissolve under the intense heat. The Refinement Simulation Technique revealed a subtle imbalance. The cores, mismatched in size, would add volatility to the process.

"Careful, now," I murmured, adjusting the heat. "Balance, balance . . ."

I didn't dare to blink, taking in every detail of the mixture.

Maintaining a steady flow of qi into the furnace, I kept the temperature stable. The effort was demanding, but thanks to my recent breakthrough in cultivation, I could manage it. I eyed the arrays glowing faintly on the table, crafted by Elder Zhu to enhance stability. They offered a safety net, providing some reprieve if I were to make a mistake.

The Breezesong Fruit followed, a burst of vibrant green amid the swirling energies.

But it proved more volatile than I anticipated. As its essence reacted with the Wind Serpent core, the flames within the furnace surged, threatening to overwhelm the concoction. This was bad; my Refinement Simulation Technique wasn't perfect, and predicting the reaction between such volatile ingredients wasn't always correct. Whether it was my timing or some other factor, the mixture had surpassed my expectations.

But before I could react, Elder Zhu swiftly traced a series of symbols in the air with his fingers. The glowing lines on the wall pulsed, and the flames subsided, returning to a controlled burn. I let out an unexpected breath. He was incredible, and I could feel my respect for him growing. Being able to observe the slightest sign of the mix becoming out of control all while maintaining the stabilizing array . . . I still had a long way to go.

The ginseng joined the dance, its earthy essence grounding the volatile mix. Finally, the white peony, a whisper of purity amid the chaos.

The green flames flickered, casting dancing shadows on the walls. The mixture in the furnace shimmered, a vibrant, harmonious blend of energies. I adjusted the heat one last time, ensuring the elixir reached its optimal state.

The real work began: the steady rhythm of stirring, the constant flow of qi, the unwavering focus. My muscles ached, my mind thrummed with the effort, but a quiet determination settled over me.

A bead of sweat trickled down my forehead as I struggled to maintain the delicate balance. The Refinement Simulation Technique flickered, warning me of an impending surge. Just as I braced myself for the worst, a gentle wave of calming energy washed over the furnace. I glanced at Elder Zhu and saw him subtly adjusting the flow of qi within the arrays, his brow furrowed in concentration. My decision to ask him for help was the correct one.

With his support, I can do this.

"Almost there," Elder Zhu's voice was a gentle encouragement. "Let me know if you can no longer stir; I will help."

"Thank you, Elder."

The elixir glowed, a radiant beacon in the light of the alchemy pavilion, Fatigue warred with exhilaration, but I wouldn't falter. Not now.

I could feel the strain in my arms and mind. Despite my cultivation breakthrough, the task was physically and mentally demanding. Hours passed, the ingredients gradually transforming within the furnace. The once distinct components became a homogeneous mixture, now turning into a pure-white liquid.

The liquid continued to glow brighter over time, its luminosity increasing as the refining process neared completion. The fatigue in my arms and mind was a constant companion, but I pushed through, knowing the reward was worth the effort.

"Keep going, Kai," Elder Zhu encouraged. "You're almost there."

The glow of the elixir intensified, casting a light that filled the room. Despite the exhaustion, a sense of accomplishment and anticipation fueled my efforts. The final stages required even more precision, ensuring that the elixir's purity was maintained. My hands moved with practiced ease, the Refinement Simulation Technique guiding me through each step, predicting and correcting potential mistakes.

"The elixir is almost ready," I said, my voice steady despite my fatigue. "Just a little longer."

Finally, the mixture reached a state of perfect harmony. The glow of the elixir was blinding, a pure-white light that seemed to pulse with energy. I turned off the heat and allowed it to cool, my body sagging with relief.

"It's done," I announced, forcing a tired smile. "We've completed it!"

The molten essence cooled, transforming into a shimmering elixir pulsing with a soft white glow. Its purity was undeniable, credited to the meticulous care and precision I had poured into the refinement process. Carefully, I transferred the elixir into a large vial.

Elder Zhu approached, his keen eyes studying the vial intently. "An unusual color," he remarked. "Most elixirs derived from Beast Cores carry a distinct tint, reflecting the creature's elemental affinity. But this . . . this is pure white."

A pang of worry struck me. Had I made an error, despite all the fail-safes and the Refinement Simulation Technique's guidance?

"Is that a problem, Elder Zhu?"

He placed a reassuring hand on my shoulder, his gaze shifting to meet mine. "Not necessarily," he replied, a hint of curiosity in his voice. "In fact, it might be a sign of something quite extraordinary."

Before I could question his words, Elder Zhu's hand reached out, his fingers gently brushing against my wrist. A warm energy flowed through me, a gentle probing of my qi. His eyebrows rose in surprise, his eyes widening slightly. "Kai," he said in wonder, "the purity of your qi . . . It's remarkable. I've rarely encountered such a refined essence."

I blinked, my confusion mounting. "What does that have to do with the elixir, Elder?"

He withdrew his hand. "Your qi is exceptionally pure. It seems that during the refinement process, your own essence has influenced the elixir, purifying it beyond what is typically achievable."

A wave of realization washed over me. Elder Ming's teachings, the Crimson Lotus Purification's slow accumulation had borne fruit in the most unexpected way.

"My mentor taught me an important lesson on how to utilize qi to my advantage," I explained, a sense of pride swelling in my chest. "He recognized my limitations and encouraged me to focus on quality over quantity, refining my energy until only the purest essence remained."

Elder Zhu nodded, a genuine smile gracing his lips. "A wise approach," he said. "Your mentor's insight is evident in your accomplishments. This elixir, Kai, is proof to your dedication and unwavering pursuit of excellence."

Excitement bubbled within me, a potent mix of anticipation and nervous energy. "Elder Zhu, may I consume the elixir now?" I asked, barely containing my eagerness.

He nodded, his smile widening. "Indeed, Kai. You have earned this moment."

With a newfound sense of purpose, I swiftly cleaned the workspace, my movements efficient and precise. The Two-Star Pagoda Pill Furnace vanished back into my storage ring, leaving the room bathed in the soft glow of the lantern. I turned to Elder Zhu, bowing deeply.

"Thank you, Elder. For everything."

"Go on, then." He chuckled, a warm light in his eyes. "Fulfill your potential."

As I made my way back to my quarters, the vial of elixir clutched tightly in my hand, my thoughts drifted back to the moment I first acquired the Beast Cores. I had known from that moment that they held the key to a significant breakthrough, not just for me, but for my companions as well. This goal had driven me, a beacon of hope and determination.

Tonight, I would finally accomplish it.

As I entered my room, I was greeted by the familiar sight of Windy and Tianyi waiting patiently for my arrival. Their presence, as always, brought a sense of comfort and purpose.

"Tianyi, Windy," I called softly, drawing their attention. "I have a special gift for us."

Their curiosity was palpable, Tianyi fluttered her wings excitedly while Windy slithered closer, his tongue flicking out to taste the air. I set down the Beast Core elixir and retrieved three bowls, carefully pouring the prized mixture into each one.

"I know I'm still weak," I confessed, my gaze sweeping over my two spirit companions. I remembered Xu Ziqing's words, and the night I was cornered by the Narrow Stone Peak disciples. I closed my eyes tightly, shaking off the memory.

"And I'm determined to change that. Not just for myself, but for you, my friends. I want to ensure your safety, to give you the strength to protect yourselves—and, hopefully, to protect me as well."

Tianyi's emotional link pulsated with a warmth that melted away any lingering doubt. It was a wave of pure gratitude and unwavering trust. Windy nudged his snout against my hand, a silent acknowledgment of my words.

I picked up my bowl and held it out to them. "Cheers," I said, clinking my bowl with theirs before bringing it to my lips.

The elixir was cool and smooth, a rush of potent qi flooding my system as I drank. Tianyi unfurled her proboscis, and Windy placed his snout by the bowl, taking small sips.

The room filled with a soft, radiant light as the power of the elixir coursed through us, binding our fates even closer together.

CHAPTER FIVE

When the Student Outshines the Master

If there was one thing Liang Feng's novels were accurate about, it was the process of cultivation. Ingesting pills, and making the potent energy within them your own . . . He portrayed it as a surreal experience, and I always wondered if it was subject to puffery, much like when he wrote about alchemy practices.

The elixir melted the instant it touched my tongue, releasing a burst of intense flavors—bitter, with earthy undertones. It was a complex taste, like a blend of fresh herbs and potent spices, leaving a cooling minty sensation that quickly transformed into a subtle warmth as it slid down my throat.

But then, the warmth turned into a torrent. The initially soothing flow of qi transformed into a raging river, and then into a terrifying waterfall, cascading through my body with overwhelming force.

I gasped, feeling the sheer volume of qi flooding my system.

This was the essence of the Wind Serpent.

The qi surged in like an explosion, nearly suffocating me with its intensity. It was hard to comprehend how such a small amount of liquid could produce such immense energy.

Focus!

I instantly abandoned all other thoughts, concentrating on my dantian and guiding the surging qi from the elixir.

It felt like a dam had burst within me. The rushing qi was violently expanding my meridians, forcing my qi circulatory system to widen and adapt. I trembled, feeling as though my entire body might tear apart under the pressure.

Control it . . . carefully.

The qi began to move beyond my control, coursing through my meridians with a will of its own. Yet, rather than panic, I felt a surge of exhilaration. The immense qi was clearing away impurities and revitalizing my very essence. My meridians widened, even the smallest blood vessels and the most clogged pathways were being forced open and purified.

> *Your Qi has advanced to Qi Initiation Realm—Rank 3.*

Every fiber of my being came alive with the fresh sensation of renewal.

I finally understood why such elixirs were so highly coveted. No amount of training could replicate this feeling. The elixir was doing what years of cultivation could not achieve, pushing my body and qi to new heights.

But . . .

This is too much.

The qi continued to flow within me. I couldn't absorb it all at once; it needed to be guided and assimilated slowly over time. Greed would lead to disaster—Qi Deviation could result if I tried to rush the process.

Slowly, I gathered the swirling qi, directing it with careful precision. I cycled the energy throughout my body, ensuring a steady flow and preventing any stagnation or imbalance. With every breath, I utilized the Crimson Lotus Purification Technique, purifying my energy, relieving the pressure.

Elder Zhu was correct: The elixir was incredibly pure and barely reduced as I sifted through to ensure the qi was as pure as could possibly be. It was the ideal panacea for someone pursuing purity like me.

Finally, the storm calmed. I opened my eyes, feeling my body shake with the residual energy. I was filled with more qi than ever before, a sensation of boundless vitality and strength.

> *Your Qi has advanced to Qi Initiation Realm—Rank 4.*

It felt like I could achieve anything.

I opened my eyes to see Windy in front of me with an empty bowl. It seems he had finished his share of the elixir, with significant changes to his status.

> *Name: Windy*
> *Race: Wind Serpent (Aberrant)*
> *Affinity: Wood and Metal*
> *Cultivation Rank: Qi Initiation Stage—Rank 4*
> *Special Abilities:*
> *Tail Whip: Delivers a swift and powerful tail strike infused with Qi.*
> *Paralyzing Venom: Injects venom that temporarily paralyzes the target.*

> *Moonlight Empowerment: Gains increased power and vitality*
> *under the moonlight.*
> *Bond Level: 2 (Friend)—Windy has developed a closer relationship*
> *with you, displaying increased trust and*
> *willingness to assist in your cultivation journey.*

He had gone up by three stages! Incredible! Perhaps his compatibility with the Wind Serpent Beast Cores had something to do with it.

"Whoa," I mumbled, flexing my fingers experimentally. "I feel like I could punch a hole through a mountain."

I tilted my head as I continued to observe his face.

Snakes were relatively expressionless, but Windy's eyes were uncharacteristically wide, his jaw hanging open in shock. He was staring intently at something on the ceiling.

I followed his gaze and nearly jumped out of my skin.

Tianyi, normally a delicate wisp of blue, was now a radiant beacon, her wings blazing with an otherworldly light.

What the hell?!

"What in the heavens?!" I yelped, scrambling back from the bed. "Tianyi, are you trying to blind us?!"

No response. Just more harsh light. It was like staring into the sun, except the sun was a giant glowing butterfly.

"Windy, cover!" I yelled, grabbing the still-stunned serpent and diving behind the bed. "I think she's about to blow!"

The air crackled with energy, and I braced myself for an explosion. But instead of a deafening boom, a gentle hum filled the room, growing louder and louder until it resonated in my very bones.

What was happening to her? Was this a breakthrough or something more dangerous?

Seconds felt like hours as I waited, tense and ready for anything. The light seemed to reach its peak, an intense, almost blinding blue that filled every corner of the room. The energy in the air was palpable, a living force that pressed down on us.

Then, as suddenly as it had intensified, the light began to fade. I peeked over the bed, cautiously lowering my arm. Tianyi hovered in the air, her wings still glowing softly, but the intense brightness had subsided.

"Are you okay?" I asked.

She fluttered down gracefully to my eye level. Whatever had happened, it seemed to have been a positive transformation.

> *Name: Tianyi*

> *Race: Mystical Butterfly*
> *Affinity: Wood*
> *Cultivation Rank: Essence Awakening Stage—Rank 1*
> *Special Abilities:*
> *Qi Haven: Transforms frequented areas into concentrated qi zones, boosting recovery and cultivation efficiency for those within its boundaries.*
> *Moonlight Empowerment: Gains increased power and vitality under the moonlight.*
> *Qi Siphon: Can absorb small amounts of qi from its surroundings to sustain itself.*
> *Qi Transfer: Can imbue living beings with energy by transferring its qi, providing a small boost to those who receive it.*
> *Qi Infusion: Infuse your body with qi, strengthening and making it faster.*
>
> *Bond Level: 3 (Close Companion)—Tianyi has formed a deep bond with you, displaying loyalty and commitment to your shared journey.*
> *Her abilities may strengthen in response to your connection, and she will be more attuned to your emotions and needs.*
> *Additional abilities or enhancements may become available as your bond continues to grow.*

"Holy—"

I couldn't help but gawk at her status.

Essence Awakening Stage?

Kai . . .

A small voice cut through my thoughts, so quiet that I thought it was a hallucination. I turned around to see if anyone was there.

I froze, glancing around the room. The voice had been faint, almost like a whisper carried on the wind. But there was no one else here—just me, Windy, and Tianyi.

Kai . . . you can hear me?

The voice was clearer this time, distinctly female. I whipped my head back toward the glowing butterfly.

This . . . This was unexpected.

"You've surpassed most third-class disciples in qi reserves. And the energy radiating from Tianyi . . . It's on par with a first-class disciple."

It was rather late now. The process of creating the elixir took the entire morning and afternoon, and my evening was spent consuming it. The heavens clearly favored me, as I had run into Feng Wu just as I had left my quarters to find someone to tell.

Feng Wu took the butterfly from my hand, and she happily perched on his finger, teeming with pride and joy. The glow around her had grown even stronger, the snowflakes melting before they even touched her.

"Her qi reserves have far surpassed mine," he said. "I'm honestly a bit jealous."

I blinked, trying to process his words. "Wait, how is that possible? I split the elixir evenly between the three of us. I should be the one with the most impressive result, but I only went up two stages, while Windy went up three. And Tianyi . . . Well, she's in the Essence Awakening Stage now! What gives?"

Feng Wu chuckled, a knowing smile playing on his lips. "Kai, have you really thought about how different your bodies are? You're a human, Windy's a snake, and Tianyi's a butterfly. The same elixir isn't going to have the same effect on such vastly different entities."

Oh. Right. Forgot to consider that in my musings.

"And don't forget, your body doesn't ingest all the elixir at once. Some of it has yet to fully integrate into your body."

Feng Wu's words hung in the cold air, and I could feel my thoughts spinning. "Wait, so you're saying . . . there's more of the elixir's qi still in me?"

He nodded, his eyes studying me with that same knowing look. "Exactly. You should check how much of it is yet to be incorporated into your dantian. It's not uncommon for a powerful elixir like this to take time to fully integrate."

I closed my eyes, focusing inward. Almost immediately, I noticed a profound change. My qi circulatory system, which had once been weak and thin, was now robust and cycling energy continuously. The pathways that had felt fragile and narrow before were now wider and stronger, allowing the qi to flow more freely.

Then, I turned my attention to my dantian. What I felt nearly took my breath away. It had grown many times over in just a single night. The space inside was vast, like an ever-expanding reservoir of pure energy. But what really caught my attention was the residual energy surrounding it—a thick, dense cloud of qi, still waiting to be fully absorbed.

When I opened my eyes again, I met Feng Wu's gaze. "I'd say about thirty percent of the elixir is left, still slowly integrating itself."

He raised a brow, clearly intrigued. "That's odd. Most people aren't able to ingest that much qi in one session. Tianyi likely absorbed the qi all at once, not needing to integrate it slowly because her body is far more compatible with qi.

She's a Spirit Beast, after all, and one that's used to cycling qi naturally. Her entire being is designed for it."

"And Windy?" I asked, looking down at the snake coiled around my wrist.

"Windy's situation is probably closer to yours. He's young, and while he's advanced rapidly, he might not have been able to integrate all the qi yet. His body will absorb it as he matures, so he's still got a lot of growth ahead of him."

I let out a breath I didn't realize I was holding. "I know . . . but it's still unbelievable how quickly things changed after that elixir. I mean, I've spent months cultivating, and this . . . this was just one night."

The man nodded, his expression turning serious. "That's why I was so shocked when you tried to surrender the Beast Core after winning the wager against Elder Jun. And even more so when they sent another to you as a gift of congratulations for placing so highly in the Gauntlet."

I couldn't help but chuckle at the memory, the absurdity of it all finally hitting me. "Yeah, I guess I didn't realize what I had in my hands back then."

I shook my head, the realization settling in. "So, how long does it usually take to fully integrate the rest of the qi?" I asked, curiosity laced with a hint of impatience. The idea of having all this untapped energy just sitting inside me was tantalizing.

He shrugged, his expression turning noncommittal. "It varies. It can take anywhere from a week to a few months, depending on your inclination and the amount of qi left. But," he added with a gleam in his eye, "there is one way to speed up the process."

My ears perked up at that. "How?"

"Through training, of course. By pushing your body and your qi to their limits, you can force the integration to happen faster."

I felt a grin spread across my face. "Are you willing to show me how?"

Feng Wu laughed, a deep, hearty sound that echoed through the chilly air. "I thought you'd never ask. Come on, let's see what you're really made of, Kai."

CHAPTER SIX

Sparring and Spirit Beasts

Elixirs were *stupid*.

"Rooted Banyan Stance!"

I unleashed my technique once more, clenching all the muscles in my body and shielding myself with qi as Feng Wu struck.

The kick to the stomach pushed me back a couple feet, but I held my stance without flinching. I grinned at the second-class disciple.

"This changes everything!"

It had been an hour since we began my training to integrate the qi of the elixir into my dantian.

I couldn't help but marvel at the difference. The Rooted Banyan Stance, a technique that used to drain me completely after just two uses, was now something I could perform seven times with ease. The increase in my qi reserves was astounding, but what struck me even more was how quickly they replenished. During our hour of sparring, I'd regained enough qi to perform another Rooted Banyan Stance, which I didn't notice with my paltry reserves back then.

As I stood, breathing heavily but still full of energy, I glanced to the side. There, Tianyi and Windy were engaged in their own little sparring session.

Windy's serpentine body whipped around with surprising speed, his tail striking out like a coiled spring. But Tianyi, with her delicate butterfly wings, parried each strike with graceful ease. Her wings shimmered with a soft blue glow, deflecting his attacks as if it were the most natural thing in the world. The contrast between the two was almost ridiculous—a powerful, aggressive snake against a fluttering butterfly—but Tianyi held her own, her movements fluid and precise.

Feng Wu's voice broke through my thoughts. "You good to keep going, Kai?"

I shook my head, wiping sweat from my brow. "I'm out of qi to use any more of my moves. Rooted Banyan Stance drains a lot, even with my increased reserves."

He nodded thoughtfully. "That's normal, but you're not done yet. Here's what I want you to do—infuse your body with qi, all of it, until you bottom out. You need to push yourself to the very limit, just like muscles. They have to be worked until they're torn down to grow back stronger. Your qi works similarly."

I took a deep breath and nodded. "All right."

Focusing inward, I began to infuse my body with the remaining qi, letting it flow into my muscles, bones, and skin. With an unspoken signal, I launched forward to continue the spar.

"Qi infusion is about enhancing your physical abilities," Feng Wu explained between punches. "It makes you stronger, faster, and more resilient. But it's also inefficient compared to techniques like your Rooted Banyan Stance."

I ducked under one of his punches, trying to process his words. "I can feel that . . . The amount of 'defense' I get from just infusing my body with qi versus using the stance is like night and day. But why is that?"

The man stepped back, lowering his fists. "Let me show you." He adopted a relaxed stance and threw a simple punch toward me, without using any qi. "This is just a normal punch. No qi, no technique. Basic."

He then infused his fist with qi, throwing another punch. This one was faster, stronger, and I could feel the difference in the air as it rushed past my face. "This is a punch infused with qi. Notice the increase in speed and power."

Finally, Feng Wu assumed a proper stance. His feet slid into position, his fist drew back in a precise movement, and his entire body seemed to coil with potential energy. When he released the punch, it drew up a small gust of wind, blowing my hair out of place as it landed right in front of me.

"That," he said, straightening up, "is the difference. The Rooted Banyan Stance is like that last punch. It's not just qi infusion—it's a mix of technique and qi that makes it much more effective. The proper form, the right movements, they all work together to amplify the effect. It's the difference between just throwing energy at something and using it with purpose."

"So, it's about refining the use of qi, not just relying on raw power?"

"Exactly," Feng Wu said with a grin. "Raw power is good, but refined power? That's where you start to see real results. And now that your qi reserves are larger, you can start focusing on honing that refinement."

I couldn't help but smile at the possibilities. This was the next step in my cultivation journey, and I was eager to see where it would take me.

The sparring continued, but it didn't take long before I truly reached the bottom of my qi reserves. Each punch, each kick became heavier, more sluggish, until I was barely able to lift my arms. My vision blurred, and I could feel myself teetering on the edge of exhaustion.

"I suppose you're done," Feng Wu said firmly, catching me as I stumbled.

I nodded weakly, too drained to respond. My legs wobbled, threatening to give out entirely, but Feng Wu supported me, guiding me back toward my quarters. The world seemed to spin around me, and it took everything I had just to stay conscious.

In the comfortable silence that settled between us, I mustered enough strength to speak. "Thank you, Feng Wu. For everything. I know I wouldn't have gotten this far without your help."

Feng Wu chuckled. "My contribution was minimal. You're the one who put in the effort, Kai. You're the one who's growing, who's pushing past your limits."

I managed a tired smile. A Taoist to the core. "Maybe, but I still owe you."

He waved it off with a grin as we reached my room. "Get some rest. We'll pick this up later."

"Yeah . . . see you," I mumbled as I sank into my bed, the fatigue pulling me into a deep sleep almost immediately. I didn't even get to register whether Tianyi or Windy followed me back.

As I drifted off, thoughts of how I could repay Feng Wu swirled in my mind. He had given me so much, and I wanted to find a way to show my gratitude, even if it was just a small gesture.

The darkness of sleep enveloped me, offering a reprieve from the exhaustion that had seeped into my bones. But it wasn't long before a soft, almost musical voice cut through the haze of my dreams.

Kai . . . wake up.

The voice was gentle but insistent, pulling me from the depths of my slumber. I woke up feeling more refreshed than I had in a long time. My qi reserves were brimming with energy, and as I checked my dantian, I noticed that the cloud of qi surrounding it had dissipated slightly. Feng Wu's guidance had been right—it was working. The integration of the elixir's qi was accelerating, and I could feel the benefits already taking root.

Something fluttered in front of my face, breaking me out of my thoughts. Tianyi, her wings shimmering with a soft blue light, hovered above me.

Morning, she chirped.

I blinked, trying to reconcile the image in front of me. She was perched delicately on my nose, her tiny form seemingly more vibrant than ever. But it wasn't just her appearance that caught me off guard—it was her voice. The fact that she could speak, that we could communicate like this now, made her feel . . . more human.

"Uh . . . morning," I replied, my brain thick with sleep. I couldn't shake the strange feeling that had settled over me. It wasn't unpleasant, just . . . different. "You can talk now, huh?"

Tianyi fluttered off my nose and hovered just above my chest. *Yes. Does it bother you?*

"No, it's just . . ." I rubbed my eyes. "I'm still getting used to it."

A tinge of relief sparked between us. It seemed that the emotional link didn't weaken, even with this.

As I thought about her newfound ability to speak, the word "human" flitted through me. The memory of an old notification from when the Heavenly Interface first appeared resurfaced. I had almost forgotten about it.

> *Your companion Tianyi cannot transform until she reaches*
> *Essence Awakening Stage—Rank 1.*

I stared at Tianyi, realization dawning on me. "Wait a minute . . . Does this mean . . . ?"

She tilted her head, her wings fluttering slightly. *Does it mean what?*

I sat up, suddenly wide-awake. "You can transform, can't you? Into a human form."

There was a pause, and she stood still for a brief moment, as though searching for something.

I . . . don't know how. Maybe someday.

I couldn't help but wonder what she would look like in human form. Would she retain some of her butterfly traits, like her wings? The thought was both intriguing and a little unsettling. She had always been a small, delicate creature, and imagining her as a human was . . . strange.

"Don't worry about it, Tianyi," I said quickly, not wanting to make her feel uncomfortable. "You don't have to do anything you're not ready for. But if you ever do figure it out, I'd be curious to see it."

Her wings picked up speed again as if the brief moment of pensiveness had passed. *I'll think about it.*

I smiled at her, trying to put her at ease. "Take your time. There's no rush."

Feeling the need to change the subject, I glanced over to where Windy was coiled up, still sleeping soundly after the intense sparring session from the previous day. His breathing was slow and steady, and I could tell he was exhausted.

"I'm going to be gone for most of the day," I told Tianyi. "Can you keep an eye on Windy? Make sure he's okay."

She fluttered over to Windy, landing gently on his tail. *I'll make sure he's safe.*

With that settled, I got dressed and made my way out of the room, leaving Tianyi to watch over Windy. As I walked through the quiet halls of the sect, my mind turned to the task I had set for myself today—creating a batch of the healing hydrosol I had developed before the Gauntlet. It was a simple but effective remedy, and I wanted to give something back to the sect that had given me so much.

As I carefully plucked the moss, I made sure to leave some behind, ensuring the patch would continue to thrive.

Before leaving, I took a moment to infuse the remaining moss with a gentle pulse of qi. The energy seeped into the plants, encouraging their growth and vitality. The moss glowed faintly in response, the qi working to replenish what I had taken. Satisfied that I had done my part to sustain the environment, I stored the harvested moss in my storage ring and made my way back to the sect.

I made my way to the alchemy pavilion, where I set to work extracting the essences from the moss in a private room. The process was familiar and soothing.

With the essences extracted, I wrote down the recipe, detailing each step with precision. I intended to give the recipe to Elder Zhu, so that the sect could produce the hydrosol on a larger scale and make it available to the disciples, sell it—whatever they wished to do.

I glanced upward, checking the position of the sun in the sky.

"They should be done with their classes by now," I muttered to myself.

Outside, I waited patiently as throngs of disciples poured out to attend different classes. Many of them tilted their heads to acknowledge me, and I responded in kind.

Then two familiar figures approached me, shouting in jubilance, "You're back?!"

Han Wei and Li Na threw themselves at me, and I caught them with ease.

"I arrived yesterday; had some loose ends to tie up. But now, this young master has returned! Stronger than ever!" I posed, flexing my biceps to show my physique. It wasn't anything like Ping Hai's, but I could still feel the difference. The strength in my limbs, the way my qi pulsed with energy just beneath the surface—it was all there, even if it wasn't visible to the naked eye.

Han Wei raised an eyebrow, a skeptical grin tugging at the corner of his mouth. "You're looking pretty much the same to me. You sure you've grown, Kai?"

Li Na playfully jabbed me in the ribs. "Yeah, don't tell me you've been slacking off while we've been training our butts off!"

I chuckled, shaking my head. "I promise I've grown—maybe not in a way that's easy to see. But trust me, I've come a long way."

Her teasing softened into genuine curiosity. "How did you do in the Gauntlet, anyway? We haven't heard anything; it's hard to get information from outside the sect."

I hesitated for a moment, the memory of the Gauntlet finals still fresh in my mind. But I didn't want to dwell on it too much. "I came in second place," I said, trying to sound nonchalant. "Lost to Jingyu Lian in the finals."

Their eyes widened in shock, and for a moment, there was silence as they processed what I'd just said.

"You're kidding, right?" Han Wei finally blurted out in both disbelief and admiration. "Second place?! You went up against someone from the Lian family and made it that far?"

I shrugged, a small smile tugging at my lips. "Yeah, it was close, but she got the better of me. But that's not the only thing I brought back from the Gauntlet."

Li Na leaned in, her eyes sparkling with curiosity. "Oh? What else did you get?"

I reached into my storage ring excitedly. "Let me show you."

CHAPTER SEVEN

Surprise—I Leveled Up!

Their reactions were priceless.

After pulling out the Golden Bamboo seeds from my storage ring, I could barely contain my grin as Han Wei and Li Na tilted their heads at the small, unassuming seeds in their glass display. I explained my quest to revive the long-lost species and how I'd been entrusted with their cultivation. The way their eyes widened told me all I needed to know—they were impressed.

But the real fun began when I brought out the Two-Star Pagoda Pill Furnace. The moment it appeared, I could see the curiosity in their expressions, but that curiosity quickly shifted to something else as I tried to explain the nuances of its operation.

"See, the furnace is designed with a dual-layer qi compression system that allows for more precise temperature control during refinement," I began, my enthusiasm barely contained. "And the thousand-page manual it came with is crucial for understanding the full range of its capabilities—"

Their eyes glazed over almost immediately.

I tried not to laugh as they nodded along, clearly lost somewhere around the mention of "dual-layer qi compression."

Li Na shot Han Wei a look, and he simply shrugged, just as bewildered.

I sighed, deciding to spare them further details. "Basically, it's a really advanced pill furnace. Way more efficient than anything I've used before."

"That's . . . nice, Kai," she managed, though I could tell she was still trying to process everything I'd said. Han Wei just gave me a thumbs-up, clearly out of his depth.

But it wasn't until I suggested we spar that I saw their biggest surprise yet.

"Are you sure, Kai? You just got back from . . . well, everything. Maybe sparring after a long trip and all that isn't the best idea."

I flashed him a confident grin. "Nonsense! I'm feeling invigorated. Besides"—I winked—"I've got a few new tricks up my sleeve."

"What could you have learned in that month you were away?"

"That's for me to know and for you to find out!"

We moved to a clearing in the bamboo forest, the crisp winter air biting at our cheeks.

"Han Wei, you're up first!"

He nodded, a determined glint in his eyes. "Ready when you are, Kai."

Li Na stepped back, giving us a wide berth. "Don't hold back, you two," she called out, a mischievous grin on her face. "Give it your all!"

Here we go.

Feeling a surge of adrenaline course through my veins, it was time to put my new skills to the test.

Han Wei and I faced each other, a distance of about ten paces separating us. We bowed slightly, acknowledging the tradition of respect before a spar. The air crackled with anticipation, the only sound the rustling of bamboo leaves in the gentle breeze.

"Start!" Li Na said.

We dove forward at the same time, him blocking my kick and me parrying his palm strike.

After a few light jabs and parries, I decided to unleash the surprise.

"Rooted Banyan Stance!"

His palm strike landed with a resounding thud, but I stood firm, rooted like an ancient tree. A flicker of surprise crossed his face, but he didn't hesitate, launching a swift kick aimed at my legs.

Again, I held my ground, the impact barely registering. Then another strike, and another. With each blow, their astonishment grew.

Each time, I could see their shock growing as they realized I wasn't tiring out. I kept using the Rooted Banyan Stance, demonstrating the sheer increase in my qi reserves.

"Wait a minute," Li Na said, rising from where she sat. "How are you not exhausted by now? You've used that stance so many times . . ."

I let the stance dissipate, smugness replacing my earlier concentration. "My qi reserves have expanded a bit," I said, trying to sound casual. "Fourth rank of Qi Initiation Stage, to be precise."

Their jaws practically hit the floor. For a moment, they just stared at me, completely speechless. Then Han Wei burst out laughing, shaking his head in disbelief.

Han Wei's laughter rang out across the training grounds, a genuine, hearty sound that was contagious. "Kai, did you find some legendary pill lying on the ground during the Gauntlet? Because this is insane!"

I chuckled, shaking my head. "Nothing so dramatic. I just refined a potent elixir from a couple of Wind Serpent Beast Cores. Split it with Tianyi and Windy, too."

Li Na's eyes widened. "Wait, you said *cores*? Plural?"

I nodded. "Yep, two of them. The first from the wager, and the other was a . . . *gift* from the Silent Moon Sect. Guess they wanted to rub in how I lost during the Gauntlet. I can show you guys the letter Elder—no, *Sect Leader*—Jun sent with it."

The mention of the rival sect sucked the air out of the clearing. Their earlier excitement evaporated, replaced by a tense silence.

"Two Beast Cores," Han Wei muttered, as if trying to wrap his head around it. He rubbed the back of his neck. "And you made an elixir out of them? That explains so much."

I nodded, with a cheeky grin on my face. "Yeah, but that's not even the craziest part. Come on, I want to show you something."

We reached my guest quarters, and I carefully pushed open the door. The room was quiet, save for the soft sounds of birds chirping outside. I motioned for them to keep their voices down as I led them inside.

I turned to the two third-class disciples with a whisper. "All right, take a guess. What ranks do you think they're at now, after ingesting the elixir?"

Han Wei squinted at the two sleeping creatures, scratching his head. "Windy's got to be at least the same rank as you, right? Fourth rank?"

Li Na seemed more hesitant, glancing at the butterfly resting atop the serpent's head. "And Tianyi . . . maybe the third rank? She's always been a bit more delicate, so maybe she didn't absorb as much."

I chuckled softly, shaking my head. "Close but not quite. Han Wei's right, but . . . Tianyi? She's in the Essence Awakening Stage."

For a moment, the room was dead silent. Then, as if on cue, their jaws dropped in unison, their expressions a perfect blend of disbelief and awe.

"Essence Awakening?" she whispered, as if saying it too loud might wake Tianyi. "But . . . that's . . ."

"Impossible?" I finished for her, grinning like a proud parent. "I know, right? And now you must bow before your superior!" I puffed out my chest and pointed down at them.

Li Na looked between us, her expression serious. "That's . . . that's big. There's been so much happening lately, especially with Sect Leader Shaotian Ye entering seclusion. Things are getting hectic."

I blinked, my focus narrowing in on her words. "Wait, what? What did you just say about Sect Leader Shaotian Ye?"

She glanced at Han Wei before answering. "Sect Leader Shaotian Ye's been in seclusion for a week now. It's likely because he's preparing to breakthrough to the Spirit Ascension Stage."

The words hit me like a ton of bricks, and I felt my thoughts racing. The Spirit Ascension Stage?

The sect leaders I knew were like towering mountains, their strength a natural barrier that no ordinary person could cross. At the peak of Essence Awakening, they were like dragons perched on clouds, capable of feats that defied the mortal realm—running faster than the wind, lifting boulders as if they were mere pebbles. They were the pinnacle of what our province had to offer.

But the next realm after . . . I only knew one person that was rumored to be there.

The Wind Sage. A man rumored to equal the power of a sect just by himself, and the one who could claim to be the strongest of our region.

"Spirit Ascension Stage," I murmured, the words almost foreign on my tongue. It was a stage that seemed more myth than reality, a level of power that belonged to the stories of the ancient cultivators, not something within reach of the present generation. Yet, here we were, with Sect Leader Shaotian Ye on the cusp of such an achievement.

The Verdant Lotus Sect, already one of the most prestigious in the province, could rise to even greater heights. But that wasn't all. With the ambient qi in the environment rising, and the Heavenly Interface's existence making breakthroughs easier, meant that others would be attempting to rise along with us. It was both an opportunity and a challenge.

"And what about the other sects?" I asked, voicing my concern. "If we're seeing such rapid advancements here, they must be experiencing similar phenomena, right? The balance of power could tip in any direction."

I remembered Feng Wu's words. The new elders of the Silent Moon, powerful, unknown cultivators serving under Sect Leader Jun.

Han Wei shrugged. "That's true, but we're strong. We won't fall short against the other sects!"

His confidence was like a bonfire on a cold night, bright and reassuring, but I knew better than to let its warmth lull me into complacency. The Verdant Lotus was strong, yes, but I had seen the rising stars of other sects—their potential as vast as the heavens.

The Silent Moon was a storm gathering on the horizon, its power undeniable. There was Ping Hai, several years younger than me, yet with a physique that seemed carved from stone. Xu Ziqing, the blade that had cut through the Wind Serpents in Qingmu like a scythe through wheat. And then Tian Zhan, the genius whose light eclipsed all others in the Whispering Wind Sect. I rubbed my arm, the memory of his strength still fresh, a reminder that the path ahead was fraught with challenges.

Even as I grew, so did they. The river of time flowed ever forward, and I couldn't afford to be a pebble swept away in its current. I had to be a boulder, unmoving, resolute.

Li Na's voice pulled me from my thoughts. "We're really fortunate, you know? To start cultivating in a time when growth is . . . well, easier than it's ever been."

She was right—this was a time of opportunity, but with opportunity came uncertainty. The status quo, long held in place like ancient stone, was now crumbling, its pieces falling into an abyss of unknown depth. The province, the sects, the very balance of power—all of it was shifting like sand in the wind, and there was no telling where it would land.

A sense of resolve settled over me. I couldn't just sit back and let this moment pass. I had to do something to ensure we, the Verdant Lotus Sect, and my friends could not just survive but thrive in this changing world.

I straightened my back. I had made my decision. "I'm going back to the pavilion," I said, making my determination clear.

They both looked at me, their curiosity piqued.

"What for?" Han Wei asked.

"Healing hydrosol. It's not all-powerful like the Beast Core elixir, but it'll accelerate your training and hopefully help the sect maintain their position during these times."

His brows furrowed in confusion. "Healing hydrosol?"

Li Na, on the other hand, nodded in understanding. "You mean the one you made before the Gauntlet, right? The one that worked wonders on wounds?"

"Exactly," I confirmed. "But this time, I'm going to refine it further, make it even better. If the sect has something like this, it could make a real difference, especially if things get as hectic as they seem to be."

Han Wei's expression cleared as he grasped the importance. "That's a good idea, Kai. With everything that's happening, we're going to need every advantage we can get."

Li Na's eyes softened as she looked at me, a small smile playing on her lips. "You've really thought this through, haven't you? You're not just thinking about yourself—you're thinking about all of us."

I shrugged, feeling a bit embarrassed under her gaze. "We're all in this together, right? Besides, it's not just about making something useful. It's about being ready for whatever comes next."

Han Wei thumped me on the back, his usual exuberance returning. "Well, if you're going to be in the pavilion, then maybe I'll stop by and see if I can learn a thing or two! And who knows, maybe I'll get inspired and create something amazing myself!"

Li Na rolled her eyes, but there was affection in her teasing. "Sure, Han Wei. Just don't blow up the pavilion while you're at it."

I chuckled at their banter, feeling a warmth in my chest. These were my friends, my comrades. And amid all this uncertainty, it was good to know I wasn't alone.

"All right," I said, turning to leave. "I'll see you two later. And don't worry— I'll make sure this hydrosol is something worth bragging about."

As I walked away, I couldn't help but feel a sense of anticipation. The future was uncertain, yes, but that didn't mean it was out of my control. There were things I could do, steps I could take to prepare.

And if the world was going to change, then I would make sure I was ready to change with it.

CHAPTER EIGHT

A Mark of Trust, a Promise of Return

Two days had passed since I'd made my decision to refine the healing hydrosol, and I now found myself seated across from Elder Zhu in one of the smaller, more private rooms of the alchemy pavilion. The air was filled with the faint, lingering scent of herbs and fresh ingredients.

Elder Zhu studied the vial in his hand, turning it slowly to catch the light. The liquid inside shimmered with an ethereal, turquoise glow.

"You've made significant improvements," Elder Zhu said, his voice calm but with an undercurrent of approval. "The increased purity and concentration will undoubtedly increase its effectiveness. This is a fine contribution to the sect."

I felt a surge of pride at his words, but I kept my tone humble. "Thank you, Elder Zhu. I left some essences in storage as a small token of my gratitude. Let me know if you need more."

I've already made Instructor Xia Ji aware of my healing hydrosol and how they could incorporate it into their training regimen. It wouldn't be long before the disciples would sing praises in my honor!

Elder Zhu's eyes flickered with something akin to surprise before he nodded appreciatively. "That is most generous of you, Kai. The sect will certainly put them to good use."

I couldn't help but reflect on how much time I had spent in the past two days extracting essences. The repetition had led to a surprising result.

> *Spiritual Herbalism has reached level 4.*

"The extraction process turned out to be quite a learning experience for me as well," I continued with a hint of amusement.

"The heavens often rewards those who act with sincerity and purpose. It seems your efforts to help the sect have led to your own advancement as well. That is the essence of true cultivation—growing in harmony with the world around you. Now, have you made all the necessary preparations? You don't want to leave anything behind."

I nodded, feeling both excitement and melancholy. "Yes, I think I have everything. I just want to do one last check in the guest quarters to make sure I didn't forget anything."

"Good. It's always better to be thorough," Elder Zhu remarked, his tone practical but with a trace of affection. "Safe travels, Kai. And remember, the Verdant Lotus Sect will always welcome you back."

"Thank you, Elder Zhu," I replied, bowing respectfully. "I'll make sure to carry the lessons I've learned here with me, wherever I go."

With that, I left the pavilion, stepping out into the familiar paths of the sect grounds. The late morning sun bathed everything in a warm, golden light, and the air was filled with the distant hum of disciples going about their daily routines. As I walked, I exchanged nods and greetings with those I passed, each interaction bringing a wave of nostalgia.

I was going to miss this place.

As I approached the guest quarters, my eyes were drawn to the roof, where Tianyi was perched on the roof, as she often did, her tiny form solemn against the vast sky. I had caught her here more often over the past few days.

"Tianyi," I called softly, not wanting to startle her.

She turned her entire body slightly, acknowledging me with a gentle flutter of her wings. *Kai,* she replied, her voice as delicate as her appearance.

I smiled up at her. "You've been quiet lately. Is everything all right?"

There was a brief pause before she answered, her voice carrying something I couldn't quite place. *I'm just . . . thinking.*

"About what?"

About change. About what's to come.

It was discomforting to realize even a butterfly could suffer an existential crisis, but I suppose her heightened intelligence as a Spirit Beast came with that.

"Well, there's one thing that won't change, and it's that we're in this together. Right?"

Right.

Although her tone didn't sound fully convinced, I could feel her contentment through our bond. Hopefully, my words provided some comfort.

With a final glance up at Tianyi, I headed into the guest quarters. The room was as I had left it, neat and tidy, with everything in its proper place.

It was hard to believe that I'd spent so much time here, and now it was time to leave.

I moved through the room, checking the drawers and shelves to make sure I hadn't overlooked anything. My mind drifted as I did so, thinking about the experiences I'd had in this room—the late nights spent refining pills, the early mornings preparing for training, the quiet moments of reflection. It was hard to let go of a place that had become so familiar.

Finally, I patted my pockets, making sure I had all my essentials. My hand brushed against the cool surface of the jade amulet, and I pulled it out, examining it closely. The jade felt warm in my hand, a reassuring weight that I slipped back into my pocket.

I didn't want to forget this one.

With everything in order, I called out softly to the butterfly perched on the roof. "Come on down, Tianyi. Time to go."

She fluttered from her perch, landing gracefully on my shoulder. I could feel her wings brush against my cheek.

Next, I approached Windy, who was curled up on the floor, still in a deep sleep. His scales gleamed in the soft light, a subtle sheen of blue reflecting off his white body. I crouched and gently lifted him, feeling the warmth of his small coiled form in my hands.

Windy stirred slightly as I picked him up, his eyes blinking open. He slithered up my sleeve, curling around my arm and poking his head out from behind my collar. His tiny tongue flickered in the air, tasting the cool breeze, and I could sense his displeasure at the temperature.

"Sorry, buddy," I murmured, rubbing his head lightly. "I'll make sure to wear the coat when we're going back home."

With Tianyi perched on my shoulder and Windy nestled against my neck, I took one last look around the room. It was strange to think that this would be the last time I stood here.

As I stepped outside, the sun was higher in the sky, casting a warm glow over the sect grounds. The day was beautiful, the kind that made you want to linger, to soak in the peace and tranquility of the place. As I walked down the familiar path to the stables, I noticed something that stopped me in my tracks—a small gathering of people just outside. My cart and horses were already prepared, waiting patiently in the warm sunlight, but what caught my attention was the group standing nearby.

Feng Wu, Han Wei, Li Na, Lan Sheng, Instructor Xia Ji, and Instructor Xiao-Hu—all of them were there, watching me with small knowing smiles. They stood together, a united front of friends, mentors, and comrades who had become an irreplaceable part of my life here.

A tingle started at the tip of my nose, the telltale sign that tears weren't far behind. I swallowed hard, pushing the emotion back down. Now wasn't the time for that.

Taking a deep breath, I plastered a grin on my face and walked toward them. "You all seem a little too eager to see me go," I joked.

Han Wei was the first to respond, his grin as wide as ever. "What can we say, Kai? It's not every day we get to kick someone out of the sect!"

Li Na rolled her eyes, though the smile tugging at her lips was genuine. "Ignore him, Kai. We're here because we're going to miss you. And because we wanted to make sure you don't leave without a proper send-off."

I felt a lump form in my throat, and I forced myself to keep my grin in place. "You guys are making it really hard to leave, you know that?"

Feng Wu stepped forward, his demeanor softer than usual. "I wish I could go with you, but unfortunately, I've some obligations here. I hope Lan Sheng will be a suitable escort in my stead."

Before I could respond, Lan Sheng chimed in with a grin. "Trust me, Kai, you'll be much safer with me than with Feng Wu. At least I won't lead you into any unnecessary fights."

A round of chuckles went around the group, and I couldn't help but join in. The lighthearted banter helped ease the tension in my chest, but it was a temporary reprieve. The weight of the moment was still pressing on me, even as I tried to keep things light.

Instructor Xia Ji cleared her throat, drawing my attention back to her. Her stern expression softened as she looked at me. "Kai, your contributions to the Verdant Lotus Sect have been invaluable. You may not be an official disciple, but you've shown dedication, skill, and heart. We'd like to present you with something as a token of our appreciation."

She nudged Instructor Xiao-Hu playfully. "Don't just stand there like a statue, Xiao-Hu. Hand over the goods!"

Xiao-Hu, ever the stoic instructor, cleared his throat and attempted to regain his composure, shooting a half-hearted glare at Xia Ji. "Must you always undermine my authority in front of the young ones?" he muttered under his breath, but a faint smile betrayed his amusement.

With a dignified nod, he presented a finely crafted charm. "Kai Liu," he said, his voice gruff yet warm, "accept this token as a symbol of our respect and gratitude. May it guide you on your path and remind you of the bonds you've forged here."

I took it from him, my fingers tracing the intricate lotus design etched into the metal. It was beautiful, with fine craftsmanship that spoke of both elegance and strength. Recognition dawned on me—it was the same type of charm Feng

Wu had used to gain entry into Crescent Bay City to get discounts at shops and other privileges.

"This charm signifies your affiliations with us. It's a mark of our trust and respect. With this, you'll be recognized as one of us, no matter where your journey takes you."

The tears I'd been holding back finally spilled over, hot and stinging. I tried to blink them away, but they kept coming, a relentless stream that blurred my vision.

"I . . . I don't know what to say," I stammered, my voice cracking. I looked at each of them, their faces a blur through my tears.

My words were clumsy, inadequate, but they were the only ones I could manage. The gesture, the recognition, the love and support they had shown me . . . It was overwhelming, a tidal wave of emotion that threatened to drown me.

"I promise . . . I'll make you all proud."

A chorus of warm laughter erupted from the group. Han Wei slung an arm around my shoulders, pulling me into a bone-crushing hug. "You already have, you oaf!" he exclaimed, his voice booming with affection. "Now come here and let us give you a proper send-off!"

Li Na joined the embrace, her hug surprisingly firm despite her petite frame. "Come back and visit us soon. If you make us wait until we're second-class disciples to visit you, I'm going to be mad."

Even Feng Wu, usually reserved and calm, offered a smile and patted my head. "Safe travels, Kai. May your journey be filled with adventure and good fortune."

The instructors, maintaining a more professional distance, stepped forward to shake my hand. Instructor Xiao-Hu's grip was firm.

"Remember everything you've learned, Kai," he said, stern yet kind. "And don't hesitate to reach out if you need anything."

"You've got a bright future ahead of you," Instructor Xia Ji said, clapping me on the shoulder. "Nurture it."

The horses, sensing our departure, pawed at the ground impatiently.

I looked down at Windy and Tianyi, both nestled against me—my constant companions through all of this. I reached into the cart, pulling out a cloth robe, draping it over myself and Windy to ward off the slight chill of the breeze. More than that, I discreetly used the edge of the cloth to wipe my eyes, clearing away the tears that had managed to escape.

Enough of this! This is unbecoming of a genius like myself! What would the world think if they saw me like this? A future legend, blubbering like a child?

I sniffed one last time, straightened my back, and pointed dramatically at the sky. "All right, Lan Sheng!" I declared. "It's time to depart! The heavens are waiting, and so are the great deeds I'm destined to accomplish! Let's go!"

Lan Sheng chuckled, clearly amused by my antics, but played along, giving a mock bow. "As you command, young master."

With a butterfly on my shoulder and a snake nestled against my neck, I climbed onto the cart, sad and excited. As we rolled through the sect gates, I couldn't help but glance back one last time. The rolling hills, the sprawling training grounds, the familiar faces—it all felt like a part of me, a home I was leaving behind.

But I knew I would always return.

CHAPTER NINE

Footprints in the Snow

The road stretched out before us, a winding path bordered by thick forests and rolling hills. The decision to bypass Crescent Bay City was a simple one—time was precious, and the journey back to my village was long enough without unnecessary detours. Besides, the thought of dealing with the city's bustling streets and watchful eyes didn't exactly thrill me. So, Lan Sheng and I stuck to the quieter path, our cart trundling steadily along.

He sat beside me, his usual easygoing demeanor making the journey feel less daunting. We'd been chatting since we left the sect, mostly about my recent advancements.

"You know," Lan Sheng said, breaking the comfortable silence, "what you've done with your qi reserves is pretty impressive. It's not every day someone raises their level to that of a second-class disciple after just one elixir."

I shrugged, trying to play it off. "The Beast Cores did most of the heavy lifting."

Lan Sheng chuckled, shaking his head. "You're too modest, Kai. Sure, the Beast Cores were potent, but not just anyone could have absorbed that power without some serious consequences. Your reserves are comparable to those of a second-class disciple, and Tianyi? She's at a rank that rivals a sect *elder*, albeit on the lower end, but that's nothing short of remarkable."

"When you put it like that . . . I suppose it is pretty crazy. I wonder what would've happened had I drunk the whole thing myself."

He grinned, leaning back against the cart's wooden seat. "Let me put it this way: We had a senior disciple in our sect who took an elixir just like yours. His qi surged, his power grew, and for a brief moment, he was the strongest in the sect."

My interest was piqued. "What happened to him?"

The man's expression turned grave, his voice dropping to a low whisper. "He exploded."

I nearly choked. *"What?!"*

"Yep. Boom. Bits and pieces everywhere," Lan Sheng continued ominously. "The sky was filled with his remains for days. Birds wouldn't go near the place where it happened for years."

My heart skipped a beat as I stared at him, horrified. "You're joking, right?"

The serious expression on his face cracked, and he burst out laughing. "Of course I'm joking! Come on, Kai, you really think Elder Zhu would let you take something that risky?"

This is why I didn't like Lan Sheng. He was a mischievous man, almost the complete opposite of Feng Wu in some ways.

"You really had me there for a second."

"Lesson learned—don't believe stories that sound too dramatic."

"All right, all right. What's the real story? What would've happened if I drank it all?"

Lan Sheng's tone shifted, though the amusement lingered. "It's about more than just a potent elixir. Compatibility is key. Some people—or Spirit Beasts—are hyper-responders. Their physique, affinities, and the medicine all align perfectly. When that happens, the effects are amplified. It's rare, but it happens."

"So it's not just the elixir's strength but how well it meshes with the person?"

"Exactly. Your body and affinities were in sync with the Beast Cores. Everything lined up perfectly. Tianyi must have had an even higher compatibility, which is why she ascended so fast. If you'd taken it all, your reserves would've been higher but not as drastic as you might think."

I glanced at Tianyi, who fluttered around while Windy was huddled under my robes. "So, a perfect storm—right place, right time, right conditions."

Lan Sheng nodded. "But even with that, there's a limit. The more you use one type of elixir or pill, the less effective it becomes as your body gets used to it. That's why you can't keep taking the same pills and expect endless growth."

"That's why variety matters," I added. "Different ingredients, different effects."

"Exactly. You keep your cultivation on its toes. But even then, you'll eventually run out of pills that give significant gains. That's why the path gets harder the further you go. You have to rely more on your own efforts and less on external aids."

The further we traveled, the more convinced I became that sharing the elixir with Tianyi and Windy had been the right decision. Sure, I could've hoarded it all for myself, raised my own power to ridiculous heights—but what kind of legend would I be without my companions by my side? The tales they'll tell won't just be of Kai, the lone cultivator with his two Spirit Beasts trailing behind him. No, we'll be known as something far grander—a trio that defies the heavens together, a force of nature that leaves entire sects trembling.

"And qi can only do so much. Even though your reserves are comparable to mine, it doesn't mean you could hang with me in a fight."

I turned to him with a raised brow. "Is that a challenge?"

"Is that what you think it is? I didn't mean it that way," he said amiably, scratching the back of his head. "Just meant it as a cautionary tale. Can't have you challenging second-class disciples with your head getting too big, they'll make minced meat out of you!"

"Oh, you look down upon this young master? How about you see if you can make minced meat out of me? I challenge you to a spar!"

Of course, it was all in jest. But having the opportunity to let loose against someone of Lan Sheng's caliber . . . It was an opportunity that was rather hard to come by. It might be the last until I go and visit the sect again.

He looked at me in surprise, before looking left and right. There was nothing but rolling hills covered in a blanket of frost and snow.

"Well, I suppose we've covered enough distance. This would give the horses a chance to rest."

We stopped at a nice, flat area and made a small camp. I placed Windy in my fur-lined coat beside the campfire while Tianyi fluttered around aimlessly. After I made sure the horses were well-situated with some food and water, I stood in front of Lan Sheng with no small amount of apprehension.

I still remembered our first spar; boosted with potions to enhance my mental acuity and physical prowess, I still had no chance against him.

But what about now?

With the Memory Palace technique, I had the opportunity to review his tells, habits, and moves over and over. Having the second-class disciples to practice against in my mindscape was crucial for refining my techniques. They were on a different level, both physically and mentally, from the younger generation like Li Na and Han Wei.

"As per tradition, I'll give you the first three moves." He rolled his shoulders, shaking his legs, before transitioning into an open palm stance.

With his demure grin and half-lidded eyes, it would've been easy for the average person to think he wasn't on guard.

But I knew. It was just a facade. One hiding a hand-to-hand combatant superior even to Feng Wu.

Without giving a signal, I dashed forward starting the fight with a swift jab to his solar plexus.

He parried it with ease, although he whistled at the punch. "Fast. You didn't take that potion of yours, did you? What's it called . . ." He casually ducked under my kick, scratching his head. "The Ambrosia of Glowing Sunrise?"

"That's not what it's called!"

I threw another punch, but this time, he caught it, pulling me forward to take me off-balance.

"Ha, sorry about that. It's a mouthful, you must admit."

As I stumbled, I could see the incoming leg sweep, which would inevitably leave me face-planting onto the snowy ground.

Just as I expected.

ROOTED BANYAN STANCE!

I tensed my core muscles, yanking my arm back in a hasty, incomplete version of the Rooted Banyan Stance. The defense was weak, but enough to keep me from being swept off my feet.

His lower shin made contact with my ankle, grinding against each other for a brief, painful moment. But I stayed standing.

Before he could respond, I let loose a burst of qi, infusing it into my next punch. The air cracked as my fist shot forward, aimed straight at his chest. But Lan Sheng, ever the seasoned warrior, sidestepped at the last possible moment, his movements fluid and precise.

My fist sailed past him, and before I could recover, he countered with a swift palm strike to my solar plexus. The force of the blow sent a shockwave through my body, knocking the wind out of me and making me heave as I staggered backward, clutching my stomach.

Lan Sheng's eyes widened, and he immediately stepped back, his hands raised in apology. "I'm so sorry! My muscle memory kicked in. I didn't mean to hit you that hard."

I waved him off, still trying to catch my breath. "N-no worries. Just . . . give me a second."

He waited patiently as I composed myself, the sharp pain in my chest slowly subsiding. Finally, I managed to straighten up, offering him a wry smile. "Guess I'm not quite there yet."

He returned the smile, but he was apologetic. "I won't lie, that was impressive. I didn't expect you to react like that. But remember, it's not just about the qi. Your body and mind need to improve in conjunction with it. Qi is like the fuel for your attacks, but if the vessel isn't built to handle it, you're going to crash."

He paused, then added, "Think of it like a bow and arrow. Your qi is the string, your body the bow, and your mind the arrow. If the string is strong but the bow is weak, the arrow won't fly true. And if your mind isn't focused, even the strongest shot will miss its mark."

I nodded, the metaphor sinking in. "So, I need to strengthen all three—body, mind, and qi—to truly become formidable."

I'd always understood it to be that way. It's why I strived for a balance rather than specializing in one particular area.

"Although, your growth rate . . . It's quite frightening. Perhaps there is some merit in your title as a genius, eh?"

I couldn't suppress the grin spreading across my face. I puffed up my chest, a playful swagger entering my step. "At this rate, I'd be able to take on Ping Hai in a straight fight, wouldn't I?"

He paused, a thoughtful expression crossing his face.

Then, he looked up at the sky and spoke. "Ah, the snow is falling so beautifully today, don't you think, Kai?"

I stared at him, my jaw agape. "That's not an answer!"

He simply shrugged, a mischievous glint in his eyes. "We can rest here for about an hour, then continue. Qingmu isn't far now."

"Lan Sheng!" I groaned, playfully shoving his shoulder. "Don't dodge the question!"

The snow continued to fall, a silent witness to our lighthearted banter as I relentlessly pestered him for a straight answer.

As the village of Qingmu came into view, a surge of nostalgia washed over me. The last time I had seen this place, it had been under siege by Wind Serpents, its streets filled with fear and uncertainty. Now, as I breathed in the crisp winter air, I could see that the damage from those attacks had been repaired. The houses stood tall and sturdy, their walls freshly mended, and life had returned to the village.

Excitement bubbled up inside me as we drew closer. The village was more vibrant than I remembered. Children played in the snow, their laughter ringing out through the cold air, while adults tended to their tasks, their expressions relaxed and content. It was a stark contrast to the tense atmosphere I had encountered before.

As Lan Sheng and I strolled down the main path, I noticed how quickly the villagers recognized me. Whispers spread like wildfire, and before I knew it, people were approaching us with broad smiles and words of gratitude.

"Kai! It's really him! The one who saved us from the Wind Serpents!"

"The hero of Qingmu has returned!"

In no time, I was surrounded by villagers, their faces glowing with appreciation. They crowded around me, some clasping my hands, others bowing their heads in thanks. The attention was overwhelming, and I could feel the familiar warmth of embarrassment creeping up my neck.

The second-class disciple, never one to miss an opportunity to tease, leaned in with a grin. "So, how does it feel to be the village's savior? They might start building a statue of you next."

I chuckled awkwardly, trying to deflect the praise. "I'm just glad I could help. No need for statues, really."

But just as I was beginning to accept the adulation, a piercing scream cut through the air, shattering the celebratory mood. The villagers around me froze, their expressions shifting from joy to alarm as they turned to look at the source of the scream.

A woman stood a short distance away, her eyes wide with terror. She was pointing directly at me—or rather, at something near me. Confused, I followed her gaze and realized what had caught her attention.

My ever-curious companion had poked his head out from my collar, his serpentine eyes gleaming innocently as he took in the scene.

Perhaps bringing a Wind Serpent into a village that had been attacked by Wind Serpents wasn't my brightest idea.

CHAPTER TEN

Fear's Lingering Bite

The crowd's joyful murmurs turned into hushed whispers, and the warm smiles I had been receiving moments ago faded into wary stares. It didn't take long for me to understand why. Windy, though far smaller and less menacing than the serpents that had attacked Qingmu, still bore a striking resemblance to them. His white scales and blue eyes were different, yes, but to the villagers, he was still a Spirit Beast serpent—a creature they had every reason to fear.

I forced a smile, trying to dispel the growing tension. "Please, everyone, calm down. This is Windy. He's not like the Wind Serpents that attacked the village. He's a different species entirely."

It was a bit of a fib. He was undoubtedly a Wind Serpent but, as listed by the Interface, an aberrant. One clearly influenced by Tianyi's abilities, infusing him with energy since he was just an egg.

The villagers exchanged uncertain glances, their apprehension palpable. I could see the fear in their eyes, the memories of those terrifying days resurfacing. I couldn't blame them; after all, it wasn't every day that a snake—especially one resembling a Wind Serpent—showed up in your village.

"He's harmless," I continued, my tone as reassuring as I could make it. "Look at him. He's smaller, his scales are pure white, and his eyes are blue, not red like the ones that attacked the village. He's not aggressive at all."

But my words seemed to do little to soothe their fears. The villagers continued to murmur among themselves, their eyes darting between me and Windy. I could hear snippets of their conversations—

"Can we trust him?"

"What if it turns on us?"

"It looks just like them . . ."

Lan Sheng, sensing the rising tension, stepped forward. His presence, usually relaxed and easygoing, took on a more authoritative air as he addressed the crowd. "People of Qingmu, I understand your concerns, but I assure you, this serpent is not a threat. On the honor of the Verdant Lotus Sect, I swear that Windy is under complete control and can be trusted."

For a moment, his words seemed to have some effect. The murmurs quieted slightly, and a few of the villagers glanced at each other, as if trying to gauge whether they should believe us. But the fear was still there, lurking just beneath the surface.

One of the older men, his face lined with years of hardship, stepped forward. "He may be different, but he's still a serpent. We've seen what those creatures can do. Can you guarantee that it won't harm us?"

I opened my mouth to respond, but the words caught in my throat. I knew he wouldn't hurt anyone, but how could I convince them? How could I make them see that he wasn't like the others?

An idea struck me. If I could show the villagers that Windy was fully under my control—tamed and harmless—they might start to see him differently. I swallowed my nerves and glanced down at the serpent, who was still nestled in my collar, his blue eyes watching the villagers with a curious but indifferent gaze.

"Of course I can guarantee it," I said firmly. "In fact, I'll prove it to you right now."

I cleared my throat, trying to sound confident. "Windy, come out and show everyone how well behaved you are."

He blinked at me slowly, and for a moment, I thought he was going to cooperate. But then he just stayed where he was, his expression unreadable. The villagers watched closely, their unease palpable, as I tried again.

"Come on, Windy," I urged, my tone a little more pleading. "Do something, uh, cool. You know, like you did back at the sect."

I swore I saw a hint of reproach in those blue eyes. He didn't move an inch. My confidence began to falter, and I could feel the sweat starting to bead on my forehead. This was not going as planned.

"Please?"

I couldn't believe I was begging a snake to perform tricks in front of a crowd, but here I was, with half the entire village watching me.

Windy finally stirred, but instead of doing something impressive or even remotely useful, he slithered out of my collar and lazily coiled around my arm, then rested his head on my shoulder. His eyelids heavy, he looked more like he was ready to take a nap than to impress anyone.

And then, I felt it—a wave of icy disdain washing over me, but it wasn't my own. It was sharp, cold, and pointed, cutting through the fog of my thoughts like a blade. My breath caught in my throat. *Tianyi?*

The realization hit me like a splash of cold water, and I turned my gaze toward her. The usually delicate butterfly was hovering in the air, her wings barely moving as she stared intently at Windy. Her entire form seemed to radiate an icy aura, and it became clear that she was the source of the frigid pressure I was feeling.

The serpentine Spirit Beast, who had been perfectly content to ignore my requests, suddenly stiffened. His gaze shifted from me to Tianyi, and for the first time, I saw a flicker of something akin to nervousness in his blue eyes. It was as if they were having a silent conversation, one where Windy was being firmly reprimanded.

His body coiled tighter around my arm, his tail twitching as if he was trying to resist whatever command the butterfly was giving him. But the pressure from Tianyi's silent will was unrelenting, her icy determination pressing down on him. I could feel the tension in Windy's small body, a silent battle of wills between the two Spirit Beasts.

For a moment, I feared Windy might openly defy her, but then the resistance in his posture softened. With a resigned huff—if snakes could huff—Windy uncoiled himself from my arm and leapt into the air. The movement was fluid and graceful, a stark contrast to his earlier laziness. He formed a perfect circle midair before landing back on my shoulder with an effortless flick of his tail.

The villagers, who had been holding their breath, erupted into applause. Their earlier apprehension began to dissolve, replaced by awe at the display.

I exhaled a long, tight breath. The icy pressure in my mind subsided as Tianyi's presence softened, her intent satisfied. Windy, on the other hand, shot the both of us a reproachful look, as if to say, *There, happy now?*

I offered him an apologetic smile in return, grateful that he had gone along with the plan, even if reluctantly. He would be receiving a nice feast when I could provide it for him!

As the villagers approached again, this time with less fear and more curiosity, I allowed myself a moment of relief. Things hadn't gone exactly as planned, but they had worked out in the end. Still, I made a mental note: Bringing a Wind Serpent into a village that had been terrorized by Wind Serpents? Probably not the wisest course of action.

They slowly returned to their routines, though their eyes still lingered on me and my serpent companion. A few even managed hesitant smiles as they gave us space to pass through.

Lan Sheng, ever the lighthearted one, clapped me on the shoulder as we continued toward the village's inn. "Well, that was a close one. It's a good thing Windy knew what 'cool' meant."

I chuckled, more out of relief than anything else. "Yeah, well, I suppose I should've anticipated that reaction. Not every day you bring a Wind Serpent into a place that barely survived an attack by its kin."

We reached the inn, a modest establishment that looked like it had seen better days but had clearly been patched up with care since the last time I'd visited. I pushed the door open with a casual swing, hoping to brush off the day's excitement.

As soon as we stepped inside, the familiar warmth of the inn enveloped us. The smell of hearty stew and fresh bread wafted through the air. The innkeeper glanced up from behind the counter, ready to greet us with the usual pleasantries. But then, recognition flickered across his face, and his words caught in his throat.

"Welcome! What can I—Elder Brother Kai?!" he exclaimed, his eyes widening in disbelief.

I grinned, already feeling more at ease. "Hua Lingsheng! You've grown!"

The boy I'd saved from the Wind Serpents, now a bit taller and certainly more confident, was standing right in front of me. It was good to see him again, especially under better circumstances.

His face lit up as he rushed forward, grabbing my hands with an enthusiasm that nearly knocked me off-balance. "Elder Brother Kai!" His voice trembled with awe. "You've returned!"

I smiled at him and patted his shoulder. "I have, and it's clear you've grown while I was away."

"Of course! I've been training! So that one day, I can protect the village just like you did!"

I chuckled softly, trying to ease his intensity. He was buzzing so much so that I thought he'd explode. "No need to rush. Just take your time and focus on your training. Cultivation is a lifelong journey, and you have plenty of time to grow."

He nodded before glancing at Tianyi, Windy, and Lan Sheng. He strained his neck to see two horses and a cart behind us. "I'll have the rooms prepared for you immediately! Just give me a few moments!"

"Thank you," I pulled out my coin satchel, heavy with change. "How much will it b—?"

But Hua Lingsheng wasn't about to be calmed down so easily. "Nonsense!" he declared with a fervor that made me blink in surprise. "I owe you my life, and allowing you to pay would bring shame upon my family for generations! Let me take care of your horses and cart—I'll make sure they're well looked after."

Before I could protest, he darted out of the inn, leaving me standing there, slightly stunned by his energy. I could hear him shouting orders to the stable hands outside, his tone brimming with purpose.

I sighed inwardly, feeling embarrassment and pride. It was touching, really, to see how much of an impact I'd had on him. But at the same time, I couldn't help but feel a bit uncomfortable about the hero worship.

Lan Sheng, who had been watching the whole exchange with barely contained amusement, finally lost his composure. He burst out laughing, his shoulders shaking with mirth. "You've really made an impression on him, haven't you?"

I shot him a glare, though I couldn't help the smile tugging at the corners of my lips. "Oh, shut up. I didn't ask for this."

He wiped a tear from his eye, still chuckling. "Oh, I know. But it's just too good. The mighty Kai, revered by the villagers and idolized by the young. Who would've thought?"

"Yeah, yeah," I muttered, trying to brush off the embarrassment. "Let's just focus on getting a room for the night."

Within minutes, we were situated and placed in the biggest rooms in the inn. It was early in the evening still, and I decided to get some training done outside. If I wanted to incorporate the rest of the Beast Core elixir into my dantian quicker, I'd need to keep on training hard and deplete my reserves.

My two companions came with me, although Lan Sheng stayed in his room, likely cultivating in peace or sleeping.

We sneakily made our way out of the inn as a group, traveling into the outskirts, but close enough where the village was in plain sight. I closed my eyes and took a deep breath, remembering Lan Sheng's words.

Qi alone is not enough.

The memory of our sparring session replayed in my mind, a relentless loop of feints, parries, and missed opportunities. I had dissected every movement, every subtle shift in his stance, every telltale twitch of his muscles. I had the advantage of familiarity, of countless hours spent replaying our encounters within the vast expanse of my Memory Palace. Yet, despite my knowledge, he had effortlessly outmaneuvered me.

What was it that kept him so far ahead of me?

I understood now. More than ever. It wasn't just about having the strongest techniques or the most potent reserves. It was about knowing when to strike, when to yield, when to adapt. It was about reading your opponent, anticipating their next move, and responding with a calculated counter.

A fierce determination ignited within me. This was a challenge I couldn't overcome with shortcuts or clever tricks. This was a battle that would be won through sweat, blood, and countless hours of practice.

And the only solution to that was gaining experience of my own. To adapt and consider the nuance of each technique I knew, when to use them and when not to. This wasn't something I could cut corners with.

I turned to Tianyi and Windy, grinning. "You two ready?"

Indeed, the butterfly said in my mind, her voice a melody carried on the crisp winter air.

Windy uncoiled, his sleek body a blur of white against the snow as he tested his newfound agility. The elixir had ignited a spark within him, a hunger for challenge and growth. And perhaps a hint of resentment for being forced to do tricks at my and Tianyi's behest.

A thrill coursed through me. The prospect of sparring with partners who could match my newfound strength was exhilarating. No more holding back, no more cautious exchanges.

"Let's go!" I roared, launching myself forward.

The snow-covered clearing became our battlefield. Tianyi darted through the air, her wings a blur. Windy, a serpentine whirlwind, weaved and lunged, his tail a whip of pure force. I met their attacks with equal fervor, my movements fueled by a newfound confidence and agility.

The night air crackled with energy, the clash of our powers echoing through the silent clearing. Under the watchful eyes of the moon and stars, we danced, we fought, we grew.

Like a dragon's claws tempered against steel scales, we honed our skills, each strike a step closer to mastery.

CHAPTER ELEVEN

A Taoist's Forbidden Feast

I groaned as I slowly became aware of my surroundings, every muscle in my body protesting even the slightest movement. It felt like I'd been run over by a herd of stampeding Spirit Beasts.

Although admittedly that wasn't too far from the case.

The dull ache in my limbs was a stark reminder of the sparring session from the night before, where I had faced the brutal onslaught of my own companions.

Windy's qi-infused tail strikes had been far more powerful than I anticipated. The sheer force behind each whip of his tail had nearly knocked the wind out of me, and I was pretty sure I'd have quite a few bruises had it not been for the Rooted Banyan Stance.

As I slowly stretched out my arm, I winced, feeling the soreness in my muscles. Tianyi had been no less formidable. Her lightning-fast bladed wings had forced me to stay on my toes, dodging and weaving as best as I could. The cuts on my robes—and the few shallow ones on my skin—were a testament to her precision.

As I lay there, staring up at the wooden ceiling, I couldn't help but replay the events of the previous night in my mind. Lan Sheng had been right, of course. Just because someone had immense qi reserves didn't mean they could wield them effectively in battle. Tianyi, despite having reached a rank comparable to a sect elder according to the Interface, wasn't yet a seasoned fighter. She had the power, yes, but her lack of experience was evident. Her attacks were fast, her wings sharp enough to slice through wood, but there was a predictability to her movements that I could exploit—if I was fast enough.

But even knowing that, I couldn't ignore the reality of our sparring session. If we had been fighting for real, with the intent to kill, there was no doubt in my mind that Tianyi would have left me in a puddle of my own blood. She was strong, far stronger than me in terms of raw power, but it wasn't an insurmountable strength. There was still a gap between us, but it wasn't the kind of gap that left me feeling hopeless. Instead, it was a challenge—a challenge to close that distance, to grow stronger alongside her.

Good morning, the butterfly said. She fluttered over, perching atop my nose.

"Good morning to you too, Tianyi."

I decided not to disturb Windy, as he was content, sleeping. Getting dressed and tying my hair into a bun, I made my way downstairs, yawning all the while.

A massive breakfast awaited me, several dishes piled high, along with the sight of Lan Sheng eating noodle soup.

Beef noodle soup.

He stilled, as though detecting my presence.

My jaw dropped. "Lan Sheng," I sputtered, pointing at the Taoist. "Is that . . . *beef* noodle soup?"

He froze, chopsticks hovering midair, a noodle dangling precariously from his lips. His eyes darted between me and the bowl. "It's, uh . . ." he stammered, clearing his throat. "It's a . . . medicinal broth. Yes, a medicinal broth made with, uh, beef essence. For strengthening the body and . . . and cultivating yang energy."

"You're the worst liar I've ever met!"

He sheepishly lowered his chopsticks, a blush creeping up his neck. "All right, all right, you got me," he admitted, a sheepish grin spreading across his face. "But it's been *ages* since I've had a good bowl of beef noodle soup. And besides," he added conspiratorially, "a little indulgence never hurt anyone, right?"

I shook my head, still chuckling. "You're incorrigible," I said, taking a seat across from him. "But I guess I can't blame you. That smells amazing."

He beamed, pushing the bowl toward me. "Try some," he offered. "It's better than anything I've tried in Crescent Bay."

Did that mean he was a repeat offender? Was this guy really a Taoist?

"Why not?" I said. "After all, a little indulgence never hurt anyone."

As I slurped up the flavorful broth and savored the tender beef, I couldn't help but grin. Maybe a little deviation from the path of strict discipline wasn't so bad after all. Especially when it involved a steaming bowl of beef noodle soup.

"I hope you're enjoying the meal," someone said from the kitchen. I turned to my right and found a familiar face. "I apologize for not meeting you last night."

"Ah . . . ! Hua Yin, right?"

Hua Lingsheng's father was looking at me with a small smile.

I wiped my mouth with the back of my hand and quickly stood up to greet him with a respectful bow. "No need to apologize. It's good to see you again."

He waved off my formality with a warm smile, stepping closer to the table. "I'm glad to see you've recovered from your journey. We've all been working hard here in Qingmu, repairing the damage from the Wind Serpents before winter truly sets in. But we wouldn't have had the chance to do any of it if it weren't for you."

His words were humbling, and I felt a flush of embarrassment creep up my neck.

"I only did what anyone would have done in my place," I murmured.

Hua Yin shook his head, his expression earnest. "You did more than that. You saved this village. My family, my son . . . We owe you a debt we can never truly repay. Your stay here, as well as your meals, are on the house. Please enjoy yourself freely."

I opened my mouth to protest, but the look in his eyes told me that arguing would be futile. Instead, I nodded, grateful for their kindness. "Thank you. That's very generous of you."

Lan Sheng, who had been quietly enjoying his meal throughout the exchange, suddenly chimed in between bites of his beef noodle soup. "Well, I have to say, this is the best hospitality I've had in a long time! You've got yourself a top-notch inn here."

I shot him a sideways glance, unable to suppress a smirk. He was eating like he'd been the one to save the village, completely at ease and clearly relishing every bite. "You do realize it wasn't you who saved Qingmu, right? Maybe leave some food for the *actual* hero."

The second-class disciple grinned, not the least bit ashamed. "I'm just making sure none of this delicious food goes to waste. Besides, if you think about it, I'm doing the village a favor by keeping my strength up. What if another Wind Serpent comes along?"

I rolled my eyes but couldn't help laughing. "Yeah, sure. Keep telling yourself that."

Hua Yin chuckled as well, clearly amused by our banter. "It's good to see you both in high spirits. You're welcome to stay as long as you like, Kai. Qingmu is always open to you."

I smiled, appreciating the innkeeper's generosity and the warmth in his voice. It was comforting to know that I had a place where I was always welcome.

"Thank you," I said again, feeling grateful. "But if I could ask for one more favor . . ."

"Anything you need. Just say the word."

"Could I trouble you for a cup of sugar water? It's for Tianyi. She prefers something sweet to start the day."

"Ah, for your companion. Absolutely. I'll have it prepared right away."

As he headed back to the kitchen, I settled back into my seat, now more at ease. The butterfly fluttered down from her perch and landed delicately on the edge of the table.

Thank you.

Lan Sheng, meanwhile, continued to eat with gusto.

"You're really making the most of this, aren't you?" I asked.

"I'm ensuring that the savior of Qingmu doesn't have to eat alone. That counts for something, right?" he replied.

I laughed, shaking my head. What a character. I wonder if Feng Wu deviated from his Taoist practices when he was alone like he did. Although something tells me Lan Sheng is an . . . exception among the rest of the second-class disciples.

As I leaned back in my chair, savoring the warmth and comfort of the inn, my thoughts drifted back to the time when the Silent Moon Sect had visited Qingmu. The memory of first seeing them was still fresh in my mind—their presence had been overwhelming.

The way they had been so adamant that Feng Wu and I not interfere when the Wind Serpents attacked . . . They wanted no uncertainty about whose territory this was, even at the cost of potential casualties.

I wondered if the Silent Moon Sect had visited again since then. Had they come to collect more tributes? The thought made me uneasy, as well as the idea of seeing Xu Ziqing.

Knowing my luck, I'd come the same day they're collecting tribute.

Just as I was about to ask Hua Yin, I noticed Hua Lingsheng entering the inn from outside, his cheeks flushed from the cold.

He spotted me and immediately brightened, rushing over with the same enthusiasm he'd shown the day before. "Elder Brother Kai! Did you sleep well?"

"I did, thanks to your family's hospitality," I replied warmly. "Actually, I was just thinking . . . Have you or anyone else in the village seen the Silent Moon Sect since they last came?"

"No, we haven't seen them since they came to help after the Wind Serpents attacked. They collected their tribute, and then . . . nothing. Which is odd, since they collected it regularly."

That was a relief, at least for now. But I couldn't shake the feeling that their absence wasn't entirely benevolent.

Lan Sheng, still working his way through another bowl of noodles, finally spoke up. "It's likely they're focusing their manpower inward after Elder Jun took power. Consolidating their strength, dealing with any internal challenges . . . It makes sense that they wouldn't be too concerned with a small village like Qingmu for the time being, as valuable as it is."

I blinked, confused at the last part of his sentence.

"Valuable? How so?"

"Well, it's a crossroads for many traders traveling to farther villages, including your hometown," he explained, setting down his bowl. "It might look unassuming, but it's a vital hub for trade in this region. The merchants pass through here, bringing goods from all over and distributing them to smaller, more remote villages. It's a lifeline, really."

I blinked, taken aback by the information. And even more so by Lan Sheng's articulate reply. "I had no idea. It didn't seem like much when I first arrived."

The man chuckled, giving me a knowing look. "Ah, Kai, are you looking down on Qingmu? Just because it doesn't look like Crescent Bay or some bustling city doesn't mean it isn't important. I thought you'd know better than to judge a book by its cover."

I quickly shook my head, panic blooming in my chest. "No, that's not what I meant! I just—"

Before I could finish, Hua Lingsheng burst out laughing, the sound light and genuine. "It's all right, Elder Brother Kai! We know Qingmu doesn't look like much. The truth is the area isn't rich in natural resources, so it's hard to expand or accommodate a larger population. We're heavily reliant on the trade that passes through here, which is why the village is smaller than you might expect."

The younger boy beamed at me. "That's why we're so grateful to you, Elder Brother Kai. Without you, we might not have had the chance to rebuild and keep the trade routes open. You've done more for us than you know."

"I . . . I'm glad I could help," I replied softly, "and I'll do my best to continue supporting Qingmu however I can."

Just as the warmth of the moment settled in, a sudden, sharp feeling of wariness pierced my thoughts—an emotion that wasn't my own. I immediately recognized it as coming from Tianyi. Her usually serene presence had become taut, like a bowstring drawn too tight.

At the same time, Lan Sheng paused, his easygoing demeanor shifting as his eyes narrowed at the door. "Something's happening outside," he said, his voice low and serious.

Without another word, we all rose from our seats and moved toward the door, the tension palpable. As we stepped outside, the source of Tianyi's unease became clear. A commotion was brewing in the village square, and a crowd was quickly forming.

Pushing our way through the gathering villagers, we soon saw what had drawn their attention. A group of cultivators, dressed in deep orange robes, were parading through the square. At their center was the massive corpse of a boar, its thick hide marred with fresh wounds. The beast's tusks gleamed in the morning light. It was clear it wasn't any regular beast.

Standing proudly atop the boar's carcass was a young cultivator, his posture exuding arrogance as he addressed the crowd.

"Behold!" he declared, his voice booming across the square. "This mighty beast was felled by none other than I, Shan Huai of the Iron Claw Sect!"

The villagers murmured among themselves, clearly impressed, but Shan Huai's bravado made me inwardly groan. Of course something like this would happen the moment I arrived. Why did events always seem to spiral out of control when I was nearby?

Lan Sheng shot me a wry knowing glance. "Looks like we've got ourselves a show-off. What do you think, Kai? Should we see what all the fuss is about?"

I sighed, already feeling the headache coming on. "Might as well. But something tells me this is going to be more trouble than it's worth."

With that, we moved closer to the front of the crowd, ready to see just what kind of spectacle the cultivators were planning to put on.

CHAPTER TWELVE

The Rumbling Thunder, Shan Huai

The crowd's chatter swelled around us as the man leading the group stepped forward, his orange robes fluttering slightly in the morning breeze. The arrogance radiating from him was palpable, and it wasn't hard to see why. With a cocky grin plastered on his face, he planted his foot callously on the corpse of the beast, his posture exuding the self-assurance of someone who had no doubt about his superiority.

"People of Qingmu!" he called out, his voice reverberating across the square. "I am Shan Huai, the Rumbling Thunder, second-class disciple of the Iron Claw Sect! This beast you see before you—a vicious Iron Boar—was stalking the outskirts of your village, threatening your very lives. But fear not, for I and my comrades have vanquished it, ensuring your safety!"

"Iron Claw Sect?" I turned to Lan Sheng beside me. He shrugged, likely having never heard of the name himself.

The villagers gasped, murmuring among themselves as they regarded the massive beast's corpse. Both of us stepped closer to get a better look at the Iron Boar.

As we approached, I could see the boar's body in greater detail.

It was the genuine article, all right.

I searched my memory; not as mythical as the Wind Serpent but undeniably a Spirit Beast, the Iron Boar was a formidable monster known for its thick hide that was said to be as tough as metal—hence the name. But what caught my attention were the wounds that marred its side. Three deep gouges ran along its flank, the flesh torn clean through to the bone. The blood that had seeped from the wounds was dried now.

Lan Sheng leaned in slightly, his voice low. "Those gouges . . . They're not from some wild, flailing attack. Those are precise strikes, deep and lethal."

The realization settled in, heavy and undeniable. Shan Huai wasn't just blowing hot air. They had actually defeated this monster, a feat that shouldn't be underestimated. If they were able to carve its hide like soft tofu, then they weren't to be taken lightly.

Tianyi fluttered slightly on my shoulder, her wings giving off a faint, uneasy hum. I felt a prickle of unease myself. This guy wasn't just some arrogant braggart.

The man, oblivious to—or perhaps reveling in—the attention he was receiving, continued his proclamation. "The Iron Boar is known for its resilience and power, but it was no match for the might of the Iron Claw Sect! We have saved your village from certain destruction. Remember this day, for it is the day the Rumbling Thunder of the Iron Claw Sect ensured your safety!"

Shan Huai's voice boomed across the square as he continued, his tone shifting from boastful to derisive. "But where was the Silent Moon Sect, huh? The so-called *protectors* of Qingmu? Nowhere to be seen, of course. They've left you to fend for yourselves, only showing up when it's time to collect their tribute. It's clear they don't value this village—don't value *you*. But don't worry! The Iron Claw Sect will not stand for such neglect and injustice."

The villagers exchanged uneasy glances, the tension in the air thickening as Shan Huai's words settled over them.

"We, the Iron Claw Sect," he continued, his voice rising with righteous indignation, "are willing to step in where the Silent Moon Sect has failed. We will take our rightful place as your protectors, and unlike them, we won't demand exorbitant tributes. We ask for far less—only what is fair and just."

Ah. So this is where he's going.

Lan Sheng and I exchanged a sharp look. It was clear now what Shan Huai was up to. This wasn't just about showing off his skills or gaining the village's admiration. This was a calculated move to undermine the Silent Moon Sect and seize control of Qingmu. The implications were dangerous—if the Silent Moon Sect discovered that the Iron Claw was encroaching on their territory . . .

Before I could voice my concerns, the village head, an older man with a weathered face and a humble demeanor, stepped forward. His hands trembled slightly as he clasped them in front of him, bowing deeply to Shan Huai. "We are grateful for your help, truly we are," he began, respectful and anxious. "But—"

Shan Huai's expression darkened, his eyes narrowing as he cut the village head off. "But what? Are you rejecting the favor of the Iron Claw Sect? Are you spitting in our faces after we saved you from certain death?"

The village head's eyes widened, his face paling as he realized the gravity of the situation. He tried to backtrack, his words tumbling out in a rush. "No, no, of course not! We are thankful, it's just that . . . we cannot so easily switch our allegiance. The Silent Moon Sect has protected us for years, and—"

"Protected?" the man sneered. "They've done nothing but take from you! And now, when another Spirit Beast comes—because make no mistake, it *will* come—what will you do? Beg the Silent Moon Sect to save you again? And if they don't come? What then?"

His words hung in the air, heavy and oppressive. The villagers murmured anxiously, their fear palpable. I could almost see the doubt creeping into their minds, the seeds of mistrust being planted.

Lan Sheng shifted beside me, his expression hardening. "This isn't good," he muttered. "If they push this too far, the Silent Moon Sect will retaliate, and Qingmu will be caught in the crossfire."

I nodded, my mind racing as I tried to think of a way to defuse the situation. Spirit beast sightings had been rising throughout the region, and Shan Huai's threat wasn't just an empty boast. The village was vulnerable, and the fear of being left unprotected was a powerful motivator.

My thoughts raced as I took in the scene. The villagers were being cornered, coerced into accepting protection they didn't fully understand. The implications were dire—if they agreed, it could be seen as a betrayal by the Silent Moon Sect. If they refused, they risked angering the Iron Claw Sect. Either choice seemed to lead to ruin.

Then something caught my eye. The deep gouges on the Iron Boar's side . . . the younger disciples surrounding Shan Huai. Their clothes, demeanor, and cleanliness.

The pieces started to fit together, and I realized there was a way to turn this situation around.

But how?

Wait . . . That's right!

I glanced at Lan Sheng, wondering if I should involve him in my plan, but quickly decided against it. This needed to be my move. And I had to do it quickly.

Leaning slightly toward the second-class disciple, I whispered, "I have an idea. Trust me on this."

Lan Sheng's brow furrowed, clearly confused, but he gave a slight nod. "All right, I'm with you."

Taking a deep breath, I stepped forward, raising my hand in an extremely meek manner. I even forced a slight stutter into my voice as I spoke. "E-excuse me . . . I, um—I have a suggestion."

Shan Huai's eyes snapped to me, a mixture of annoyance and curiosity flickering in them. He made a brief glance at Lan Sheng, but quickly turned his eyes back to me. "Who are you?"

"I'm just an alchemist, visiting family here," I said, keeping my voice small and unthreatening. "But, uh, I couldn't help overhearing your conversation, and I think there's a way to resolve this . . . for both sides."

Shan Huai raised an eyebrow, clearly intrigued but also skeptical. "Oh? And how do you propose we do that?"

I took another deep breath, forcing myself to maintain the timid act. "With a demonstration," I said, my voice trembling just enough to make it sound like I was nervous. "A simple contest . . . between you and me."

"A contest?" Shan Huai repeated, his tone dripping with incredulity as a smirk played at the corners of his lips. The crowd's murmurs grew louder, the villagers exchanging uneasy glances, unsure of what to make of my proposal.

"Y-yes," I stammered, playing up the meekness as much as I could. "A spar—"

"Sorry, could I speak with my friend here for a moment?"

Just as I got the word "spar" out of my mouth, Lan Sheng suddenly stepped forward, grabbing me by the arm and pulling me aside, a few steps out of the crowd of villagers. His grip was tight, and I could see the panic in his eyes.

"Are you out of your mind, Kai?!" he hissed, shaking me. "Have you lost your mind somewhere along the way to Qingmu? Why in the world are you picking a fight with a second-class disciple? Did you forget everything I told you about how increased qi reserves don't automatically mean you can fight against us?"

I swallowed hard, trying to stay calm despite the intensity of his reaction. "Trust me on this," I whispered, grabbing his arms to steady him. "Just look closer at them. Fighting a beast of the Iron Boar's caliber should have left some visible signs of struggle—torn robes, bloodstains, or at least some dirt and grime. But they're completely unscathed. Doesn't that raise any red flags for you?"

Lan Sheng frowned, his eyes narrowing as he cast another glance at Shan Huai and his group. I could see the wheels turning in his mind, his expression shifting as he began to piece together what I was suggesting.

"Think about it," I continued urgently. "They're not even carrying weapons that would be capable of piercing the Iron Boar's hide. They're claiming they took it down with their bare fists. Now, either they attacked the boar when it was already weakened, or they're powerful enough to dispatch such a beast without breaking a sweat. Either way, something's off."

Lan Sheng's grip on my arms loosened slightly, his gaze growing more thoughtful as he processed my words. "So, what's your plan, then? Why the sparring challenge? Why don't I spar in your stead? It's basically the reason why I'm here. So *your* ass doesn't get itself into trouble."

I took a deep breath, shaking my head as I tried to explain. "That's exactly the problem, Lan Sheng. If you take up the challenge, he'll be more on guard, knowing you're a second-class disciple like him. He won't let his guard down so easily. But me? I'm just an unassuming alchemist—no sect affiliation, no reputation to worry about. He'll underestimate me, and that's what we need right now."

Lan Sheng's eyes searched mine, still full of doubt, but I could see that my reasoning was starting to get through to him. "Kai, this is risky. If they really did take down that Iron Boar with their bare fists, then we're dealing with some seriously powerful people here."

"Exactly." I kept my voice firm. "*If* they're as strong as they claim, they would've already challenged the Silent Moon Sect directly. But they haven't. Instead, they're trying to exploit the death of the Iron Boar to gain leverage over the village. That's a red flag. If I'm right, and this is all just a bluff, then I can expose them and drive them away without bloodshed. And if . . . If I'm wrong, then at least we'll know the village is under the protection of someone who's actually strong enough to stand against the Silent Moon Sect."

Lan Sheng let out a long sigh, his shoulders slumping slightly as he finally relented. "All right, Kai. I don't like it, but I'll trust you on this. Just be careful, okay?"

"I will," I promised, giving him a reassuring nod. "And if things start to go south, don't hesitate to step in."

With that, I turned back to the crowd, trying to keep my nerves in check as I approached Shan Huai once more. The man was watching me with a curious, almost amused expression, as if he were trying to figure out what my angle was.

"You're awfully close to the second-class disciple of the Verdant Lotus Sect," Shan Huai remarked casually, his tone laced with thinly veiled disdain. "But you should know that just because our titles are the same doesn't mean our skills are. The Verdant Lotus is full of scholars and alchemists, not warriors."

I bit my tongue, forcing down the urge to snap at him. Instead, I kept my expression meek and nodded in agreement. "You're right, of course. The Verdant Lotus is known for its knowledge and alchemy, not for its martial prowess." I took a deep breath, then added, "That's why a sparring demonstration would be so valuable. It would help us common folk better understand and appreciate your incredible skills. I mean, it's almost hard to believe that you defeated such an incredible beast with just your bare hands."

I could see the hint of a smirk forming on the second-class disciple's lips, and I knew I had him. I decided to sweeten the deal. "And to make it more interesting, if you win, I'll offer you a selection of my finest potions as a reward. After all, I may not be much of a fighter, but I am an alchemist."

Shan Huai's eyes gleamed with interest at the mention of potions, and I knew I had him hooked. "All right, alchemist." His voice dripped with condescension. "I accept your terms. What are the rules?"

"Simple," I replied, keeping my tone deferential. "All I have to do is land one hit on you to win, but for you to win, you must make me yield. But, uh, I have a small request." I hesitated, as if unsure whether I should even be asking. "Since I'm no warrior, I was hoping I could have my Spirit Beast companions support me in the spar. It's the very least I'd need to hold a candle to the mighty Rumbling Thunder."

His smirk widened, his ego clearly stroked by my words. "Spirit Beasts, huh? Fine. Let's see what your little pets can do. It won't make a difference, but I'll humor you."

I nodded gratefully, gesturing to Tianyi, who fluttered innocently on my shoulder. "This is Tianyi." I introduced her, watching as she gave a delicate flap of her wings, the very picture of harmlessness. "And as for the other . . . Would you mind waking him up?"

Of course.

I hesitated, realizing I would have to call Windy out from where he was still curled up, sleeping in the inn. She fluttered slowly over to the closed window, glowing subtly as she did so. Not even a moment later, the window clicked open with a smooth move, and the hatchling slithered out with indifferent eyes.

"This is Windy," I said, gently patting the serpentine Spirit Beast's head. "With them by my side, I might just be able to give you a challenge worthy of your title."

As Windy coiled around my shoulders, I couldn't help but notice the flicker of greed and desire that crossed Shan Huai's eyes. He hid it well, but for a moment, it was there—an unmistakable glint of avarice as he took in the sight of my Spirit Beasts. However, the smug grin quickly returned to his face, and he seemed unconcerned, as if dismissing the idea that my two companions could pose any real threat.

"You know, the world is vast, full of mysteries and hidden dangers," Shan Huai said patronizingly. "But if you think a couple of minor Spirit Beasts and an untrained alchemist will change anything, then you're sorely mistaken."

I met his condescending gaze, my heart pounding in my chest, though I kept my expression composed. His arrogance was a double-edged sword— dangerous, yes, but also something I could use to my advantage. He saw me as insignificant, someone barely worth his attention. And that was exactly what I needed him to believe.

Windy shifted slightly, his cold scales brushing against my neck, a silent reminder of the stakes. Tianyi hovered at my shoulder, her delicate wings shimmering in the light. We were ready, even if Shan Huai didn't think so.

"Perhaps," I replied quietly, letting just a hint of uncertainty creep into my voice.

Shan Huai smirked, clearly enjoying his perceived superiority. He glanced at his disciples, who chuckled at my words as if they were nothing more than the ramblings of a fool. "We'll see about that," he said. "Prepare yourself, alchemist. I'll make sure this is over quickly."

I nodded, swallowing the nerves that threatened to bubble to the surface. The crowd was silent now, all eyes on us, waiting for the clash that could determine the future of their village.

CHAPTER THIRTEEN

A Meek Facade, a Strong Strike

Lan Sheng stepped forward, moving in between Shan Huai and me with a sharp breath. "I'll serve as witness and mediator for this spar," he commanded as his eyes flicked over to Shan Huai. "Kai Liu's task is to land a single hit on you, while your goal is to make him yield."

He barely acknowledged Lan Sheng's words, raising a hand to pick his ear as if the whole affair were beneath him. "Yeah, yeah," Shan Huai muttered dismissively, clearly not concerned. His eyes flickered back to me, filled with the same smug confidence he had worn since the moment he arrived.

Lan Sheng, however, wasn't having it. I could see the way his jaw clenched, how he gave Shan Huai a pointed stink eye that lingered just a second too long. He then turned back to me, his posture subtly shifting as he planted himself firmly in the space between us, almost as if he was positioning himself to jump in the moment things went wrong.

For a second, I caught the second-class disciple's eye. It was a fleeting moment, but the message was clear.

I'm watching. If this gets out of hand, I'll stop it.

There was comfort in that, but I couldn't afford to rely on him. This was my fight, my wager. If I wanted to win, I had to do it myself. Windy and Tianyi had their roles to play, but the burden ultimately rested on my shoulders.

Shan Huai's voice snapped me out of my thoughts. "Hurry up and begin," he sneered, tapping his foot impatiently on the ground. "I've got better things to do than waste time playing games with an alchemist."

Lan Sheng looked at me, giving me a brief, sharp nod, his expression all business now. "Whenever you're ready," he whispered, stepping back to give us room.

The older disciple smirked, his posture shifting as he clasped his hands behind his back, adopting a stance of complete and utter arrogance. "I'll even give you the first three moves. Consider it mercy," he declared, oozing condescension. His eyes gleamed with self-assuredness, the assumption that this fight would be over before it even began.

I swallowed, keeping up my meek facade as I bowed slightly in thanks. "Th-that's very generous of you," I stammered, putting on my act. Inside, my thoughts raced.

He's already written me off. Perfect.

Straightening up, I cast a glance at my companions. "Well, if that's the case, let's not waste any time," I said softly, then gestured to the two Spirit Beasts. "Tianyi, Windy, would you two be so kind as to begin?"

The butterfly's wings glowed brighter in response, her slight form radiating with a sudden intensity. She flapped once—just once—but it was enough to stir the air into a violent gust. The snow, dirt, and debris that littered the ground were whipped up in an instant, swirling toward Shan Huai with alarming speed.

Surprised, he instinctively raised his hand as the wind hit his face, sending dirt into his eyes.

That single moment of blindness was all Windy needed.

With a sharp hiss and uncoiling of his powerful muscles, the serpent sprang into action. He closed the gap in an instant, his jaws snapping open as he aimed straight for the man's face.

"Urgh!"

The second-class disciple barely managed to twist his head aside, avoiding Windy's fangs by the width of a hair. But before he could fully recover, Windy's tail lashed out in midair, slapping across his eyes.

"Argh!" Shan Huai stumbled back, blinking furiously. His smug confidence wavered, confusion on his face.

I hadn't even moved yet, still rooted in place as I watched the scene unfold.

Tianyi wasn't finished. As Shan Huai reeled from the blow, she darted forward with shocking speed, her wings cutting through the air with the sharpness of blades. The glow surrounding her flared, and she dove forward in the gap between his arm and torso, ripping open his orange robe.

The man snarled as the fabric of his robe tore, his expression shifting from confusion to fury. His arrogance was now replaced with a burning frustration. He planted his feet, his body tensing as he dropped into a low, crouched stance. His fingers curled into claw-like shapes.

With a sharp growl, Shan parried Windy's next tail strike, his reflexes sharp despite the debris in his eyes. There was power in his movements, but he was still off-balance, still reacting to the unpredictable assault from both beasts.

Before he could capitalize on the parry, Tianyi darted in front of his face once again, her shimmering wings flickering with light, obscuring his vision. Shan Huai flailed her, his hands slashing through the air, but she was already gone—retreating just as quickly as she had appeared.

That brief distraction gave Windy the time he needed to retreat, his serpentine body curling back toward me as he readied his next strike.

They're toying with him.

Windy and Tianyi were moving around Shan Huai with a speed and precision that I hadn't even fully grasped until now. Their coordination was flawless, their agility far beyond what I had expected. Shan Huai was left swinging at nothing, his strikes falling short as they made him look like a bumbling child trying to swat at flies.

My heart pounded in my chest as I stood there, frozen. I hadn't expected the fight to be so one-sided. A second-class disciple had come in with all the confidence in the world, but now . . . now he was being humiliated.

And the most shocking part? I hadn't even made a move yet.

BAP!

"Wh—"

CRACK!

I caught myself midstep, realizing I was about to rush in. But for what? To help? They didn't need me. In fact, I was starting to wonder if they had been holding back in our sparring sessions the entire time. How else could I explain the absolute thrashing they were giving Shan Huai now?

"ENOUGH!"

His roar reverberated through the air as he slammed his hands into the snow-covered ground. The force of his qi-infused strike sent a plume of snow billowing up around him, obscuring everything in a swirling vortex of white. My vision blurred, and for a moment, all I could see was the blinding curtain of snow swirling through the air, separating us.

I blinked rapidly, trying to make out what was happening through the chaotic flurry. The intense energy from the man was palpable, even from this distance. But then, through the haze, I felt it. A strong sense of urgency.

Not mine but Tianyi's. The bond between us flared with emotion, her telepathic voice cutting through the haze like a blade.

Watch out!

The warning hit me just as Shan Huai's form emerged from the snow, crouched low, his hand drawn back for a strike, qi visibly swirling around his fingers like claws. His speed was shocking, his movements silent and swift.

In that instant, I dropped into my stance, rooting myself into the earth, my legs spreading wide into the Rooted Banyan Stance. With practiced ease, I activated the technique, feeling the qi surge through my body, anchoring me deep into the ground. I braced myself as the strike came down with terrifying precision, aiming straight for my gut.

The blow landed, and for a split second, I felt the impact ripple through my body. But it didn't hurt. I stood there, rooted and steady. His triumphant expression quickly twisted into one of utter disbelief as he realized I hadn't moved an inch.

"W-what?"

I could see the confusion in his eyes as he tried to process what had just happened. Before he could pull back, I shifted my weight, planting my back foot firmly and turning in a swift, fluid motion. I launched a spinning hook kick toward his chin.

CRACK!

The kick connected with a satisfying thud, sending Shan Huai's head snapping back as his body crumpled beneath the force of the blow. His legs gave out under him, and he collapsed onto the snow-covered ground, his limbs trembling as he tried—and failed—to stand.

The snow settled, the chaotic whirlwind of white dissipating into a gentle fall. Heavy silence followed as the villagers and Iron Claw disciples stared in stunned disbelief. Shan Huai, the proud and arrogant second-class disciple of the Iron Claw Sect, lay bruised and beaten at my feet while I remained untouched.

"The match is over. Victory goes to Kai Liu!" Lan Sheng announced.

My heart was still hammering in my chest, the adrenaline from the fight coursing through my veins despite how easily it had ended. I glanced down at Shan Huai, crumpled in the snow, struggling to regain his footing. The man was strong; individually, he would've beaten the three of us handily. But together? No chance.

"You hid your strength!" he spat hoarsely. "I demand a rematch—this was a trick!"

I shook my head, stepping forward slowly, my gaze steady and locked on him. "I didn't hide anything," I said calmly. "You underestimated me. That's all."

"Lies!" Shan Huai roared, his face twisted with fury. "You're no mere alchemist—you're a disciple of a sect, aren't you?!"

I met his eyes, snorting. "I swear on my name, I'm not a disciple of *any* sect. I've only been learning martial arts for less than a year."

Lan Sheng stepped forward, his arms crossed over his chest as he nodded in agreement. "It's true," he conceded. "He's an alchemist, one who participated in the Grand Alchemy Gauntlet."

Shan Huai's eyes darted between the two of us, his disbelief clear. But I could see it—he was rattled. His entire worldview had just been upended by what he thought was an insignificant alchemist.

I bent down, lowering my voice as I leaned closer to him. "And I know you didn't kill that Iron Boar."

His eyes widened, a flicker of panic crossing his face for the briefest of moments. I continued my words, just loud enough for him to hear. "If you don't want to be exposed here and now—losing to a mere alchemist in front of everyone—then I suggest you take your disciples and leave. Quietly."

Shan Huai's expression twisted with a mix of anger and shame. He opened his mouth as if to retort, but no words came. He knew I had him cornered.

I straightened up, turning to face the gathered crowd. "Is there anyone else who would like to challenge me?" I called out, my voice carrying through the still air. My gaze swept over the third-class disciples of the Iron Claw Sect, each of them turning away, their eyes downcast and shoulders slumped in defeat.

There was no response. The fight had been won, and everyone knew it.

Shan Huai grit his teeth, his body shaking with barely suppressed rage. But he knew he had no choice. "Retreat," he growled, barely audible as he gave the order to his disciples.

In an instant, the group of Iron Claw disciples moved to follow him, their previous arrogance now replaced by a humbled silence. They left the Iron Boar's corpse behind as they made their swift departure, their retreat echoing the sound of their defeat.

The villagers, who had been watching in tense silence, began to murmur among themselves, relief and awe flooding the air. I could feel their eyes on me, but all I felt was the chilly breeze brushing against my skin.

As I stood there in the falling snow, watching the Iron Claw Sect disappear, I couldn't help but feel a small flicker of satisfaction settle in my chest.

I won.

Not one where I was left bruised and broken, like my encounter with Ping Hai of the Silent Moon Sect. That fight had ended with me barely able to stand, and Ping Hai had walked away nearly unscathed. But this? This was different. I had won—against a second-class disciple, no less—and I stood here, untouched.

It wasn't just a fluke, either. This wasn't a narrow escape where I had managed to pull victory from the jaws of defeat. And yet, the irony of it wasn't lost on me. I had barely even fought. It was Tianyi and Windy who had humiliated Shan Huai, who had toyed with him and shown their strength in a way that I hadn't anticipated.

But still, I'd come a long way.

A year ago, I wouldn't have dreamed of standing in a situation like this. I was no Lan Sheng, no Feng Wu, no Ping Hai, but I had won. And for the first time since the Gauntlet, I felt the subtle burn of accomplishment, that taste of victory lingering on my tongue, sweeter than anything I could have imagined.

Lan Sheng stepped beside me, his arms crossed, and his usual playful demeanor softened by a quiet respect. "You really surprised me there," he muttered, glancing sideways at me. "I was ready to step in at any moment, but . . . I guess I didn't need to, huh?"

I let out a breath. "It wasn't just me. Windy and Tianyi were incredible."

Lan Sheng nodded, a faint smile tugging at the corner of his lips. "They were. But don't sell yourself short, Kai. That Rooted Banyan Stance . . . You held strong, even when he went in for the kill."

I blinked, absorbing his words. I'd reacted purely on instinct, relying on the stance I'd practiced countless times. It had worked, and yet, there was still a sense of disbelief washing over me. I wasn't used to feeling victorious like this. Not when the stakes were so high.

"First Ping Hai, and now this? You're making a habit of pissing off sect disciples. If we leave you alone for a little longer, I can see you finding a way to provoke the Whispering Wind Sect as well!"

I chuckled softly, shaking my head. "I didn't ask for this."

"No one ever does," he replied, giving me a knowing look. "But you handled it like a pro. You've come a long way, Kai. And you're only going to keep getting stronger."

Stronger. The word echoed in my mind as I looked out at the villagers, at the snow-covered ground where Shan Huai had fallen, and at my companions who stood by my side. I wasn't sure what the future held or what other challenges would come my way, but one thing was certain—I wasn't the same alchemist who had stumbled into the Jianghu nearly a year ago.

I had changed.

And for the first time, I was starting to believe that I could stand my ground.

"We should get inside before we freeze to death," Lan Sheng added with a smirk, shaking the snow from his sleeves. "Victory's sweeter with a hot bowl of soup."

I nodded, feeling the cold seep into my bones now that the adrenaline was fading. But beneath it all, that spark of victory remained, warming me from the inside out.

As we made our way back toward the inn, I couldn't help but glance back at the Iron Boar's corpse, still lying in the square. It was a reminder of the lie Shan Huai had tried to sell, a lie I had seen through from the beginning.

I smiled to myself, the taste of victory still fresh.

"Next time," I murmured under my breath, "it'll be even easier."

CHAPTER FOURTEEN

Price of Pride

Elder Brother Kai! You were amazing!" Hua Lingsheng exclaimed, bouncing on his feet. "You didn't even break a sweat!"

"Let this be a lesson," I said, pausing to swirl the rice in my bowl before taking a bite. "Underestimating your opponent is like grasping fire with your bare hands—by the time you realize the danger, the damage is already done."

Lan Sheng chuckled, swirling his own cup of wine as he raised an eyebrow. "That's rich coming from the same guy who declared himself the rising genius of the province not too long ago."

I shot him a playful grin. "It's not arrogance if you can back it up."

Laughter rippled through the inn, blending with the hum of voices and the clatter of dishes. The atmosphere was lively, a far cry from the tense showdown that had unfolded just hours earlier. Now, the villagers crowded around, offering smiles and congratulations as platters of food and jugs of wine made their rounds. Our table, in particular, was filled to the brim with delicacies—roasted meats, steamed buns, fragrant broths—and at the center of it all, Windy and Tianyi were being treated like royalty.

The hatchling preened under the attention, happily scarfing down whole, roasted chickens, his white scales shimmering in the firelight as he flicked his tail in contentment. A young girl with bright eyes held up another plate of meat, offering it to him with a wide smile. Windy's tongue flicked out as he accepted it, swallowing the bird whole.

Tianyi, however, was daintier in her indulgence. She perched elegantly on the edge of a wine bowl, using her delicate proboscis to slurp the drink with a regal air. Her wings shimmered with a faint glow, and I could sense her satisfaction as the crowd around us marveled at her beauty and grace.

The inn buzzed with cheerful chatter, the villagers eager to share their stories of the day's events. "That Shan Huai, he got what he deserved!" a burly farmer declared, raising his cup of alcohol. "Tried to cheat us, he did! But our hero Kai put him in his place!"

"Hear that, hero?" Lan Sheng said with a smile.

I put a finger to my lips and closed my eyes, pretending like I didn't hear it. "Don't. Say. A. Word."

I couldn't help but feel a twinge of embarrassment despite the lively celebration around me. Inwardly, I knew I could have approached the situation better. A more careful plan, one that didn't involve wagering with someone like Shan Huai, would have been smarter. But there had been a part of me that had wanted to throw myself into that danger, to prove something.

Not just to the village, not even to Lan Sheng, but to myself.

Ever since the Gauntlet, my confidence had been shaken. Today's victory over Shan Huai felt like regaining a sliver of that lost belief in myself, but it didn't sit as well as I'd hoped. There was a selfishness in what I did, a need to reclaim something personal through this fight.

But that victory didn't come without its consequences. As I chewed on a piece of meat, my thoughts drifted back to Shan Huai. He wouldn't forget this. And if the Iron Claw Sect was truly looking to expand its influence, there was a chance they wouldn't let this humiliation slide. That brought me to a bigger problem—the rising tensions between the sects. Qingmu was just one small village, but I felt like it was caught in the middle of something much larger.

I leaned closer to Lan Sheng, lowering my voice to ask what had been nagging at the back of my mind. "What do you think? Will Shan Huai come back and try to get revenge? Do you think the Silent Moon Sect would protect the village if things escalate?"

Lan Sheng's expression turned serious, the humor and ease that had filled the evening fading as he considered the implications. He put down his cup of wine and looked out toward the quieting inn, his brow furrowing slightly. "It's possible," he said quietly. "If the Silent Moon Sect doesn't step in, Qingmu is going to face more trouble. And Shan Huai . . . He might not be strong enough to take revenge on his own, but sects don't act alone. He could bring others."

The weight of his words settled over me like a stiff wind. The Iron Claw Sect had proven they weren't above flexing their power, and if they decided to press the matter, the villagers would suffer the most.

Lan Sheng gave me a sidelong glance, his lips pressed into a thin line. "But that's why I'm here. As a second-class disciple, it's my job to ensure things like this don't spiral out of control. I'll send a letter to the Silent Moon Sect as soon as I can, informing them of the situation. If they know what's at stake, they might intervene."

"And if they don't?" I asked, though I had a sinking feeling I already knew the answer.

"If they don't," Lan Sheng said grimly, "then I'll stay. I'll make sure the Iron Claw Sect doesn't try anything while we wait for the Silent Moon Sect's decision. But one way or another, I'll see to it that Qingmu isn't left defenseless."

His confidence was reassuring, but the uncertainty of it all still weighed heavily. Sect politics, ambitions, and power plays were beyond anything I'd been prepared to face when I first left my village. Yet here I was, in the thick of it, with the fate of an entire village possibly hanging on what came next.

Lan Sheng clapped me on the shoulder, rubbing it affectionately. "You did well today, Kai. You bought the village time. Now it's my turn to make sure that time isn't wasted."

Shan Huai lashed out, his voice cutting through the night air as his third-class disciples trudged through the dense forest. "Move faster!" he barked with venom. Each breath he took was accompanied by pain where that wretched alchemist's kick had landed.

He clenched his teeth, his fists trembling. The humiliation burned hotter than any of his wounds. How had it come to this?

How had *he*, a second-class disciple of the Iron Claw Sect, been brought so low by an alchemist and his pet Spirit Beasts?

His thoughts churned, spiraling back to the fight, to the mocking laughter of the villagers, to the boy's calm, confident gaze as he issued that ultimate challenge.

But more than the shame, there were the relentless questions that gnawed at him—how had that alchemist seen through their scheme? How had he known they hadn't killed the Iron Boar?

He envisioned himself returning to the sect, laden with the spoils of the hunt, the elders praising his prowess, his rival disciples seething with envy. Instead, he realized with a sickening lurch in his stomach, that he was returning with nothing but disgrace. A disgrace that would spread like wildfire through the Jianghu. They'd whisper about the second-class disciple who was humiliated by a mere alchemist, a boy from a backwater village. The thought was unbearable. He had gambled everything on this scheme, and now he was facing utter ruin.

The very thought made Shan's stomach twist. The Iron Boar had been a stroke of fortune, a gift from the heavens. When they had stumbled upon it already dying from injuries sustained in a battle with another beast, it had seemed like the perfect opportunity. Claiming the kill would earn them glory, influence, and leverage over Qingmu Village. They hadn't anticipated that anyone would question the story. Who would dare challenge the might of the Iron Claw Sect?

But that damn alchemist had. Somehow he had seen through the ruse, and now that knowledge hung over Shan Huai like a blade. The very thing that should have been a boon had turned into a weapon of blackmail—something Kai Liu, and by extension, the Verdant Lotus Sect—could use against him.

"Senior Brother Shan . . ." one of the third-class disciples trailed off, hesitating as he sensed the fury radiating from Shan Huai.

"What?" he snapped through a clenched jaw. "Spit it out!"

The disciple flinched, his gaze darting away. "D-do you think . . . we'll be in trouble with the sect if they find out about . . ."

"Shut up!" Shan Huai growled, his eyes narrowing into dangerous slits. He didn't need reminding. He already knew the consequences. If the elders of the Iron Claw Sect learned of this, his position—his very future—would be at risk. And worse, if Kai Liu decided to spread that knowledge, it could ruin everything. He'd be seen as a fool, a liar, and worse still—a weakling.

"Keep moving," he hissed, barely keeping his composure. "We'll regroup, and I'll figure out a way to fix this. But mark my words, that alchemist will regret the day he ever crossed me."

The disciples quickened their pace, none daring to speak further. As they moved deeper into the forest, Shan Huai's mind spun with plans and counterplans, desperate to control the situation before it spiraled further.

"Kai Liu . . ." he whispered with venom.

He could still hear the villagers muttering the name, their awe palpable. They celebrated his humiliation. The shame twisted in his gut like a knife.

The Iron Claw Sect couldn't afford this kind of disgrace, and neither could he. But how could they handle it?

The snapping of branches underfoot drew him out of his thoughts. The third-class disciples trudged behind him, slower than he liked, their eyes wary as they glanced at their surroundings.

"Move faster! You slow, useless bastards!" Shan Huai barked, the sharpness of his voice startling them into action. He grit his teeth, fury and frustration fueling him. He needed a way to reclaim what had been stolen from him.

But as they trudged onward, his eyes caught something ahead—a figure standing in the middle of their path.

A frail old man, his tangled hair draped over his face like a curtain of neglect. He wore a tattered robe, his bare feet planted on the cold forest floor.

The man was muttering something, low and unintelligible. His presence felt unnatural—out of place in the stillness of the woods.

"What is this?" Shan Huai growled, irritation flaring as he clenched his fists. His hands curled into tight fists, ready to strike. "Out of the way, old man," he barked. "Move before I make you regret it."

The figure didn't move. His head hung low, and his body swayed gently as if the wind itself was pushing him. He continued mumbling, the words slipping through his cracked lips, but they made no sense.

Shan Huai's patience, already stretched thin, snapped. "I said move!" He stepped forward, his arms tensing with barely contained qi, ready to unleash a strike.

Slowly, the old man's head lifted. His eyes were clouded, vacant, and his smile twisted into a grin that seemed to crawl up his face like it didn't belong there. His voice, though still soft, became clear enough to understand, sending a cold shiver through the group.

"Are you the ones . . . who took it?"

Shan Huai's fists tightened. "I'm not in the mood for your riddles. Move, or I'll make you regret standing in my way."

The old man's smile widened into something eerie, almost otherworldly. "Then . . . *you* will take its place." Then his voice dropped to a whisper, his eyes gleaming with a dark, chilling intent. "You . . . will become our nourishment."

The second-class disciple felt the surrounding air change, a chill creeping in, unnatural and foreboding. His instincts screamed at him, but his fury overpowered the warning. "Enough! You're wasting my time," he growled. His eyes flashed to his disciples, his patience long gone. "Take him down."

The third-class disciples hesitated only for a moment before they obeyed, cracking their knuckles and spreading into their stances. They were martial artists, their hands were their weapons, and they were used to breaking bones with a single blow. Without hesitation, they surged forward, fists and claws ready to strike the old man down.

But as they closed in, something in the air shifted again—something darker.

CHAPTER FIFTEEN

Winds of Change, Roots of Home

The night had settled over Qingmu, quiet and cool, the air filled with the faint scent of woodsmoke. Most of the villagers had retired for the night, but I was still awake, crouched next to the cart as I double-checked the supplies. We would be leaving soon, continuing the long journey back to my home village. If Lan Sheng wanted to be present in the village before the Iron Claw Sect could cook up a scheme, we'd need to speed things up.

I hadn't expected to stay in Qingmu this long, and part of me was eager to get back on the road, away from the looming threat of sect politics and Shan Huai's bruised ego.

I tightened the ropes on a bundle of hay and sighed. Despite the victory, my mind was restless, running through the events of the past few days. Sure, I'd won, but it wasn't the kind of victory I could take lightly. They wouldn't forget the embarrassment I'd caused them.

Damn cultivators and their obsession with face . . . But then again, I was partially to blame for taking advantage of it.

I glanced around, the silence of the village only broken by the occasional rustle of leaves in the night breeze. The shadows seemed longer now, stretching out from the trees like old memories.

As I was about to secure another bundle, a soft voice called out from behind me, "Elder Brother Kai."

I turned to see Hua Lingsheng walking toward me, his usual bright energy somewhat subdued in the dim light. His hands were clasped behind his back, and he wore a slightly awkward expression, like he had something important to say but wasn't sure how to approach it.

"What are you doing up this late?" I asked, standing up from the cart.

He smiled sheepishly. "The villagers wanted to give you something. It took them a while to prepare it."

Before I could ask what he meant, he stepped forward and handed me two large, rolled-up pelts. The moment I touched them, I felt the surprising weight of the gift. My hands sank under their density, and I immediately recognized the texture—thick, coarse, and sturdy.

"Iron Boar pelts?" I blinked, unrolling a section to confirm. The dark fur had a metallic sheen under the moonlight, and the leather beneath felt almost like armor. "They kept this from the boar?"

Hua Lingsheng nodded, his smile widening. "It's our way of saying thank you. We know how valuable these pelts are. They worked fast to preserve them for you."

I ran my fingers over the fur, feeling the strength of the hide beneath. These pelts were no ordinary gift—Iron Boar leather was known for its toughness, often used in crafting armor for cultivators or reinforcing robes for battle. It could fetch a high price in the right market, and here I was, holding two pristine pelts, freely given by the villagers.

I stared at the pelts, feeling the weight of them in more ways than one. The villagers had given these to me as a sign of gratitude, but my mind drifted to Feng Wu, his unwavering righteousness, the kind of Taoist who would never accept such a reward. He would have refused it outright, saying that a true cultivator doesn't act for reward or recognition.

A twinge of guilt gnawed at me. I didn't deserve this kind of gratitude, not when my motives weren't purely selfless either.

"I—I can't accept these," I stammered, thrusting the pelts back toward Hua Lingsheng. "Really, I didn't do this for a reward."

He blinked at me in surprise, then shook his head with a knowing smile. "I refuse your refusal, Elder Brother Kai."

"Wait . . . What?"

He grinned, stepping back as if to dodge my attempt to return the pelts. "The villagers worked hard to prepare these, and they want you to have them. It's their way of showing gratitude, and it would be disrespectful to refuse. So, I refuse your refusal!"

I stared at him, half-exasperated, half-amused. "That's not how it works, you know."

"It is now," he said, crossing his arms with a self-satisfied nod. "So you'd better just take them before you make things awkward."

I chuckled despite myself, shaking my head.

As if on cue, Lan Sheng appeared from the inn, carrying a half-asleep Windy draped around his shoulders and Tianyi perched on his arm.

"You ready?" he asked, adjusting Windy, who let out a lazy hiss and stared at me sleepily.

I gave the cart one last tug to make sure everything was in place, then turned to him with a nod. "Yeah. Let's get going."

Hua Lingsheng waved with both hands, a small but happy smile lighting up his face. "Farewell, Elder Brother Kai! Safe travels!"

I waved back from the seat of the cart. No grand send-off, no crowd of villagers, just Hua Lingsheng standing there in the quiet village under the soft glow of the full moon.

"See you soon," I called back as I clicked the reins, urging the horses forward. The cart began to move, wheels creaking as they rolled over the dirt path, and the horses picked up their pace into a brisk trot.

The boy stood at the edge of the village, waving until he was just a small figure in the distance. The road stretched out before us, dark and empty, illuminated only by the moon hanging above. The village of Qingmu quickly faded behind us, leaving nothing but the soft sounds of hooves clattering against the earth and the occasional rustling of leaves in the night breeze.

Lan Sheng, sitting beside me with Windy curled on his lap, was quiet. He didn't seem to have much to say now that we were on the move. Maybe, like me, he was lost in his thoughts.

But there was no use dwelling on what had already happened. We were on our way to Gentle Wind Village now, and there was still a long road ahead. Instead of letting my mind wander, I focused on something more productive.

I shifted in my seat and closed my eyes, letting out a slow breath as I started cycling my qi, drawing it in from the air around me, focusing on its flow. It had been a while since I'd had a quiet moment to cultivate, and I needed to keep refining my techniques if I wanted to improve.

Tianyi, resting lightly on my shoulder, seemed to sense my intent. Without a word, her wings glowed faintly, and a soft, calming energy radiated from her. It was as if the entire world around us had shifted, the flow of qi becoming more vibrant and responsive. I felt a sudden rush as I drew in more than I expected.

It wasn't just my imagination. Her powers had grown stronger since ingesting the Beast Core elixir. Her presence magnified the qi around us, making it easier to cycle larger amounts at once. I could feel it pouring into me with a smoothness I hadn't experienced before, like a river widening to accommodate a flood. My breathing slowed, and I focused on guiding the qi through my body, following the familiar paths but pushing them further, deeper.

The cart moved steadily beneath me, the horses trotting along, but all I could feel was the warmth of the qi filling my core, my dantian, flowing in perfect harmony with her power.

Hours passed as the cart rumbled steadily along the dirt road, the moon still shining brightly overhead. The brisk pace of the horses continued without faltering, their hooves striking the ground rhythmically as the miles melted away. At first, I thought nothing of it, too caught up in the flow of my cultivation, but as the night dragged on, a subtle unease crept in.

The horses hadn't slowed once. In fact, they were moving faster than they should been have at this point. Their breath, visible in the cool night air, came in regular puffs, but something about the way steam continuously rose from their flanks concerned me.

Frowning, I looked over at Lan Sheng, who was still sitting beside me, quietly observing the passing landscape. "Let's stop for a moment. The horses have been keeping this pace for too long. I need to check on them."

He nodded, glancing toward the horses as if just now realizing what I'd pointed out. With a quick tug of the reins, he slowed the cart to a stop, and I hopped down to inspect the horses.

Their coats were slick with sweat, but oddly enough, they didn't look tired. I ran a hand over their sides, feeling the heat radiating from their bodies. Despite how long they had been running, they weren't even panting heavily. It was strange.

Tianyi fluttered lightly from my shoulder and landed near the horses, her wings glowing faintly in the moonlight. The horses nuzzled her affectionately, their breath still steady. It was as if her presence had soothed them.

"They're not worn out," I muttered to myself. But even if they seemed fine, I wasn't going to take any risks with their health. Elder Wen would have my head if I let something happen to these two.

I walked back to the cart, retrieving a few key ingredients from the supplies: licorice root and ginseng, both known for their restorative properties. With quick hands, I pulled out my Two-Star Pagoda Pill Furnace from my storage ring and crouched down, gathering a handful of fresh snow from the ground and melting it.

As the furnace heated, I prepared the ingredients, grinding the licorice root and slicing the ginseng thinly before adding them to the water. The mixture bubbled gently, and soon a simple yet effective supplementing feed was ready. I mixed it into some hay, letting the scent of the herbs infuse the feed.

Approaching the horses once more, I offered them the enhanced hay, watching as they eagerly devoured it. Their calm demeanor reassured me, but I couldn't shake the feeling that something more was at play.

I turned to the butterfly, who was still perched on the cart, her wings shimmering in the moonlight. "Tianyi," I asked quietly, "do you have something to do with this?"

She fluttered closer, her glowing wings brushing against the horses. A soft pulse of energy washed over them, and I could feel the faint echo of her response through our bond.

Yes, her voice echoed gently in my mind. *I can help restore their energy, just like I do for you.*

I couldn't help but smile at the realization. Tianyi's powers had grown immensely, more than I'd even noticed until now. She wasn't just aiding in my cultivation; she was amplifying *everything* around her.

"You're incredible," I said, earning a soft hum of agreement from our bond.

With the horses now resting and eating contently, I turned back to Lan Sheng. "They're in better shape than I expected." I climbed back into the cart. "We should be good to keep going after this break."

The cart rolled steadily through the night once again, and as the hours passed, the familiar landscape of Gentle Wind Village in the distance finally began to take shape. The familiar silhouette of the place I once called home came into view—tall trees swaying gently, casting long shadows over the quiet path. Everything looked just as I remembered, but as I sat there, watching it all come into focus, I felt an odd sense of distance settle within me.

The village was the same, but somehow different. The narrow dirt roads, the simple homes, the fields beyond . . . I had walked these paths a thousand times, yet now they felt like memories I was only visiting. I had left this place as one person and returned as someone else entirely.

I wasn't sure what I had expected. A small part of me had clung to the naive notion of a triumphant return, like a hero coming back from distant lands. But there was no grand celebration waiting. Just the quiet, the steady creak of the cart, and the gentle rustling of trees as the wind moved through them.

This was home, yet it wasn't. The village was a river, flowing just as it always had, but I was no longer the boy who had lived here. The battles I'd fought, the lessons I'd learned . . . they had changed me. I wasn't the same, and neither was this place, even if it looked the same on the surface.

I inhaled deeply, letting the cool morning air fill my lungs. The road stretched ahead, leading me back to where I started, but it didn't feel like a return. It was a continuation, another step forward into the unknown.

"We're here," I murmured, pulling the reins gently to slow the horses to a stop just before the main path leading into the village.

Lan Sheng smiled at me. "What now?"

"I'll take the horses to Elder Wen's and visit Elder Ming." I gestured to my home on the outskirts of the village. "Can you take the cart, Windy, and Tianyi there? It'll be a quick thing, I promise."

He nodded without hesitation. "Of course. I'll take care of everything while you finish up."

I handed him the reins and hopped down from the cart. As the horses snorted softly, I gave their necks a reassuring pat before guiding them down a narrow path toward Elder Wen's place. The quiet surrounded me as I walked, the only sound being the soft crunch of my boots on the dirt.

Arriving at Elder Wen's home, I tied the horses to the post near the small stable and headed toward the door. But before I knocked, I felt a tug toward Elder Ming's house. Knowing Elder Ming, the old man would probably already be awake, tending to his garden and sipping tea.

"If I have to bother someone first, it might as well be him," I muttered to myself.

Giving one more glance at the horses, I jogged over to the village head's home.

As I neared Elder Ming's house, the familiar creak of the old wooden gates echoed faintly in the early morning quiet. But instead of the usual peaceful dawn silence in the village, I heard unexpected sounds—grunts of exertion and the rhythmic thudding of feet. It reminded me of the training grounds back at the Verdant Lotus Sect.

Curiosity piqued, I approached the slightly ajar door of the courtyard, my brow furrowing as the noises grew louder. I cautiously pushed the door open just enough to peer inside.

There, in the courtyard, were two familiar figures.

Wang Jun and Lan-Yin, fully engaged in martial arts conditioning exercises, sweat dripping down their foreheads as they moved through forms with a surprising level of precision. Wang Jun focused his usually carefree expression, executing each strike with sharp movements, while Lan-Yin mirrored him, her slender frame flowing with an intensity I hadn't seen before.

I blinked, feeling a wave of confusion wash over me.

"What the hell?"

CHAPTER SIXTEEN

Growing in Absence

Neither of them had ever expressed the slightest interest in cultivation before. I could hardly wrap my mind around the sight of them practicing martial arts so diligently, especially not in Elder Ming's courtyard.

This wasn't the return I had imagined, and yet, it was just another reminder of how much things had changed while I was away.

And clearly, I wasn't the only one who had been changing.

"What the hell?" I blurted out.

Both of them turned toward me, their faces lighting up. In a flash, they rushed at me faster than I could react. Lan-Yin reached me first, her arms wrapping around me in a tight hug.

"Kai! You're back!" she exclaimed happily.

The force of her hug almost knocked me off-balance, and I quickly noticed how much stronger she felt. Gone was the delicate, refined aura she used to carry. Now her hair was tied back in a practical bun, her shoulders were broad and defined, and her grip was strong—far stronger than I'd remembered.

Before I could comment, Wang Jun barreled into me next, laughing as he tackled me to the ground. "Kai, you bastard! You didn't even tell us you were coming!"

I grunted under his weight. Wang Jun had always been big, but now he was even more robust, his frame solid as a mountain. The roundness that used to soften his features was gone, replaced by hard lines and a square jaw. He looked like a completely different man.

"Okay, okay! You two are gonna crush me at this rate!" I gasped, trying to wiggle free from their combined weight.

They both scrambled to their feet, helping me up with wide smiles plastered on their faces. As I stood, brushing off the dirt from my robes, I couldn't help but admire how much they'd changed. Wang Jun's physique had sharpened into something more than just raw muscle—he moved with a deliberate grace that hadn't been there before. And Lan-Yin, who once held herself with a delicate air, now exuded strength and confidence, her muscles toned and firm.

"You two look . . . different," I said, catching my breath. "When did this happen?"

Before either of them could answer, a familiar voice spoke up behind me. "Kai, it's been some time."

I spun to see Elder Ming standing at the threshold of the courtyard, watching us with a warm, knowing smile. His presence was the same as I remembered—calm and wise—but there was something about seeing him now, after all I'd been through, that stirred me.

Elder Ming wasn't just the village head to me; he was my first mentor, the one who had put me on the right path when I didn't know where to turn. Without his guidance, I wasn't sure I'd be standing here today.

Without thinking, I stepped forward and bowed deeply, my voice quiet but filled with emotion. "Elder Ming . . . I'm back."

There was a long pause, and when I finally straightened, I found Elder Ming's eyes had softened, his gaze resting on me with pride and affection. "It's good to see you've returned safely, Kai. You've come a long way since you left, but I can see that your journey isn't finished yet."

I smiled. "No, it's not. But I owe much of it to you."

Elder Ming's expression didn't change, but his eyes twinkled with quiet amusement. "I simply pointed you in the right direction. The rest was up to you."

He stepped closer, placing a hand on my shoulder, and I felt a sense of peace settle over me. This was the man who had given me my start, and standing before him now, I realized just how far I had come.

Wang Jun's voice broke the moment, full of playful energy. "We're not the only ones who've changed, Kai. I mean, look at you!"

Lan-Yin nodded in agreement, her wide eyes amazed. "You look different too. Stronger. It's like . . . you carry yourself differently now."

I blinked, unprepared for their words. I hadn't really thought about how much I had changed since I left. Hard to notice when I saw myself every day.

"I don't know . . ." I rubbed the back of my neck awkwardly. "I think you two have changed more than I have."

Wang Jun laughed, shaking his head. "Not a chance, Kai. You're not the same guy who left the village. We can see it."

Lan-Yin smiled warmly. "It's true. You've grown in more ways than one."

I glanced down at myself, suddenly aware of the lean muscle I'd developed from the training, the callouses on my hands, the way I stood a little taller, a little straighter. They were right—I wasn't the same.

Elder Ming looked between the three of us, a small, satisfied smile on his face. "Now, I think that's enough training for today. You two can resume tomorrow."

Wang Jun and Lan-Yin both bowed to him, and as they straightened, the blacksmith grinned. "Guess that means we can catch up with Kai now."

I couldn't help but smile back, still processing everything. "You'll have to explain to me how this all started." I glanced between them. "The last time I left, you were both still . . . well, *you*."

Wang Jun chuckled, looking at his betrothed with an amused smile. "It started after that conversation we had. Remember? About using qi for things other than cultivation?"

I did remember. After learning the Crimson Lotus Purification Technique, I had gone on rambling about the potential of the Heavenly Interface; how it could help them in their respective careers. I didn't think it would unfold like *this*.

Lan-Yin nodded brightly. "That's when it clicked for us. We realized we didn't have to give up everything to cultivate. We did it just like you, doing it side by side with our regular lives. Elder Ming's help was crucial, and we started training bit by bit. It certainly wasn't easy, the first month or so."

I winced. I still remembered the first time I trained with him. I had thought I was going to die.

She continued, "But it's worth it. I've never felt better! I can run your shop, help at the Soaring Swallow, and still have the energy to train without feeling completely drained. It's like my body's finally caught up with everything my mind wanted to do."

"How about you both come to the shop later? I'll introduce you to a friend of mine, Lan Sheng. He's waiting there now. But . . ." I tried to hide my amusement. "I'll save the other introductions as a surprise."

Lan-Yin raised an eyebrow. "A surprise?"

I nodded. "You'll see."

As we began walking back toward the village center, they pelted me with questions, most of them revolving around the Gauntlet and my travels.

"Come on, Kai," Wang Jun prodded. "Tell us how the Grand Alchemy Gauntlet went. Did you win?"

I took a steadying breath. The Gauntlet was a subject that had once made my chest tighten with frustration, but now . . . well, it still stung, but I'd come to terms with it. Somewhat.

"No." I allowed a small, comfortable smile to appear on my face. "I didn't win. I lost in the final round."

Wang Jun and Lan-Yin exchanged glances, surprised by how casually I answered.

"But," I continued, puffing up my chest and flipping my hair back, "I only lost by a razor-thin margin. The heavens themselves wept at the injustice of it all!" I flourished my hands dramatically, trying to get a rise out of them.

Wang Jun laughed out loud, shaking his head. "There it is. The Kai we know."

Lan-Yin chuckled, her eyes twinkling. "So close, huh?"

I dropped the act with a chuckle of my own. "Still, I learned a lot. It wasn't the victory I wanted, but it was the loss I needed, I think." As I said the words, I realized I was more at peace with it than I'd ever been. Even if a small part of me still ached at the memory, I was moving past it, slowly but surely.

The blacksmith clapped me on the back. "Well, win or lose, you've done more than we could've imagined. We're proud of you, Kai."

Lan-Yin nodded in agreement. "And we're even prouder that you're back."

The warmth in their words caught me off guard. I had spent so long pushing myself to be stronger, to prove something, that I hadn't realized how much support I had from the people I cared about. It was a grounding feeling.

"I missed you both," I said softly. "It's good to be back."

We continued down the path together, and I couldn't help but feel like, despite everything, this was exactly where I was meant to be right now—home, with the people who had helped shape me.

And soon enough, they were going to meet the rest of my family. Windy was sure to leave an impression.

As we walked, I couldn't help but notice the little things—Wang Jun's hand finding its way to the small of Lan-Yin's back, the soft smile she gave him in return.

I suppose I'd have to prepare to be called "Uncle Kai" soon.

When we arrived, Lan Sheng was already outside, leaning against the cart with his usual easygoing demeanor. He straightened up when he saw us, smiling. "These your friends?"

The two immediately noticed him and exchanged respectful bows. "Greetings, senior," Wang Jun said with formality.

Lan Sheng waved them off with a chuckle. "No need for all that. I'm just a friend of Kai's."

As they relaxed, I couldn't help but grin, holding back the surprise I had in store. Before I could say more, a distinct hissing filled the air, and Windy slithered up from behind the second-class disciple. His white scales gleamed in the light as he flicked his tongue, surveying the newcomers.

They jumped back, shocked. "What in the—?!"

I held up a hand, suppressing a laugh. "Relax, relax! That's Windy. He's . . . well, technically my Spirit Beast now."

Lan-Yin's eyes narrowed as she took a step forward, staring at the serpent. "That's your pet?!"

Windy hissed angrily, making them flinch backward. I quickly corrected them.

"Not a pet, my companion!"

At that moment, Tianyi fluttered out from the cart, her shimmering wings glowing faintly as she perched on my shoulder. Lan-Yin smiled at the butterfly, obviously more comfortable with her.

"Tianyi," she greeted softly. "Good to see you again."

Wang Jun, however, was still eyeing Windy with skepticism. "You brought back a snake? It's not gonna swallow up one of the kids in the village, right?"

I couldn't help but laugh this time. "He won't. Windy's harmless . . . mostly. Found him as an egg after a Spirit Beast attack in Qingmu. Been taking care of him ever since."

He crossed his arms, still looking uncertain but curious. "You really come back with all sorts of surprises."

"You've got no idea," I said, amused. I wasn't even getting started.

As their initial shock faded, their gazes softened. Lan-Yin still gave Windy a cautious glance, but Tianyi's presence reassured them, especially since they'd met her before. I turned my attention to the garden, catching sight of the plants that had thrived in my absence. The Moonlit Grace Lilies I'd planted were blooming beautifully, their petals glowing under the light. Seeing them alive and well brought a sense of calm over me.

The sight reminded me of the Golden Bamboo seeds I had tucked away to wait for the right time to plant. I'd need to expand the garden for them, and now that I had the funds from the Azure Silk Trading Company's advance, I could finally afford to expand and add a greenhouse!

I turned back to my friends, smiling. "Seems like the garden's been doing well without me. Thank you for taking care of them."

Lan-Yin closed her eyes, waving me off. "It was no trouble at all. The guide you left us made it easy. Elder Ming and I worked on it together, and every-thing's been thriving."

I nodded, feeling a strange sense of nostalgia wash over me as I gazed at my small shop. The air inside was warm, filled with the faint scent of herbs and dried flowers.

For a moment, I stood there in the quiet, letting it sink in: I was finally back home.

The nostalgia hit harder than I expected, memories flooding back from my idle days here, keeping up my shop. This was where I found my footing.

Lan Sheng's voice brought me out of my reverie. "Well, now that you're back, what's the plan?"

"How about we all sit down for a grand meal together? You'll all be graced with the privilege of hearing about my *many* glorious exploits in Crescent Bay City."

The second-class disciple leaned casually against the doorframe, amused. "Oh? You mean the tales of you narrowly avoiding getting yourself in trouble every other day? Poor Feng Wu had a headache telling me of all you did."

"Nonsense! Such slanderous statements made on my name. This Feng Wu shall bear the might of my ire!"

"All right, all right." Wang Jun clapped me on the back. "You've convinced me. Let's go eat and hear about your 'legendary' trip."

With everyone in good spirits, we made our way out of the shop, the laughter lingering in the air. As we headed toward a meal together, the warmth of home and the joy of being surrounded by my closest friends settled into my heart.

CHAPTER SEVENTEEN

Building Bridges and Mending Bonds

You're sure you don't need more supplies?" I held out an extra pouch of dried food. "It's a long road."

Lan Sheng glanced at the pouch, then at me, grinning in that easy way of his. "I appreciate it, but that'll only slow me down. The lighter I travel, the quicker I'll be there."

"Quicker, maybe, but you'll be starving when you arrive."

He chuckled and dipped in a mock bow. "I've survived worse. Besides, I could use the challenge. Don't worry about me."

I frowned, still holding the pouch out to him. He just gave me a wave, already stepping away from the village gates. "Kai," he called over his shoulder, his voice drifting on the wind, "you focus on getting things settled here. I'll be fine."

Before I could argue further, he dashed forward, his silhouette growing smaller by the second. I watched him disappear down the road, his form nothing but a streak as he bounded over the horizon.

"He's as fast as a horse," I muttered. "I wonder when I'll be able to do something like that."

I turned and headed back toward the Soaring Swallow Teahouse, my mind still half on Lan Sheng's effortless departure. I shook my head, dismissing the thought as I approached the teahouse. Inside, Lan-Yin and Wang Jun were seated, each with a cup of tea in hand. The atmosphere was relaxed, though the two of them perked up when they saw me enter.

"Did Lan Sheng leave already?" Lan-Yin asked, raising an eyebrow.

I nodded. "Took off like a gust of wind. I tried giving him some extra supplies, but he wouldn't take them. Said they'd slow him down."

The blacksmith snorted, amused. "On foot? Cultivators are crazy."

"You should've seen it. He'll probably get to Qingmu before the day ends." I took a seat across from them. In a corner, Windy was curled up, chomping down on raw fish, completely oblivious to the world around him. Nearby, Tianyi was perched daintily on the table with her small cup of alcohol. Somehow her tiny frame was gulping down far more than seemed reasonable.

Lan-Yin followed my gaze and laughed. "Looks like Tianyi is enjoying herself. Didn't think butterflies could hold their liquor."

Wang Jun leaned forward, resting his arms on the table. "Enough about her, though. We want to hear more about *you*. Specifically, about that run-in with the Silent Moon Sect." His eyes gleamed with curiosity. "Something about a wager?"

I sighed, having known this was coming. "Right, the Silent Moon Sect. Well, let's just say I may have gotten myself into a bit of a situation."

"You? In a situation?" he teased. "Shocking."

I recounted the entire tale. How I put myself in and provoked Elder Jun, the month I spent preparing for the wager, and my eventual victory over that mountain of a man, Ping Hai. Their jaws seemed to drop with every word I spoke.

"And this was *before* the Gauntlet even began?" she asked in a shrill voice.

I waved a hand nonchalantly, trying to downplay the intensity of the situation. "Yeah, it was resolved easily enough. Nothing too crazy."

I neglected to mention the fact that I'd been bedridden for days afterward, barely able to move from the pain of that battle. They didn't need to know every little detail, and besides, the end result was what mattered.

"But what came out of it was worth it." I leaned back in my chair. "I got my hands on a Beast Core after the fight, and I managed to use it to craft a powerful elixir. It wasn't easy, but yeah. I shared it with Tianyi and Windy. And thanks to that, I broke into the fourth stage of the Qi Initiation Realm. Windy's at the same level, and Tianyi . . . Well, she's now in the Essence Awakening Stage."

I waited for their jaws to drop, or for them to drop to the ground, coughing out blood in sheer surprise, but all they did was tilt their heads, exchanging a confused glance.

"Qi Initiation? Essence Awakening?" Lan-Yin asked. "I'm not really familiar with all the cultivation terms. Elder Ming didn't really explain much about that."

I rubbed the back of my neck. "Right, right. I guess those terms don't mean much unless you're deep into it. Okay, let me simplify it. Qi Initiation is basically when the body starts to understand how cultivation works, learning the basics of harnessing qi. It's . . . well, it's the level I'm at right now."

"And Essence Awakening?" Wang Jun asked, his brows furrowing.

"It's the stage where those myths and stories about cultivators come to life. You know, lifting boulders, cutting through stone, that sort of thing. When you see people causing gouges in the ground with their attacks, it's because they've hit the Essence Awakening Stage."

Lan-Yin looked at the relaxed butterfly in the corner. "So, that's where Tianyi's at now?"

I nodded. "Yep. There are some nuances to the whole situation, but rest assured, she's far more dangerous in a fight than I am."

Wang Jun gave a low whistle. "And what comes after Essence Awakening?"

I hesitated for a moment, thinking. "There's Spirit Ascension, where the cultivator starts to understand the connection between their spirit and the world around them. Then there's Earthly Transcendence, but . . ." I trailed off, scratching my chin. "I've only ever heard of that one in Liang Feng's novels. I'm not even sure if it's real or just something he made up." I quickly brushed off the deeper complexities of cultivation. "But enough about that. There's something else I wanted to show you."

They watched as I held out the hand with my storage ring. There was something oddly satisfying about their wide-eyed reactions to the transparent case popping out of thin air. As I set it on the table, their curiosity deepened.

"What's in there?" Wang Jun leaned in closer.

"Golden Bamboo seeds." I grinned. "A rare species thought to be extinct. I got them as one of my rewards from the Gauntlet. The method to cultivate and reproduce them has been lost, but I'll figure it out. If I can revive the species, it'll be worth the effort."

He whistled again, regarding the seeds with a newfound appreciation. "So, you're planning to grow these in your garden?"

I nodded. "That's the plan. I'll need to expand the garden first, though. Maybe even build a greenhouse to protect them while I figure out how to bring them back. I'll probably need to send a message to the Azure Silk Trading Company to find a capable artisan and carpenter who can handle glass and construction. It's not going to be easy, but I've got some connections now."

As I spoke, I noticed the two of them exchanging a knowing glance. Lan-Yin grinned. "You might not need to look too far for that, Kai."

I blinked. "What do you mean?"

"Well, we're not the only ones who learned a thing or two. I think it's better to show you."

"A greenhouse, surrounded by glass? That's doable. You'd have to consider humidity control, sunlight exposure, and temperature regulation, though," Li Wei said nonchalantly, barely looking up as his charcoal pencil sketched rapid lines on a piece of parchment. His hands moved with practiced ease, already outlining the rough dimensions of the structure.

I stared at him, still somewhat stunned. The boy sitting in front of me, barely thirteen years old, had grown so much. He had messily tied up his scruffy hair, as if he couldn't be bothered, and sawdust and wood shavings streaked his clothes. The interior of his family's home, which doubled as a carpentry workshop, was a mess of tools, beams, and unfinished projects.

I watched him work, still trying to wrap my mind around the fact that this was the same kid who used to trail after Wang Jun and me, barely tall enough to carry a hammer. Now he was talking about humidity control and construction details with the ease of a seasoned craftsman.

"You can really handle this?" I asked, my doubt probably showing on my face.

Li Wei glanced up blankly. "Yes? Why can't I?"

I remembered vaguely that he had mentioned something about his skill level when the Interface first arrived; he was already far beyond what most people his age could do. Still, I hesitated. A greenhouse wasn't exactly a small project.

"Well, it's just . . ." I paused, wanting to make sure I didn't sound too skeptical. "Glass is a difficult material to work with. I know that, at least."

Before Li Wei could respond, Wang Jun cut in, a proud grin spreading across his face. He gestured toward the forge where he worked. "You see the forge? That used to be a real problem for me. The bellows were old and uneven, and the airflow was weak—made it hard to control the temperature in the furnace. Li Wei came by, took one look, and designed an entirely new airflow system. He crafted a bunch of wooden ducts and levers to direct the wind more precisely into the furnace. Now I can adjust the heat exactly how I need it, no wasted air, and the forge gets hotter, faster. It's made my work easier, and I save hours every week."

He leaned closer, ruffling the boy's hair, much to Li Wei's chagrin. "I've worked that forge for years, and even his old man wouldn't have thought of that. He would have just built a new set of bellows or told me to replace the whole system. He made a solution that's not just better but smarter."

The blacksmith pointed out of the door once more. "And you remember the grain storage building near the village center? It was sinking into the ground. Li Wei designed a system to lift it without cracking the walls and reinforced the base with treated wood. Took him two days, and now it's more stable than it ever was. The kid's not just skilled—he thinks ahead, solves problems no one else even sees."

Li Wei, still scribbling on the parchment, shrugged like it was nothing. "It's all about knowing the materials. Wood, air, fire . . . They all have their own paths. If you work with them instead of against them, you can make anything last."

With Wang Jun's endorsement, my doubts faded completely. I patted the teen on the back with a grin. "All right, I'm convinced. We'll make this greenhouse happen, and I have no doubt it'll be the best one anyone's ever seen."

"It'll take some time to prepare the measurements, but I'll come down to your shop later to check the viability of the greenhouse. I'll need to see the space myself."

I nodded, satisfied. "Sounds like a plan."

With that settled, we left Li Wei to his work, and as Wang Jun and Lan-Yin followed me out, the village was already coming alive. The morning light filtered through the trees, casting long shadows as people started their daily routines. The familiar sounds of the market stalls being set up, carts rolling over the dirt paths, and villagers calling out to one another filled the air.

I turned to my two friends with a grin. "All right, it's time for the second most important matter of the day: giving gifts."

We moved from house to house, distributing the items I'd brought back from Crescent Bay City. Every gift was met with excitement and gratitude, and the joy on their faces was contagious.

Wang Jun's eyes sparkled as he unwrapped a finely crafted set of calligraphy brushes, each bristle perfectly tapered. "Kai . . . these are incredible," he murmured, his fingers gently brushing over the delicate wood.

Lan-Yin, on the other hand, marveled at the skin-care goods I'd picked up for her from Bai Hua's shop. She let out a delighted laugh, holding up the bottles of fragrant oils and creams. "You remembered! These will make my skin glow like a Moonlit Grace Lily!"

The other villagers received more practical items—tools, herbs, and even some finely woven fabrics that would make their lives easier in the coming months. Many of the gifts I received from merchants and other companies were useless to me, so I decided to give them to the villagers who'd appreciate it more.

Distributing the gifts was an incredible moment, watching as their faces lit up, knowing that I'd brought back a small part of the world beyond the village. It felt good to give back, to share what I'd gained from my travels.

By the time the morning turned to afternoon, the village had returned to its usual rhythm but with a renewed energy. Everyone had greeted me warmly, commenting on my transformation, Tianyi's newfound power, and, of course, Windy, who had become an unexpected source of fascination. They were adjusting, though, and the joy in their eyes reminded me of why I'd come back in the first place.

Once things had settled down, I found myself making my way to Elder Ming's abode. The village head was exactly where I thought he'd be; sitting in his courtyard, sipping tea with a peaceful expression on his face. As I approached, Windy curled around my neck and Tianyi resting on my shoulder, Elder Ming's sharp eyes caught sight of us. He smiled faintly but raised an eyebrow at Windy.

"I see you've picked up a new companion, Kai," he said, gesturing to the serpent. "You'll have to explain this to me later."

I chuckled softly, taking a seat across from him. "I will. But first, I wanted to show you this."

Elder Ming tilted his head, curious. Without another word, I reached into my storage ring and pulled out a bundle of bound novels.

Liang Feng's latest works.

"For you." I handed them to him with a grin. "I thought we could read these together. Like old times."

Elder Ming's eyes softened as he took the bundle, carefully running his fingers over the spines. "I've been looking forward to this," he murmured, a rare smile tugging at his lips.

And just like that, the weight of my travels, struggles, and victories seemed to melt away in the comfort of home.

CHAPTER EIGHTEEN

The Daily Grind

Weeks had passed since I returned, and life had finally settled into something resembling normalcy. At first, it was overwhelming. Between catching up with the villagers, setting the shop back in order, and making time for training, I felt like I was trying to juggle a hundred different tasks all at once. But now? Now it felt effortless, like slipping back into an old routine.

Of course, "effortless" didn't apply to everything. Not when it came to Elder Ming's training regimen, which had, without a doubt, turned into my own personal hell.

Every morning, like clockwork, I'd wake up before dawn, join Lan-Yin and Wang Jun for training, and face whatever new form of torment Elder Ming had concocted. He'd wave us off with a smile, then add, "Oh, and, Kai? No using qi today."

At first, I thought it was a joke. But after one too many mornings of running through the hills with rocks strapped to my limbs, I realized he was serious. Dead serious. He said that if my body couldn't keep up with my cultivation, I was doomed to hit a wall later on. He kept harping on about building a strong core and lower body. Apparently, it didn't matter what martial art you practiced—whether you were a sword master or a fist-fighter—if your legs were weak, you'd collapse like a rotting log.

"Maybe he's secretly a sadist," I muttered under my breath, trying to keep pace as we sprinted uphill yet again. "There's no way any normal human could come up with this."

"Did you say something?" Wang Jun panted beside me, already lagging. He wore similar weights on his legs, albeit lighter than mine, while being allowed to use qi.

"Just . . . thinking about how much I love early mornings."

Lan-Yin, farther ahead and looking as fresh as ever, threw a glance over her shoulder. "Keep up, boys. You're falling behind!"

I gritted my teeth, putting everything I had into each step. No qi, no shortcuts—just raw, burning muscle. By the time we finished the sprint, I was seeing stars and couldn't feel my legs.

And this was just the warm-up.

Next came the body-weight exercises. Push-ups, squats, planks—all with Elder Ming standing off to the side, watching like a hawk. He even had the nerve to sip tea while we were on the verge of collapse. Meanwhile, Lan-Yin and Wang Jun were working hard too, but it was clear I was on another level of suffering. Elder Ming had tailored my training to be, well, particularly brutal.

"Five more, Kai!" Elder Ming called, as if that were supposed to motivate me.

"What kind of sadist did you learn these from?" I muttered into the dirt as I struggled through my last push-up. I felt my arms shaking with every movement, heavy as lead.

He only chuckled in response. "That's for me to know and you to experience."

As I finally collapsed onto the ground, face first, I relished the cool winter air that washed over my skin. Steam rose from my body as the sweat evaporated in the chilly morning breeze, and for a moment, I just lay there, savoring the sensation. There was something almost liberating about being utterly, completely exhausted. My mind was too tired to worry about anything else. It was just me, the dirt beneath me, and the cold air above.

"I'm alive," I groaned, rolling onto my back. Lan-Yin, who had finished her own set of exercises, stood nearby with a smirk.

"Barely," she teased, offering me a hand to help me up.

I took it, groaning as my legs protested. "Remind me again why we do this every morning?"

"Because you're obsessed with getting stronger?"

"Right. I knew there was a reason."

Wang Jun, looking equally wrecked but far more cheerful about it, clapped me on the shoulder as I wobbled to my feet. "By the way, I took a good look at that Iron Boar pelts you brought back."

"Yeah?" I asked, wiping sweat from my brow.

He nodded. "It's an incredible specimen. The hide is thick, durable, and has just the right amount of flexibility. I'll be able to make something great with it, but it's gonna take some time. Working with material that tough requires precision."

"No rush," I said, waving him off. "Take your time. As long as it keeps me from getting skewered in the future, I'm happy."

He chuckled. "Oh, it'll do that and more. Just leave it to me."

With that, our training session ended, and we all parted ways for the day. Lan-Yin was attending to tasks at the Soaring Swallow, and Wang Jun was going to the forge. As for me, I was looking forward to collapsing in my shop and maybe catching a break from Elder Ming's 'sage wisdom.' But before we split up, I couldn't resist one last jab.

"By the way," I said, letting a sly grin creep onto my face as we walked, "you two seem closer these days. All that 'cultivating together,' eh? Must be quite the experience, sharing your energy flows, synchronizing your qi . . . bonding in such an *intimate* way."

Wang Jun groaned, rolling his eyes, while Lan-Yin's face flushed. "Kai . . ." she warned, already clenching her fist.

"What?" I asked, feigning obliviousness. "I'm just saying—cultivating side by side, your breathing in perfect harmony, feeling each other's presence, the warmth of your combined—"

Before I could finish, I felt a swift gust of air as Lan-Yin's hand came swinging toward the back of my head. But I was ready. My legs locked, my body bracing against the earth like the ancient roots of a tree.

ROOTED BANYAN STANCE!

Her palm met my skull with a resounding smack, but instead of the impact sending me sprawling, I stood firm, unmoving, with a triumphant smirk.

"Really, Kai? You're using an advanced defense technique just to avoid getting smacked?"

I shrugged, still grinning. "When you're as fragile as I am, you've gotta take precautions. Besides, your strength has been on the rise lately. I wouldn't want to be knocked out before breakfast."

She huffed and crossed her arms, clearly unimpressed. "You're ridiculous."

"Thank you," I said, offering a mock bow before turning to Wang Jun. "Now, if you'll excuse me, I have a shop to collapse in. Just make sure the pelt looks good on me. After all, a young master has a reputation to uphold."

The blacksmith snorted with an amused smile. "Reputation? Is that what you're calling it now?"

"Of course," I said, flipping my hair back dramatically. "Why else would I use all these advanced techniques to keep my perfect form intact?"

And with that, we split up, each heading off to face the rest of the day. Another morning survived.

After a peaceful walk, I finally made it back to my shop. The familiar smell of herbs and dried flowers greeted me, grounding me in the present. Despite my exhaustion, I knew there was no time to rest. The deal with the Azure Silk Trading Company wasn't going to fulfill itself, and I had a massive batch of potions to prepare.

The Two-Star Pagoda Pill Furnace gleamed in the morning light as I set to work. It had become my constant companion, its efficiency allowing me to brew multiple batches at a time. With a flick of my wrist, I activated it, watching as the furnace hummed to life with a small pulse of qi.

I gathered the ingredients, my hands moving automatically as I measured out the exact amounts for each concoction. Ginseng, goji berry, Morning Dew Herb—all essential for the various potions I'd promised to the company. With the pill furnace and my Refinement Simulation Technique, the process was practically seamless. I tossed the ingredients into the furnace, feeling a small sense of satisfaction as the flames flared higher, wrapping around the materials and breaking them down into their purest forms.

As the potion brewed, I checked my mail. It had become a daily habit—thanks to the post station that the Azure Silk Trading Company provided, I had access to fast communication with Crescent Bay City and beyond. It was a luxury I hadn't used prior to leaving the village, but one I learned to appreciate now.

I sifted through the letters: one from Tao Ren, another from Bai Hua, and—ah, there it was—a letter from the trading company. I opened it first and scanning through it.

"Good news," I muttered to myself, still skimming the details. They had found an artisan capable of producing high-quality glass, and the pieces would be ready within a month, just in time for Li Wei to use them in constructing the greenhouse. Perfect timing.

The next letter was from Tao Ren, updating me on his efforts. After plenty of back-and-forth and some long nights, he'd finally secured the permit for the shop he'd been planning in Crescent Bay. There was a hint of pride in his words, and rightfully so! Hopefully his father approved.

Then there was a letter from Bai Hua, of course. As usual, he was tinkering with new skin-care concoctions, experimenting with more potent formulas meant to protect against extreme conditions. I'd have to try them out at some point; Lan-Yin and the other women in the village I bought cosmetic goods for have been practically glowing since I arrived.

Finally, there was a letter from Guowei Wang. He thanked me for my recent note and, as always, encouraged me to keep balancing both alchemy and martial arts. *Even the most elusive plants,* he had written, *need time to root before they grow strong.*

He then mentioned my work with the Golden Bamboo and included a few excerpts from texts he thought might provide clues about its lost cultivation method. There were references to rare qi conditions and unique soil compositions, but nothing concrete yet. Still, it was more than I had before.

By the way, he'd added, *the Wandering Wind Press has some new releases that might interest you. If you find yourself back in Crescent Bay, stop by. You never know what you'll find in those old books.*

I leaned back in my chair, letting my thoughts wander. So much had changed since I returned, and yet, the day-to-day tasks were strangely comforting. As chaotic as life had become, I was thriving amid it all.

With the letters out of the way, I turned my attention back to the potions. The mixture inside had reached the right stage, and it was time to transfer the liquid to cooling containers. I carefully lifted the cauldron's lid, the fragrant steam rising in gentle swirls, and ladled the concoction into several glass vials.

The next step was letting them cool and infuse over the next several hours. I placed the vials in their cooling racks and left them undisturbed, trusting the natural process to do the rest.

With the potions now set aside, I needed a break. The sun had risen fully by now, bathing the village in a soft winter light. I stepped outside, making my way toward the small garden Lan-Yin and Elder Ming carefully tended to. Most of the plants had entered a dormant state, their growth slowed by the cold, but they were still alive, hanging on in the harsh weather.

I crouched by the Moonlit Grace Lily, a delicate yet resilient flower that had been thriving despite the winter chill. Its silvery petals shimmered faintly, even under the pale sunlight. I placed a hand near its stem and channeled my qi into it.

The lilies responded, their petals perking up as the qi reinvigorated them. I repeated the process for the rest of the garden.

As I worked, something caught my eye—a small, twisted form lying near the base of one bush. I flinched when I realized what it was: a rodent, wrapped up in thick webs. The creature's glazed-over eyes and lifeless body were clear signs it was dead.

"Oh no," I muttered, stepping back. That had to be the work of that strange spider I'd seen skittering around the garden a few times.

The thing was terrifying, being able to subdue animals many times larger than itself. Clearly, it had been busy while I was gone. And unlike Tianyi or Windy, it didn't seem enthused about meeting me. It would skitter away as soon as I saw it. I'd have to give it a name soon. Calling it the "strange spider" all the time was rather cumbersome.

"Hm. Perhaps Yin Si?" I mused aloud, then sighed and shook my head, wondering how long it would be before the regular farm animals in this village turned sentient or magical too. "One day, it'll be chickens. I just know it." I imagined a qi-infused rooster unfolding the Silent Moon Sect's techniques, like the Twelve Form Harvest Moon. It was rather comical.

For some reason, the image fit incredibly well.

As I stood there, shaking my head at the ridiculous image of battle-hardened chickens wielding martial techniques, something heavy dropped right beside me. I jumped back, startled, as the bisected form of a magpie lay at my feet, twitching slightly. My stomach twisted.

Sorry.

I glanced up just in time to see Tianyi fluttering lazily overhead, her delicate wings shimmering with soft blue light.

Before I could get a word out, Windy slithered into view, his tongue flicking in the air. In one smooth motion, the serpent swallowed the magpie's remains whole. I grimaced but said nothing. Between Tianyi, Windy, and that unsettling spider, my shop was turning into something of an invincible fortress—one that dealt with pests in its own gruesome way.

"Could you at least give me some warning next time?"

Tianyi fluttered down to perch on my shoulder, her small presence a familiar comfort despite the odd situation. I shook my head and turned back to the garden, deciding it was better to focus on something a little more peaceful.

Slowly but surely, my plants drank in my qi, ensuring they'd be ready to flourish when spring came.

As I worked, a few customers passed by, seeking potions or salves for winter ailments. It wasn't a busy day, so the work went by quickly. The villagers had become accustomed to my shop's pace, and the flow of people seemed steady but without the rush I'd experienced when I'd returned.

Just as I was finishing up another round of tending to the herbs, a familiar sound reached my ears: the high-pitched chattering of children. Sure enough, Xiao Bao and Mei-Li, two of the more rambunctious village kids, appeared at the gate, followed by a gaggle of their friends.

"Kai!" Xiao Bao called out with excitement. "Tell us more about the Gauntlet! How you fought the Five Fists of Narrow Stone Peak!"

Mei-Li joined in, bouncing on her toes. "Yeah, you never told us what happened!"

I suppressed a grin, already feeling the urge to embellish my tale. "Ah, the Five Fists, huh? Well, let me tell you, those were some of the toughest foes I've ever faced."

The kids gathered around, completely enraptured. I knew this was my moment. Of course, I didn't mention the minor detail that I had help from Xu Ziqing. Why ruin the magic of the story?

"And then," I continued, standing tall, "with a single blow, I shattered their formation. The very ground trembled beneath our feet, and the heavens wept at the sight of my victory!"

The kids gasped in awe, and I couldn't help but smile.

As the children ran off, no doubt to reenact my grand battle with the Five Fists, I rested my elbows against the fence and took in a deep breath. The beauty of a normal life, a life I'd once thought too small for my ambitions, was finally settling back into my bones. The rhythm of the village had tempered that constant wanderlust that used to gnaw at me.

But as the sun dipped lower, painting the sky with shades of amber, I knew my day wasn't done yet.

Once the shop was closed and the village had quieted for the night, I made my way to the small clearing next to my home. The moonlight filtered down through the bare branches, casting soft silver shadows across the ground.

Tianyi hovered beside me, her wings shimmering in the moonlight, while Windy coiled lazily near the base of a tree. I stretched my limbs, preparing for the last task of the day—training.

My qi reserves were brimming, which was exactly what I needed. Tonight, I would spar, pushing myself to the edge of my physical and mental limits. The remaining Beast Core elixir I had consumed needed to settle, to fully integrate into my dantian. And the best way to ensure that was through the grind of battle.

Taking a deep breath, I slipped into my stance, the energy swirling within me as I prepared to test everything I had. The night was still, the world quiet, as the three of us charged at each other, sharpening our skills.

Rooted Banyan Stance has reached level 3.

Another day. Another step closer.

CHAPTER NINETEEN

A Flower of Dread

Xu Ziqing sat across from Elder Fang, the dim light of the lanterns swaying gently with the motion of the carriage. The soft clinking of the wooden wheels against the uneven dirt road was the only sound breaking the silence. Despite the calm exterior of the ride, his thoughts churned, each turn of the wheel fueling his growing unease.

The lanterns cast flickering shadows across Elder Fang's face, further emphasizing the sharp lines of the man's expression. Though the man had not spoken a word since they had set off, his mere presence dominated the carriage. The second-class disciple could feel the heavy weight of the elder's qi pressing against the space, thick and suffocating.

These elders are not from here, Xu Ziqing thought grimly, confirming once again what he had suspected from the start. Powerhouses like them wouldn't have gone unnoticed for so long if they had. *So how did Sect Leader Jun bring them here?*

Decades ago, the province lost the route to the other continents, an event woven into the history of their world. Yet these men, bound to Jun's cause, hailed from those distant lands. What price had Jun paid to forge such alliances? The possibilities churned the disciple's stomach.

From the front of the carriage, Ping Hai guided the horses, his quiet grunt audible as the reins creaked in his large hands. The Azure Moon Marauder watched his junior brother from the shadows, his heart heavy. The third-class disciple had changed since losing to Kai Liu, and not for the better.

Once, he had been full of potential, a disciple on the rise. But that defeat, paired with Sect Leader Jun's manipulation, had twisted Ping Hai's trajectory. The boy had thrown himself into mission after mission, each more dangerous than the last, risking life and limb hoping to reclaim some shred of honor. His rapid growth had come at a cost—a deep, jagged scar now marred his face, cutting across his left eye, and his once-bright spirit had been replaced by a hollow devotion to the sect's cause.

To most, Ping Hai's transformation showed his dedication and remarkable rise through the ranks. But to Xu Ziqing, it was a tragedy. His junior brother had become little more than a pawn in Jun's growing web of control.

He had to protect him, even if it meant doing so from the shadows.

Observe Elder Fang, Sect Leader Jun had told him before the mission began, as cold and cutting as a winter wind. *Do not offend him under any circumstance.*

Those words lingered in the second-class disciple's mind as he studied the elder sitting across from him.

But how had such men come to serve Jun? What had the sect leader offered them? The answers were elusive, yet Ziqing couldn't shake the growing certainty that whatever Jun's plans entailed, they were far more dangerous than anyone realized.

The carriage rolled on, the silence heavy, as they approached the outskirts of Qingmu. Xu Ziqing kept his thoughts tightly contained, stealing glances at Elder Fang, but the man remained motionless, his presence as ominous as ever. Although neither spoke, there was palpable tension between them.

At the front of the carriage, Ping Hai suddenly called back, his voice breaking the stillness. "We're here, Senior Brother. Elder."

Ziqing straightened as the carriage slowed to a halt. The third-class disciple brought the horses to a stop, his broad shoulders hunched slightly. He jumped down from the driver's seat, his scarred face barely visible in the dim light of the lanterns. To anyone else, Ping Hai would look like a loyal disciple eager to serve. But Ziqing could see the shadows behind his eyes—shadows that deepened with every mission Sect Leader Jun sent him on.

Elder Fang finally stirred, his sharp gaze sliding to Ziqing. Without a word, the elder rose from his seat, stepping down from the carriage with the quiet grace of a predator.

This mission wasn't just about the Iron Claw Sect's transgressions. This was about sending a message. A message that the Silent Moon Sect, under Jun's rule, would not tolerate any insult—no matter how small.

The second-class disciple stepped out of the carriage, the cold air of Qingmu biting at his skin. Lanterns flickered along the village path, casting a dim glow on the waiting figures of the villagers. As he scanned the crowd, his eyes fell upon Lan Sheng, the second-class disciple of the Verdant Lotus Sect who informed them of the situation.

"Welcome to Qingmu," Lan Sheng said smoothly, his gaze sliding over the group. "I figured you were arriving today. Fortunate timing too. The Iron Claw Sect has been . . . pressing their luck lately. If it weren't for Kai Liu stepping in, things could have gone much worse. *You* were supposed to be the ones handling it, correct?"

The subtle dig made his stomach churn.

Again, it's him. Every time Xu Ziqing turned around, the young alchemist was there, involving himself in matters far beyond his reach. The village, the Gauntlet, the wager with Ping Hai—it was as if Kai's very existence was a constant reminder of the chaos that trailed him.

"How *convenient* for Qingmu that Kai Liu just happened to intervene," the second-class disciple replied coolly.

Lan Sheng's smile didn't reach his eyes. "It's becoming a habit, isn't it? Him cleaning up after your sect. One might think the Silent Moon Sect has more important matters than keeping its promises."

His words cut deeper than Ziqing cared to admit. He hated that Lan Sheng was right—hated that they were here again, playing catch-up to an alchemist who seemed to always find himself at the center of everything.

The tension simmered, the conversation teetering on the edge of over-formality. But Elder Fang wasn't interested in their verbal sparring.

The elder's bitter voice broke through the tension. "This is not our concern. The Iron Claw Sect is. We'll deal with them directly. Where do they reside?"

"They live a few hours northwest of here, Elder," Xu Ziqing replied. "The Iron Claw Sect has a small stronghold near the base of the Crescent Hills. If needed, I can send a request for reinforcements immediately."

He already had the plan forming in his mind: he could quickly mobilize a small contingent of Silent Moon disciples, fortifying their position and ensuring they had a backup if the situation escalated. It was the logical move, and one Sect Leader Jun would approve of. But before Xu Ziqing could act on it, Elder Fang dismissed the idea with a wave of his hand, his face unreadable.

"There's no need," he said, his voice casual, as though they were discussing something as mundane as the weather. "I will be enough deterrent."

He spoke with such certainty, as if the idea of needing reinforcements was laughable. And perhaps, for him, it was.

The more Xu Ziqing thought about it, the more disturbed he became. What had Sect Leader Jun promised this powerhouse? What had they given to have three other men like Elder Fang on their side, or, more terrifyingly, *were they really on their side?*

As these thoughts swirled in his mind, Xu Ziqing glanced at Ping Hai, who was now interacting with the villagers, accepting what the disciple assumed to be the tribute the Silent Moon demanded for their so-called protection. The villagers were anxious, but Ping Hai handled the exchange with mechanical efficiency, his expression devoid of warmth.

He could feel the weight of it pressing down on him—his own powerlessness, the slow realization that the sect he had dedicated his life to no longer existed. He had failed not only as a disciple but as a guardian of its values.

"Let's move," the elder said sharply, already turning toward the carriage.

Lan Sheng made no further remarks but nodded at Xu Ziqing before taking his leave, his presence lingering like a shadow.

Without another word, Xu Ziqing climbed back into the carriage, Ping Hai following closely behind. As they set off once more, the oppressive silence of the journey resumed.

The journey continued in tense silence as the carriage rattled along the uneven path, each bump jostling his thoughts into further disarray. The trees thinned, revealing a clearing up ahead. As they drew closer, something felt off—an oppressive stillness hung in the air, and the scent of dried earth mixed with something more sinister.

The carriage jolted to a halt, its sudden stop jarring Xu Ziqing from his grim thoughts. He leaned forward, glimpsing Ping Hai climbing down from the driver's seat, his broad form a silhouette against the dim lantern light.

"What is it?" Xu Ziqing stepped down from the carriage.

Ping Hai stood frozen a few paces ahead, staring at something in the distance, his brow furrowed in confusion. "There's something strange here," he muttered, pointing at the ground.

He followed his junior brother's gaze, his boots crunching against the dry, uneven dirt as he moved closer. Clear signs of movement marked the path before them—many footprints, some heavy and deep, others lighter, all converging on this exact spot. There was no mistaking it; this was the site of a struggle. Yet something was off.

The second-class disciple crouched down, his hand brushing the earth. The ground had been disturbed but not violently—no gouges from weapons, no splashes of blood, no debris from armor or clothing. Just footprints. Dozens of them, spread in every direction but leading to a single point where they simply vanished.

"Over a week old," he murmured, trying to make sense of the scene. "But there's no sign of a battle. No blood, no broken weapons—nothing."

But the tracks simply ended here. As if those who made them had disappeared into thin air.

Xu Ziqing's mind raced. This wasn't normal—no sect battle he'd ever seen ended like this. Even a retreat would leave clearer signs. A scattering of belongings, perhaps. But here, there was only this ominous silence, and the footprints, cut short as though swallowed by the earth itself.

Just as he was about to say more, Ping Hai's sharp intake of breath drew his attention. "Senior Brother," he called, his tone grim, "look."

Xu Ziqing turned to where the bald disciple pointed, and the words died in his throat.

There, nestled in a patch of disturbed earth, was a flower. But it was unlike anything Xu Ziqing had ever seen. A reddish hue pulsed faintly in the bloom; its petals were grotesquely fleshy, almost as if formed from raw muscle. Dark veinlike tendrils snaked through the flower's body, and with every pulse, a faint, malevolent energy seemed to radiate from it, twisting the air around it.

"What in the world . . . ?" he whispered, unable to hide the revulsion creeping into his voice. His instincts screamed at him to back away, but his feet remained rooted to the spot, transfixed by the eerie sight. Even with all his years of experience and battles fought, the sight of this flower unnerved him in a way he couldn't explain.

Elder Fang approached silently, his stony gaze fixed on the flower. For the first time since they'd begun the journey, his expression twisted—not with fear but with a mix of recognition and disgust.

From his sleeve, a long spear appeared as though summoned from thin air, the weapon gleaming in the dim light.

In one swift motion, he brought it down with enough force to obliterate the flower entirely. The ground erupted as the spear struck, and when the dust settled, nothing remained of the strange bloom but a blackened scar on the earth.

"This mission is complete. Let's head back," Elder Fang decided. He was as cold and measured as ever, as if the flower's existence had been a mere inconvenience.

Xu Ziqing's mind reeled, struggling to process the implications of Elder Fang's words. Was that it? Was this strange flower, this unsettling emptiness, truly the only clue left behind? No. There had to be more to it than that.

"But . . . the Iron Claw Sect . . . ?" Xu Ziqing started. "There's no trace of them. No remains, no—"

Elder Fang turned toward him slowly. For a moment, Xu Ziqing saw something strange in his expression.

"Their fate was sealed by forces beyond their understanding. Or ours. We need not concern ourselves with the Iron Claw any longer."

"But if we press forward," Xu Ziqing persisted, unable to hide his unease, "we can at least find answers. We should—"

"No," Elder Fang cut in with sharp finality. His gaze distant, he looked to the northwest, where the Iron Claw Sect's stronghold was hidden among the hills. "There is no need. Whatever claimed those disciples will claim the rest. The Iron Claw Sect will likely no longer be a bother. Pursuing them any further would be unwise."

The second-class disciple's heart pounded in his chest, an unsettling realization dawning on him. Elder Fang, the man who had been so willing to confront an entire sect on his own, was now backing down. Retreating. For a man of such power, such confidence, to suddenly turn cautious—it sent an icy wave of fear over Xu Ziqing.

"Unwise?" Xu Ziqing echoed barely above a whisper. "But we were sent to—"

"We've seen enough. This matter is concluded."

Xu Ziqing's mind raced, but no more words came. Elder Fang, who only moments ago had dismissed the need for reinforcements, was now suggesting they retreat. That the threat, whatever it was, wasn't something they could face—or *should* face.

"We return to the sect," Elder Fang said as if in warning. "Do not speak of what you have seen. Understand?"

The atmosphere thickened with an oppressive, dark energy. It felt as though the world itself held its breath, waiting for the slightest misstep. A cold sweat formed on Xu Ziqing's brow.

Then he felt it—a faint, almost-imperceptible shift in the air. It was subtle, like the distant rumble of a storm on the horizon, but the second-class disciple recognized it instantly. Killing intent. It was so faint that most wouldn't even register it, but to someone as attuned as himself, it might as well have been a blade at his throat.

He resisted the instinctive urge to reach for his sword, knowing full well that if he did, he would be dead before he could even unsheathe it. The pressure that radiated from the cultivator in that moment wasn't just a warning—it was a promise. A reminder of the power the man held, the kind of power that could snuff out lives in an instant.

Ping Hai, despite his towering frame, visibly faltered. His head dipped low, and his shoulders trembled slightly under the weight of the elder's intent. Xu Ziqing could see the strain in his eyes, the struggle to keep himself composed in the face of such overwhelming force.

For a brief, terrifying moment, he thought that the killing intent would consume them both. That Elder Fang had lost his patience, dooming them to die in the forsaken clearing, killed by forces they couldn't understand or resist.

But Xu Ziqing couldn't allow that to happen. Ping Hai—his junior brother—wouldn't survive this alone. And Xu Ziqing knew that if there was any hope of getting out of this alive, it was on him to act now. If he was to fall here, it would be on his terms, not because he had been too afraid to act.

The second-class disciple stepped forward, moving between his junior brother and the elder. Forcing himself to stand tall, his eyes locked with Elder Fang's cold, unreadable gaze.

"We won't say a thing. You have my word, Elder."

For a moment, there was only silence, the tension in the air so thick it was almost unbearable. The killing intent hung like a guillotine's blade, poised to strike.

The older man's gaze lingered on him for what felt like an eternity. Then, as suddenly as it had appeared, the killing intent dissipated, like a storm passing over. The suffocating pressure lifted, and the second-class disciple could finally breathe again.

"Good," Elder Fang said, calm and detached as ever. "See that you don't forget."

With that, he turned away, as if the exchange had been of little consequence to him. As if he hadn't just come within a hair's breadth of ending both their lives. He walked back to the carriage, his movements as fluid and composed as ever, leaving them standing in the eerie quiet of the clearing.

Ping Hai, still visibly shaken, straightened himself, his hands trembling slightly as he tried to regain his composure. Xu Ziqing placed a hand on his junior brother's shoulder, offering a silent reassurance before they both followed Elder Fang back to the carriage.

The mission was over, but as Xu Ziqing climbed back into the carriage, a bitter taste lingered in his mouth. The truth of what they had witnessed in the clearing would remain buried, but the darkness surrounding Elder Fang had only deepened.

CHAPTER TWENTY

Seeds of Fortune

Y ou sure you don't need any help?" I asked, mostly because it felt polite at this point.

Li Wei didn't even look up from the wood he was chiseling. "Kai, would you want me to help you make an elixir?"

I blinked, surprised by the rhetorical question. "Probably not . . . ?"

"Exactly," he said, giving me a quick side-eye before going back to work. "We've got this covered. Go play with your plants or something."

I glanced over at his father, who gave me a nod of agreement, hammering down another beam without missing a beat. Clearly, this was their domain, and I was just some guy who showed up with ideas and seeds. They were the professionals. Plus, they looked like they were in their element—thick coats, sawdust everywhere, and not a single break in their rhythm. Meanwhile, I was just standing there feeling, well, unnecessary.

Tianyi fluttered curiously near the half-built foundation, her wings shimmering in the frosty morning light, while Windy slithered around the edge of the garden, eyeing the woodpile like it was a challenge. Probably deciding whether he could knock it over with his tail.

"All right, all right," I said, holding my hands up in surrender. "I'll leave you to it."

Li Wei didn't respond, too focused on whatever intricate wood sorcery he was working on. His dad gave a grunt, which I assumed meant *thank you for not getting in the way.* With one last glance at the growing structure that would soon be my greenhouse, I turned and headed back inside my shop, leaving the carpentry duo to their magic.

Once inside, the familiar smell of herbs and dried flowers greeted me, grounding me back into my world. I shut the door behind me, blocking out the cold and noise, and made my way to the table where the Golden Bamboo seeds sat, waiting for me.

Time to get back to the real puzzle.

I plopped down into my chair and pulled out the stack of notes Guowei Wang had sent me. Despite the many failed attempts recorded in the letters, the information had been invaluable. Every failure was a clue, showing me what didn't work. Cultivating Golden Bamboo was like asking the heavens to hand over a divine treasure. The seeds would sprout, yes, but then they'd just stop. No growth, no energy. Just . . . there. A tiny little shoot that gave up on life before it even started.

I flipped through the pages, reviewing the detailed notes. One of the more promising attempts mentioned a seed that had sprouted—full sun, well-drained soil—basically treated like any other bamboo. It had even grown a few inches before it stubbornly refused to grow any more. That had led me to my current theory: The soil probably needed to be treated just like regular bamboo but required something more than just sunlight.

"More sunlight," I muttered to myself. How do you get *more* sunlight when it's already been planted in full sun? Build a second sun? Did there used to be another celestial body in the sky that disappeared centuries ago?

I stared at the seed in my hand, rolling it between my fingers. There had to be something I was missing, something I wasn't seeing. Maybe I was over-thinking it? I closed my eyes and activated my Plant Whisperer skill, feeling the familiar tingle crawl down my spine, spreading out to the tips of my fingers.

The seed hummed with life beneath my touch. It wasn't dead, not by a long shot. It felt eager, like it was just waiting for the right conditions to explode into growth. But those conditions were still a mystery.

I let out a sigh, dropping the seed back onto the table.

My head was spinning from all the cross-referencing and thinking, so I took a quick break. Grabbing a few herbs from the shelf, I began preparing a revitalizing tonic. The herbs mixed easily in my hands, their aromas familiar and calming. Within minutes, I had extracted their essence, creating a potent, energy-boosting drink.

Tossing it into a couple of vials, I headed back outside, where Li Wei and his father were still hard at work. They hadn't slowed down in the slightest, but even carpenters needed a boost now and then.

"Thought you could use a pick-me-up," I called out, holding up the vials.

Li Wei finally stopped chiseling long enough to give me a skeptical look. "What's in it?"

"Trust me, you'll feel like you could build ten greenhouses after this."

His dad took the vial without hesitation, downing it in one go. A second later, his eyes widened slightly, and he straightened up, his energy clearly restored. "Not bad, Kai," he grunted, giving me a nod of approval.

Li Wei followed suit, taking a swig and blinking in surprise as the tonic hit. "Okay, maybe you're good for something," he admitted, handing back the empty vial.

"Glad to be of service," I said with a smirk.

As they got back to work, their energy noticeably renewed, I couldn't help but grin. It wasn't every day I got to play a supporting role in someone else's craft. Maybe I couldn't build a greenhouse, but I could keep the builders going strong. Watching them work, I noticed an obvious difference in their working styles.

Jian Wei, Li Wei's father, worked with the steady, methodical precision that came from years, no, decades of experience. He used marking knives with familiar ease, carefully outlining the wood with smooth, deliberate cuts. Each motion was purposeful, measured, as if the wood itself were an old friend, and he knew exactly how to coax the best out of it.

Li Wei was like a storm. Where Jian Wei was slow and deliberate, Li Wei moved quickly, his hands flowing over the wood in almost a blur. He didn't even bother with marking knives. Instead, he cut freehand, trusting his instincts and skills without a second thought. And yet, despite his speed, his cuts were precise—almost unnervingly so. He'd pause occasionally, step back to examine his work, then dive right back in with a quick change that brought everything perfectly into alignment.

It was mesmerizing to watch, the way the two styles contrasted yet complemented each other. The father, with his years of expertise, and the son, with his natural talent amplified by something more.

As I watched, Li Wei suddenly looked up from his work and called out to his father. "That guideline's off by a fraction. Left by two millimeters."

Jian Wei paused, squinting at the wood before adjusting it slightly. I blinked. From where I was standing, I couldn't see any difference at all, but somehow Li Wei had caught it from across the foundation.

"Wait," I said, narrowing my eyes. "How did you even see that?"

Li Wei shrugged, casually wiping his hands on his tunic. "Harmonic Carpentry."

"What?"

"The skill I unlocked about a month ago," he explained, as if this were the most normal thing in the world. "It's called Harmonic Carpentry. Helps me see the balance in materials or visualize grid lines or paths in the things I'm working on."

"Grid lines?" I leaned in, intrigued. "So it's like your vision has boundaries?"

"Sort of." Li Wei gestured to the beam he'd been working on, and I swear I could imagine the faint outlines he was describing. "It lets me dabble in other things too, like masonry, even metalworking. All the materials, they've got their own rhythm. It's just a matter of tuning into them."

I couldn't help but feel a sense of awe as I listened. It reminded me so much of my own skills, like the Refinement Simulation Technique—how I could visualize the reactions inside the furnace, see the paths ingredients would take before I even added them.

"Have you learned the Memory Palace technique?" I asked, suddenly curious if his skill set paralleled mine even more closely.

Li Wei's eyes flicked over to me, a grin tugging the corner of his mouth. "I did, actually. Got it as a quest reward. It's been useful, especially when working on more complex structures. You?"

When everyone was special, no one was, I supposed. First Feng Wu, then Zhi Ruo, and now him? Everybody was getting all these supposedly rare skills, even though Elder Ming said it was unheard of to have unless you were an Essence Awakening Stage Cultivator!

I nodded. "Yeah. I use it for remembering a lot of things, and revising recipes, techniques, and whatnot."

"Huh." Li Wei scratched his chin pensively. "I guess we're more similar than we thought."

That realization struck me harder than I expected. How had Li Wei, someone who had been a promising carpenter until recently, reached such a high level so quickly? What had prompted the Heavenly Interface to give him these quests and abilities, allowing him to eclipse his father in skill in just a few months? Was it something in his potential, or had the Interface been waiting for him to tap into it?

Before I could ponder it further, Li Wei gave me a curious glance. "What about you? What abilities did you get?"

"Well, since you asked . . ." I plucked a sprig of mint from a nearby plant, holding it up as I activated my Essence Extraction skill. Instantly, the essence of the mint flowed from the plant, gathering into a shimmering ball of energy at the top of my palm.

Li Wei's normally aloof expression brightened, his eyes sparkling with interest. He reached out to touch the essence, his hand brushing against the surface.

The moment his fingers made contact, the energy dropped from my palm, liquefying into a glowing liquid that slid off my hand and onto a nearby astragalus plant. The plant shuddered as it absorbed the liquid, its leaves taking on a strange, vibrant hue that shimmered under the light.

I stared at the plant, my brain struggling to process what had just happened. "Uh . . . that's not supposed to happen."

"My bad. I'm sorry."

"No, it's okay." I crouched to observe the astragalus, which stood out prominently among its standard purple counterparts. "It just . . . absorbed it?"

The plant's now-vibrant and odd shade of bluish green pulsed slightly, almost as if it was breathing. The realization struck me like a bolt of lightning.

Have I been able to do this all along?

I looked up at the teen, who was still watching curiously. "Do you know what this means?"

He shrugged, unaware of what had just transpired. "The plant's gone bad now?"

I waved my hand dismissively. "No, no. I can put these essences into other plants! I could create entirely new hybrids! Imagine the possibilities! What if I could make pills and elixirs using these hybrids that no one has ever seen before?"

Li Wei's expression changed little, but his eyebrow raised a fraction. "You mean like a mint-astragalus hybrid?"

"Yes!" I exclaimed, my excitement building. "But bigger! What if I took the essence of a rare herb and merged it with a common plant? Or combined two powerful herbs into one super plant? I could make pills and potions that don't lose their effectiveness as quickly because they're unique every time!"

Lan Sheng's words echoed in my mind about how most pills lose their potency with repeated use because the body grows accustomed to them. But what if I could make entirely new variants, hybrids with never-before-seen properties? I could create pills that retained their potency regardless of how often they were taken, because each batch would be unique.

The clinking of gold coins rang in my ears. My mind flashed to the possibilities. Creating a line of hybrid elixirs, selling them far and wide, becoming renowned as the alchemist who discovered a new way to enhance herbal medicine. My face split into a wide grin as the fantasy of endless riches formed in my head.

Suddenly, I couldn't contain myself. I shot to my feet, arms flung wide, and shouted at the top of my lungs, "I'm rich! I'm rich!"

Before Li Wei could react, I lunged forward and hugged him tightly, nearly knocking the poor guy over with the force of my enthusiasm. "Li Wei! This is the luckiest accident of my life!"

Well, second luckiest. Running into the ancient ruins where the Heavenly Interface laid dormant was even more ridiculous.

Li Wei, clearly startled by my sudden outburst, stiffened for a second before awkwardly patting me on the back. "Uh, yeah, sure. Congratulations."

"Do you understand what this means?" I pulled back, practically bouncing on my feet. "This changes everything! I could make an entirely new branch of alchemy! I'm going to be a legend! An immortal alchemist known across the land for creating life-changing elixirs!"

"You sure you're not getting ahead of yourself?"

"Nope! Not even a little!" I beamed, spinning around to look at the astragalus plant, still marveling at it. "This is just the beginning!"

Tianyi fluttered over, sensing my excitement. She landed softly on my shoulder, and her wings glimmered with a soft blue glow, reflecting the mood of the moment. Even Windy slithered closer, curious about what had happened.

"Just think of it," I said, grinning from ear to ear. "Unique elixirs, unheard-of pills. I'll change the world of alchemy! And all because of one little accident."

"Well, good luck with that," Li Wei said, returning to his work on the greenhouse. "Let me know when you've made a mint-ginger hybrid. Might help with the cold."

I laughed, my mind already racing ahead with ideas. There was no turning back now. If this worked, the possibilities were endless. I was going to make history, one plant at a time.

CHAPTER TWENTY-ONE

Sweat, Seeds, and Spiritual Growth

I trudged up the path to Elder Ming's house, the first rays of sunlight just beginning to peek over the horizon. I felt as if my legs were made of lead, and my eyes . . . Well, if I had to guess, they probably looked as tired as I felt.

But I didn't care.

Every single batch of herbs in my garden had at least one or two miscolored hybrids. Now, even as exhaustion gnawed at the edges of my consciousness, the thrill of my discoveries kept me going.

As I approached, I spotted Elder Ming already seated in the courtyard, a small cup of tea in his hands. He glanced up as I neared, his sharp eyes immediately noticing my disheveled appearance. One eyebrow raised, just enough to let me know he saw right through me.

"Kai," he said, calm but curious. "You're early. Did you even get any sleep?"

I let out a breathless laugh, dropping onto the nearest seat without so much as a greeting. "I didn't sleep," I admitted, grinning like an idiot. "I've been up all night. You won't believe what I figured out!"

Elder Ming sipped his tea, clearly amused by my state. He silently poured me another cup, and I gingerly accepted it, letting the warmth envelop my cold fingertips.

I could hardly sit still as I recounted my accidental discovery with Li Wei yesterday, dropping a ball of extracted mint essence onto one of my plants. How it absorbed into the astragalus, infusing itself with the essence.

Elder Ming's eyebrow raised slightly higher, but he said nothing, just gestured for me to continue. He was used to my ramblings by now.

"So I started small," I went on, my words tumbling over each other in my excitement. "I took some dried ginger, infused its essence into Morning Dew Herb, and created another hybrid! I've been trying it with all the different plants in my garden."

The older man gently set down his tea; his expression was unreadable, but I sensed his intrigue. "You can create a hybrid plant by infusing the essence of another into it? And it survived the process?"

I nodded vigorously. "Not just survived—it thrived! The mint essence didn't just mix with the astragalus; it changed it! I tested the plant afterward and discovered that it now has the potential to treat both internal injuries and minor poisons. Normally, astragalus wouldn't be nearly as effective in that category. And get this—it grows faster too! After adding a second ball of mint essence, it reached full maturity right then and there!"

For the first time, a flicker of something like pride crossed Elder Ming's face. "Impressive."

"And that's not all," I added quickly, unable to contain myself. "I've got big theories. What if I did this with rarer herbs? Or—or—what if I infused *multiple* essences into one plant? I could create entirely new species, Elder Ming! This could revolutionize how we cultivate! Think of the potions, the salves, the elixirs!"

I knew I was babbling now, but I couldn't stop. My mind had been racing all night, and now that I had someone to talk to, it all just spilled out.

Elder Ming, to his credit, didn't laugh. He didn't even smirk. He just watched me with that calm, wise expression of his, his hands folded in his lap. But I could see it—the glint of pride in his eyes, the way his lips curved ever so slightly.

"This discovery could indeed be groundbreaking . . . if handled properly. But you must be cautious. Such experimentation, while innovative, is also unpredictable. The balance of nature is delicate, you know."

I nodded, but my mind was already on my next idea. "Right, right. I'll be careful. But this could open doors we didn't even know existed!"

Elder Ming smiled softly, but his gaze drifted past me, settling on the horizon where the first light of dawn was spreading across the sky. His usual calm demeanor seemed slightly distant, as if his thoughts were far away, lost in some deeper reflection.

I sipped my tea, the warmth of it calming the buzzing in my mind. But something about his expression gnawed at me. Was he unhappy with what I was doing? Did he think I was getting too reckless?

"Is something bothering you?" I asked carefully, unsure if I had overstepped. "You don't seem too thrilled about this."

His eyes softened, but he didn't respond right away. Instead, he looked down at his tea, swirling it lightly in the cup before letting out a quiet sigh. "It's not your discoveries, Kai," he finally said. "In fact, I'm proud of what you've accomplished. But there's something else. Something in the air these days . . ."

"What do you mean?"

"So much has changed in the past year after decades of normalcy. The Heavenly Interface suddenly appeared, the sects rising in power, strange events occurring all over the province . . . It's as if the world itself is shifting. And not just gradually, but rapidly. Like we're all being pulled toward something."

The weight of his words settled heavily on me. I remembered my conversation with Han Wei and Li Na before I left. Things *had* been moving fast—too fast. My thoughts drifted to the Silent Moon Sect, how they'd grown so powerful so quickly, how the Heavenly Interface had placed a new pressure on everyone, and how everything seemed to race toward an unknown end.

"One falling leaf heralds autumn for the entire world," Elder Ming said quietly.

For a while, neither of us spoke.

He broke the silence. "You've done well, Kai. And you'll need to keep doing well, because the world we're in now . . . it's not the same one you grew up in. It's changing faster than any of us can keep up with. But change brings opportunity too."

I looked at him, nodding slowly. A strange sense of foreboding now tempered the excitement I'd felt earlier. "I understand," I said quietly, more to myself than to him.

The tension hanging in the air was gnawing at me. I needed to change the subject before I got swallowed by it. "Well, since I'm already here, how about we get started on training early?" I asked, forcing a grin onto my face. "No point in sitting around when we could work on my 'roots,' right?"

Elder Ming's eyes twinkled at my attempt to lighten the mood. "Ah, so you're eager to torture yourself, I see," he said, setting down his cup and standing. "Very well. Let's begin."

We started with the basics; horse stance, balancing rocks, the familiar drills that always seemed deceptively simple until you were halfway through and your legs were screaming in protest. And as usual, without using my qi. Even with the exhaustion gnawing at me, I pushed through, determined not to let the lack of sleep slow me down. My mind kept wandering back to Elder Ming's words, but I channeled that unease into my movements, keeping my focus sharp.

As the morning progressed, we moved on to practicing basic forms. I felt my body resisting, the weight of the sleepless night pulling at my limbs, but I gritted my teeth and kept going. There was no way I was going to let fatigue stop me. How could I call myself the rising star of the Tranquil Breeze Province otherwise?

Elder Ming watched me with his usual calm, occasionally offering corrections, but mostly let me push myself. It was only when we moved on to sparring that the real challenge began.

"Let's see how far you've come," he said, taking up his stance.

I nodded, positioning myself across from him. Despite his injury, Elder Ming moved with the fluidity of someone who had spent a lifetime mastering his body. I had never truly seen him fight at his peak, but even now, with his dantian destroyed, his movements were precise, every strike calculated.

We began slowly, trading blows and testing each other's reflexes. But soon enough, I felt the familiar heat of competition rising within me. I pushed harder, quicker, my strikes aimed with more precision. To my surprise, Elder Ming's defenses held, parrying and dodging with ease.

Then, I saw my opening.

As he shifted his weight for another strike, I dropped my guard and allowed his fist to hit. I redirected his momentum, using the force of his attack to fuel my own counterstrike.

BAMBOO REPRISAL COUNTER!

My fist shot forward, aimed straight for his chest, but at the last second, I held back, stopping just short of making contact.

Elder Ming's eyes widened in surprise, and for a moment, I caught a flicker of something in his eyes. But it was gone as quickly as it appeared, replaced by a small, approving smile.

"Lucky strike, I guess," I said sheepishly.

He shook his head, his smile widening. "Luck has nothing to do with it. You've come far."

Before I could respond, the weight of the sleepless night finally caught up with me. My legs gave out from under me, and I felt the world tilt as I collapsed toward the ground. Before I hit the dirt, Elder Ming's hand shot out, catching me by the arm and pulling me back up to my feet.

"You've pushed yourself too hard," he chided, though there was a hint of amusement in his voice. "You can't just stay up all night and expect to be invincible by morning."

I let out a tired laugh, leaning heavily on him for support. "I blame you. You're the one who makes me do all these ridiculous exercises every day."

"Ridiculous exercises that are clearly working," Elder Ming countered, raising an eyebrow. "And I didn't tell you to stay up all night playing with plants."

We both chuckled, the tension from earlier easing into something more comfortable. For a moment, it felt like everything was back to normal, like the world wasn't changing so fast, and all that mattered was the familiar routine of training and teasing each other.

"You're a slave driver," I muttered, a grin tugging at my lips.

"And you're stubborn," he responded simply, giving a light chop to my head before guiding me to the edge of the courtyard.

We sat in silence for a moment, letting the quiet of the early morning settle over us. The world may have been changing around us, but for now, at least, this felt like a rare moment of peace.

As I sipped the last of my tea, I heard the faint sounds of Lan-Yin's and Wang Jun's voices echoing from the village path. They'd be here soon. But before they arrived, I glanced at Elder Ming again, noticing the quiet stillness in his gaze. He was staring off toward the horizon, his expression distant, as though his thoughts were far away.

For a moment, I wasn't sure if I should say anything. But then, with the faintest hesitation, I spoke. "I get it, you know. The world's changing fast, and it's unsettling. It feels like we're standing on the edge of something big."

He didn't move, but I could tell he was listening, his eyes still focused on the rising sun. I set my tea down, leaning forward a bit. "But I've been thinking," I continued, "about the village, the way everyone looks out for each other. We've all built something strong here, something that can weather change. And knowing we have each other . . . It makes all of this easier to face."

His gaze shifted ever so slightly toward me, and I saw a flicker of surprise in his eyes. I wasn't used to being the one offering reassurance, but it felt right. I'd always looked up to Elder Ming; his wisdom, his strength, but even he wasn't immune to anxiety.

"Master Qiang, Lan-Yin, Wang Jun, even Li Wei . . . Everyone's doing their part, lifting each other up. It's hard to feel like we're alone in all this when there's so much strength in the people around us."

He was quiet for a moment, the early morning light casting long shadows across the courtyard. Then he finally spoke, his voice softer than usual. "Yes. We face it together."

Before I could say anything more, the familiar sound of Lan-Yin's teasing voice broke the quiet.

"Well, look at this!" she called out as she and Wang Jun entered the courtyard. "Kai's early for once. What did I miss? Has the world turned upside down?"

Wang Jun wasn't far behind, smirking as he took in the sight of me slouched over, visibly exhausted. "Did Elder Ming wear you out before we even got here? You look like you're about to pass out."

I straightened up, trying to muster some dignity despite the dark circles under my eyes. "I came early, so I get to leave early, right, Elder Ming?"

Elder Ming, ever the picture of calm, raised an eyebrow, feigning thoughtfulness. "Leave early? Not so fast. One more exercise before you're free to go."

I groaned, throwing my head back dramatically. "You're relentless, you know that?"

I hobbled away from Elder Ming's courtyard, cradling my bruised stomach and wincing with every step. Each inhale felt like I was sucking in a bunch of angry bees, thanks to Lan-Yin's 'payback' punches. Wang Jun, mercifully, had gone easy on me, but she had been waiting for that moment.

Every step felt like a reminder of just how ruthless my friends could be when given an excuse.

The morning was still young, and the village was stirring. I waved at some of the early risers with my free hand, trying to maintain my composure, but internally I was already scheming to beg Tianyi for some healing the moment I got back.

"Good morning, Kai!" Xiao Bao called cheerfully.

I waved back, trying not to grimace. "Morning."

I trudged along, every muscle in my abdomen screaming for relief. There was no way I could keep this up on sheer willpower alone.

Despite the complaints running through my head, there was a strange sense of accomplishment bubbling up inside me. I had survived the training—barely—and pushed through my exhaustion. And, of course, I couldn't let them know how much it actually hurt.

As I neared my shop, thinking longingly about collapsing onto a soft surface and possibly never moving again, a familiar sensation washed over me—a soft chime echoed in the back of my mind.

> *Quest: Mastery of Spiritual Plant Cultivation—Cultivate and grow fifty viable and different plant hybrids. (0/50)*

I stopped dead in my tracks, blinking. My head snapped up, all thoughts of resting evaporating as I tried to make sense of the notification. A quest? Now?

I glanced around, half expecting something to leap out of the bushes, but the village looked as calm as ever. Still, I couldn't ignore the quest, especially with the weight of recent changes lingering over everything.

"Well," I sighed, straightening up as best as I could despite my aching body, "I guess rest will have to wait."

CHAPTER TWENTY-TWO

Hybrid Horizons

I knelt in the forest, staring at the small plant in front of me. My fingers brushed the rough bark of a gnarled winter vine, its curled tendrils barely clinging to life in the cold.

The extracted cinnamon essence swirled in my palm, glowing faintly, but I hesitated. I had already tried infusing two different plants, and each one had wilted within minutes. I wasn't going to let that happen again.

At least, not without understanding why.

"All right," I muttered to myself. "One more try. And if this fails, well . . . at least we're learning something."

Behind me, Tianyi fluttered silently, her healing aura faint but warm as it brushed against my sore muscles. The combination of her presence and the crisp forest air worked wonders to clear the fog of exhaustion from my mind. She reached out to me through our bond, her voice gentle as a breeze.

Can I help? she asked.

I smiled softly, feeling her concern radiate through our connection. "I'm okay, Tianyi. Just need to figure this out. Besides, I'm actually enjoying this. It's been a while since I got to experiment like this, out in the wild."

It had started with the wintergreen but after an infusion of cinnamon essence I had, it had shriveled in seconds, its petals blackening like scorched paper. Next was the frostroot, a plant known for thriving in harsh winters. It had fared better, lasting a few hours before wilting, its roots turning brittle and useless.

Each failure gnawed at me, but they were failures with purpose. There was a pattern forming, a commonality in each plant's collapse that I hadn't seen before. All the plants I'd experimented with shared something in common; they were all aligned with yin energy. But when I infused them with the essence of herbs aligned with yang energy, they wilted.

"So there's a limit," I murmured. "Incompatible plants die when combined with the wrong essence. That's what the quest meant by 'viable' hybrids."

Tianyi drifted closer, her healing aura intensifying slightly, soothing the lingering soreness in my muscles. I exhaled, letting the warmth seep into my bones. She always knew when I needed that extra support, even when I tried to brush it off.

Despite the setbacks, there was something oddly calming about this process. I felt like the herbalist I used to be, before the Heavenly Interface changed everything. Back when it was just me and the forest, before Spirit Beasts, sect politics, and alchemy tournaments became the norm. The failures didn't bother me as much as they might have back then. This was part of the work. Part of the journey.

I ran my fingers over the winter vine again, feeling the rough texture of its bark, its dormant energy barely clinging to life in the cold. This vine wasn't like the others. It wasn't aligned with yin energy or skewed toward either. It was hardy but simple, growing wherever it could find a foothold, surviving on minimal resources. If any plant could handle an infusion of yang energy, it was this one.

"Okay. Let's try this again."

I focused on the essence, holding it above the vine. Slowly, carefully, I released the essence, letting it drip down in small, controlled pulses. The vine trembled slightly, its tendrils reacting to the infusion, but it didn't wilt. Not yet.

"That's it," I said. "Slow and steady."

The vine absorbed the essence gradually, its bark darkening slightly as the energy soaked in. Tianyi watched closely from her perch, her wings fluttering gently in the breeze.

I still remember that day clearly. Much like today, I had been wandering the forest looking for Moonbeam Petals. Until I found her fluttering around daintily and setting me on a path that changed the trajectory of my life.

I glanced over at her now, seeing the strength she carried in her delicate frame. So much has changed since then.

The vine absorbed the last of the essence, its tendrils twitching as they adjusted to the new energy. This time, it hadn't wilted. It was still alive.

Quest: Mastery of Spiritual Plant Cultivation
—Cultivate and grow fifty viable and different plant hybrids. (1/50)

I smiled at the notification, feeling a rush of excitement despite the exhaustion weighing down my limbs. Finally, some progress.

Tianyi fluttered closer, her presence warm and reassuring. I reached out to let her land on my finger. "Looks like we're on the right track now."

As I gathered my tools and prepared to infuse more plants, I realized I had run out of cinnamon essence. With a sigh, I glanced around the forest, deciding it was time to gather more. The plants that thrived here were abundant, more so than I remembered from my herbalist days. Even in the dead of winter, green life covered the forest floor. I realized then how much the increased flow of qi through the province had changed the landscape. Everything was growing stronger, faster—like the world itself was waking up.

A cold gust of wind swept through the trees, carrying with it the scent of snow and something else, almost imperceptible. But I brushed it off. No need to be paranoid. It was winter, and most animals were hibernating, which explained the eerie silence in the woods.

Still, the absence of small critters scurrying through the underbrush felt . . . unnatural. I hadn't seen so much as a bird or a squirrel since I entered the forest.

"Relax. It's just winter. Animals hide away this time of year."

I kept walking, scanning the undergrowth for plants to infuse. Wintergreen, wild sage, frostroot—they all thrived here, and I could extract their essence easily enough. I knelt beside a patch of wild rosemary, its spindly leaves surviving against the odds in the frost. With a flick of my wrist, I drew out its essence, watching as the shimmering energy pooled in my palm. A quick glance over my shoulder showed Tianyi circling above, monitoring the surroundings.

Still, no animals. The silence nagged at me, an uneasy weight settling in the pit of my stomach. It was far too quiet, even for this season. Not even a single birdcall.

I pressed on, delving deeper into the forest. As I walked, I infused different plants, carefully selecting each one for their properties, and testing new combinations. A few more failures followed; an ice thistle shriveled after I infused it with wild sage, and a winterflower's petals withered when I combined it with frostroot, but I learned from each mistake.

"All right." I knelt by another patch of wild rosemary. "One more infusion, and then I'll head back to go over the results."

But just as I reached for the plant, Tianyi's voice echoed sharply through our bond.

Something's coming.

I froze, my fingers brushing the leaves of the rosemary. Her warning sent a chill down my spine, and I straightened, scanning the tree line.

There was rustling in the bushes ahead.

A young wolf stepped out, its fur matted and thin, ribs showing beneath its coat. Its eyes locked onto mine with a mix of fear and caution, as though it wasn't sure whether to approach or flee. It hesitated, sniffing the air, then bared its fangs at me.

Tianyi fluttered down to my shoulder, her presence a comforting weight against the sudden tension in the air. The wolf was young, too young to be hunting alone. Where was its pack?

I stayed perfectly still, my eyes locked on the wolf as it observed me with a mix of fear and aggression. There was a desperate edge to its posture. One paw lifted hesitantly as if it wanted to flee but couldn't afford to. Its nose twitched, catching my scent, and for a moment, I saw a flash of recognition in its eyes, but that only seemed to confuse it more.

"Tianyi," I whispered through our bond, my voice low and steady. "Can you try to calm it? Maybe we can avoid a fight."

She fluttered from my shoulder, her wings glowing faintly as she projected a calming aura toward the wolf. Her ability to communicate with animals hadn't failed yet, and I was hoping it would work now. Her essence spread like a gentle breeze, brushing against the wolf's mind, trying to ease its tension.

But the wolf didn't calm. Instead, it flinched, stepping back as if something about me repulsed it. It growled low in its throat, a sound that sent a ripple of unease through the quiet forest. Its eyes were wide with terror, and yet, instead of running, it lowered itself into a crouch, muscles coiled and ready to spring.

It's too scared, the butterfly said. She was concerned. *Not responding like most animals.*

"Dammit," I muttered, shifting my stance as the wolf prepared to lunge. I clenched my fists, shifting my stance. I didn't want to hurt it. This wolf wasn't a genuine threat, just a starved, frightened creature lashing out. But I couldn't let it get too close.

The wolf charged.

It was fast, faster than I expected for something so weak. I barely had time to react, dodging to the side just as its jaws snapped at where my leg had been. The move was clumsy, driven by hunger and desperation more than skill, but it was enough to keep me on edge.

"We've got to subdue it—without killing it if we can," I called out to Tianyi, barely dodging another frantic lunge. My muscles screamed in protest, remnants of Elder Ming's brutal training session dulling my edge.

She dove from the air, wings shimmering as she released another wave of soothing energy, but the wolf was too far gone. Whatever happened to it, whatever drove it to this point, broke something in its mind. It was too consumed by fear and hunger.

The wolf circled me, snarling, saliva dripping from its bared fangs. Its eyes were wild, darting between me and Tianyi, as if it was still unsure whether to attack or flee. Then, with a guttural growl, it made its choice.

It leapt.

I barely had time to think, only to act.

ROOTED BANYAN STANCE!

My body locked into position, my feet anchoring me to the earth as the wolf's jaws snapped shut around my neck. But instead of the sharp, searing pain I expected, I felt only the tug of fabric—its teeth punctured my robes, but my skin remained unscathed.

The wolf thrashed violently, trying to tear into me, but I remained rooted, unmoving. The stance held firm, but it came with a cost—I couldn't move either. All I could do was brace myself and wait for an opening.

Tianyi, seeing my predicament, didn't hesitate. In a split second, she darted forward, her wings shimmering with a sharp edge of condensed qi. She struck with swift, deadly precision, slicing across the wolf's eyes in one clean motion.

The wolf yelped in pain, its grip on my robe loosening as it stumbled back, blinded and weakened. I could see the agony in its movements, the way its body trembled with each step. It wasn't long for this world now.

She fluttered beside me, her wings dimming as the threat faded.

I knelt beside the wolf, its body limp, its breaths shallow. There was no longer any fear in its eyes, only pain and confusion. My heart clenched. I hadn't seen wolves in this forest for years, and now this young one had died alone, far from its home. I wasn't angry—not at it, not even at the situation. Only sadness filled me.

Quickly scanning the forest floor, I spotted a patch of frostroot. I plucked a few leaves, crushing them in my fingers to release their essence. With gentle hands, I applied the essence to the wolf's wounds, hoping to ease its passing, even if I couldn't save it.

"It's okay," I whispered. "You don't have to fight anymore."

The wolf let out a low whine, its body shuddering as it struggled to take one last breath. I cradled its head in my lap, my hand resting gently on its thin neck. There was no anger in me, no resentment for the bite that could have been far worse.

This creature hadn't stood a chance. It was lost, scared, and starving. And now it was passing on, not in a frenzy of violence but with a moment of peace, surrounded by the quiet of the forest.

Its breathing slowed, then stopped altogether. I stayed there for a long moment, my hand resting on its fur.

Tianyi perched on my shoulder, her presence comforting but subdued.

I'm sorry.

"It's not your fault," I told her, brushing my hand gently over the wolf's fur. "You saved me."

What had driven the creature to such desperation? It wasn't injured, just starved—its fear palpable even in death.

I carefully examined its frail body but found nothing to explain its madness.

"I know," I said, glancing around the eerily quiet woods. "Something's wrong here."

I couldn't take the wolf back with me, so I buried it. Slowly, I gathered dirt and snow, covering its slight form with care. It was a simple act, but it felt right, an offering of peace after its life of suffering.

When I finished, I stood over the grave for a moment, hoping the wolf would find rest.

"It's time to go," I said, turning back to the village. The forest had changed; it was no longer safe. I made a mental note to warn the others. Something dark was at work here, and the villagers needed to be cautious. No one should go out alone.

As Tianyi perched on my shoulder, we headed back. The path felt different now, more dangerous.

The world was shifting, and the forest was only the beginning.

CHAPTER TWENTY-THREE

Silent Threats and Steady Hands

I sat cross-legged on the floor of my shop, surrounded by a dozen potted plants in varying states of growth. Some were familiar species I'd foraged from the forest, while others were native to my garden, now transformed by the essence infusions I'd been experimenting with.

Not bad, but not nearly enough.

I leaned over the newest batch, inspecting the leaves of a wild ginseng plant I had infused just the day before. Its roots, once spindly and pale, now had a faint glow, and the leaves shimmered with a vitality that hadn't been there before.

The infusion had taken, but it wasn't enough. It needed more.

"Resilient plants," I said, running my fingers gently along the ginseng's stalk. "That's the key."

Plants like this one, hardy and built to survive in tough conditions, seemed to absorb essence more easily. Not like the delicate wintergreen or frostroot that had withered as soon as I tried to infuse them with anything even slightly mis-aligned. Ginseng, though—this one had potential. I'd have to infuse it at least one more time to make sure the changes settled in, but it had already made more progress than some of my earlier experiments.

I sighed, rubbing the back of my neck. "Gotta find that balance. Too much essence and they burn out. Too little and there's no effect."

I glanced over at the cinnamon tree in the far corner. I'd nearly given up on that one, figuring a plant of that size and strength wouldn't take to an infusion. But after several attempts, I realized it just needed more infusions of essence. Subtle, gradual infusions had altered it, the bark darkening in some places, the leaves becoming more robust, their edges curling slightly as they absorbed the new energy.

The trick wasn't overwhelming it with essence all at once. I had to be patient, layering the energy in stages, and allowing the tree to adjust before adding more.

"Like growing roots deeper before reaching for the sky," I said to myself, feeling a small smile tug at my lips. This was the kind of discovery I lived for.

Tianyi fluttered overhead, her wings shimmering softly in the afternoon light as she circled the shop, keeping a watchful eye on the garden just outside. Windy, meanwhile, slithered lazily along the edge of the potted plants, his blue-tinted scales glinting as he flicked his tongue at each one as if assessing their viability himself.

He gave a slight flick of his tail, barely acknowledging me, his attention focused on whatever invisible threat he thought might be lurking outside.

I turned back to the plants, picking up a small vial of essence from the table beside me. This one was wild sage, carefully extracted and ready for infusion. I uncorked the vial and held it over the ginseng plant, letting a single drop fall onto the soil near its roots. The plant trembled slightly as it absorbed the essence, the glow around it intensifying.

"Slow and steady," I whispered. "Let it take root."

I repeated the process, careful not to overwhelm the plant. Patience had always been the hardest part for me while exploring this ability, but if I'd learned anything in the past few weeks, it was that rushing wouldn't get me anywhere.

The cinnamon tree was next. I approached it, admiring the subtle changes that had already taken hold. The bark was tougher now, its scent stronger, more fragrant.

I tipped the vial over the base of the tree, watching as the essence soaked into the soil, and took a step back.

> *Quest: Mastery of Spiritual Plant Cultivation*
> *—Cultivate and grow fifty viable and different plant hybrids. (12/50)*

"Thirty-eight to go," I said, but I wasn't frustrated, only determined. "Piece by piece."

I stood, stretching my arms over my head as the late afternoon light streamed through the windows. "Well, I think that's enough for today."

With the plants infused and the day's experimentation wrapped up, I turned my attention to the other task at hand—the contract with the Azure Silk Trading Company. My first batch was due today.

Stacks of elixirs sat neatly on my workbench. At first, the contract had seemed like a mountain to climb. I'd promised a larger supply than I probably should have in exchange for a bigger advance, but with the improvements in my techniques, the challenge was easier than I initially thought.

Thanks to the Refinement Simulation Technique, I cut off the unnecessary steps. Combined with my Two-Star Pagoda Pill Furnace, the work had become almost seamless. What would've taken a full month before now took only a fraction of the time.

I began carefully organizing the vials, securing each one with padded cloth and placing them inside small wooden crates. As I stacked the last few, a small crate of essences caught my eye, a gift I'd prepared for the Verdant Lotus Sect I'd be sending off alongside this. It was a personal touch, something to show appreciation for the opportunities they had provided me with.

The crate was filled with purified essences: ginseng, wintergreen, cinnamon, and even some Moonlit Grace Lily, a batch that I was proud of. Each one was carefully bottled, glowing faintly with the raw power of the plants they'd been extracted from. It was a simple gesture, but one I hoped would build a stronger relationship with the sect that gave so much without expecting anything in return.

With the last vial stored, I moved everything outside, placing the crates onto the wooden cart that sat just outside my shop. The cart creaked under the weight, but it held steady as I double-checked the straps, making sure nothing would shift during transport.

As I stepped back to inspect my work, my eyes drifted toward the unfinished greenhouse. Expertly fitted together, one side of the greenhouse joined seamlessly to my shop wall, forming what looked like a single, downward-sloping piece of wood. It would allow rainwater to run off easily, something I hadn't even considered until Li Wei pointed it out in the initial design.

The craftsmanship was impeccable, each beam and joint meticulously designed to serve a purpose.

"That kid's a genius," I said, a smile creeping onto my face as I ran my hand along one beam. "I'd be drowning in waterlogged plants if he hadn't fixed that."

Windy and Tianyi moved cautiously around the perimeter, their attention focused outward, vigilant as ever. I'd noticed how on edge they'd been lately, and while I had seen nothing to warrant concern, I trusted their instincts. Tianyi's wings shimmered softly in the fading light as she circled above the garden while Windy slithered gracefully between the pots, his bluish-white scales gleaming in the evening sun.

The elixirs were complete, this month's quota fulfilled, and the greenhouse was on its way to becoming a reality. I'd even made solid progress on my quest, with twelve successful hybrids now under my belt. Things were moving forward, slowly but surely.

"Guard the place well!" I shouted to the two Spirit Beasts.

I grabbed the handles of the cart and set off toward the village square, the wheels creaking softly as I pushed it along the well-worn path. The late afternoon air was crisp, carrying the scent of damp earth and woodsmoke. As I made my way through the village, familiar faces greeted me, some waving, others nodding in acknowledgment. I smiled and waved back.

What used to be a simple tent had now transformed into a proper building, a sturdy wooden structure that suggested permanence. The company wasn't just passing through; they were here to stay. Finally! It only took my brilliance and potential for them to see how Gentle Wind Village was a hidden gem!

As I approached the outpost, Huan stood outside, talking animatedly with one of the villagers. He waved when he saw me coming, a broad smile spreading across his face.

"Kai! Here to drop off the batch?" he asked as I parked the cart near the entrance.

"Yep, all ready to go," I replied, gesturing to the crates on the cart. "How've things been on your end?"

"Busy, as usual." Huan chuckled, his eyes gleaming with the usual merchant's cheerfulness. "But you'll be pleased to know that something else arrived for you this morning."

He stepped back and gestured toward the side of the building, where several large bundles were stacked. "The glass you ordered finally made it in."

My eyes widened as I took in the sight. Layers of straw, hay, and thick cloth securely wrapped the bundles, but the faint shimmer of glass showed through. It was enough to fill a cart much larger than the one I had now, easily doubling the load I'd brought.

"That's more than I expected," I said, excitement bubbling up inside me. "This is going to be perfect for the greenhouse."

Huan grinned. "Figured you'd be happy to see it. We packed it extra carefully for the journey; don't want any cracks, especially with glass this fine."

He handed me a small stack of letters, tied together with a thin piece of string. "These came with it as well. From Crescent Bay, I believe."

I untied the bundle, immediately recognizing the familiar emblem on one of them. One was from Feng Wu, the other from Zhi Ruo. A surge of curiosity filled me, but I'd save those for later. For now, there was business to handle.

"Thanks, Huan," I said, tucking the letters away in my robe. "I'll read these later. How's the payment looking?"

"Should be processed by the end of the week," he replied, nodding toward the crates of elixirs on the cart. "And the ingredients for the next batch are due to come next week."

"Good to hear. Also, while you're at it, place an order for Tranquil Breeze Farm," I said casually, rattling off a list of herbs. These were ones I couldn't grow in my garden because they were too temperamental or required special conditions I hadn't yet mastered. Perfect for infusion experimentation, but there was no need to mention that part just yet.

Huan scribbled down the list quickly, nodding. "Consider it done."

I glanced over at the large bundles of glass, already picturing how they would look installed in the greenhouse. "All right, I'll take these to Li Wei's place. He'll want to know the glass has arrived."

"Need a hand with the transport?" Huan offered.

"Nah, I've got it. I'll take it slow. No sense rushing and breaking something after all this effort."

"Fair enough. Well, let me know if you need anything else."

With that, I carefully loaded the bundles of glass onto the cart, securing them with extra ropes to keep them from shifting. It was a tight fit, but the cart held everything without issue. I gave the straps one last tug, making sure they were secure before setting off toward Li Wei's family home.

As I ambled through the village, careful to avoid any bumps or rough patches in the road, I couldn't help but admire the craftsmanship of the glass itself. Each piece had been wrapped with care, its faint shimmer visible even through the thick layers of cloth.

The sun was setting as I arrived at Li Wei's home, casting a warm orange glow over the village. I parked the cart outside and knocked on the door. Within moments, Li Wei appeared, wiping his hands on a rag. He blinked in surprise when he saw the cart full of glass.

"It's here already?"

"Yep. Just arrived this afternoon," I said, gesturing to the bundles. "Figured you'd want to see it for yourself."

Li Wei's eyes lit up as he approached the cart, examining the bundles. "This is going to be perfect. We can start installing the glass as soon as we finish the framework."

I grinned. "Glad to hear it. I'll leave this with you, then. Let me know when you're ready for the next step."

He gave a nod of thanks, his focus already shifting to the task at hand. I could tell his mind was working through the logistics of installing the glass, and I trusted him to handle it with the same precision he had shown with the rest of the greenhouse.

I made my way back toward the shop. The evening air was cool, and the fading light cast long shadows across the village paths. My mind wandered back to the letters Huan had handed me earlier.

Upon settling back in my shop, I untied the string around the letters and read Feng Wu's first.

As expected, Feng Wu's letter was full of the meticulous detail I'd come to associate with him. He confirmed what I had been hoping to learn: Master Li Tao, the originator of the Essence Extraction technique, had never been able to infuse plants with the extracted essences. This solidified what I had suspected; this ability to fuse essences with living plants was unique to the Spiritual Plant Cultivation skill.

"So it really is tied to me," I muttered dumbly.

The fact that this infusion ability was something even legendary alchemists hadn't mastered made me feel both proud and a little apprehensive. There was no precedent for what I was doing. But that was as unnerving as it was exciting. There was no blueprint for what I was doing. Just me, feeling my way through it.

After finishing Feng Wu's letter, I opened the second one, from Zhi Ruo. I hadn't heard from him since we last saw each other in the Gauntlet. I leaned back in my chair as I read, expecting a long debrief.

But as my eyes moved over the words, my mood shifted. The parchment felt rough under my fingers.

Hey, Kai,

First off, I hope things are going well back at home. I've been busy getting acclimated to my new position here at the Whispering Wind Sect. They move quite fast compared to a library, you see. I've secured a position as a junior alchemist under Jingyu Lian.

My smile froze.

Jingyu Lian. Her name stirred up something complex within me. I still remember our battle, her techniques so flawless, her composure so unwavering. I'd convinced myself I'd moved past that loss, but clearly, the bitterness hadn't entirely faded.

"Wonder what that's like. Working with her . . ." If her approach to alchemy was anything to go by, working with her must be quite demanding. But undoubtedly a good place to learn.

I continued reading, bracing myself.

I know what you're probably thinking right now, but listen: This is an opportunity I couldn't pass up. She may be ruthless, but she's got knowledge that runs deep. Being in her shadow is better than being in anyone else's spotlight, you know what I mean?

He wasn't wrong. Jingyu Lian was one of the best, and if he could learn from her, it would only strengthen his skills.

"Well, good for you, Zhi," I muttered without conviction.

That being said, something's going on over here that doesn't sit right with me. You probably haven't heard yet, but there's been some serious turmoil regarding the Iron Claw Sect. They've either gone completely silent or . . . something worse. No one's heard from them in weeks. They're a minor sect about a few hours northwest of Qingmu, if you didn't know.

I paused, the weight of his words settling in. Shan Huai. Wasn't he part of the Iron Claw Sect? That wasn't normal, especially for a sect that had been vying for control of Qingmu. What could have happened?

I leaned forward, reading on, my grip tightening on the parchment.

The rumor is that the Silent Moon Sect might be involved. Nothing's confirmed, but let's be real: Those rumors didn't come out of nowhere. People are scared, Kai. Sect politics have always been messy, but this? This feels different. There's talk of retaliation, of sects mobilizing.

The Silent Moon Sect. Of course they'd be tied to something like this. I'd suspected them from the start, but if they were responsible for an entire sect's disappearance . . . this could be bad. Very bad.

I'm telling you this because you need to be careful. You're out there in that village, building your reputation and all, but if things escalate, places like Gentle Wind Village won't be overlooked. You and I both know how quickly sects move when they feel threatened.

I ran a hand through my hair, trying to process it all. He was right. If the Silent Moon Sect was really behind the Iron Claw Sect's disappearance, and if the rumors of retaliation were true, things could spiral out of control. And fast.

I could already see the pieces falling into place. Gentle Wind Village might be small, but it wasn't insignificant. With the Azure Silk Trading Company investing in the area, the attention I was bringing to the village with my alchemical work, and the growing tensions between the sects, it wouldn't take much for us to get caught in the crossfire.

Anyway, keep your head down for now, and don't do anything too flashy. I know that's hard for you, but try. Next time we meet, remind me to show you a new elixir I've been working on. It's not bad, if I do say so myself.

Stay safe, Kai.

—Zhi Ruo

I sat back, the letter resting on my lap as I let out a long breath.

"Don't do anything too flashy, huh?" I shook my head.

Easier said than done, when I lived the way I did. Being the center of attention was as natural as breathing!

Tianyi fluttered over, landing lightly on my shoulder. Her presence was a comfort, but I could feel the tension radiating from her as well. She must've sensed my unease.

What's wrong?

"Nothing, just stupid politicking," I said quietly, more to myself than to her. I folded the letter and set it aside, staring at it for a long moment. "Don't worry about it."

I stood up, looking at my array of ingredients with a critical eye.

Everything had been progressing well, slowly, carefully—just the way I liked it. Plants needed time to adjust, to take root before reaching for the sky. I had to be patient, layering essence in small doses to let them thrive.

But this world I was in? It didn't seem to share my fondness for patience.

"Slow and steady," I said again. But as much as I wanted to stick to that, I had a sinking feeling that slow and steady wasn't going to be enough this time. Not with sects disappearing and power plays being made in the shadows.

It looked like I'd have to speed things up after all.

CHAPTER TWENTY-FOUR

The Unfolding Path

The sky above was a pale wintery gray, casting a muted light over the village below. From her perch on the branch of an old, sturdy oak tree, Tianyi surveyed the scene unfolding beneath her. The villagers moved about with hurried purpose, their footsteps crunching lightly on the snow-covered ground.

Her small wings fluttered lightly, catching the air as she hovered silently, her gaze fixated on the figure of Kai in the distance. He stood at the edge of the village, deep in conversation with a younger boy. *Li Wei*, she recalled. Though she could not hear their words, she could feel the undercurrent of urgency that hung between them.

The world of immortals was once again stirring. Kai always seemed entangled in something beyond her, something grander than her former, simple life. But there was something different this time. She had been beside him for long enough to notice it. The unrest wasn't just a passing storm. It was a gathering one, dark and heavy on the horizon.

Her wings stilled, and she landed softly on the branch, folding them close to her body. She looked to her left, where she saw Windy coiled lazily on a rock below, basking in the faint sun's warmth. He looked peaceful, but Tianyi knew how quickly the serpent could strike. Agile and deadly. Windy was strong, even in his youth. His strength came naturally.

Tianyi's gaze lingered on the serpent for a long moment, and a familiar feeling sprouted in her chest.

Envy.

Not a bitter envy, but a quiet, yearning kind. He had been born with the power to protect, to fight. It was part of his nature, a gift that came effortlessly. Yin Si, too—the spider she befriended, whom Kai had honored with a name— had their own power, webs spun with precision, movements calculated and purposeful.

And I . . . I was born with wings that fluttered delicately in gardens, meant to dance in the air, not battle in it.

Yet even as envy coiled within her chest, a softer, warmer feeling stirred alongside it. Kai's voice echoed in her thoughts, his steady encouragement and belief in her unwavering despite her doubts. He never saw her as weak. To him, she was a companion, an ally, someone he relied on—not a burden. That thought both comforted and stung. How could he believe in her so deeply when she struggled to believe in herself? How could she continue to flutter by his side, knowing she wasn't enough to shield him from the dangers ahead?

The thought gnawed at her. Every day, the world seemed to grow darker, the threats looming larger, and she could feel the weight of the unspoken expectation pressing down on her.

The pressure to evolve, to become something more, twisted inside her, feeding her doubt. The more she dwelled on it, the heavier it felt, until it spiraled into a loop of uncertainty and frustration, each thought more desperate than the last.

Even with the gifts Kai had given her, the mysterious liquid that had sharpened her wings and enhanced her speed, it didn't feel like enough. She had grown faster, yes, but that speed couldn't shield Kai from the dangers that lurked beyond the village. The memory of that fierce beast just a few days ago came unbidden.

Her wings twitched in frustration. It wasn't as though she hadn't tried. Time and again, she had pushed herself to the limits, testing her new abilities, hoping they would be enough. But every time the immortals clashed—every time Kai faced danger—she felt herself limited, helpless in her current form. She was no longer a mere butterfly, and yet . . .

It's still not enough, she thought bitterly, glancing down at her delicate frame.

Even though she had surpassed her original limits, she knew deep down that her current form would never be enough to stand by Kai's side, not against the likes of the immortals and the dangers that came with them. No matter how fast she flew or how sharp her wings became, she remained small, still fragile compared to the beings Kai now moved among.

You can transform, can't you? Into a human form.

She remembered Kai's words, spoken in a tone of quiet assurance. He had told her about Spirit Beasts that, through enlightenment, could change their forms. They could take on shapes that allowed them to fight alongside immortals, to walk the world on two feet rather than wings or claws.

But how? How could she find that path within herself when it felt so distant, so impossible? For weeks, she had tried to focus, to meditate as Kai did, but it all seemed so far out of reach. And every time she looked at her small fluttering wings, the doubt crept back in, stronger than before.

I don't know how, she whispered, her wings drooping as the realization settled into her body. *I don't know how to become more.*

Her gaze flickered back to Kai. He was laughing now, shaking his head at something Li Wei said, though the tension still lingered beneath his smile. Kai differed from the boy she had first bonded with. He had grown so much in the time they had been together, evolving into someone she hardly recognized yet admired even more. He was powerful, resourceful, and a protector.

And me? What am I now? Tianyi wondered. *Am I still just the butterfly in his shadow?*

She knew Kai didn't see her that way. He valued her, cared for her. But that wasn't the issue. It was her own perception, the way she felt every time she fluttered above his shoulder, watching him face dangers she could never hope to fight head-on like he did.

I want to stand beside him, she whispered to herself, her wings fluttering softly. *Not behind him.*

But the path to that dream still felt hidden, lost somewhere deep within her. She had to find it. Somehow.

As the chilly breeze swept through the village, carrying with it the scent of pine and snow, Tianyi spread her wings again and lifted into the air, leaving the garden in her wake.

She was fast—faster than any of them could hope to achieve. She could slice through the air like a blade, nigh untouchable at her full power. But was that enough? Could speed alone protect Kai? Could it defend the garden when real danger arrived?

How could she find it? She had tried everything the immortals did. Meditating, focusing, pushing her qi, but nothing had worked. The form she longed for, the strength she knew she needed, was elusive—just beyond her reach.

But why? What was she missing?

For a long time, she had been content with simply being beside Kai. Flying in the skies, keeping watch, bringing him comfort when needed. But now . . . now everything was changing. The world was growing more dangerous, more complex, and the simple joys she had once known no longer seemed enough. Kai needed her to be more, whether or not he admitted it.

Tianyi descended slowly, landing on a large boulder near the edge of the forest, her wings folding tightly against her back. The faint smell of frost and damp earth filled her senses, grounding her, even as her mind raced. Her gaze flickered to her reflection in a small, frozen pond at the base of the boulder.

A butterfly. That was all she saw. A beautiful, fragile thing. And yet, that image felt . . . incomplete.

Her thoughts spun in circles, frustration building. It was like trying to catch the wind, this feeling of becoming something greater, of breaking free from her current form. It was close, tantalizing, but every time she reached for it, it slipped away.

What am I missing? she thought, her wings twitching in agitation.

Her eyes fell on her reflection again, and suddenly, a memory flashed through her mind. Not of Kai but of Yin Si—the spider. When Kai had first named her, Tianyi had noticed a change in the creature. It was subtle, but there was a shift in the way Yin Si carried herself, the way it spun its webs with more confidence, more purpose. The name had given the spider a sense of identity, of recognition.

A name. An acknowledgment of existence. Of purpose.

Her wings fluttered slightly as the realization dawned on her. All this time, she had been looking outward, trying to force herself into something greater. But perhaps . . . perhaps the answer lay not in pushing for change, but in accepting herself as she was now.

I was never just a butterfly.

She was more. She had always been more. It wasn't about transforming into something else, something entirely different. It was about embracing everything she had become and everything she had yet to be. She wasn't Windy, born a predator. She wasn't Yin Si, weaving webs of instinctual precision. She was herself, with her own path.

The strength she needed wasn't about shedding her wings. It was about owning them. Owning the journey that had brought her here, beside Kai, and the journey that would carry her further.

It's within me.

Your understanding of the dao has deepened.

She had been waiting for some grand sign, some moment of enlightenment, to strike her like lightning, but perhaps enlightenment wasn't always so dramatic. Sometimes, it was quiet. A slow unfolding, like the opening of a flower's petals. A transformation that started not with a flash, but with a whisper.

She stilled, feeling the pulse of her qi. It flowed through her like a river, steady and sure. And there, in the quiet of the forest, with the cold air swirling around her, she let go of her doubts.

And in that moment, something shifted.

The air seemed to thrum with energy, and her body glowed, a soft, ethereal light radiating from her wings. It wasn't forced. It wasn't something she was trying to do. It was happening naturally, as if her body had been waiting for her mind to catch up.

Her form changed.

It was a gentle transformation, her wings elongating, her body stretching, reshaping. She remained grounded, her wings growing larger, more vibrant, like an unfolding promise of something new.

As the transformation began, she felt a deep shift in her core. Her six legs, once designed for nothing more than clinging to leaves and flowers, quivered.

Two of them slowly retracted into her body, disappearing entirely, while the remaining four began to elongate and reshape. Muscle and bone formed where before there had only been delicate limbs. She felt herself stretching and reforming, her lightweight, fluttering frame becoming something more grounded, more substantial.

It wasn't a painful change, but it was strange, both exhilarating and unnerving. Each movement, each ripple of change, felt deliberate, as if her body had always known how to grow into this new form. Her soft butterfly abdomen slimmed and reshaped, giving way to a slender, humanoid torso.

Her arms formed from the two remaining upper limbs. What had once been thin legs meant for perching now shifted, growing into lithe, graceful arms. Hands emerged, fingers unfurling at the tips, though they still kept the faint, iridescent sheen of her butterfly heritage. These were not the fragile appendages she once had—they were tools of precision and power, capable of wielding the strength she had always known lay dormant inside her.

Tianyi's antennae receded slightly, disappearing into the thick, silken strands of hair that cascaded down her back, gleaming with a subtle, otherworldly glow. Her compound eyes, once suited for her insect form, reshaped themselves but didn't lose their sharpness. They retained an iridescent sheen and a wide field of vision, though now they had a new, focused clarity, able to see details with a precision she had never known before. She could sense movement, feel the world around her with a sensitivity far beyond her previous form.

Her wings changed too. They didn't vanish but became even grander, fanning out behind her. Larger, more intricate, they shimmered with every subtle movement, no longer just tools for flight, but symbols of the strength and beauty she had grown into. These wings were still her essence, an integral part of her being.

Her legs, now fully formed, were long and lithe, designed not just for standing but for running, leaping, moving with an agility her butterfly form had never known.

When the transformation was complete, Tianyi stood on two legs for the first time. She glanced down at her hands.

What had once been legs meant for clinging to flowers had transformed into strong, dexterous fingers. The faint bioluminescent markings along her arms and legs pulsed gently. Her body, though slender and graceful, thrummed with hidden strength, the chitinous sheen of her skin shimmering under the faint winter light.

Tentatively, she took a step forward, her feet meeting the earth with a new-found solidity. Her wings fluttered lightly behind her, still a part of her but no longer the only way she could move. She didn't need them to carry her any-more. She could walk, run, leap, and face whatever challenges came her way.

Her gaze shifted to a small frozen pond nearby, and for the second time, she caught sight of her reflection. The figure staring back at her was not entirely human. Her eyes still had their mesmerizing, iridescent glow, and faint chitin-ous plates shimmered just beneath the surface of her skin.

A wide, disbelieving smile spread across her lips. This was her. Not just a butterfly, not just a companion, but something more. She had found her path, not by shedding who she was, but by embracing every part of herself, allowing her transformation to grow from within rather than forcing it.

"I've found it," she whispered, a soft smile spreading across her face. "I've found my path."

And now she could stand beside Kai—not behind him.

CHAPTER TWENTY-FIVE

Training amid Stillness

I waved goodbye to Li Wei as he disappeared back into his family's workshop, his excitement about the greenhouse infectious. The glass panes had arrived in perfect condition, and he was eager to install them first thing in the morning. As I turned to head home, the evening air was crisp, carrying the subtle scent of pine and woodsmoke. The village was settling down for the night, but my mind was anything but quiet.

Walking along the familiar path, I couldn't help but replay Elder Ming's words from this morning's training session.

"Conditioning isn't just about toughening your body. It's about understanding the mechanics, the flow of energy, and how to deliver power without harming yourself."

At the time, I'd nodded along, thinking I understood. But the more I mulled it over, the more I realized I'd missed a crucial nuance. My approach had been all wrong. I was so focused on hardening my fists and shins by striking unyielding surfaces that I'd overlooked the essence of the practice.

I paused midstride and threw a punch into the open air, imagining the impact against a solid, unmoving tree trunk. My knuckles twinged at the thought, having experienced it far too often. Then I visualized the same punch connecting with something that had a bit of give, like a flexible piece of wood or bundled reeds. The difference was palpable, even in my mind. Striking a surface that absorbed some of the impact would allow me to focus on technique, ensuring proper alignment and energy transfer without the immediate risk of injury.

"A perfect punch shouldn't hurt the one throwing it," I said, recalling Elder Ming's mantra. It made sense now. By practicing on something with slight resistance, I'd not only improve my form but also condition my body more effectively.

A smile tugged at the corners of my mouth as a plan began to form. I needed to build a training apparatus that embodied these principles; a target that could mimic the resistance of an opponent while still offering enough flexibility to prevent self-injury.

"Perhaps a post wrapped in layers of bamboo strips or padded with woven fibers . . ."

The last rays of sunlight painted the sky in hues of orange and purple as I reached my home. The familiar sight of my shop and the partially constructed greenhouse brought a sense of comfort. I stepped inside, expecting to hear the soft flutter of Tianyi's wings or glimpse her darting through the rafters. But the space was quiet, save for the gentle creaking of the floorboards beneath my feet.

"Tianyi?" I called out, glancing around. No response. Odd. She usually greeted me the moment I returned.

Shrugging it off, I reasoned she might be tending to the garden or off bisecting another bird. She was a free spirit, after all. I made a mental note to check on her later.

Setting my thoughts back on the training apparatus, I rummaged through my supplies, gathering materials that might serve my purpose. As I worked, Windy slithered into the room, his blue-tinted scales catching the light.

"Have you seen Tianyi around?" I asked him.

He paused, then flickered his tongue before giving what could only be described as a serpentine shrug.

I chuckled softly. "Thanks for the help."

Back outside, I began assembling the training post. I planted a sturdy stake firmly in the ground. Around it, I layered thinner branches, binding them tightly with cord to create a surface that was solid yet yielding. Testing it with a light tap, I felt it give ever so slightly.

"Perfect," I whispered.

I took a stance, feet shoulder-width apart, grounding myself as Elder Ming had taught me. Drawing a deep breath, I executed a series of punches, each one deliberate and controlled. The post absorbed the blows, the slight resistance allowing me to focus on the mechanics—alignment of my wrist, the rotation of my hips, the grounding of my stance.

The difference was immediate. Without the harsh jarring of striking an immovable object, I could sense the flow of energy from my core to my fist. It felt right.

After a few minutes, I shifted to practicing knife-hand strikes, something I had devoted little time to before. Positioning my hand with fingers straight and tight together, I struck the post's surface with the edge of my hand. The unfamiliar motion sent a mild sting up my arm, but I adjusted my technique, ensuring proper form.

"Every part of the fist needs conditioning," I reminded myself. "Not just the knuckles."

I continued alternating between strikes, slowly building a rhythm. The evening air cooled the light sheen of sweat on my brow, and for a moment, all distractions faded away. It was just me, the post, and the steady cadence of my training.

Time slipped by, and the sky deepened into twilight. Finally, I lowered my hands, flexing my fingers to ease the slight stiffness settling in. There was a satisfying ache—a sign of muscles worked but not overstrained. This would have to do for now, especially since my supply of healing hydrosol was running out.

Glancing back toward the house, I expected to see Tianyi's soft glow or hear the gentle buzz of her wings. But the yard remained quiet, shadows stretching across the ground.

I frowned, a nagging feeling creeping up my spine. She was never gone for this long. Her usual flitting about the garden or appearing to hover near me had become a staple of my day, a constant that I relied on more than I realized. But now . . . nothing.

"Tianyi?" I called out again, louder this time, as I approached the house. Still no answer.

A flicker of unease stirred within me. I glanced around the yard, scanning for any sign of her, but the fading light made it hard to see much. I reached out through the bond we shared, closing my eyes to focus. It was faint, like trying to grasp at a fading echo, but I could sense her. Barely.

With my heart beating faster, I centered myself and tried to focus on the faint pull of our bond. It led . . . toward the forest. The same direction where that wolf had attacked just days ago. A cold realization hit me, and my chest constricted.

No. She couldn't have—

I didn't finish the thought. Without another moment's hesitation, I infused qi into my legs and bolted, sprinting toward the tree line. Each stride felt like I was covering several li, the world blurring as I pushed myself harder. Wind roared in my ears, but I didn't stop.

The thought of finding her hurt, or worse, sent a chill down my spine. My breath quickened, turning ragged as my chest tightened, and for a moment, I thought I might choke on the air itself.

The forest loomed ahead, the trees dark silhouettes against the deepening night. The quiet was unnerving. No birds, no insects, only the sound of my heartbeat, too loud, in my ears.

"Tianyi!" I shouted desperately.

My breaths came in sharp bursts as I focused harder on our bond, sensing her presence nearby, though still faint. My eyes darted left and right, scanning the darkened underbrush. The tension in the air felt thick, palpable, and every shadow seemed to whisper danger.

Then, through the thicket, I spied movement.

I froze.

A figure stood amid the trees, small and seemingly fragile, but there was something deeply unnatural about them. My breath stilled as I took in the sight.

At first glance, it seemed like a girl, but the more I looked, the more I realized that wasn't right.

The wings were the first thing I noticed, bright blue and shimmering in the pale moonlight, sprouting from her back and fluttering gently.

Her skin was smooth and pale, but it wasn't quite right. Lines ran across her body in sections, like the joints of finely crafted lacquered wood or the seams of porcelain figurines. Each segment was slightly raised, as though her skin had been formed in pieces and fitted together. Her hair cascaded down, with two distinct strands falling down and framing her face.

It was her eyes that unsettled me the most—far too large for a human face, dark and shimmering, holding a depth that felt more animal than person. And though her body was otherwise naked, it lacked any real detail, as if sculpted from jade.

And yet, her wings . . . Those wings were undeniably familiar.

My mind struggled to comprehend what I was seeing.

I took a step forward, my mouth dry, words caught somewhere between disbelief and confusion. And then, the possibility hit me like a wave.

"Tianyi?"

The figure turned, her too-wide smile gleaming with unnatural brightness. My pulse quickened as she locked her gaze on me. My mouth went dry, and a prickling sensation crept up the back of my neck. It felt like the earth itself was tilting beneath me.

The air shifted with her movement, a blur of blue wings and shadow. One moment she was distant, the next, her wings stirred the wind around me, her fingers wrapped around my wrists before I could blink.

But there was no attack. Instead, she grabbed my wrists, her grip gentle yet firm, and a warm, soothing energy flowed from her touch. The cuts and bruises from my training earlier healed, the pain fading away almost instantly.

"I figured it out," she said softly, her voice surprisingly clear yet carrying an otherworldly echo. "I figured out how to become human."

My vision swam, blurring the world around me as the realization crashed into me like a tidal wave—this was Tianyi. Somehow, impossibly, she had transformed—become something beyond what I could comprehend. But my mind struggled to keep up, the flood of emotions and disbelief colliding with the stark reality in front of me.

A sharp heat surged through my body, too intense for the winter chill that clung to the air. Sweat trickled down the back of my neck, soaking into my collar despite the icy breeze. My heart pounded violently in my chest, each beat louder than the last, echoing in my ears like the relentless drumming of war. I felt the world tilting, my legs unsteady, my skin burning as if the very air had thickened, pressing down on me.

The cold that should have been biting at my skin barely registered; instead, I felt fevered, my breath coming in shallow, ragged bursts. Every nerve in my body tingled with confusion, panic, and awe, all tangled together in a mess I couldn't unravel.

Her smile, a smile that was too wide, too perfect, never faltered as she watched me, but the edges of my vision darkened. The world around me dimmed, the sound of the forest fading into a muffled hum. My legs trembled, the strength in them slipping away as my knees buckled under the weight of everything.

"Tianyi . . ." I whispered, strained. My head felt too light but too heavy at the same time, and I knew I was losing the battle to stay conscious.

With my sudden rush of adrenaline, along with the shock of seeing my longtime companion standing before me in an uncanny human form, my eyelids fluttered shut. As the darkness rushed in, the last thing I saw was her standing there, her wings shimmering faintly in the moonlight.

The training, the exhaustion, the adrenaline, and the sheer shock of seeing Tianyi not as the butterfly I had always known but as something greater. My body, pushed beyond its limits, was giving out. My mind, overwhelmed by the impossible reality before me, had followed.

And then everything went black.

CHAPTER TWENTY-SIX

Wings of Change

I woke up with a start, gasping as my eyes flew open, my heart pounding so hard it felt like it would break through my chest.

My bed. I was in my bed. The familiar scent of herbs and woodsmoke clung to the air, and I could see that the sky was pitch black outside.

I sat up, rubbing my eyes. The last thing I remembered . . . Tianyi. The forest. That strange form with her wings.

"Was it just a nightmare?" I ran a hand through my hair. Maybe I had been overworked. Too much training, not enough sleep. It wouldn't have been the first time my mind played tricks on me.

Just as I started to convince myself that I'd imagined it all, something darted toward me with such speed that I barely had time to react. I jerked back, scrambling against the headboard as a scream tore from my throat.

It wasn't a dream. She stood by my bedside, her wings fluttering rapidly, her too-large eyes wide with concern. That same unsettling, too-perfect smile stretched across her face, frozen there as if she wasn't entirely sure how to change it.

"I'm . . . sorry!" she said, her voice quiet but carrying that odd echo, almost too clear for this small room.

I stared at her, heart still racing. She looked at me with those mesmerizing eyes, alien and human at the same time. I opened my mouth to speak, but no words came out. What was I supposed to say? What *could* I say?

Windy, curled up near the foot of my bed, flicked his tongue out lazily. He gazed at Tianyi for a long moment before turning away with an air of indifference. Typical. He didn't seem to find her new form worth any more of his attention.

Tianyi, meanwhile, hovered there, her wings twitching awkwardly, her expression still that eerie, unwavering smile. My brain finally started to catch up with everything, and I forced myself to take a deep breath.

"It's . . . it's okay," I mumbled shakily. "I just . . . wasn't expecting . . . you." I stared down at the blanket, still processing.

She tilted her head, watching me intently. The smile faltered for a second, as if she were trying to adjust her expression, but it didn't quite land. It was clear she was struggling with this new form.

As I stared at her, something else dawned on me. She was still completely—

"Oh!" I jumped out of bed, avoiding her eyes and feeling heat rush to my face. I had to cover her up. "Hold on, just . . . wait here."

I scrambled over to the corner of my room, rifling through my storage.

"Where was that robe? The one that one of the merchants had gifted me . . . Here it is!"

I yanked it out from beneath a pile of folded linens. The deep blue silk practically shimmered in the light as I hurried back toward Tianyi, keeping my gaze firmly averted.

"Uh, here," I said, offering her the robe as I gestured at her form. She tilted her head again, but after a moment, she seemed to understand. With a soft flutter of her wings, she folded them back, shrinking them enough to let me drape the robe over her shoulders.

The wings shifted, folding so smoothly it was like they'd always been a part of her, perfectly aligned. The robe fit her well, though her inhuman form made it look more regal than I'd anticipated. She looked like Lady Xiao Yun, a daughter of a wealthy merchant, so long as I ignored the raised lines on her skin.

"Thank you," she said, her voice still echoing strangely. Her smile was still too wide, too perfect, but there was an earnestness in her eyes.

I nodded, still not entirely sure what to say. Everything felt too surreal. Just a day ago, she was the small butterfly I'd known for so long, flitting around the garden, bringing a sense of calm to my world. Now she was . . . this.

I was just getting used to the idea of her talking, too!

My gaze flickered toward her wings again. Even under the dull morning light, her wings shimmered, catching every beam as if made from the sky itself. Her form, while humanoid, was clearly not human. The lines running across her skin, the smoothness where I expected human details—it was all so . . . alien. Yet somehow undeniably Tianyi.

"How did this happen?"

"You . . . said I could transform," she began softly. "You told me about Spirit Beasts that could take on human forms. I wanted to be like them. To stand beside you, not just fly above or behind you."

Her voice still carried that strange, clear echo, but what stunned me most wasn't her voice, it was how deeply my words had affected her. She had taken something I'd said so casually and made it her goal. The weight of that realization sank into me like a stone.

"You . . . did all this because of me?" I said, dumbfounded. "Tianyi, I never meant—" I broke off, unsure how to even finish the thought. I wanted to tell her she didn't need to change, that she was enough as she was. But now, looking at her, I realized that this transformation wasn't just about me. It was about her, too. Her own journey, her own growth.

She tilted her head again, watching me intently, her too-wide smile still plastered on her face, though it faltered slightly, as if she wasn't sure if it was the right expression.

"I . . . I thought it would make you happy," she said, her voice softening. "I wanted to protect you better."

I stared at her, the weight of her words hitting me like a blow. How long had she been silently working toward this, keeping to herself despite her newfound ability to speak?

I sighed, rubbing my temples. "I'm sorry, Tianyi. I didn't realize . . . I didn't know how much this meant to you."

I took a closer look at her, this time with more focus. Her irises shimmered in segments, catching the light in a way that made them seem like the facets of an insect's compound eyes. The raised lines along her arms and fingers weren't just surface markings, they were like separate segments, dividing her skin into intricate, interconnected sections. Even her hair . . . Two strands that fell in front of her face twitched slightly in a way that normal hair never would.

Despite the warmth of the room, her hand was cool to the touch when I finally held it. Her skin, pale and smooth, was hard, almost rigid—like polished stone rather than flesh. It was as if she had grasped the essence of what it meant to be human but missed the finer details.

"Tianyi, you did nothing wrong," I said, my voice softening. She looked at me with that same wide, unsettling smile, though I could see the hesitation behind it. "I was just . . . worried. I didn't know where you were."

Her smile faltered, and for a moment, it seemed like she was struggling to control her new form, her wings fluttering slightly as she leaned in closer.

"I didn't mean to scare you," she whispered apologetically.

I shook my head quickly. "No, it's not your fault. I just . . . wasn't ready for this."

At my words, her expression brightened, though the too-perfect smile remained. Before I could react, she lunged forward, wrapping her arms around me in a surprisingly gentle hug. "You're very warm," she said, sounding almost pleased.

I hesitated for a second, my mind still reeling from everything that had happened. But then, slowly, I returned the hug, my arms wrapping around her unfamiliar frame. Despite everything, there was a strange sense of comfort in the embrace.

"Thank you, Kai," she said softly, her voice muffled against my shoulder.

I smiled weakly, exhaustion creeping over me as the events of the day finally caught up. "You're . . . welcome, Tianyi," I murmured, my voice barely a whisper as the last of my strength faded away. "I think I need to lie down."

Without another word, I collapsed back onto the bed, with her still holding me. My mind swam in a haze of fatigue, the day's events blending into a blur of confusion and awe. Within moments, sleep claimed me.

I woke up to the sensation of something watching me.

Slowly, I blinked, my eyes adjusting to the dim morning light filtering through the window. I turned my head to the side and nearly jumped when I saw Tianyi sitting there, her large, shimmering eyes locked on me, her expression unchanged.

"Good morning!" she chirped the moment she saw I was awake.

"Did you even sleep?"

She nodded cheerfully, her wings fluttering slightly beneath the robe. "I don't sleep like you do. I just . . . rest."

I narrowed my eyes, feeling a shiver crawl up my spine as I realized something. "You haven't blinked once."

She tilted her head, seemingly unbothered. "I don't need to. Is that a problem?"

I opened my mouth, then closed it again, deciding not to question it further. At that moment, Windy slithered up onto the bed, his tongue flickering out as he studied Tianyi with new interest. For the first time since her transformation, he moved closer, curling around her neck as she greeted him with a soft smile. The sight was strange but oddly fitting.

While they interacted, my mind raced. Zhi Ruo's letter flashed in my thoughts: *Don't stand out.*

How was I supposed to keep Tianyi's new form hidden? If anyone saw her like this . . .

I sighed, my pulse quickening again. I had to figure out what to do.

"Tianyi," I began, "do you think you can change back into your butterfly form? You know . . . to keep things less . . . complicated?"

She looked thoughtful, her wings twitching slightly. "I'm . . . not sure. I haven't tried."

Before I could ask further, a sudden knock on the door made my heart leap into my throat.

"Kai! You're late!" Lan-Yin's voice rang out. "Elder Ming's going to punish you if you don't hurry!"

My eyes widened in panic. "Hide!" I hissed, already scrambling out of bed.

She looked confused for a split second but then darted beneath the bed with surprising speed, her wings folding up tightly against her back. Just in time, too, as Lan-Yin and Wang Jun burst through the door a moment later, oblivious to the chaos they had narrowly missed.

The door creaked open, and Lan-Yin and Wang Jun stepped into the room, both grinning like foxes sniffing out trouble. I stood frozen for a moment, still catching my breath from the earlier panic, my clothes damp with sweat. My hair clung to my forehead, and I must have looked a mess. I opened my mouth to explain, but Lan-Yin's eyes gleamed with mischief as she leaned casually against the doorframe.

"Well, well," she began. "What's this?"

Wang Jun's grin widened as he crossed his arms. "Seems like someone's been dedicating themselves to their own, uh, private pursuits."

I felt my face burn instantly, the embarrassment hitting me like a slap. "No, no, it's not—" I stammered, but the words fumbled out of my mouth uselessly.

Lan-Yin raised a brow, clearly enjoying the moment. "No need to be so shy, Young Master Kai. Everyone's got to practice refinement one way or another, right?" She chuckled lightly, nudging her betrothed in the ribs.

The two exchanged a knowing look, and I groaned inwardly. "No!" I finally managed, my voice a bit too loud. "I wasn't—I mean—!"

The words stuck in my throat, and I felt the sweat beading on my forehead again. My heart raced, not from the accusation, but because Tianyi was still hiding just a few feet away, underneath the bed. If they caught on to her presence . . .

I forced a grin, waving my hands in front of me in a desperate attempt to clear the misunderstanding. "I was just . . . doing some physical training last night! Conditioning, you know, working on endurance. Nothing improper."

Lan-Yin tapped her chin, pretending to be deep in thought. "Oh, conditioning, was it? That must be why you're soaked through like a steamed dumpling, hmm?"

Wang Jun snickered behind her. "Pretty intense training to leave you looking like *that*."

I felt the blood rushing to my face. This was not how I'd imagined starting my morning. I tried to shift the conversation, anything to divert their attention.

"Look, I'm running late, right?" I said, trying to sound calm as I wiped the sweat from my forehead. "What's the punishment this time? Can't have Elder Ming thinking I've been slacking off."

"Oh, I'm sure Elder Ming will forgive you if you tell him you were working on some . . . more personal cultivation techniques."

Lan-Yin gave me a mock serious look, crossing her arms. "Though you might want to clean up before heading out. No one wants to train next to someone who's still in the throes of their, um, solo cultivation."

I sighed deeply, giving up on explaining and hoping they'd just drop it. "Right. I'll clean up. See you both out there."

They finally took pity on me, turning to leave, though not without a few more snickers and winks thrown in my direction. As the door closed behind them, I let out a long, exasperated breath, slumping down onto the edge of the bed.

I had a long day ahead of me.

CHAPTER TWENTY-SEVEN

Beneath the Stone, the Fist

I staggered back, hands on my knees, gasping for breath. My whole body ached, muscles screaming in protest after the brutal session Elder Ming had just put me through. Punishment for being late, of course. I wiped the sweat from my brow, trying to ignore the burning in my legs. Every step felt like I was walking on hot coals. It hadn't helped that Lan-Yin and Wang Jun kept up a steady stream of snickers the entire time, making sure to remind me about my so-called self-cultivation.

I'd ignored them, or at least, I pretended to. It was hard enough staying focused with my muscles strained to their limits, let alone with everyone joking about what they thought I was doing last night. But I couldn't let it bother me—not now.

Because, despite everything, my thoughts kept drifting back to Tianyi.

The thought gnawed at me. She couldn't stay hidden forever, especially not in a village as close-knit as this one. But perhaps I wouldn't need to hide her completely. I mulled over the idea, straightening up as it took shape in my mind. If I kept her presence low key, only telling those I trusted—Wang Jun, Lan-Yin, and a few others who frequented my shop—then maybe we could manage without raising too many questions. She didn't need to be seen by everyone, after all.

I had just opened my mouth to mention the idea to the others when a small voice cut through the small courtyard.

"Elder Ming!"

I turned just in time to see Xiao Bao, one of the village kids, sprinting across the courtyard toward us, his face flushed from the effort. His wide eyes flicked between us before settling on Elder Ming, who was calmly wiping down the training posts.

"There's someone asking for you. They said it's important!"

Elder Ming's expression shifted, his brows furrowing as he exchanged a glance with me. "Who is it, Xiao Bao?" he asked, his voice steady despite the sudden tension that seemed to fill the air.

"I don't know!" Xiao Bao shook his head, still catching his breath. "They didn't say much, but they look important. They look like cultivators!"

He set down the towel he'd been using, his gaze sharpening. "All right. Let's see what this is about."

I shot a quick glance at Wang Jun and Lan-Yin, both of whom seemed to have dropped their teasing demeanor, watching Elder Ming carefully. I didn't know what this was about, but a knot of unease was already twisting in my gut. Something told me this wasn't just a casual visit.

"Should we come with you?" I asked, stepping forward.

Elder Ming looked at me for a moment before nodding slightly. "Yes. You three should come along."

We followed Elder Ming out of the training grounds, my muscles still protesting with every step, but the knot of unease in my stomach had me pushing through the discomfort. I couldn't shake the bad feeling that had settled over me since Xiao Bao's arrival. There was something about the urgency in his voice that stirred a sense of foreboding.

As we stepped out into the open courtyard, the sun was peaking, casting long shadows over the village. I scanned the faces of the villagers. Some were gathered in small clusters, their eyes wide with curiosity or concern, others standing back cautiously as they watched a group of unfamiliar men near the edge of the square.

And then I saw them.

Six men stood in a semicircle, clearly the source of the disturbance. Five of them were strikingly similar. Large, muscular builds with shaved heads, their presence imposing and hard to ignore. They loomed over the villagers, their expressions blank but watchful. Their bodies exuded a quiet strength, but it wasn't just their size that caught my attention. There was something oddly familiar about them.

I narrowed my eyes, studying their faces, trying to place where I'd seen them before. The recognition hovered just out of reach.

At the front of the group, a sixth man stood, far shorter than the others but was no less intimidating. His receding hair was tied into a tight bun at the back of his head, and despite the loose robes he wore, the outline of his broad, muscular figure was unmistakable. He was speaking animatedly with a group of villagers, his voice carrying a smooth, confident tone. Some villagers seemed drawn in by his words, but there was an air of caution around them, a reluctance to fully engage.

As we approached, the shorter man's gaze snapped toward Elder Ming. His face brightened immediately, and he gave a low bow, his voice oozing respect. "Village Head! Thank you for taking the time to meet with me."

Elder Ming, always composed, nodded. "Who are you, and what brings you to Gentle Wind Village?"

The man straightened, still smiling. "My name is Wei Long; a first-class disciple of Narrow Stone Peak. We've come to offer protection to your village during these uncertain times."

"Narrow Stone Peak . . ." Elder Ming echoed, his expression unreadable.

Wei Long gestured toward the five men behind him. "And these are my subordinates, the Five Fists. They've made quite a name for themselves."

That name—Five Fists of Narrow Stone Peak—hit me like a hammer to the chest. Suddenly, everything clicked into place. Crescent Bay City. The fight. Duan Jian. These were the same five brutes that tried to cause a ruckus at Spirited Noodle until Feng Wu scared them off.

My hands clenched into fists at the memory.

"You," I muttered, my pulse quickening. They were trouble, I knew that much. I narrowed my eyes, locking onto the familiar faces of the Five Fists of Narrow Stone Peak. That day at Spirited Noodle, they had been loud, arrogant, and looking for trouble, but they'd backed off when things didn't go their way.

Before I could voice my thoughts, one man with a shaved head suddenly stiffened, his eyes widening in recognition. He pointed a thick finger directly at me.

"You! It's him!" he said, his voice cutting through the air like a blade.

The other members of the Five Fists glanced at me, their expressions a mix of surprise and confusion, but I could see it. At least one of them had recognized me too.

Elder Ming's gaze slid toward me, a question in his eyes. "Kai," he said, his tone calm but firm. "How do you know these men?"

I hesitated for a moment, then exhaled sharply. "We crossed paths in Crescent Bay City. They were causing trouble at a noodle shop, trying to intimidate the waiter. I may have gotten involved, and things escalated." I glanced at the Five Fists, their expressions hardening as I continued. "Later, they cornered me in an alley while drunk. Let's just say it didn't end well for them."

Wei Long's pleasant demeanor shifted almost imperceptibly. His smile tightened, and his eyes darkened. I braced myself, fully expecting him to lash out or reveal his true nature, especially after hearing what had happened between me and his subordinates.

His fist trembled slightly, and I could feel the tension building in the air.

But instead of an outburst, the first-class disciple pivoted on his heel and backhanded the nearest of his subordinates, sending him staggering back with a shocked grunt.

"Idiots!" Wei Long's voice was low and venomous. Without missing a beat, he slapped each one of them upside the head, his movements swift and precise. "How dare you disgrace our name with such dishonorable behavior! Attacking someone in a drunken stupor? Have you no shame?"

The Five Fists flinched under his blows but remained silent, their heads bowed as they endured the berating. To my surprise, they didn't argue or retaliate. They just stood there, taking it.

This wasn't the reaction I had anticipated at all.

Once Wei Long had finished his reprimand, he pointed toward me. "Line up in front of him. Now."

Without hesitation, the Five Fists scrambled to obey, forming a line directly in front of me. One by one, they bowed their heads in unison.

"We're sorry," they muttered, their voices subdued.

Wei Long turned back to me, offering a slight bow of his own. "I hope this is enough to put the matter behind us. They are still maturing, and it is clear they have much to learn. I ask that this incident not affect our current discussion."

The weight of the moment pressed down on me. Everyone's eyes were on me now; the villagers, Elder Ming, Lan-Yin, Wang Jun. It felt like the entire village was waiting for my response, and the tension in the air was palpable. I could feel their gazes burning into me, expecting me to decide.

I swallowed, my mouth dry. There was no reason to escalate this further, especially not in front of Elder Ming and the rest of the village. I forced myself to nod. "I . . . I won't hold it against them. Let's put it behind us."

Wei Long smiled, the tension in his posture easing ever so slightly. He gave another respectful bow before turning his attention back to Elder Ming.

"Now that this unpleasant business is behind us, Village Head," he said smoothly, "we have come here with a genuine offer of protection for your village. There has been a sharp rise in bandit activity in the region, and recent sightings of Spirit Beasts have only added to the danger. Narrow Stone Peak has already taken steps to safeguard nearby villages, and we would like to extend that same protection to Gentle Wind Village."

Protection. The word hung in the air, as smooth as Wei Long's voice, but it grated against me like sandpaper. The Five Fists certainly hadn't been offering protection back then, just throwing their weight around, preying on the weak. And here they were again, wearing the same false smiles but with different words.

I glanced at the Five Fists. They stood there, silent and disciplined now, but I knew better than to trust appearances. I'd seen what they were like when no one was watching.

And Narrow Stone Peak? They reminded me too much of the Iron Claw Sect—sect disciples showing up with grand offers of security, but always with a price. I couldn't shake the feeling that this "protection" was just another way to control the village. If we accepted, we'd owe them. No matter how friendly Wei Long seemed, I could feel the strings being pulled behind the scenes.

Elder Ming listened carefully, his expression thoughtful but unreadable. "Why offer protection now?"

Wei Long inclined his head slightly, his tone smooth and diplomatic. "We have reason to believe the bandit activity will spread soon, and Spirit Beasts are drawn to areas of concentrated qi, such as this village. Gentle Wind Village may be small, but it is not insignificant. Our sect wishes to maintain stability in the region, and it would be in everyone's best interest to prevent trouble before it arrives at your doorstep."

I watched Elder Ming closely, trying to gauge his reaction. He was cautious, as he should be, but I could tell he was weighing Wei Long's words.

"And what would this protection cost us?" Elder Ming asked.

Wei Long's smile remained steady, but there was a gleam in his eye, a subtle shift that spoke volumes about his calculated nature. "The cost would be fair, of course," he said. "We ask for nothing unreasonable, just an exchange of services. Perhaps your village's skilled craftsmen or herbalists could lend their aid when needed. A mutually beneficial arrangement, nothing more."

He selected his words carefully; they were neither overbearing nor too humble. It was a clever play, one that implied an offer of protection while hinting at future obligations without being explicit about what those obligations might entail.

Elder Ming crossed his arms, his face still unreadable as he considered the proposal. Around us, the gathered villagers murmured among themselves, some nodding in agreement, others casting uncertain glances.

Wei Long seemed to notice the mixed reactions. His smile widened slightly, as though anticipating this. "If it would put the good people of Gentle Wind Village at ease," he continued, "I could arrange a demonstration of our capabilities. A simple show of strength, to prove that your village would be in capable hands."

I could see the mixed reactions in the surrounding villagers. Some looked intrigued, others unsure, but none of them knew what I knew. I'd seen what sects like this were capable of when they thought no one was looking. They weren't here out of goodwill—they were here to expand their influence, and our village was just another stepping stone, even if they had a more diplomatic approach than the Iron Claw.

Elder Ming's eyes narrowed just slightly, his gaze fixed on Wei Long. But after the odd happenings within the forest, the political unrest . . . a little protection didn't sound too bad.

My gaze shifted to the Five Fists. The last time I'd run into them, they'd cornered me in an alley, drunk and full of bravado, thinking they had the upper hand. But when Xu Ziqing showed up, they scattered like frightened rats, unwilling to stand their ground. I remembered the way they'd tried to gang up on me, only to flee when faced with real opposition. These weren't men willing to put their necks on the line for anyone, least of all this village. No matter what their leader promised, I knew they'd cut and run the moment things turned dangerous, even if the village had paid for their so-called protection.

Still, something in me wanted to test them. To see how far I'd come since our last encounter. I'd trained hard under Elder Ming, pushed myself to the limit, and yet, a part of me still wondered how I'd fare against them now. I didn't have Windy or Tianyi at my side this time, but maybe that was the point. It was time to see what I could do on my own.

I could feel the weight of the moment pressing down on everyone. And in that silence, a spark of an idea ignited in my mind.

Before anyone else could speak, I stepped forward, the words leaving my mouth before I had fully thought them through.

"If I may . . ." My voice sounded more confident than I felt, and all eyes turned to me. I kept my gaze steady, focusing on Wei Long. "Perhaps I could indulge in this demonstration. A sparring match, to see your strength firsthand."

The tension in the air shifted immediately. A few gasps and murmurs rippled through the crowd, and I could feel Elder Ming's gaze on me, heavy with unspoken questions. I knew the dangers of challenging a sect. Especially one as ambitious as Narrow Stone Peak. But if we didn't stand up now, this village would end up like so many others, tied to the whims of a sect that didn't truly care.

I wasn't about to let that happen.

Wei Long's smile didn't falter, but his eyes flickered with something— amusement, perhaps. He nodded slowly, his voice low and measured. "A spar, you say? Well, I wouldn't want to discourage your enthusiasm. But are you sure this is what you want?"

I held his gaze, my heart pounding in my chest, but I couldn't back down now. "I'm sure. I've had some experience with martial arts of my own."

Elder Ming's brow furrowed as I stepped forward. I could sense his unease, his gaze heavy. Perhaps he knew, just as I did, how quickly things could escalate from a simple sparring match to something much worse.

He placed a hand on my shoulder, his voice cutting through the moment. "Kai, you don't have to do this. You haven't recovered from the training."

I met his eyes, appreciating the concern, but I gave a slight shake of my head. "I know. But I think it's the best way to see what we're dealing with. I'm not doing this for a victory."

Wei Long chuckled softly. "Very well. Let's give the village something to watch."

CHAPTER TWENTY-EIGHT

More than a Win

The Five Fists of Narrow Stone Peak stood in a line, each one towering and built like a stone wall, their expressions unreadable. My eyes scanned the group, and Wei Long's sharp voice cut through the air like a blade.

"Gu Bei," he called, stepping forward with an air of authority. The name echoed in my mind. Gu Bei stepped out of line, his movements deliberate yet restrained. His gaze met mine, and I could see the wariness there. He wasn't one of the men who had attacked me in Crescent Bay City. No, he'd been passed out drunk, according to the other four, missing the brawl entirely.

I tempered my anger, keeping my breathing steady. This wasn't about personal grudges. Not today. I had to stay calm.

The man before me was a giant, easily a head taller than me, and built like an ox. His shaved head gleamed in the afternoon light, and as I studied him more closely, I noticed a burn mark trailing from his neck to his shoulder, a discolored patch of skin that stood out against his otherwise rough-hewn exterior.

I gestured toward the line of the Five Fists behind him. "You all look strikingly similar. Are you related?" The question slipped out before I could stop it, half curiosity, half an attempt to gauge the dynamic between them.

Gu Bei shook his head, his voice gruff but not unfriendly. "No. Not brothers, not by blood. Just brothers in training."

I nodded slowly, taking in the way they stood together. Their appearance was almost uncanny. Same shaved heads, same muscular frames, but now that I looked closer, I could see the subtle differences: Gu Bei with his burn scar, another missing a tooth, one with a nose that looked like it had been kicked in by a horse, and the last bearing a scar that ran from his ear down his jawline. Despite their similarities, each of them bore the marks of their past struggles, minor details that set them apart from each other.

I don't recall them having those when I first encountered them. Perhaps they've been through much since our last meeting.

Wei Long's voice broke through my observations. "Since this is a demonstration, you will be given the first three moves, Kai." His tone was smooth, diplomatic, but there was an edge to it. "If it becomes too heated, I *will* step in. This is a demonstration first and foremost. Safety is paramount."

I nodded, my mind already working through possible openings. Gu Bei's presence loomed over me like a mountain, but I couldn't let his size intimidate me. I had trained too hard for that.

The ground beneath my feet felt solid, familiar. My fists clenched at my sides, and I could feel the quiet hum of qi stirring within me, waiting to be called upon.

I shifted into my stance, keeping my posture loose, my palms open and facing up. It was a position of readiness, a stance that would let me adapt, stay fluid.

To my surprise, I felt calm. Not cocky, just reassured.

Gu Bei stood across from me, his arms hanging loose at his sides, but I could sense the coiled strength in him. But size wasn't everything.

"Begin!"

I moved first, closing the distance between us in three quick strides. My first strike shot toward his torso, a feint, testing his defense. Gu Bei's arm came up to block, solid as a brick wall. No surprise there.

But the next two hits were the real ones.

I twisted my hips, throwing a sharp hook to his ribs. My fist connected with a satisfying thud, and I followed it immediately with a palm strike to his chest, sinking the blow into his sternum. Gu Bei staggered back, his eyes widening, clearly not expecting the speed or precision of my attack.

And in that moment, I realized how far I'd come.

He was strong; there was no denying that. But he was slow. His size and power were impressive, but they didn't intimidate me anymore. Not after everything I'd been through.

I saw it clearly now—something that had eluded me when fighting opponents who either overwhelmed me with superior skill or were too familiar. It wasn't about how many techniques I had or how strong my punches were.

It was about knowing when to use them.

> *A surge of clarity washes over you.*
> *Your Mind has advanced to Qi Initiation Realm—Rank 2.*

Gu Bei's next strike came, a heavy, wide punch aimed straight at my head. It was powerful but predictable. I sidestepped, my body moving with a fluid grace I had honed through endless training, and I flowed into the first principle of the Bamboo Reprisal Counter, deflecting his blow with my forearm, redirecting the force of his strike away from me.

He grunted in frustration as he overextended, his fist passing harmlessly by. He followed up with a swing of his other arm, but I stepped into his guard, using Rooted Banyan Stance to brace myself as I blocked the strike with ease.

He was getting flustered, I could feel it. His attacks were powerful but clumsy, each one leaving an opening. I wasn't letting him adjust. The harder he hit, the softer I became, dispersing his force with calm precision. When he tried to slow down and tighten his movements, I switched to the Rooted Banyan Stance, throwing him off-balance again.

Another wild swing came, and this time, I ducked beneath it, slipping low and driving my fist upward in a sharp uppercut. I tapped him on the chin, barely a touch, pulling the punch at the last second. It was enough to let him know that if I hadn't held back, he'd be flat on his back.

His face flushed with embarrassment. I could see it in his eyes. He felt humiliated. With a growl, he rushed forward, his massive arms spreading wide as he tried to crush me in a bear hug, intent on ending the fight with brute force.

But brute force was predictable.

I slipped under his arms, moving low and fast, feeling the flow of his momentum as he overreached. In the same motion, I brought my fist into his solar plexus, driving it deep with a solid punch infused with qi. I stood firmly rooted, my lower body stable from all the conditioning. It didn't matter that my frame was smaller—this blow was well placed and perfectly timed.

Gu Bei gasped, his breath knocked out of him as he stumbled backward, clutching his chest.

I didn't press the attack. The fight was over.

As I stood there, I realized for the first time I could truly say it.

I had become strong.

Not because of tricks or Spirit Beasts, but through pure martial skill.

Gu Bei, still clutching his chest, looked up at me with disbelief.

I met his gaze, offering him a slight nod. "Good match."

The tension broke, the crowd exhaling in a mixture of awe and relief, and for a moment, I allowed myself the smallest of smiles. It wasn't like before—when my victories had been reckless or desperate. This was different. I wasn't the same person who had faced Ping Hai, terrified of being utterly crushed, or the one who'd felt overwhelmed at every turn in the alchemy tournament. Today, I had controlled the fight. I'd dictated the pace.

I had grown.

I turned to face the first-class disciple, keeping my stance relaxed but my mind sharp.

"Thank you for the opportunity to spar," I began, my tone measured. I didn't want to come off as disrespectful, but I also needed to show that Gentle Wind Village wasn't weak. "Your disciple fought well, and it's clear that Narrow Stone Peak has a tradition of producing powerful fighters. But I think this match has shown that our village has its own strength too."

His expression didn't shift, but I could see a flicker in his eyes, like he was sizing me up. I kept my voice steady, choosing my words carefully.

"We've faced our share of hardships here," I continued, glancing toward the villagers who were watching closely. Among them, Lan-Yin and Wang Jun, who stared at me with proud gazes. "We may be small, but we're resilient. We've had to be."

I met Wei Long's gaze directly, refusing to back down, but without being confrontational. I wanted him to understand where I stood, without turning this into a challenge.

"I appreciate what your sect has done for other villages, and I understand your offer of protection," I said, softening my tone slightly, "but Gentle Wind Village isn't defenseless. We've always found ways to look out for our own."

Wei Long's smile didn't waver, but there was a slight tightening at the edges of his lips, as though he were trying to gauge how much of what I said was for the village's benefit, and how much was directed at him.

"You speak well. Kai, correct?" he replied smoothly, his voice carrying a hint of admiration. "Your village is fortunate to have someone as capable as you. And it's clear you've trained hard to reach this point."

His eyes gleamed, and I could sense the shift in his tone. "But strength, as you know, can always be refined further. Narrow Stone Peak has a wealth of resources and knowledge, especially for those who are ready to take the next step in their cultivation journey. Have you ever thought of joining a sect? With your potential, the training we could offer would be invaluable."

His offer hung in the air like a well-set trap, but I kept my expression neutral, giving myself a moment to respond.

"I appreciate the offer," I said slowly, making sure my words were deliberate. "But my place is here, with my village. The people I care about, the people I've grown up with, they're here. And for now, that's where I belong."

"Your loyalty is commendable. But the doors of Narrow Stone Peak are always open, should you ever decide to walk a different path."

With that, he stepped back, signaling for his disciples to fall into line.

"We'll stay in the area for a few more days," he announced, his tone as diplomatic as ever. "Should anyone reconsider or wish to discuss the matter further, you'll know where to find us. Your safety and prosperity, after all, of the utmost importance to us."

With that, he turned on his heel, his disciples following closely behind, leaving the village square in a disciplined formation. As Wei Long turned, his gaze lingered on me for just a moment longer, his expression unreadable. A chill ran down my spine, but I forced myself to stand tall.

The villagers slowly began to disperse, murmuring among themselves, but I caught Lan-Yin and Wang Jun moving toward me, admiration plain on their faces. I could feel the pressure in my chest ease just a little, though not entirely.

But the more I let that thought settle, the more I realized just how far I'd come in such a short time. Gu Bei wasn't nearly as fast or skilled as Ping Hai, but he was still a cultivator. And here I was, standing victorious. Me—a village boy, barely a year into my training. Yet, despite all that, I had won.

The realization swelled inside me, and with it came a surge of pride, a warmth that spread through my chest. All my training, all the hours spent bruising my hands and legs, had paid off. It hadn't been for nothing.

A few clapped me on the back, offering their congratulations, but the warmth of their praise didn't sit as comfortably as I expected. Wasn't this what I wanted? Their respect, their approval? I had finally earned it, but now it felt fleeting.

I caught sight of Elder Ming standing at the edge of the square. I made my way over to him, feeling a mixture of pride and exhaustion settle over me.

"You've come far, Kai," he said, his voice quiet yet firm.

"Today proved it. All the training, all the effort, it wasn't for nothing. It's proof that it mattered."

Elder Ming's brow furrowed slightly, a soft sigh escaping his lips as he turned to face me fully. "Kai," he breathed, his gaze searching mine, "you don't need proof that your efforts bore fruit. That's not what truly matters."

I blinked, not fully understanding his meaning. "But . . . isn't that the point of all this? To get stronger, to show that the training worked?"

He shook his head, his expression still calm but hinting something deeper. "It's not about showing anything to anyone, Kai. Strength, real strength, is found in your effort, not in the results. Whether you become a heaven-defying genius or simply a man with a strong heart, I'll be equally pleased."

"But if . . . if I failed, if I didn't live up to expectations—"

"Expectations are fleeting," he interrupted gently. "What matters is how you walk your path, not where it leads. If you put your heart into what you do, whether you rise to the heavens or never make it beyond these village walls, that is enough. I would be just as proud of you if you never became a great cultivator, so long as you gave everything you had."

His words sank deep into me, settling like stones in a still pond. I had focused so intently on proving myself and showing everyone my training wasn't wasted that I hadn't considered that perspective. I'd conditioned myself to believe that only success mattered, that victory was the only proof of my worth. That's why every failure felt so sharp, so devastating.

I'd built my entire perception of myself around the outcome. Around winning, around proving myself.

I met his gaze, my mind replaying my losses . . . I realized now why each defeat had stung so much. I hadn't accepted them as part of the journey. I'd seen them as failures, as proof that I wasn't enough.

"Detach from the outcome, Kai. Be pleased that you're growing, that you're walking your path earnestly. That's the real reward."

"You're right," I whispered, the words carrying more weight than I expected. I looked at him with new clarity. "I've spent so long tying my success to whether I win or lose that I'd forgotten why I started in the first place."

That was what Elder Ming did. He tempered me, whether it was pulling me back when I was riding high on a wave of success or lifting me up when I sank into shame after a failure.

As the villagers slowly dispersed, murmuring about the spar and glancing my way with admiration, I stayed rooted in place, Elder Ming's words lingering like a steady drumbeat in my mind.

I didn't need to prove myself to anyone. Not even to him. My journey wasn't measured by how others saw me, but by the quiet satisfaction of knowing I was giving it everything I had.

And for the first time, that was enough.

CHAPTER TWENTY-NINE

Dripping Water Wears Through Stone

I walked along the quiet path back home, Elder Ming's words still echoing in my mind. The village was settling down as the sun dipped lower in the sky, casting long shadows across the ground. The warmth of the earlier spar had faded, and now I found myself in a strange state of calm, more thoughtful than triumphant. I'd won the fight, but the lesson went deeper than the victory.

As I approached, I saw someone moving near the greenhouse. It was Li Wei, working steadily by himself, carefully installing one of the new glass panes. His hands moved with an almost unnatural precision, the glass sliding into place without so much as a scratch. For a moment, I stood there and watched him.

"Where's your father?" I called out, stepping closer. "I thought you two were working together on this."

Li Wei glanced over his shoulder, nodding slightly before turning back to work. "He's at the shop. Doesn't know much about working with glass, so I'm handling this part. Figured it was better this way."

I watched as he continued with the next pane. His hands were steady, and there was a quiet confidence in the way he handled the fragile material. I couldn't help but notice how motivated he looked, more focused than I'd seen him before. There was no hesitation in his movements, no second-guessing.

"Have you worked with it before?" I asked, folding my arms and leaning against the wooden frame of the greenhouse.

Li Wei shook his head, never breaking from his work. "Nope. First time. But I've learned enough about it from studying. Plus, with the Heavenly Interface, it's helping me get familiar pretty fast."

The Heavenly Interface. Of course. That system had a way of speeding up progress in ways that still surprised me sometimes. But watching him now, it wasn't just the Interface at work. There was something in the way he handled the glass—careful but not cautious, like he knew exactly where to apply force and when to let it be.

"Looks like you're doing pretty well," I said, genuinely impressed.

Li Wei let out a chuckle, stepping back from the pane he'd just finished installing. "Thanks. It's coming along, but it's not without its hiccups." He nodded toward a shattered pane resting against the wall, shards of glass glinting in the fading light. "That one broke earlier. But it was expected, so I ordered extra just in case."

I raised an eyebrow at that, my lips twitching into a small smile. "So you planned for it to break?"

"Well, yeah. Glass is fragile. It's bound to happen when you're still learning how to handle it. Better to plan for failure than to pretend it won't happen at all."

I couldn't help but shake my head, inwardly bemoaning how audacious he was. Ordering extra glass knowing he'd break some? And on my tab? But I supposed it made sense. The boy was clever, no denying that.

"You've got some nerve," I muttered, half joking. "But I guess it's smart."

Li Wei shrugged, clearly unbothered. "Failure's part of the process, right? As long as you learn from it, it's not really a failure."

I watched him for a moment, admiring how easily he shrugged off the broken glass as just another step in the learning process. There was something refreshing about it, how he didn't seem weighed down by mistakes the way I often was. It wasn't just the glasswork. It was his whole approach. Failure wasn't an obstacle for him, it was a tool. He used it, learned from it, and kept moving forward.

"You're right," I said, nodding thoughtfully. "You're doing good work, Li Wei. Really."

"Thanks," he replied casually, as though my compliment hadn't surprised him in the slightest.

It made me think about how I reacted to failure. For all the pride I felt in my victories, I realized how much more sharply I felt my losses. How I conditioned myself to expect success, and when it didn't come, it grated at me far more than it should. But watching him, I saw another way. He expected setbacks, even planned for them, but they didn't slow him down. If anything, they spurred him on.

And maybe that's what I needed to do too.

Just as I was about to speak again, I heard Tianyi's voice call out from inside the house. "Kai, are you back?"

Li Wei glanced toward the sound, and before I could warn him, She stepped out from the doorway. She moved with that strange grace, her wings flickering faintly in the dimming light. Li Wei's eyes went wide, and I saw the glass pane he was holding slip from his hands. Instinct kicked in, and I darted forward, catching it just before it hit the ground.

"Careful!" I snapped, setting the glass aside safely.

Li Wei stood frozen, his mouth hanging open. "W—Who is that?" he stammered, pointing at Tianyi, who tilted her head in confusion.

"She's, uh," I hesitated, unsure of how to explain this without making things worse. "All right, let me explain from the beginning."

I spent the next little bit recounting what had happened over the past few days. How I found Tianyi in the forest, having turned into her current form, and how I've been hiding her, trying to figure out the best way to reveal Tianyi to the others.

"So she really turned into a human?" His eyes filled with awe as they flickered between her wings and her humanoid form. "She's . . . she's . . . pretty." A slight blush bloomed across his cheeks.

I cleared my throat, stepping between them. "She's my companion," I said sharply. "She might look different now, but she's still a butterfly at heart. Don't get any ideas."

Li Wei's eyes widened as he hastily shook his head. "No, no! I wasn't—I didn't mean—" He was clearly embarrassed, but he couldn't keep his eyes off Tianyi.

Tianyi, for her part, seemed entirely oblivious to the tension. She looked at the young boy curiously, as if trying to figure out what had him so flustered. "Why does he keep staring?"

I sighed. "He, uh, probably just wants to be friends. Please put the robe on. You'll get cold!"

Li Wei laughed nervously, scratching the back of his neck. "Yeah . . . friends."

I shot him a stern look, and he glanced away, mumbling something about getting back to work. After a moment, I let the tension fade and decided it was time to shift the conversation. I quickly shooed Tianyi back in, cautiously checking if the cultivators from Narrow Stone Peak were nearby. I couldn't let them see her, after all.

"So, you missed a bit of excitement today," I began, stepping back toward the house and motioning for Li Wei to follow. "Narrow Stone Peak's disciples are staying in the village."

Li Wei's brow furrowed, his attention snapping back to me. "Cultivators? They're here?"

I nodded, watching as his expression shifted from surprise to cautious interest. "Yeah. They offered protection for the village, but I don't know . . . something feels off about the whole thing. They're too eager, too smooth. Wei Long, their leader, he's . . . I don't trust him. Please keep Tianyi a secret for now. I don't want them to find out about her."

He considered this with a thoughtful face. "Of course. I'll keep quiet. It's good to be cautious, but they could be genuine, right? Maybe they really do want to help. Then again, I can see why you'd be wary."

"I think it's just too soon to say for sure," I said. "But I don't want to rely on them without knowing their true intentions."

Li Wei nodded slowly, then paused, his expression brightening as an idea struck him. "Hey, why don't you reach out to the Verdant Lotus Sect? You've got connections there, right? If they send word, maybe even a few cultivators to support the village."

I hesitated, the idea immediately sparking a wave of embarrassment. Asking for help from Verdant Lotus . . . It felt like admitting I couldn't handle things on my own. That's why I trained so hard, after all.

But Li Wei had a point. It would be a smart move, and I needed to be practical.

"You might be right," I admitted a little reluctantly. "I'll write to them tonight. If nothing else, they could give us some advice."

Li Wei gave me a small smile. "Better safe than sorry."

As he returned to working on the greenhouse, I lingered for a moment, watching him handle the glass with careful precision. The evening breeze rustled through the trees, and the sound of his tools tapping against the frame echoed softly. Everything seemed so calm, but I couldn't shake the tension that had been steadily building in my chest.

I had been so focused on my progress, on pushing myself harder, faster, that I hadn't taken the time to stop and really think about what I was chasing. Success? Strength? Respect? It all felt important, yet now, standing here in the fading light, I wasn't so sure anymore.

The truth was that I had conditioned myself to only accept one outcome: victory. Anything less felt like failure, and that ate at me, lingered far longer than it should. Watching Li Wei shrug off his mistakes, I realized how different we were. He embraced failure, saw it as part of the process. Me? I avoided it like the plague, and when it happened, I let it consume me.

It's not the outcome that matters. It's the effort.

I exhaled slowly, letting the thought sink in. Maybe Elder Ming was right—maybe it wasn't about proving myself, about showing the world what I could do. Maybe it was about something deeper.

But I wasn't there yet. Not completely.

I turned away from the greenhouse and began walking back to the shop, the quiet settling in around me like a thick fog. I needed to push forward, to keep going. The people of this village depended on me. And as much as I hated to admit it, asking for help, writing to the Verdant Lotus Sect, was probably the smartest thing I could do right now.

I guided Tianyi back into the shop, glancing over my shoulder to make sure no one was around. Once inside, the house felt oddly quiet. The earlier rush of adrenaline from the sparring match, and the conversation with Li Wei faded, leaving me with the weight of my growing concerns.

Her wings fluttered faintly, brushing the doorway as she stepped inside.

"I'm sorry, Kai," she whispered. "I didn't mean to reveal myself like that."

I shook my head, sighing softly. "It's all right. Just . . . for now, try not to leave the house unless you absolutely have to. There are people here, bad people, who would hurt you if they found out what you really are."

She nodded, her wings folding neatly behind her. "I'll stay inside, but what are you going to do, Kai? About them?"

I let out a slow breath, the weight of it all pressing down on me. "I have to speed up my progress. What I've achieved so far . . . it's not enough. If these Narrow Stone Peak cultivators are staying longer than expected, I need to be ready for whatever comes next."

With that, I moved toward the back of the shop, pulling open the wooden door that led to my alchemical workstation. The scent of herbs and fresh soil filled the air, a sharp contrast to the tension lingering in the village. On the table before me were the hybrid plants I'd been cultivating. Their vibrant leaves shimmered faintly.

I don't know how long we have before things go sideways, but I can't afford to wait and find out. If I'm not ready when they make their move, the village won't stand a chance.

Tianyi followed me in, watching curiously as I set up my tools.

I nodded. "They're ready. These hybrid plants will be the foundation for my next batch of pills. If I can refine them properly, they'll enhance my qi reserves even more." I glanced at her, offering a small determined smile. "It's time to take the next step."

The exhaustion from the day's events still tugged at me, but there was a fire burning inside me now. I pulled my hair into a messy bun, securing it out of my face as I prepared for a long night of work. I couldn't afford to be complacent. Not anymore.

These hybrids were my pride and my gamble. They were unlike anything I'd ever worked with before, and that was both exhilarating and terrifying.

I closed my eyes and waited for the Refinement Simulation Technique, anticipating the usual flood of visions and calculations.

Nothing.

My brow furrowed as I tried again, concentrating harder, willing the simulation to kick in. Still, the familiar network of glowing lines and interactions refused to appear. A pang of frustration sparked within me, but I shoved it aside. I was missing something.

No, ignorant of something.

These plants were uncharted territory for me. Their properties and temperament were unknown to me.

And the technique couldn't work with that, not when it's something I've never seen before with any precedent.

I stood, reaching for my notebook and ink brush. "All right, if the Refinement Simulation Technique won't work, I'll start from scratch. Break each plant down to its core properties, compare them to their originals, and figure out how their essences interact."

It was going to be tedious. A pain in the behind. But I smiled regardless, knowing that trial and error was part of the process.

CHAPTER THIRTY

Sending Charcoal in the Snow

"Here."

Lan-Yin and Wang Jun looked cautiously at the two pills I presented to them, both of them eyeing the small, round objects like they might suddenly explode.

"What are these?" Wang Jun asked warily. His breath hung in the frosty air, the chill of the winter morning seeping into the training ground around us. The sky was a pale gray, and the snow, packed under our feet, crunched with every shift of weight.

I stretched, rolling my shoulders casually as I tossed them each a pill. "Pills for you, obviously. Don't ask too many questions, just be grateful and kowtow before me in thanks for my superior alchemical prowess."

Lan-Yin raised an eyebrow, smirking at my dramatic tone. "Oh? You want us to worship you now?"

"You should've been doing it earlier," I said, grinning as I dusted off my robes. "But seriously, I made these for you both. Took your elemental affinities into account, so they should work well for your cultivation."

Wang Jun and Lan-Yin exchanged a glance, their skepticism palpable.

Lan-Yin gave the pill in her hand an experimental sniff. "And just how do you know our elemental affinities, O Wise and Powerful Alchemist?"

I crossed my arms, adopting my best haughty expression. "It's an educated guess, of course. But if you check your Interface, it should say. I made Wang Jun's pill with Metal and Fire in mind."

Wang Jun blinked, looking down at the pill in his hand before raising an eyebrow. "Metal? Fire? What, just because I spend my days hammering metal, that's my personality now?"

"Pretty much," I shot back with a grin.

"And me?" Lan-Yin interjected, holding up her pill. "Let me guess—water?"

I raised my brow. "Am I wrong?"

They looked at each other, their faces carefully kept blank. It seemed I was right.

"You shouldn't base your guesses on careless stereotypes," she remarked.

"Well," I admitted, rubbing the back of my neck, "it's not a perfect science. But your affinity is usually determined from the beginning and dictates much of your personality and future career. And I can't be entirely sure, but based on everything I know about you both, it seemed like the best guess. Worst-case scenario, if I'm wrong, they just won't be as effective. But you won't die, if that's what you're asking."

Wang Jun gave me a flat look. "I was about to ask exactly that."

I rolled my eyes. "Relax. It's not poison. If your elemental affinity doesn't match the pill perfectly, it'll just have a weaker effect. No big deal. I'm not here to kill off my only friends."

Lan-Yin twirled the pill between her fingers, her expression thoughtful. "So, if I take this, I'll get stronger, right?"

"That's the hope." I leaned back against a nearby post, my breath fogging the air in front of me. "Think of it as a boost to help you push through the next level of cultivation."

They both stared at the pills in their hands for a moment, the early winter sun barely peeking through the clouds as a soft breeze swept through the courtyard. The cold bite of the air was creeping into my bones, but I didn't show it. I wanted them to take the pills, to trust in what I'd made.

"Well," Wang Jun finally said, flipping the pill up and catching it in his palm, "here goes nothing." He popped the pill into his mouth and swallowed without hesitation, before lurching over and making a disgusted face. "Ugh! It tastes like blood! What'd you put in this?"

"I didn't say it'd taste good!"

Lan-Yin, a little more tentative, followed suit, though she made a point of shooting me a mock suspicious glance before swallowing hers. "You'd better be right about this, Kai."

I waved them off, a smirk tugging at the corners of my lips. "Just sit down and start circulating your qi. You'll feel the effects soon enough."

They both grumbled a bit, but did as I instructed, crossing their legs on the snow-covered ground, their breaths still visible in the chilly air. Wang Jun closed his eyes first, settling into his cultivation stance, and Lan-Yin followed soon after, her expression softening as she focused inward.

I joined them, but I wasn't there to cultivate. Instead, I monitored their qi circulation, stepping forward to ensure everything flowed smoothly. Elder

Ming, who had been observing from a distance, came over as well, standing silently beside me. His presence was steady and reassuring. I was glad for it.

Wang Jun was the first to react. I felt as the energy flowed through him, his qi pathways circulating properly. I discreetly analyzed the rhythm of his circulation, noting how easily the pill had integrated with his natural qi flow. I couldn't help but smile, pleased that my guess had been right.

Lan-Yin seemed to benefit as well, with Elder Ming nodding in satisfaction from inspecting her qi circulation. I could tell she was adjusting well.

Elder Ming broke the silence, his voice low but thoughtful. "These pills . . . Were they made using those hybrid plants?"

I nodded, feeling a surge of pride. "Yeah, I've been experimenting with them for the past week. I finally found a combination that works, though I had to throw out more batches than I care to admit." I winced a little, remembering the countless failed attempts. I'd need to order additional ingredients from Huan. Foraging in the forest wasn't ideal, and I couldn't use my *entire* garden for this experiment.

He raised an eyebrow but smiled slightly. "And yet, you don't seem too bothered by those failures."

I shrugged, waving him off. "I'm learning not to let it get to me. It's better to plan for failure than to expect perfection. I prepared extra ingredients, knowing full well some of it would go wrong."

"Wise beyond your years, it seems."

I stood there, watching Wang Jun and Lan-Yin as they cultivated, the winter air crisp around us. Their auras slowly grew stronger as the pills worked, and it was hard not to feel a quiet sense of satisfaction.

Having learned the intricacies of pill-making and its effect on the body, I knew how important it was to give the right medicine to the right person. People reacted differently, depending on their elemental affinities. Lan Sheng's mention of hyper-responders, people whose bodies soak up the benefits of a well-aligned pill like dry soil absorbing water, stuck with me.

I'd crafted these pills with care, considering what I knew about Wang Jun and Lan-Yin.

But it wasn't just about the pills. Watching them now, I knew that hoarding power and knowledge would not help anyone. These were dangerous times. The disciples of Narrow Stone Peak still lingered in the village, their presence a constant reminder of the lurking threats. It was better to make sure everyone around me was capable of defending themselves, at least somewhat.

Elder Ming must've sensed where my thoughts were drifting. "The Narrow Stone Peak disciples . . . They've been persistent, haven't they?"

I nodded, recalling how they'd tried to persuade the villagers over the past few days. They weren't overtly hostile, just persuasive. They'd come to me too, of course. I had stood my ground, politely but firmly refusing their offer, but there was a lingering doubt in my mind. Was I right to refuse them?

"They're persistent, but not pushy," I said, trying to find the right balance in describing them. "It's strange. They aren't unfriendly, but they won't take no for an answer either."

Elder Ming's face remained unreadable for a moment, before he gave a slight nod. "That's the way of most cultivators. Righteous sects, like the Verdant Lotus, are exceptions rather than the norm. Narrow Stone Peak may not mean any harm, but . . . you're right to trust your instincts. Especially from what you told me of their character."

"I guess so," I muttered, still feeling that nagging doubt. Had I turned down something that could've been helpful? Maybe they really did just want to protect the village. But something about their smoothness, their persistence— it didn't sit right with me.

"Your instincts are often sharper than you realize, Kai. Trust them. You've been through enough to know when something doesn't feel right."

I sighed, my breath fogging up in the cold air as I looked out at my friends, still sitting there in peaceful cultivation. "Yeah, I guess. It's just hard to know for sure, sometimes."

"That uncertainty is part of the journey," Elder Ming replied, smiling softly. "But one thing is certain. What you've done here, for them, is more valuable than any protection they could've offered. These pills, your support, your presence, it's enough."

I glanced at Wang Jun and Lan-Yin again, feeling the warmth of his words settle over me. Maybe he was right. I didn't need to rely on outside forces to protect those I cared about. I had my own strength, my own knowledge, and I wasn't alone.

"Thanks," I said quietly, the weight of the conversation slowly lifting. "And one day," I added, almost impulsively, "I'll make something to fix your dantian, Elder Ming."

He chuckled, shaking his head. "You've got enough on your plate, Kai. Don't worry about an old man like me."

I wasn't just making pills for the sake of power. I was making them to give those around me a fighting chance to share the strength I was gaining with the people I cared about. It was as simple as that.

There were so many ways I could use this power to help my village. With enough time and effort, I could make hybrids for different purposes, like barley infused with Entangling Vine essence to make them grow faster or infusing a paddy field with Sunfire Blade Grass so it can resist the cold, allowing us to grow rice during the winter. It gave me more than just martial power.

"You should get out of here," he said, his voice light now, almost teasing. "I'll watch over them while they cultivate. Go, take a break."

I smiled at Elder Ming's words, giving a grateful nod before turning away, the cold air cutting through my robes as I made my way back to the shop. His reassurance settled into me, quieting the doubts that had lingered. Still, there was always more work to be done. Always another step to take.

As I scanned the village on my way back, the absence of the Narrow Stone Peak disciples gnawed at me. They'd been persistent before, always hovering around the square, trying to convince the villagers. Perhaps they were taking the day off or, better yet, left the village. The unease prickled at the back of my neck, but I pushed it aside. For now.

Seeing Windy patrol the garden, I waved at him with a smile. For some reason, the Five Fists of Narrow Stone Peak gave him a wide berth. Although it didn't stop their leader, Wei Long, from coming in to recruit me. Good thing Tianyi could move like lightning when she needed to, so she hadn't been exposed yet.

As I stepped inside the warmth of the shop, the familiar scent of herbs and oils greeted me. The light from the small hearth flickered against the walls, casting long shadows across the shelves packed with ingredients and tools. I let out a sigh, feeling the tension from the day slowly ease from my shoulders.

I walked over to my workstation, where the pills I'd prepared for myself sat in neat rows. They had taken time to craft, but now that I had them in front of me, I felt a sense of satisfaction. I'd been waiting to take these for a while now, especially since I hadn't fully incorporated the effects of the Beast Core elixir yet.

I held up one of the pills, studying its polished surface in the flickering firelight. This particular pill wasn't just for strengthening my qi; it was designed to target the pill residue left in my body from the Beast Core elixir.

"I suppose it's a good problem to have."

Pill residue was a subtle but serious problem. It blocked the circulation of qi, diminishing the effectiveness of future pill consumption. Even though my pure qi cultivation method meant I had far less residue than most, it still accumulated over time.

This pill would cleanse that residue, unblocking my qi channels and allowing me to absorb future medicines more effectively. It was a small step, but a crucial one.

I glanced over at Tianyi, who had been sitting quietly in her human form, reading one of the many books I'd gathered for her to keep busy. She looked up as I walked toward her.

"Guard me while I cultivate," I said with a playful grin, knowing full well I didn't need a guard in my own shop.

She nodded, her large eyes unblinking as she did so. "I'll keep an eye out for any intruders," she said, mimicking a warrior's salute.

Perhaps Liang Feng's works were a good way for her to learn the ways of a human.

I chuckled and settled down in my usual spot, crossing my legs and centering myself. I held the pill between my fingers for a moment, then swallowed it in one smooth motion. The taste was bitter, but familiar, like iron and earth mixed together.

Closing my eyes, I began to circulate my qi, feeling the pill dissolve and release its essence into my system. Slowly but surely, the energy began to flow, cleansing the remnants of old elixirs, burning away the impurities that had clogged my channels. It wasn't painful, but it was intense like a deep, internal scrubbing.

Time slipped away as I immersed myself in the cultivation process, focusing entirely on the flow of qi. I could feel the effects taking hold, the smoothness of my channels returning, my body slowly regaining that sharp, efficient edge that residue dulled.

Somewhere in the back of my mind, Elder Ming's words lingered. It wasn't about proving anything to anyone, it was about knowing that I was doing my best, that I was growing in my own way.

But still . . . there was always the push, the hunger to reach higher, to become stronger. I couldn't shake that drive. Not entirely. I wasn't sure I even wanted to.

The night deepened around me, but I didn't stop. The fire within me had been lit, and I had no intention of letting it dim.

The room had long since fallen into a deep, tranquil silence, the crackling fire in the hearth casting warm, flickering shadows across the walls. Tianyi sat in her corner of the shop, legs tucked beneath her, a thin strand of hair slipping loose from her cascading locks. She glanced at Kai, who was deep in meditation, his breathing steady, his face relaxed but focused.

But something else tugged at her attention, a nagging sensation at the edge of her consciousness.

Tianyi's delicate wings, though hidden in her human form, tingled as she stared at the two strands of hair that had fallen across her cheek. They twitched slightly, as if disturbed by the faintest breath of wind, though the room was still.

Her neck turned suddenly, her movements precise and graceful. Her sharp senses, honed over a lifetime of surviving in a world that often treated her as prey, pricked at something just beyond her immediate awareness.

There was a rustling, like leaves. The room was silent, but the world outside wasn't. Her gaze flicked toward the window, and a whisper escaped her lips.

"Someone's near."

CHAPTER THIRTY-ONE

Broken Stems

Under the pale light of the moon, the man moved like a shadow, his blade cutting through the winter air with lethal precision. The sound of steel slicing through the frozen stems and delicate plants of the garden filled the night, each swing methodical, destructive. Alongside cutting the stalks, he wedged his blade deep into the soil, twisting it viciously to sever roots and tear through the delicate network of life below. When his blade couldn't reach, he brought his boot down with brutal force, stomping on the blossoms and grinding them into the dirt, leaving only crushed petals in his wake.

His eyes narrowed as he approached the nearly finished greenhouse, the fragile structure gleaming faintly under the moon's gaze. With a smirk curling his lips, he stepped forward, set on reducing it to splinters with a single strike.

He raised his blade, preparing for the decisive blow, when he suddenly froze. A sensation crawled up his spine, prickling his skin. It was a feeling he knew well—killing intent. Cold, sharp, and unmistakable.

His grip tightened on the hilt of his sword as he slowly turned, scanning the dark garden for the source. His gaze fell on a white serpent, coiled beneath the snow-dusted bushes, its body shimmering with a faint blue sheen. The snake's hiss cut through the silence, its blue eyes gleaming with fury.

The man's shoulders relaxed slightly, a chuckle slipping from his throat. "Just the snake," he muttered, tilting his head as he considered whether to kill it as well. "It's only a matter of time before it becomes a nuisance."

He took a step toward it, but something caught his eye, movement just above the greenhouse, high on the rooftop.

There, bathed in the soft glow of the full moon, stood a figure. A woman cloaked in a flowing blue silk robe that shimmered like water. Though her face was half-hidden beneath her hood, her eyes captivated him.

Too large. Too blank. Cold, emotionless, and unnerving. She glowered at him with an intensity that sent a chill through his body, freezing him in place.

For a moment, the woman stood perfectly still, like a statue carved from ice. The wind tugged at her robe, but she remained motionless, her gaze never leaving him. There was something deeply unsettling about her presence, her stillness unnatural, her silence deafening.

His heart hammered in his chest, his fingers twitching at the hilt of his blade. "What the hell . . . ?" he whispered, backing away, his bravado faltering. "They didn't say anything about this."

Something primal told him to run.

Before he could even finish the thought, she moved.

A blur of motion, faster than his eyes could follow. The next thing he knew, she was no longer on the rooftop.

She was upon him.

The impact of her foot, like a battering ram against his chest, was so sudden and brutal that it knocked his breath out. He barely registered the searing pain in his ribs as his body flew backward, crashing past the garden fence and skidding across the cold ground. The world spun, and blood filled his mouth as he coughed violently, struggling to breathe.

The man wheezed, clutching his ribs. His mind raced as he forced himself to his feet, his vision swimming. Gritting his teeth, he lifted his blade, eyes wild with desperation.

This was no ordinary opponent.

With a growl, he swung his sword at her in a wide arc, putting all his strength into the blow. But the woman didn't move to dodge. Instead, she raised her arm, bare and delicate, and deflected the blade with casual indifference.

His sword collided with her arm, and to his shock, it bounced off, barely leaving a minor scratch. He stared, dumbfounded, as the blade trembled in his hands, the sting of the recoil shooting up his arms. "What the—"

Before he could finish, she struck.

A barrage of punches rained down on him, each one lightning fast, blurring into a flurry of strikes. The blows weren't heavy, but their speed disoriented him, forcing him back step by step as he tried to keep up with her movements. He swung wildly in an attempt to regain control, but it was futile. She was too fast, her fists hammering into him with precision, leaving him with no opening.

With a frustrated roar, he threw his sword to the ground, opting for hand-to-hand combat. His fists came up defensively, and he lashed out, striking at her midsection. To his surprise, she didn't dodge this time. His punch connected with her side, and for a moment, he thought he had the upper hand.

He pressed forward, swinging harder and faster. Without the blade, he fought noticeably better, his strikes more fluid, more familiar. His confidence surged as he blocked her next punch and retaliated with a heavy strike to her ribs. She staggered, if only for a fraction of a second, and he grinned in triumph. This was it. He had her.

The man caught her fist in his hand, squeezing tightly. "Got you now," he spat, his grin widening as he looked her dead in the eyes.

Pain lanced through his leg. He looked down, his heart sinking as he saw the small white serpent—its fangs buried deep in his calf. It hissed, eyes glowing with an eerie blue light as the venom pumped into his bloodstream.

The man's breath hitched as his leg went numb, the venom quickly spreading through his veins. His grip on the woman's fist weakened, panic flashing in his eyes. He cursed under his breath, his muscles twitching as the paralytic poison took hold. Staggering back, he tried to steady himself, but his limbs felt sluggish. He needed to escape now.

"Show yourself, intruder!"

From a distance, voices echoed, sharp and urgent. The disciples of Narrow Stone Peak were coming, drawn by the commotion. He cursed again, louder this time. He had no time. His hand trembled as he reached for his fallen sword, but his body was betraying him, stiffening with each passing second.

With a desperate grunt, he turned and bolted into the night without his blade, his movements unsteady but faster than expected, given the venom coursing through him. He disappeared into the darkness, leaving a trail of shallow footprints in the snow.

Tianyi remained where she stood, her blank gaze following his retreating figure. The danger had passed, but the sound of approaching footsteps grew louder. She couldn't stay here.

A flicker of doubt crossed her face, the memory of Kai's words flashing in her mind. He had warned her, told her not to reveal herself to these people. Her lips pressed together in a thin line, and with a swift movement, she scooped up Windy, cradling the serpent close.

Without a sound, she darted toward the house, her movements a blur as she slipped through the door. Inside, the shop was dimly lit, Kai still deep in his meditation. She hesitated for a fraction of a second, her instincts pulling her to remain on guard, but Kai's words anchored her decision.

Muttering quietly, almost as if reassuring herself, she said, "Kai said not to reveal myself."

She crawled under the bed, curling up in the shadows. Though hidden, she stayed alert, ready for anything.

I stirred from my cultivation, my senses gradually returning as the world around me came back into focus. The faint murmur of voices reached my ears, and I blinked, my vision adjusting to the dim light of the shop. Something felt off.

My muscles were stiff, a sign that I had been meditating for longer than I'd intended. But that wasn't the problem. My eyes adjusted, and I saw them— Lan-Yin and Wang Jun, standing at the doorway, their postures tense, as if guarding me. A few villagers had torches lit, looking around in concern.

"Kai," Wang Jun said the moment he saw me stir. His voice was steady, but there was something frantic beneath the surface. "You're awake."

I sat up fully, rubbing the sleep from my eyes. "What happened? Why're you all here?"

Lan-Yin stepped forward, her expression serious. "Someone vandalized your garden. It's bad."

I froze for a moment, my mind racing. Vandalized? My garden? I quickly pushed myself to my feet, ignoring the stiffness in my legs as I made my way to the door. The cold air hit me as soon as I stepped outside, and I looked toward the garden. My breath caught in my throat.

A chunk of it had been destroyed. The delicate plants I had spent so much time cultivating had been trampled, the once neat rows of herbs and flowers reduced to a mess of broken stems and scattered earth. The greenhouse, nearly finished, was untouched, but the surrounding area looked as if a battle had taken place. My chest tightened with frustration.

"Dammit," I muttered, my voice louder than intended. "Who would . . . ?"

I trailed off, noticing a familiar figure standing just beyond the fence. Wei Long. His expression was grim, his usually calm demeanor replaced with something far more serious. He approached, stopping just short of the entrance to the garden.

"The Five Fists are pursuing the trail," Wei Long said without preamble, his voice low. "We believe the culprit fled after realizing they had been discovered."

I clenched my fists, trying to keep my temper in check. "Did they see who it was?"

Wei Long shook his head. "No. The trail is faint, but they're skilled trackers. If anyone can find him, it's them."

I took a deep breath, forcing myself to remain calm. My mind was racing, though. If they didn't know who it was . . . I couldn't afford to take any chances. My eyes darted discreetly around the area, searching for any sign of Tianyi or Windy.

A flicker of movement caught my attention near the base of the shop. Windy, coiled in the snow, watching me closely. It was as if the serpent knew what I was looking for. Slowly, Windy's head tilted toward the house, his gaze fixating on the doorway.

My eyes followed, and I understood. Tianyi. She was inside, hiding. She had listened to me. Thank the heavens.

I turned back to Wei Long, doing my best to mask my relief. "Thank you," I said, nodding to him. "I appreciate your help. Let me know if they find anything."

Wei Long studied me for a moment, his expression unreadable, before nodding in return. "We'll keep you informed. Stay vigilant. Whoever did this might return."

As the first-class disciple turned to leave, his figure blending into the shadows, I remained rooted to the spot, my gaze slowly shifting back to the garden. The icy breeze stung my skin, but it was nothing compared to the ache that had formed in my chest.

The Moonlit Grace Lilies I had been cultivating for months were crushed by something, scattering their silver-white petals like remnants of a broken memory. As I walked toward them, my hands trembled, and I crouched down to gently pick up one of the trampled stems. It was limp in my fingers, the life force of the plants fading as quickly as my hope for their recovery.

The scent of crushed herbs and broken soil filled the air, but it was the sight of those lilies that hurt the most. They weren't just any plants; they were my connection to my mother. I had nurtured these flowers as a way of remembering her, of keeping a part of her with me. And now . . .

My vision blurred, a lump forming in my throat as I struggled to hold back the tears. The weight of the destruction was too much. I clenched my teeth, my breath shaky, trying to find the anger I knew should be there. But all I felt was grief.

Deep, aching grief.

"Kai . . ." Lan-Yin knelt beside me, her hand resting gently on my shoulder. "I'm sorry."

Wang Jun stood behind her, his fists clenched, a mixture of anger and sympathy on his face. "We'll help you rebuild," he vowed. "We'll fix this."

I wanted to say something. To thank them, to tell them it wasn't their responsibility . . . but the words wouldn't come. Instead, I just nodded, my hand still holding the ruined stem of a lily, its once-vibrant glow now nothing more than a dull shimmer under the moonlight.

I had worked so hard, pouring my time and energy into these plants, hoping to create something beautiful, and a potent medicine in the case of an emergency. But this . . . this was beyond fixing with just effort. In one careless moment, I lost months of cultivation, care, and attention. It wasn't just the garden; it felt like a part of me had been trampled as well.

Lan-Yin gave my shoulder a comforting squeeze. "We'll find whoever did this," she whispered. "And we'll make sure they pay."

But I wasn't thinking about revenge. Not in that moment. I was just thinking about the waste of it all.

"Why these?" I mumbled, barely audible, speaking more to myself than anyone. "Why the lilies?"

I couldn't shake the image of my mother's smile as she showed me how to prepare them long ago. The way her hands had moved so gently over the petals, her voice full of warmth and patience. I had carried that memory with me, and seeing the lilies bloom had been like a small piece of her living on. But now they were gone, and it felt like I had lost her all over again.

The cold pressed in, and I wiped at my eyes hastily, not wanting my friends to see the tears that had finally escaped. But they didn't need to say anything. Their presence was enough, grounding me as I mourned the loss of something more than just a garden.

Lan-Yin sat beside me, her silence filled with understanding, while Wang Jun stood vigil, his gaze scanning the surroundings as if daring the attacker to return.

The night stretched on, the moonlight casting long shadows across the destroyed garden.

CHAPTER THIRTY-TWO

Fragments and Friends

I couldn't sleep.

After the events of the night, sleep felt like a distant hope. My body was exhausted, but my mind refused to settle. I needed to do something, anything, to push away the frustration gripping me.

So I got up.

I found myself outside, standing in the wreckage. The cold air nipped at my skin, but I didn't care. I just wanted to salvage what I could. The garden had been a sanctuary for me, a place where I could nurture life, and now it lay in pieces. I knelt in the dirt, my hands brushing over the remnants of the plants, trying to figure out where to even start.

Before long, I heard the familiar crunch of footsteps behind me. I didn't need to turn around to know who it was.

"Brought some spare wood from the forge," Wang Jun said, his voice cutting through the quiet morning air. "It'll be enough to fix the fences. They needed to be replaced anyway."

Lan-Yin ruffled my hair. She was carrying a small basket with her.

I opened my mouth to tell them they didn't need to, but she beat me to it.

"Don't say anything about us needing rest," she added, shaking her head with a small grin. "I've got so much energy in me, I don't think I could sit still if I tried."

Her betrothed nodded, smiling. "Those pills you gave us . . . Well, let's just say we owe you. And besides"—he gestured to the garden—"we're not letting you handle this alone."

Lan-Yin's fists clenched as she surveyed the destruction. "Whoever did this had no respect for what you've built here. For what this garden means. If I find out who it was . . ."

I wanted to argue, to tell them it was okay, that I'd figure it out myself. But honestly? I was grateful. Grateful for their help, grateful for their presence. And maybe a little too drained to push them away.

Together, we worked in silence for a while. They didn't try to cheer me up with empty words or platitudes. Instead, they threw themselves into helping me clean up the wreckage, focusing on rebuilding the garden. Wang Jun repaired the trampled fence sections, while Lan-Yin salvaged the surviving plants.

I found myself glancing at the Moonlit Grace Lilies, or what was left of them. Every time I saw the crushed petals, that tightness in my chest returned. But seeing Lan-Yin and Wang Jun working so hard, it reminded me that there was still a chance to recover, even if it was small.

As the sun rose higher, casting golden light over the village, we paused. The worst of the damage was cleared, but much work still lay ahead. I could already feel the strain in my muscles from the work, but it was a good kind of tired. A distraction from everything else.

We finally headed back inside for a well-deserved break. I sat down at the table, exhaustion beginning to settle in. Lan-Yin excused herself, saying she'd run home to grab something for breakfast. Moments later, she returned with a steaming pot of rice porridge, and I rummaged through my shelves for some preserved vegetables and dried meats to add to the bowls.

We sat together, the morning light filtering in through the windows as we shared the simple meal. I took a quiet moment, sneaking a bowl of sugar water under the bed for Tianyi, who'd been hiding there all night. She deserved something after staying there without a sound. It was almost unsettling, knowing she was there.

As we ate, I couldn't help but glance over at Wang Jun and Lan-Yin. I set my chopsticks down and leaned back, curious. "How much stronger are your reserves after those pills?"

Wang Jun grinned proudly, his chest puffing out a bit. "According to the Heavenly Interface, I've reached the second rank of the Qi Initiation Stage."

Lan-Yin nodded, though her expression was more modest. "First rank for me, but I can definitely feel the difference."

I raised an eyebrow, impressed. They had both made solid progress, but this was the perfect moment to explain something they might not have considered.

"That's great," I said, "but I want to talk to you both about something important—pill residue."

They both looked at me, confused.

"What's that?" Wang Jun asked mid-bite.

"Pill residue," I began, "is what's left behind in your body after you take a pill. Even though pills give you a permanent boost in power and energy, they leave behind residual materials in your body. If that residue builds up too much, it can block your qi circulation. It's like clogging a river with debris, it slows everything down and eventually stops it altogether."

Lan-Yin frowned, setting her bowl down. "So, the pills aren't as perfect as they seem?"

I nodded. "Exactly. Pills are helpful, but they aren't a shortcut to power. If you rely too heavily on them without properly integrating the energy into your dantian, you'll end up hitting a wall in your cultivation. And that's not all—over time, the residue can weaken the effects of future pills. That's why detoxification pills are so important. They clear out the residue, making sure your qi flows smoothly."

They both nodded, taking the information seriously.

"And don't worry," I added with a grin. "I've got detoxification pills ready for when you need them."

The three of us shared a small laugh, but the lesson was clear.

For now, though, we enjoyed the rest of our breakfast in peace, the morning sun casting a warm glow over us. Despite everything that had happened, I couldn't help but feel grateful for friends like them.

Even in the worst moments, I wasn't alone.

But even as I sat there, trying to soak in the calm of the moment, I couldn't shake the feeling of being hyperaware of Tianyi's presence. She'd been hiding under my bed all night without a word. I don't think I even heard her when I first attempted to sleep.

I caught myself glancing toward the bed more often than I should have. Guilt ate at me. I'd kept her in hiding, and it didn't sit right with me, but I couldn't see any other choice. I was responsible for her safety, and as much as I wanted to make things right, I had to be cautious. That thought didn't ease my conscience, though. I hope the sugar water will appease her for now. I hadn't cleaned under there in a while.

After breakfast, the three of us gathered what was left of the garden and headed to Elder Ming's courtyard for morning training. The walk there was quiet, almost somber, the weight of last night hanging over us.

When we arrived, Elder Ming was sitting on his usual stone bench, his eyes closed in deep thought. He opened them when we approached, his gaze immediately falling on me.

"Kai," he said, "you look troubled. What's on your mind?"

I hesitated for a moment before stepping forward. "There was a break-in at my house last night. Someone came into my garden, destroyed a lot of the plants I'd been cultivating. They got away before anyone could catch them."

Elder Ming's expression darkened immediately, his brows furrowing. "A bandit?" His voice was low, but there was an edge to it.

"Maybe," I replied, unsure how much to reveal. "Whoever it was didn't steal anything, just wrecked the place."

Elder Ming's jaw clenched, and he exchanged a knowing look with me. "The Narrow Stone Peak disciples," he muttered skeptically. "They've been . . . persistent, haven't they? Trying to get closer to the village, to us."

It made sense. The Narrow Stone Peak disciples had been too eager to "help" the village and their constant presence had been wearing on me. But before I could respond, Lan-Yin spoke up.

"It couldn't have been them," she said, shaking her head. "We were staying at the Soaring Swallow Teahouse last night, and we noticed the commotion from the balcony. The disciples were there, watching the whole thing with us. They even pointed it out."

That gave me pause. If they weren't directly involved, then who was? A mystery wrapped around this incident, and it only deepened the growing sense of unease I had about everything lately.

I tried to think through the haze of my exhaustion, searching for other possibilities. Who else could have done this?

Duan Jian? The thought crossed my mind, but I quickly dismissed it. After the incident in the alley with Xu Ziqing, he had made himself scarce. Even if he harbored resentment toward me, he didn't know where I lived, or at least I hoped he didn't.

The Iron Claw Sect? Another possibility, but it was unlikely. They'd gone completely silent if Zhi Ruo's letter was correct. There hadn't been any reports of them resurfacing, either.

Silent Moon Sect? Another candidate, but I doubted I was on their radar. I hadn't done anything significant to attract their attention, and as far as I knew, they had no quarrel with me anymore. Not when they were looking at upending the status quo of the province and expanding themselves.

I was running out of potential enemies. It didn't add up.

Elder Ming's voice broke through my concentration. "You're thinking about who might be responsible, aren't you?"

I nodded, still unsure. "I just can't figure it out. It doesn't seem like any of the usual suspects."

"Sometimes it's not about who you've wronged, but what you possess that others covet. Keep that in mind."

Could it be about the garden itself? The herbs, the hybrids . . . But none of it seemed valuable enough to warrant an attack. Still, it was clear I needed to be on high alert.

Elder Ming studied me for a moment before he spoke again. "I don't want you to train today."

I blinked, taken aback. "What? Why?"

He gave me a knowing look. "You're not physically exhausted, Kai. It's your mind that's worn out. Cultivation can do just as much for you today as any physical training would. Take the time to meditate, absorb the qi around you, and let your body and mind heal."

His words rang true, though they stung a bit. I'd always been the type to push myself, but he wasn't wrong. My head was a mess, and maybe forcing myself through drills wouldn't help me clear it.

Lan-Yin and Wang Jun both chimed in agreement.

"I have to say," Wang Jun added with a smile, "cultivation has been a lot smoother lately, thanks to the abundance of qi in the air. Don't know how I would've gotten through morning practice without it."

Lan-Yin nodded. "It feels like it's been that way for the past few months, but it's really ramped up since you got back, Kai. I suppose he's a harbinger of good fortune. Many thanks, young master."

Come to think of it, the ambient qi around the village had grown stronger, comparable to a sect's training grounds. I was so absorbed in getting back to my daily life that I didn't notice, but even compared to the Verdant Lotus Sect, the amount here didn't fall short, did it?

I looked at Elder Ming, doing my best to keep my expression neutral. "Is it true the qi here has been steadily growing? Even while I was away?"

He nodded thoughtfully. "Somewhat, but nothing like it is now. Ever since you returned, it's been unusually strong. It's as if the village itself is becoming a prime spot for cultivation."

I felt my pulse quicken. The realization hit me like a jolt.

Tianyi's Qi Haven skill. She had broken through in cultivation. Did it mean her abilities were enhanced? I recalled when we were riding the horses back here. Her presence allowed them to run without stopping for *hours*. If her Qi Haven skill had been amplified to a similar degree, then . . .

I needed to confirm this. But the more pressing issue was the danger this posed.

My mind raced as the pieces fell into place. The increase in ambient qi wasn't just a curiosity, it was a beacon. Cultivators, and even sects would be drawn to this place like moths to a flame. And Narrow Stone Peak . . . They weren't here out of generosity.

Wei Long's words replayed in my mind. From when I first met him. He knew. Or at least, he suspected. He hadn't come to the village to offer protection; he'd come to stake a claim. A village with qi as strong as this was worth far more than its crops or timber. To a sect, it was an unguarded treasure trove.

And now I had a target painted on my back.

If I had noticed the change, surely the Narrow Stone Peak disciples had too.

I glanced at Elder Ming, my decision made. "Can I leave early today? There's something I need to check on."

He gave me a concerned look but nodded. "Go ahead. Be careful, Kai."

As I turned to leave, the tension built within me. I had to get to the bottom of this—and fast. Something much larger was at play, and it wasn't just about a break-in anymore.

It was about power.

And it was growing.

CHAPTER THIRTY-THREE

The Silent Witness

As I rushed back home, the weight of what I had just learned settled heavily in my chest. The realization of what was happening, of what *had been* happening under my nose this whole time, made my heart pound even harder. The ambient qi in the village, stronger than it should have been. And now it all pointed back to one person.

Tianyi.

When I reached my front door, I paused, quickly scanning the area for any sign of prying eyes. The last thing I needed was someone from Narrow Stone Peak catching me talking to her. The village was still quiet, early enough that most people were still eating or getting ready for their day. I slipped inside the house and closed the door behind me as quietly as I could.

"Tianyi," I called softly, approaching my bed, where she'd spent the night hidden. "You can come out now."

There was a slight rustling from underneath the bed, and then a soft sigh as she emerged, moving with that quiet grace that always unnerved me a bit. Windy was curled up beside her, his blue eyes gleaming in the dim light, as if sensing my thoughts. Tianyi's large, too-bright eyes met mine, and for a moment, we just stared at each other.

I took a breath, steadying myself. "I need to ask you something, and I need you to be completely honest with me."

Her head tilted slightly, the faintest sign of curiosity.

"I've noticed . . . the ambient qi in the village," I began, choosing my words carefully. "It's stronger now, more than it was when I left for the Verdant Lotus Sect. And since I got back, it's been getting even stronger. Stronger than it should be."

Her gaze didn't waver, but I could see the recognition in her eyes.

"It's your Qi Haven skill, isn't it? Has it changed? Has it expanded beyond just specific zones and now covers the entire village?"

For a moment, Tianyi didn't respond. Her eyes remained fixed on mine, unreadable. Then, slowly, she nodded.

"After my breakthrough," she said quietly, her voice soft but clear, "my skill grew. It no longer affects only small, isolated areas. The entire village is now within its range, creating a place where the qi is richer, stronger."

My stomach twisted at her confirmation. It made perfect sense, but it also made everything so much more complicated.

"So that's why the ambient qi is so strong . . ." I muttered to myself, my mind racing. Elder Ming, Wang Jun, and Lan-Yin had all noticed it too. But none of us had understood why until now.

Tianyi's eyes never left me, although the two strands falling in front of her face continued to twitch with nervous energy.

The reason the Narrow Stone Peak disciples were hanging around . . . The reason they were so eager to "help" the village . . . It all made sense now.

My mind flashed back to that conversation with Wei Long, the first time he came to the village. I had overlooked his words then, distracted by his smooth-talking and the obvious power he wielded. But now his words rang in my mind with new clarity.

We have reason to believe the bandit activity will spread soon, and Spirit Beasts are drawn to areas of concentrated qi, such as this village.

He knew. Maybe not the full extent of it, but he knew something was different here. He saw the village's growing significance, and now I could see why the disciples of Narrow Stone Peak were so eager to establish themselves here. It wasn't just about protecting the village from bandits. They wanted to control it. They wanted the qi.

And now that I knew the truth, I had to be careful. More careful than ever before.

I let out a slow breath, the weight of the situation sinking in deeper. "Thank you, Tianyi," I said softly, grateful but concerned. "Thank you for staying hidden and keeping yourself out of sight. I don't know what I'd do if they found out about you."

Tianyi remained still, her gaze unwavering but now tinged with something . . . hesitant. She shifted slightly, her wings twitching ever so subtly, and I could sense she had something to say. I waited, the silence stretching between us.

Finally, she spoke, her voice quieter than usual. "I didn't stay hidden the entire time."

I blinked, her words catching me off guard. "What do you mean?"

She glanced down, her large eyes showing a flicker of uncertainty. "Last night when the man came to the garden. I . . . I didn't stay hidden. He was going to destroy the greenhouse, and I know how much it means to you."

The realization hit me like a punch to the gut. She had fought off the intruder, shown her face. My pulse quickened.

"I didn't want to fight," she added quickly, as if sensing the worry rising in me. "But I couldn't let him destroy the place you've worked so hard on. So I stopped him. I stayed out of sight of the bald men in the village . . . I made sure no one else saw me."

A wave of relief mixed with panic surged through me. She had protected the greenhouse, but at what cost? If anyone had seen her, if anyone even suspected . . .

"Tianyi," I whispered, trying to keep my voice calm, though my mind was racing. "You . . . you shouldn't have—" I stopped myself, realizing that there was no point in chastising her. She had done it out of care, out of loyalty. But now this situation was far more serious than I thought.

My mind shifted focus. I needed to know more. My gaze hardened as I knelt down, closer to her level. "Tell me everything about the attacker. What did they look like? How did they fight?"

Tianyi stared at me, her eyes narrowing slightly in thought, as though she were piecing together how to explain something that didn't fully make sense to her yet. Her wings twitched slightly.

"It . . . was like Windy's fang," she started. "Sharp. He used it . . . not to bite, but to . . . slice?" She tilted her head, searching for the right word. "He cut the garden with it."

I frowned, trying to follow her logic. "A blade?"

Tianyi's face brightened at the word, and she nodded quickly. "Yes! A blade, like a bigger, meaner fang. He had it when I saw him. He was slow. Slower than I thought he would be."

My heart clenched at the thought of her facing that intruder alone. "And what happened when you confronted him?"

She glanced down at her arm, where a thin line still marred her pale skin. It was faint, but the sight of it stoked an ember inside me. I fought to keep my expression neutral as she continued.

"He dropped the fang," she said, the words coming more easily now. "He was worse with it. Better with his fists. When he fought with his hands, I couldn't hit him as much." She trailed off, her hand gently brushing the scratch. "He hit me here with the fang. But it's nothing."

I stared at the faint scratch, feeling a cold rage creeping up my spine. I wasn't sure if it was because of the intruder daring to strike her or that she seemed so nonchalant about it. My mind replayed her words: *Dropped the blade . . . better with his fists.*

It wasn't just some petty thief. Whoever this was had training.

"He hurt you," I said, the words coming out more sharply than I intended.

She tilted her head, her wings shifting slightly, confused by the intensity in my voice. "A scratch. It will heal."

But I couldn't let it go so easily. A dull roar filled my head, like a pressure building, ready to explode.

I took a breath, trying to ground myself, but the anger wouldn't go away. Not fully. Instead, it simmered just below the surface, waiting.

Tianyi's eyes widened slightly as she studied me. "You are angry?"

"I am," I said, quieter this time. "Not at you. Never at you. I'm angry at the man who hurt you. Who came here. I should've been there to stop him."

Her expression softened, as though she were trying to understand what I was saying, but couldn't quite grasp the human depth of emotion. "I stopped him. And I did not want him to destroy the place you cared about. The greenhouse."

I felt a pang of gratitude mingled with that burning anger. She hadn't acted out of aggression; she had intervened to protect the greenhouse I poured my heart and money into. And yet, the fact that she had to step in at all bothered me.

"Thank you," I whispered. "You did the right thing."

But even as I said it, I knew this situation was far more serious than I had realized. This wasn't some random act of vandalism. This was planned. Deliberate. And if Tianyi had to intervene, then it meant the threat wasn't just against my garden—it was against all of us.

I met her gaze again. "Can you remember anything else about the man? Please—everything you can remember."

She seemed to think for a moment, her eyes flicking toward Windy before returning to me. "He fought hard . . . but left when the bald men started running."

With every word that left her lips, I pushed for more, digging into each detail, dragging every drop of information I could from her memories. What did he do? How did he look when he did it? I pressed her for the smallest gestures, the flick of his hand, the pace of his movements, anything that might give me insight.

She mentioned Windy's role in the battle, how he bit him on the ankle, pumping him full of venom. The serpent in question looked at me, raising his head high like an arrogant young master.

"Windy, he can track his prey. Whenever he bites. He can tell where they go."

I took a slow breath, trying to piece together the information Tianyi had given me. Her description was fragmented, but it was enough to know that this wasn't just an amateur sneaking into my garden for a quick smash-and-grab. The man wielded a blade, expertly used his fists, and deliberately intended to destroy my work.

And if Windy could track people he attacked, then that'd mean we have a trail to follow the culprit.

Even so, I needed more information.

I turned toward her, my brows furrowed. "Was it like this?" I asked, standing up slowly. I shifted my stance, feet planted firmly, widening my shoulders to imitate a larger, more aggressive style. My arms moved in tight arcs, simulating the way the Narrow Stone Peak disciples would strike. Close-range punches aimed at grappling, their bodies leaning forward to grab or overpower their opponent. I mimicked their footwork, using firm stomps to suggest a stronger, slower approach, designed to overwhelm someone faster.

"They use their size and brute strength to get close," I explained, recalling all I remembered from my spar with Gu Bei, as well as the incident in Crescent Bay. "Locking their opponent down with grabs and crushing force."

Tianyi's wings twitched slightly as she watched my movements. Her eyes lit up with recognition, and she nodded slowly. "Yes . . . he moved like that. Not fast, but strong. It was harder to hit him when he fought with his hands, since he'd try to catch me."

I cursed under my breath. Narrow Stone Peak. Of course. Everything kept pointing back to them. Their presence, their interest in the village, and now this.

And that's when it hit me.

The blade. He dropped it according to her, but . . . where was it? Who would've taken it?

I'd been outside the entire night, cleaning up the wreckage, combing through the garden, but I never found a blade. There had been no sign of it when I woke up after the break-in, no trace of it in the garden when we were fixing the fence. Either Wei Long or one of the Five Fists picked it up in the time between Tianyi going back under the bed and the villagers arriving. But it made sense. Some plants were cut in half. This couldn't have been done with bare hands.

Just as I was about to speak, a sharp knock echoed through the shop, cutting through the tense air.

I froze, my mind racing. My eyes shot toward Tianyi, and she immediately understood, retreating under the bed without a sound, with Windy slithering to her side.

The knock came again, this time more forceful, more insistent. My heart pounded in my chest as I straightened up, trying to calm the storm of thoughts swirling in my mind.

I opened the door just a crack, and my stomach sank as I found myself staring into the grim face of Wei Long. He had tied his hair up in a tight bun, and his face looked even more severe than usual.

He wasn't here for pleasantries.

"Kai," Wei Long said. "We need to talk."

I stepped aside, forcing a calmness into my voice that I didn't feel. "Come in."

CHAPTER THIRTY-FOUR

The Mask and the Mantle

The moment Wei Long stepped inside, I felt an uneasy shift in the air. His eyes scanned the room, lingering just a beat too long on every corner and shadow. It wasn't the casual glance of a visitor; he was looking for something—or someone. I tensed, keeping my expression neutral as I gestured toward a seat near the counter.

I resisted the urge to confront him then and there. Even if I did, what could I do? He was a first-class disciple; that wasn't someone I could attack on a whim.

If he was in cahoots with the bandit that attacked my garden, then it was fair to assume he knew of Tianyi. And I had to be as cautious as possible.

"What brings you by this early, Wei Long?" I asked, careful to keep my tone light.

He smiled, but it was tight and controlled, his eyes never quite warming. "I thought it best to continue our previous conversation, especially after last night's . . . incident." His gaze was intense, unwavering. "Kai, it's time to reconsider our offer to protect the village. Gentle Wind Village needs real defenses. Our sect can provide that."

I kept my face neutral, though my mind raced with several emotions.

Why was he so insistent? And . . . why come to me?

"I appreciate that, Wei Long, really," I said slowly, "but wouldn't it make more sense to approach the village head directly?" I raised an eyebrow, trying to sound as casual as possible. "I'm just the village herbalist, after all."

He held my gaze, leaning forward just slightly. "I could speak with the village head, yes. But it's clear that the village listens to you, Kai. They trust you. They look to you." His smile grew faintly, as though he enjoyed letting this realization settle over me. "Even the village head defers to you in matters of security."

My mouth went dry. The casual tone I'd been trying to keep up wavered. I had seen myself as the herbalist, the kid who helped and sometimes got asked for advice. But the truth was there in Wei Long's words, and it clicked into place, even if I didn't fully want to acknowledge it. I wasn't just the herbalist to the people here. I was . . . someone they looked to for answers, for protection.

I'd put myself in that role without even realizing it.

"Now do you see?" Wei Long said, his voice smooth. "You're already a leader here, Kai. It's only natural that you'd be the one to make this decision." He paused, letting his words linger. "And with Narrow Stone Peak's support, you'd have even more strength to defend the village from future threats."

I let out a slow breath, careful not to reveal my true feelings. "It's something to consider, definitely," I replied, pretending to think about it. "But I'll still need some time. This decision isn't something I can rush into, and you know how people can be with change."

Wei Long's smile thinned, but he nodded. "Of course, Kai. But don't take too long. The break-in was only the first sign. There are others who will come, drawn by the qi here. With our help, you'd have no reason to worry. You'd have our top disciples deployed here, prepared to protect the village from any threat." His voice dropped a notch, his tone unmistakable. "And without us . . . Well, it's your responsibility to keep them safe, isn't it?"

I resisted the urge to scowl, forcing my shoulders to relax instead. "I understand. A few more days. That's all I ask."

He nodded, seemingly appeased, though his eyes lingered on me a moment longer than necessary. Then, in a voice nearly too casual, he added, "And remember, we're also here to support your growth. Even if you're not interested in joining Narrow Stone Peak, you could gain training, resources . . . things that would be difficult to come by otherwise. You've done well so far, Kai, but there's only so much one can achieve alone."

I held his gaze, feigning contemplation even as my resolve hardened. "I appreciate the offer, Wei Long. Really. It would be an honor to train alongside your disciples . . . but I need a bit more time to think about what's best for the village."

He studied me, but I kept my expression neutral, unyielding. Finally, he gave a small, almost reluctant nod. "Of course. But don't take too long. This isn't the kind of decision that can wait."

I walked him to the door, watching as he scanned the room one last time before he stepped out. He paused on the threshold, turning to look at me.

"All you have to do is say the word."

The door closed, and I stood there, his words ringing in my ears. As I looked around my shop, I thought about his insistence, his pressure, his probing gaze. This wasn't just about defending the village. It was about control.

But I wasn't about to let that happen.

I glanced toward the shadows where Tianyi hid, a fierce resolve settling over me. This wasn't just about a decision for the village.

I stood still, breathing deeply, willing the frustration and anger out of my system. I couldn't afford for those emotions to cloud my mind or sway my judgment. Instead, I channeled them, letting each breath calm me further, refining my resolve into something sharp and focused. Wei Long had given me a few days—every second of which I intended to use.

I could confront Wei Long, but that would only allow him to twist the narrative to his advantage. And even if I showed damning evidence, what good would it do? It'd probably even bring greater danger upon the village.

No, for this, I need allies and witnesses.

I grabbed a brush and parchment, continuing the half-written letter I had made for the Verdant Lotus Sect.

"It's time to call in some favors."

By the time I finished writing, the ink was barely dry, and predawn darkness still cloaked the sky. I knew I wouldn't find rest even if I tried, so I gathered my things, tucking the letters securely into my satchel.

"I'll be back," I told Tianyi and Windy.

The butterfly humanoid looked at me with unblinking eyes and a small nod. The serpent cradled in her lap continued to sleep, blissfully unaware of me.

Stepping out into the crisp morning air, I felt the chill nip at my cheeks. The village was silent, save for the distant hoot of an owl and the gentle rustling of leaves.

The path to the Azure Silk Trading Company's outpost was familiar, though in the dim light, the surroundings seemed shrouded in an almost dreamlike stillness.

The trading company's building came into view, a sturdy structure of dark wood and slate tiles, designed to withstand the elements and the passage of time. Lanterns hung at the corners of the building, their soft glow illuminating the frost-covered ground. Wagons were stationed neatly to the side, their wheels locked and tarps secured, waiting for deliveries and shipments.

I hesitated for a moment, guilt twinging at the thought of waking Huan at such an ungodly hour. But my task took precedence. Taking a steadying breath, I walked up the wide wooden steps leading to the main entrance. The double doors were firmly shut, but a small side door stood slightly ajar, likely left open for ventilation during the night.

I stepped lightly onto the porch and rapped my knuckles against the wood, the sound sharp against the early morning stillness. "Huan," I called softly in a harsh whisper. There was no response. I knocked louder this time. "Huan, it's Kai. I'm sorry to disturb you, but this is important."

For a moment, there was silence, and I considered knocking again. Then I heard the faint creak of footsteps from inside. Moments later, the side door opened a fraction, revealing Huan's disheveled figure. His hair was a mess, and he squinted when he saw me.

"Kai?" he murmured groggily, rubbing his face. "What in the heavens are you doing here at this hour?"

I offered him an apologetic smile. "I wouldn't be here if it wasn't urgent. I need your help."

He blinked a few times, processing my words, then nodded slowly. "All right. Give me a moment." He disappeared back into the building, and then he emerged shortly after, wearing a cloak over his nightclothes. "Come in."

Once we were inside, Huan turned to me, concern evident in his eyes. "What's going on?"

I took a deep breath, steadying myself. "I need to send these letters to Crescent Bay City," I said, pulling the neatly sealed envelopes from my satchel and placing them on the table between us. "As fast as possible."

Huan glanced down at the letters, then back at me, his brows furrowing. "To Crescent Bay? That's no simple trip. It's a day and a half, minimum, even with our fastest messengers—and that's assuming no delays. If you want speed, it'll cost more. They'll have to travel light, no heavy loads or stops along the way."

"That's fine," I replied. "Whatever it takes."

Huan's eyes dropped to the letters again, his hand hesitating over them as though he could divine their contents through the parchment. When he turned them over to read the addressees, his expression shifted. His eyes widened, and he sucked in a breath as though he'd just seen something forbidden.

"Are you . . ." He paused, his gaze darting to meet mine. "Kai, are you preparing for war?"

I met his gaze steadily, the flickering light of the lantern casting shadows across the room. "To an extent." I was resolute. "These aren't letters for pleasantries. I need these delivered without fail."

Huan nodded slowly, his face pale. He placed the letters back on the table, his hand lingering as though reluctant to part with them. "You know what this could mean, don't you? If the wrong people catch wind of this . . ." He trailed off, glancing around as though the shadows might be listening.

"That's why it's crucial no one from Narrow Stone Peak hears about this," I said, leaning forward. My voice dropped to a low, urgent tone. "They're not here to help the village, Huan. Their true intentions run deeper, and I need to be ready when they reveal themselves."

He swallowed hard, nodding again. "I understand. You've always had the village's best interests at heart, Kai. But this . . . it's risky."

"Riskier than letting them sink their claws into Gentle Wind Village unchecked?" I countered. "This is the only way, Huan. Trust me."

He studied me for a moment, then sighed heavily. "All right. I'll make it happen. Our fastest messenger will leave within the hour. But . . ." He hesitated, dropping his voice further. "I hope you know what you're doing."

I forced a small smile. "I do. And thank you, Huan. You're doing more for this village than most will ever know."

Huan picked up the letters with both hands, treating them as if they were made of carved jade. "I'll see to it personally," he said. "And . . . take care of yourself."

With that, he disappeared into the back of the building, leaving me alone with my thoughts and the faint flicker of the lantern's flame.

I stepped out into the cool morning air, the first hints of dawn creeping over the horizon. My breath puffed in the chill, my mind racing with possibilities and contingencies. This was just the first step, but it was a necessary one.

As I approached the Soaring Swallow Teahouse, its windows were dark, the faint scent of last night's revelry lingering in the air. The Narrow Stone Peak disciples were likely still deep in sleep, blissfully unaware of the storm brewing around them.

I passed quickly, my steps careful and measured to avoid the crunch of snow that might disturb the silence. The teahouse loomed like a sleeping beast, its presence a constant weight on my mind. Soon enough, I knew I'd have to face what lay within.

My thoughts drifted instead to Wang Jun and Lan-Yin. Elder Ming's morning practice would start soon, and if I knew those two, they'd already be stirring, preparing themselves for the day's lessons. And afterward, they'd go about their day: Wang Jun pounding away at the forge and Lan-Yin balancing trays and tea kettles with an effortless grace.

Wang Jun's growth had been remarkable. He'd learned to integrate the discipline and precision of martial arts into his blacksmithing. I remembered his words, how his blades had become sharper, more durable, almost as if his qi found its way into the steel, ever since he started training with Elder Ming.

Lan-Yin had blossomed in her own way. Her improved physique and refined constitution allowed her to shoulder the heavy burdens of running the teahouse with ease. Where once her parents had carried the weight of decades of service, she now stepped in, taking over long shifts with ease.

They were proof that this village wasn't just a collection of homes; it was a community of talents, each finding their path and strengthening the whole.

I couldn't let them down. Not now, when the stakes had risen so high.

A faint gust of wind stirred the stillness, and I quickened my pace.

It wasn't long before I reached Elder Ming's home, the modest structure nestled near the village square. The faintest trace of smoke curled from the chimney, a sign that he was likely awake, but I didn't dare disturb him directly. Instead, I withdrew a carefully folded letter from my satchel. It was bound with simple twine.

I glanced around, ensuring the area was still and empty, before stepping into the courtyard. Kneeling, I placed the letter just inside the gate, tucking it securely against a stone where he'd be certain to see it. As I stood, I let my gaze linger on the house for a moment, imagining the reaction this letter would evoke.

In the letter, I explained the situation succinctly. Narrow Stone Peak was involved. They were behind the destruction of the garden, and perhaps more. But I urged Elder Ming not to act. Not yet.

I promised I had a plan and that the truth would be revealed in due time. I asked him to share the contents of the letter with Wang Jun and Lan-Yin, as I knew they'd press for answers soon enough. They deserved to know, even if I wasn't ready to confront the disciples just yet.

Satisfied, I turned and slipped back into the shadows, retracing my steps toward my shop. The dawn was breaking, casting a faint golden hue over the village. Yet the beauty of the morning was lost on me as my thoughts swirled with what lay ahead.

When I arrived at my shop, I stopped in the garden—or what remained of it. Despite the effort my friends and I had poured into clearing the debris, the phantom image of its destruction still loomed in my mind. Crushed plants, overturned soil, shattered pots—my life's work reduced to chaos. My hands clenched into fists, and for a moment, the weight of it threatened to crush me.

But I took a deep breath, forcing my hands to unclench. This was no longer a matter that could be solved with words or peaceful negotiations.

This was my home. My sanctuary. My responsibility.

And I would not let Narrow Stone Peak destroy it.

I turned toward the shop, with Tianyi and Windy waiting patiently by the door. A quiet determination settled over me. From here on out, my plans would leave no room for failure.

CHAPTER THIRTY-FIVE

Moving in Silence

Days passed in a blur of preparations, every hour spent honing my plan. I moved deliberately, keeping a low profile and ensuring everything was ready.

Despite everything, I maintained the shop. Supplies were scarce, and even with my storage of dried herbs and extracted essences, it wouldn't last forever.

Still, the shop remained open. People stopped by, not to buy anything, but to offer their support in the ways they could. Mrs. Wang brought over a steaming pot of stew one morning, pressing it into my hands before I could protest.

Others dropped off small tokens; a basket of eggs, a bundle of firewood, and even a loaf of freshly baked bread. Some stayed to chat, like Xiao Bao and the other children. It was both heartwarming and humbling, but it also served as a constant reminder of why I couldn't fail.

But as Wei Long promised, he quietly left me alone, allowing me to work in peace.

As I expected, Lan-Yin and Wang Jun were among those who stopped by, though their visits were far from casual. They didn't bother with pretense, each of them entering the shop with an air of determination that left no room for pleasantries.

Lan-Yin leaned against the counter, her arms crossed as she fixed me with a pointed look. "So, are you going to tell us what's going on, or are we supposed to keep pretending nothing's wrong?"

Wang Jun stood nearby, his expression softer but no less concerned. "Lan-Yin's right. We're not blind. You've been avoiding us, and it's obvious you're planning something. Why not just tell us?"

I met their gazes, doing my best to appear calm. "I'm biding my time," I said simply, shrugging as though it were nothing. "There's nothing to worry about. When the time is right, I'll explain everything."

Lan-Yin's eyes narrowed, clearly unsatisfied with my answer. "Biding your time for what? Kai, we're your friends. If something's happening, we can help. You don't have to do this alone."

Wang Jun nodded in agreement. "Whatever it is, we're with you. You know that, right?"

Their sincerity was almost enough to make me break. Almost. But I couldn't risk involving them—not until I was certain my plan would work. The less they knew, the safer they'd be.

"I appreciate it, really," I said, forcing a smile. "But this is something I need to handle myself. Trust me, okay?"

Lan-Yin looked like she wanted to argue, but Wang Jun placed a hand on her shoulder, shaking his head. "Fine," she said reluctantly, pushing off the counter. "But don't think you're getting away with this forever. We'll be here when you're ready to talk."

To compensate for the absence of Elder Ming's morning training, I ran through the drills and visualized them in the Memory Palace technique, staying within my garden's perimeter.

With Wei Long potentially aware of Tianyi's presence, I couldn't leave my home unattended.

In the depths of my Memory Palace, I conjured the Five Fists and Wei Long. The process was painstaking, drawing from every scrap of observation I had of their techniques, their mannerisms, their strengths and weaknesses.

The Five Fists appeared first, their forms solidifying with every detail I could recall. Their brute force and tendency to favor grapples with overpowering moves stood at the forefront.

I started slow, rehearsing counters to their basic maneuvers. How they'd lunge for a grapple, or their aggressive barrages that forced me to parry and evade, my own movements calculated to exploit the slightest gap in their rhythm. Each sequence played out in vivid detail, their movements sharp and deliberate, as though they were truly alive.

But it wasn't enough. The Five Fists were third-class disciples—skilled, but far from the genuine danger.

With a deep breath, I let my imagination stretch, summoning a figure I'd never seen in action. Wei Long.

His form was hazy at first, an outline more than a man, but as I forced my mind to work, he took shape. I started with his demeanor—the way he carried himself, always calm, always calculating. I layered on what I knew of their style. Then I added the small tells I'd observed in our conversations; the way his stance shifted when he stood, balanced but ready, or the way his gaze lingered on people's weak points.

I pushed my imagination further, combining what I'd seen from the Five Fists with the refinement of a first-class disciple. Where their grapples were predictable, Wei Long's were fluid, adaptable. Where their strikes left themselves open, Wei Long's were precise, each one part of a larger strategy to corner and dismantle his opponent. I blended the Five Fists with shades of past opponents—Lan Sheng, Feng Wu, Ping Hai—to fully visualize the strength and technique of a first-class disciple.

The sparring began, and it was brutal. In my Memory Palace, Wei Long struck with a speed and ferocity that forced me to adapt on the fly. He didn't react to my moves—he anticipated them, countering before I could finish an attack. My strikes met empty air, and when I tried to evade, his grip found me anyway, locking me into a grapple that ended with me slammed into the ground.

Each defeat brought frustration, but also clarity. I replayed the scenarios, adjusting my movements, my timing. If he reached for a grapple, I visualized myself striking at his wrist, redirecting his momentum to create an opening. When his strikes came too fast to counter, I imagined myself retreating, using the environment—broken terrain, uneven footing—to slow him down.

Nevertheless, he won every single time.

But this wasn't about victory, not yet. It was about learning. Understanding. Each simulated fight sharpened my instincts, taught me to think faster, react smarter. It was a process of chipping away at the unknown, carving out a path forward.

I knew this wouldn't be enough. A Memory Palace visualization was no substitute for the real thing. The Wei Long I fought was a construct of my imagination, not the man himself. He would be faster, stronger, and far more cunning than anything I could predict. But it was a start. A step forward in the right direction.

By the time I pulled myself out of the Memory Palace, the sun was dipping low in the sky, painting the remnants of my garden in hues of gold and orange. I ached from hours of drills, and the intensity of my visualizations exhausted my mind. But beneath the fatigue was a quiet determination.

Brute strength or raw talent wouldn't take Wei Long and the Five Fists down. But with preparation, precision, and just enough unpredictability, I might stand a chance.

And then, early one afternoon, as I was preparing to head out, a familiar voice greeted me at the door.

Li Wei shifted slightly, scratching the back of his head as he met my gaze, his expression stilted, as if he were carefully choosing his words. "So . . . the greenhouse is done," he said, his tone direct but with subtle pride. "Because the structure was undamaged, we finished on time."

"I owe you and your father. What's the total? I know I've only paid for materials, and you said you'll determine the pay once it was complete."'

"No, uh—no need. It's fine. You don't . . . have to pay." I could see he was uncomfortable. "You should use the money on the garden. Getting it back on track. It'd be better that way."

I chuckled, trying again. "Come on, Li Wei. I can more than afford it. And you earned it, no question."

"The work was good. I enjoyed doing it." He paused, glancing up briefly. "It helped me gain a few levels in Harmonic Carpentry. Better than money, anyway. Think of it as paying my debt to you."

"Debt?" I barked out a laugh. "At what point have you ever owed me?"

Li Wei shifted nervously, his gaze flicking to the floor. He mumbled, as if embarrassed, "You probably don't remember." He looked up, forcing himself to continue, though his words came out haltingly. "It was years ago. I got really sick, fever was bad, thought I wouldn't . . . make it." He scratched his head, eyes darting to the side as if avoiding the intensity of the memory. "You came over and helped. Brought all these herbs, kept trying things out. Didn't ask for anything . . . except maybe help with your garden when the fences need to be fixed."

I blinked, the memory slowly resurfacing. I hadn't thought about it in years. It was just part of those early days, back when I was still figuring out how to fill the role of village herbalist. Back then, I'd taken on almost every case, desperate to learn, terrified of making a mistake after my parents had passed. When Li Wei had fallen sick, I'd been far from confident, and I'd used up nearly all my herbs trying different remedies.

"Li Wei," I said softly, remembering. "I . . . I just wanted to help. I didn't want anyone else in the village to lose family like I did. Think nothing of it."

He nodded, glancing down. "How could I? I wouldn't be here right now if it weren't for you. So, I'm . . . paying it back, I guess." He shrugged, his voice almost too casual. "Besides, now you can use the money for new seeds or plants. It's better."

A warmth spread through me, something grounding yet humbling. It was easy to forget the impact of those small gestures from so long ago, but here it was, circling back in a way I hadn't expected. I smiled, clapping him gently on the shoulder. "Thank you, Li Wei. But you're still getting those energy elixirs, whether or not you want them."

A small, awkward grin tugged at his lips. "Wouldn't say no to that." He paused, then added with more confidence, "But I'd rather you get the garden back up first."

The quiet determination in his voice strengthened my resolve. This village wasn't just a place to live; it was a community that looked out for each other, even when they didn't have to.

And now I knew exactly what I had to protect.

"Well." Li Wei shifted his weight. "What's first?"

I straightened up, feeling my focus returning. "Not planting," I said. "There's something I need to take care of first."

Li Wei gave me a small nod, his gaze lingering on me for a moment. I could see the question there, curiosity tempered by a quiet respect. But, true to his usual self, he didn't push, merely offered a quick "Let me know if you need help" before he turned and made his way down the path.

As his figure disappeared around the corner, I glanced back at the greenhouse, appreciating the sturdy, elegant structure. It was beautiful. An achievement that would nurture the future of my garden. And it only deepened my resolve to protect this village and everyone in it.

I stepped back into my house, closing the door quietly behind me. I'd made my preparations, but seeing that greenhouse completed reminded me of the responsibility I had.

It was time to act.

Pulling open a small drawer beneath my workbench, I retrieved five vials of a viscous liquid, carefully sealed and labeled, as well as two pills I'd prepared. I held each one in my hand for a moment, mentally reviewing their effects, their timing, every contingency I'd planned for. This would need precision.

"Tianyi, Windy," I called out, though I knew they were probably hiding or resting somewhere in the shadows of the house. "We'll wait until nightfall to make our move."

I tucked the vials into my satchel, ensuring they were secure. Tonight, I'd have to take my plans straight to the heart of the matter.

Narrow Stone Peak was going to get a response they wouldn't expect.

The evening passed slowly, each hour marked by a quiet tension as I went over my strategy one last time. Finally, as the last sliver of daylight faded from the sky, I made my way to the Soaring Swallow Teahouse.

As I stood in front of the door, I swallowed the two pills with a single gulp. They settled like a quiet pulse in my bloodstream, sharpening my senses and steadying my breath. Even my heartbeat felt measured, each beat a reminder of the control I needed tonight. No missteps.

I pushed the doors open.

The air was thick with the sounds of laughter and the clinking of cups as I entered. Only a few of the villagers were present. They quieted upon seeing me.

I spotted the Five Fists and Wei Long gathered at their usual table, already well into their meal, exchanging stories and toasts as if they hadn't a care in the world.

I took a slow breath, steadying myself before moving forward with practiced calm. As I approached their table, Lan-Yin noticed me first, her eyes widening slightly as I gave her a nod.

"Lan-Yin," I said with a warm smile, loud enough for the Five Fists to hear, "please serve them some of your best wine. I'll cover it."

Her brows furrowed slightly, the question clear in her eyes, but she nodded, going to fetch the bottles.

I took a cup as soon as she returned, raising it high. "I've come to a decision after these past few days. I've seen your dedication and persistence, and I'm moved. If Narrow Stone Peak is so dedicated to protecting Gentle Wind Village, then I would be honored to celebrate that commitment."

Silence fell over the table as the disciples exchanged surprised glances, Wei Long watching me with a guarded expression, as though trying to decipher my intentions.

"Let's toast to a new era for Gentle Wind Village," I directed, gesturing to Lan-Yin to fill everyone's cups.

The disciples raised their cups in a tentative toast and I mirrored their gesture, feeling the weight of my own plans solidify.

As I raised my cup to toast, I caught Wei Long's gaze. His eyes narrowed, suspicion flickering beneath his polite smile. He was trying to read me, to pick apart my words for hidden meanings. I met his gaze with a calm I didn't fully feel, letting the silence stretch just a moment too long before I took a deliberate sip of my drink.

CHAPTER THIRTY-SIX

Drinking Games and Hidden Aims

Downing another cup, I savored the taste as it spread warmth through my chest, helping to smooth out the tension that prickled along my spine. I caught Gu Bei's eye, raised my cup in a cheerful toast, and clinked it against his.

He smirked, clearly amused, but Wei Long's sharp gaze stayed fixed on me, observing with a calculating intensity that didn't waver. I felt his eyes studying every shift in my expression, every movement, as though he was peeling back my words, layer by layer.

"So," Wei Long began, his tone casual but edged with something keener, "what brought on this change of heart? Last we spoke, you seemed reluctant. Has something . . . *happened* since then?"

Feigning a thoughtful pause, I poured myself another cup, letting the silence drag out just long enough to seem genuine. I raised the cup in salute to Wei Long before taking a slow, deliberate sip, then set it down with a bright, amiable smile despite the dampening on my back.

"Well, I suppose you could say I've been a little . . . rattled. This break-in shook me up more than I expected. Just when I thought things had settled, someone comes along to tear it all apart." I chuckled, leaning back and shrugging with a bit of exaggerated exasperation. "And I realized I might have been stubborn. It's not easy admitting you need help."

Wei Long's eyes narrowed, but he let me continue, his interest piqued.

"It's strange, really," I said, raising the next cup and clinking it lightly with another member of the Five Fists adjacent to me. "I thought I could manage it on my own, but after everything, well . . . I suppose the events at the Verdant Lotus Sect only added to it."

I glanced around, catching a few curious glances from the Five Fists as I took another sip. I made sure to let the words come out casually, as if it were just an offhand detail.

"Oh?" Wei Long tilted his head, his smirk fading into a look of intrigue. "What events, if you don't mind sharing?"

I set down my cup and leaned forward, putting on a rueful smile. "I went to the Grand Alchemy Gauntlet, you know? It's where I had my run-in with these guys. I thought getting in as a sponsored contestant might open some doors, and maybe secure me a position as an official member of the Verdant Lotus Sect. But . . . they didn't want me. Said I was too old." I let a hint of bitterness seep into my tone, shaking my head slowly. "Imagine that. Too old. As if all that matters is a number."

One disciple at the table muttered under his breath, shaking his head as though commiserating with me. Wei Long, however, continued to study me, his expression caught somewhere between sympathy and suspicion.

"Of course," I continued, brightening a bit, "you all don't seem so narrow-minded." I lifted my cup again, casting an appreciative look at Wei Long. "It's refreshing to meet a sect that can see beyond age and acknowledges potential where it lies. The fact you're extending an offer of protection when they didn't is also telling."

"That's right! Narrow Stone Peak doesn't discriminate!"

Gu Bei raised his cup to that, and a few of the others followed suit, nodding along with murmurs of agreement. Wei Long, however, kept his eyes on me, his expression thoughtful as he took a slow sip from his own drink.

"A practical outlook," I added, leaning back again, crossing my arms casually. "The Verdant Lotus Sect is all well and good, but they're rigid. Bound by old customs, as you all know. A place like Narrow Stone Peak seems to value more than just pedigree or youthful promise." I allowed my gaze to drift over the disciples, as if including them all in my praise.

Wei Long's lips twitched into a faint smile, and he inclined his head slightly, acknowledging the compliment, but his eyes still hadn't left mine.

"Interesting," he murmured. "And here I thought you'd have more loyalty to the Verdant Lotus Sect, considering your history. It seems ridiculous they'd let a talent like you slip through."

I let out a light laugh, brushing the comment off with a wave of my hand. "Oh, I wouldn't say I resent the Verdant Lotus Sect for that. They have their strengths, of course, and I respect them for it. But let's just say I'm interested in exploring other options now that their door is closed to me."

I shot Gu Bei a sly grin. "After all, I might need stronger training partners to get better. If I can already beat you, I'd ask Wei Long to trade pointers with me instead."

Gu Bei scoffed, his cheeks coloring slightly. "Hold your own? You caught me off guard, that's all. I was holding back."

"Oh, sure you were," I replied, grinning as I nudged his shoulder. The table broke into laughter, the tension softening a bit as the disciples joined in, enjoying the playful back-and-forth. Even the first-class disciple's serious expression relaxed for a moment, his lips curving into an amused smile.

The laughter faded, and Wei Long refocused on me, his gaze as sharp as ever. "So . . . if you're seriously considering our offer, perhaps we should discuss specific terms. You mentioned training, but how often would you want access to our resources? And in return, what level of commitment—"

I held up a hand, cutting him off with a casual wave. "Ah, come on. Let's leave the details for later, yeah? I'd much rather focus on celebrating tonight than getting bogged down in the fine print. Besides," I added, leaning back with a languid smile, "being the village's lone protector is a heavy load. I'd prefer to enjoy the idea of a lighter burden for just a little while longer."

Wei Long blinked, surprised by the response, but quickly composed himself. "I suppose I can't argue with that." He turned to Lan-Yin and raised his hand, signaling for more food. "Then let's enjoy ourselves properly," he announced, raising his cup in another toast. "To Gentle Wind Village and new alliances."

Lan-Yin appeared moments later with plates piled high with fragrant dishes—steamed buns, sizzling meat skewers, and bowls of colorful pickled vegetables—all set out in front of us. The Five Fists wasted no time digging in, eagerly toasting to everything from village prosperity to, ironically, their "impeccable reputation."

Through it all, Wei Long's attention kept drifting back to me, but I sidestepped each of his probing questions, steering the conversation toward more superficial topics. I even teased two other disciples, laughing and joking as though I didn't have a plan brewing in the back of my mind.

For the moment, all I had to do was keep this charade going.

Hours passed, and the alcohol continued to flow.

"Next thing you know," I continued, gesturing wildly with my hands, "the furnace just starts rolling down the arena! This poor guy had no idea what hit him, just turned around, and—bam! I thought I saw his teeth fly out, but it was just the pills he was carrying!"

The table erupted into laughter, and I joined in, chuckling harder than I had in weeks. Even Gu Bei slapped the table, eyes watering as he struggled to catch his breath.

Wei Long, though, remained as sober as he had been since the night began, a faint smile playing at his lips but his gaze still piercing. He cleared his throat, standing up with a slight stretch.

"Well, it's been entertaining," he said smoothly, glancing down at his disciples, who were clearly feeling the effects of the evening's drinks. "But some of us need to keep our wits about us. I trust you will behave yourselves." He pointedly looked at the Five Fists, who were now slouched over their plates, grinning drowsily. "I'll leave you to enjoy the night, but tomorrow, we can discuss more specifics. The . . . *protection* of Gentle Wind Village should be well planned."

Feigning disappointment, I reached for another cup. "Wei Long! The night's still young! Surely you're not heading off already?"

He raised an eyebrow. "Unlike some, I have more to consider than simply feasting," he replied coolly, offering a subtle nod. "Rest well. Tomorrow, then."

I clinked my cup with his, hiding my satisfaction behind a sloppy grin. "Tomorrow it is."

Wei Long made his way out, leaving the Five Fists and me behind. The moment his footsteps faded upstairs, I turned to the disciples, a devilish glint in my eyes. "All right, gentlemen, how about I show you around a bit? You're here to help protect the village, so let me take you to the best spots."

The Five Fists looked at each other, then shrugged and nodded, clearly too tipsy to question anything. But first, I excused myself, making a show of staggering toward the counter where Lan-Yin was watching with a frown.

"Kai, what are you doing?" she whispered urgently as I handed her a handful of coins. "Have you gone insane?"

I dropped the drunken act for just a moment, leaning in close. "Trust me, Lan-Yin. Just keep things as is and pretend everything's normal."

She hesitated but nodded, watching me with worried eyes. I gave her a quick wink before slipping back into my act, stumbling slightly as I rejoined the disciples and led them toward the door.

"Gentlemen!" I called cheerfully, heading outside with them in tow. "Tonight, we see the heart of Gentle Wind Village."

Inside, though, my mind was calculating as I prepared for the next steps of my plan.

We moved through the quiet village, the soft glow of lanterns casting long shadows as I guided the Five Fists toward the outskirts where I lived. I kept up my cheerful, half-drunken facade, gesturing grandly at every corner and tree as if each held some hidden significance. The disciples seemed content, ambling along and laughing among themselves as I shared stories about the villagers as we passed by them.

Soon, we arrived at my home, and I ushered them toward the greenhouse. Its structure gleamed under the moonlight, a sturdy, beautiful reminder of what I'd worked so hard to protect.

"This," I said with a sweep of my hand, "is my pride and joy. Plants for every ailment, every condition. I even have a few that are a little . . . rare." I lowered my voice conspiratorially, winking at them. "If you're nice to me, maybe I'll share a cutting or two."

They chuckled, peering into the greenhouse with drunken curiosity. I pointed out some plants, sharing lighthearted stories about their supposed origins and effects. They laughed and jeered good-naturedly, thoroughly entertained.

As we moved farther past the village boundaries, the conversation turned to the break-in.

"You know," I began, slurring slightly for effect, "I can't believe someone had the guts to break into my garden. Middle of the night, sneaky-like, and they still didn't take anything useful. Who does that?"

One disciple chuckled. "Probably some poor idiot looking for a quick haul and got scared off."

I shook my head dramatically, stopping to turn and face them. "Scared off, huh? Then why destroy the garden? They smashed plants, trampled paths . . . like they wanted to send a message." I let the words hang in the air for a moment, glancing between them with exaggerated curiosity. "Any of you ever seen something like that before?"

Gu Bei, emboldened by the alcohol, snorted. "Happens all the time. You step into the wrong territory, you get what's coming to you."

I paused, furrowing my brow as if struggling to recall something. "Wei Long mentioned that the intruder used a weapon. He dropped a . . . a . . . What was it?" I scratched my head, exaggerating my seeming confusion.

"A blade?" one disciple suggested, filling in the blank.

"Ah! Yes!" I snapped my fingers, pretending to recall. "A blade! What a fool, dropping something so crucial during an escape." I scoffed. "But maybe he panicked, huh?"

One of the Five Fists, a bit more loosened up by the drink than the others, nodded enthusiastically. "Oh, definitely! Especially when that woman hit him, he must've lost his nerve and ran off."

There it was.

Gu Bei groaned, pulling a hand down his face. "You're drunk, Wen. Don't start talking nonsense."

"Woman?" I asked slowly. "What woman?"

The disciple's face paled as he tried to backpedal, but it was too late. I continued, my tone now icily calm. "And about that blade . . . Wei Long never actually said there was one. If there was, where would it have gone?"

They exchanged panicked glances, their intoxicated stupor vanishing as they struggled to find an answer. Behind them, a soft hiss and rustling filled the silence, and they turned to find themselves face-to-face with Tianyi and Windy, blocking their retreat to the village.

Tianyi's wings shimmered ominously in the dim light, her gaze unblinking as she held her ground. Beside her, Windy coiled, his scales gleaming, his eyes coldly watching the men stumble backward as they realized their escape was blocked.

I stepped forward, all pretense of drunkenness gone, as I folded my arms, looking at each of them in turn.

"So," I said quietly, "why don't we talk a bit more? I'm sure there's plenty you'd like to tell me."

CHAPTER THIRTY-SEVEN

The Thin Line

Gu Bei went pale, his eyes darting around, desperately searching for a way out. "It was just . . . you know . . . a slip of the tongue," he stammered clumsily. "We've all been drinking, and sometimes you say things you don't mean . . ."

I stepped closer, letting the threat hang between us. My eyes never left his. "Save it," I said, my voice cold. "I already know what happened. And unless you'd like to spend the next fifteen minutes struggling to breathe, I suggest you start talking."

I pulled out the vials from my sleeve, holding it up in the moonlight. The liquid inside was a sickly, pale yellow, catching the light with an eerie gleam.

"Do you feel it yet? The shaky breathing? The rapid beating of your heart?" I raised an eyebrow, watching as realization dawned on their faces. "In a few more minutes, that'll be the least of your problems. Soon, the spasms will start. Your lungs will burn, nausea will take over, and then the vomiting . . . and the blood. It'll be excruciating. A slow, painful death."

One of them clutched his stomach, panting, while another sputtered.

"You . . . poisoned us? When?"

A flash of panic crossed their faces. They looked at each other, half believing, half doubting. Watching them quake under my words, I felt a faint bitter satisfaction. But it left a sour taste in my mouth.

But the memory of my garden—ruined, trampled underfoot, all for control, for someone else's gain—reignited the anger within me.

Elder Ming's warning of the Jianghu was right: Righteousness could only go so far. Sometimes you had to fight fire with fire.

Is this what I'm becoming?

I pushed the thought aside, but it lingered, shadowing the edges of my satisfaction.

I saw the fear in their eyes; none of them were willing to test me. I gave the vial a little shake, letting the liquid inside slosh ominously. "And before you get any ideas," I continued, "if you try to take this antidote from me, I'll throw it on the ground. You'd be out of options, left to writhe here until morning. You have my word as an alchemist."

Their backs pressed against the greenhouse wall, and I could see them cornered, visibly rattled. Tianyi and Windy loomed behind them, each a silent threat in the darkness. Windy let out a low, venomous hiss, and I saw four of the disciples flinch, their eyes wide with a fear that ran deeper than I'd thought. Whatever it was, I could see the terror plain on their faces.

Gu Bei swallowed hard. His voice cracked when he spoke. "Fine. You win. What . . . what do you want to know?"

My fists clenched at my sides. I'd tried to keep my anger in check, but the sight of them, their deceit, their arrogance—it stirred something in me that refused to stay quiet.

"You think you can come here, threaten my village, attack my home, and I'll just *let it go*?" I sounded calm, too calm, but every word was sharp enough to cut. "I want to know why you sent someone to destroy the greenhouse. I want to know what else you're hiding and why the hell you think you can invade this place and control it."

Gu Bei's brave front crumbled as fear contorted his features. "I—I don't know why! We were just following orders. Senior Brother Wei Long told us to chase off Zhao Wen, our Senior Brother who was . . . pretending to be a bandit. Make sure he gets away. That's all I know."

I narrowed my eyes. "And where is this *Senior Brother* of yours hiding now? What does he look like?"

With a desperate glance at his companions for support, the bald disciple hesitated. They only looked back at him with wide, fearful eyes, just as trapped. He looked at me, his mouth twitching, clearly hesitant to reveal more than he should.

I slowly lifted my hand, the vials clinking faintly. I kept my gaze steady. "Last chance. You're all running out of time."

One ashen-faced disciple couldn't take it any longer. "He's staying at the Green Peak Inn! East of here, by the mountain pass leading up to Narrow Stone Peak." With desperation, he spilled words out in a torrent. "He has a scar on his upper lip—a-and bushy eyebrows! That's all we know!"

I looked over to my butterfly companion. "Tianyi?"

She glanced at Windy, and the two shared a silent conversation as the serpent stuck his tongue out repeatedly, pointing his head off into the sky—to the east.

The disciples weren't lying.

I nodded, letting the silence settle heavily before tossing the vials at their feet. They scrambled to snatch them up, frantically uncorking the antidotes and drinking the contents like men starving for air. The relief in their eyes was fleeting; within moments, their eyelids drooped. Their bodies swayed, weakly fighting against the sedative effect of the "antidote" before they finally slumped to the ground in a scattered, unconscious heap.

I took a long, controlled breath, taking in the scene before me. Zhao Wen. The final missing link in this conspiracy.

With a last glance at the slumbering disciples, I turned to Tianyi. "Help me move them."

One by one, I lugged each of the men onto the cart.

She stared at them for a moment too long, as if inspecting. "These men . . ."

"No, they're not dead." I waved her off, guessing what she was about to ask. "Fed them a sleeping aid. They'll be out for the next day, minimum."

She shook her head. "No, I recognize them. They're the ones from the . . . city. The ones who hurt you. Now they're here." Tianyi's wings shimmered, and she cocked her head, her expression turning oddly detached. "Should I kill them?"

Her question hung in the air, and for a moment, it felt like a bucket of ice water had been thrown over my rage. *Kill them?* Even in the haze of anger, the words jarred me, sank into me in a way I didn't want to admit. I'd come this far, but . . . had it really come to that?

"No," I said, and even as the word left my mouth, the doubt gnawed at me. How far was I willing to go to protect my home? What lines was I willing to cross? I'd thought I knew, but each step down this path left me wondering who I'd be at the end. "It'll make things worse for us."

She shrugged, unbothered. "Then . . . on the cart, as you said."

Once we'd loaded the unconscious disciples, I made my way back to the Soaring Swallow with the cart in tow.

Tianyi froze suddenly, antennae twitching in that subtle, telltale way. Before I could react, her form shimmered, wings folding tight against her back as she slipped out of sight with practiced grace. She was gone, leaving behind the faintest trace of glimmering qi in her wake.

When Lan-Yin spotted me and the limp bodies of the disciples, she immediately walked over, arching an eyebrow.

"They had a bit too much to drink," I explained with a casual shrug. "They'll sleep it off here. Mind watching them until the morning?"

Her expression shifted from surprise to suspicion as her gaze swept over the men and then back to me. "Kai Liu, tell me you didn't slip something into their drinks. I swear, if you poisoned our alcohol supply without telling me, I'm banning you from my teahouse for life. And how aren't you drunk? You drank half your body weight in alcohol keeping up with these oafs."

I held up my hands. "Swallowed a couple of pills with arrowroot and ginkgo leaf extract before I started; nothing short of Master Qiang's rice wine in a barrel could get me drunk right now. And it's not poison, Lan-Yin. Just a little lie. I told them they'd been poisoned, and they believed me. Desperation does the trick sometimes."

The Five Fists didn't look like the smartest or bravest. Tricking them like this, especially when they were so drunk, was easy to do.

Her narrow-eyed look cleared, but her frown didn't. "What are you planning? You've been silent this past week, and now this . . . Is it so hard to let us know when you're doing something? We can help you, you know."

She'd never seen me like this. Truth be told, I'd never seen myself like this either. Normally, I kept everything in the open. But here I was, keeping my friends in the dark, working in the shadows. I tried to shrug it off with a smile for her, but I could feel the weight of it settling deeper.

I nodded apologetically, glancing down at the slumped disciples. "It's hard. When they're patrolling the village so often, monitoring me . . . That's why I can't waste any more time. I need to get things finalized before it's too late. But don't worry. I'm not acting alone."

She paused, then leaned in, her voice hushed. "Where are you going?"

"East," I replied simply, leaving her with a slight nod before slipping away. From my peripheral, I could see her grabbing one of the Five Fists and heaving them over her shoulder, bringing them into the Soaring Swallow.

I moved through the village's quiet streets until I reached Elder Wen's stable, where the horses rested with their heads low, puffs of warm breath misting the frigid air. With an apologetic mutter, I led one out, patting its side before mounting it. Tianyi emerged from the shadows behind the stable, her pale form gliding soundlessly over the frost-bitten ground. Without a word, she leapt lightly onto the front of the saddle, perching cross-legged, while Windy coiled around my arm, his tongue flicking the air in readiness.

With a quiet nudge, the horse surged forward, and we cut a silent path toward the east.

Hours passed under the cover of night, and I pushed the horse harder, determined to reach the Green Peak Inn before dawn. I kept my gaze sharp, my mind set on the plan unfolding ahead of me. The snowfall intensified, collecting on my shoulders and the horse's mane as we pushed onward.

As the snow thickened around me, muffling the world in icy silence, my thoughts grew louder. Zhao Wen's name lingered bitterly on my tongue. Was this the right choice?

The frigid air bit through my cloak, each gust of wind carrying a chill that crept under my collar and settled deep into my bones. Tianyi huddled close to me, her wings pulled tight against the cold, while Windy coiled a little tighter around my arm, his scales warm against my skin.

The Green Peak Inn finally loomed ahead, a solitary silhouette nestled against the mountainside. It looked desolate in the pale dawn light, its wooden frame frosted over, the windows dark save for a faint glow leaking from within.

The inn was closed.

"So, how am I going about this?" I asked myself.

I couldn't just barge in, after all. I looked at my status.

> *Heavenly Interface: Kai Liu*
> *Perk(s):*
> *Interface Manipulator—Allows manipulation of the Heavenly Interface and access to special features.*
> *Dao Pioneer—Grants a unique status that softens the rigid thresholds that usually constrain skill acquisition and evolution, allowing for more fluid and spontaneous development of skills and cultivation techniques.*
> *Race: Human*
> *Vitality: Sufficient*
> *Primary*
> *Affinity—Wood*
> *Cultivation Rank: Mortal Realm—Rank 5*
> *Qi: Qi Initiation Stage—Rank 5 (. . .)*
> *Mind: Qi Initiation Stage—Rank 2 (. . .)*
> *Body: Mortal Realm—Rank 4 (. . .)*
> *Skills*
> *Spiritual Herbalism—5 (. . .)*
> *Nature's Attunement—4 (. . .)*
> *Accelerated Reading—8 (. . .)*
> *Cultivation Techniques*
> *Rooted Banyan Stance—3 (. . .)*
> *Crimson Lotus Purification—1 (. . .)*
> *Bamboo Reprisal Counter—1 (. . .)*
> *Memory Palace Technique—1 (. . .)*
> *Refinement Simulation Technique—1 (. . .)*
> *Currency*
> *Technique Token—1*

Based on the Five Fists and Tianyi's information, this Zhao Wen was a second-class disciple. Even after all my training, could I deal with someone of that caliber?

I shook my head. It wasn't the time to get cold feet.

Dismounting, I guided Elder Wen's horse to the side and gave it a grateful pat, letting it rest under the shelter of a nearby tree. I took out the Verdant Lotus Sect's charm, the proof of my friendship with them. I'd carried it around as a good luck charm, but tonight . . .

I gathered myself, tying my hair back in a style that mimicked Feng Wu's, neater and more disciplined, knowing that for this to work, I needed to look the part.

Taking a deep breath, I strode to the door and knocked, crisply and persistently, until the innkeeper finally answered. His face, flushed from sleep and irritated by the interruption, peered out into the cold, his frown deepening as he took me in.

"What is it you want at this hour?" he grumbled, rubbing his eyes.

Adopting a formal, serious tone, I replied, "I am Lan Sheng, disciple of the Verdant Lotus Sect. These two are my companions, and our presence here is a matter of urgency."

The innkeeper's irritation faltered, but his expression changed to suspicion. "The Verdant Lotus Sect?"

I held up my token from the Verdant Lotus Sect, the intricately etched lotus catching his attention immediately. The innkeeper's hesitation flickered, but I saw the faintest nod of recognition in his eyes. He knew what it meant. Even if he doubted my claim, he wouldn't risk opposing the authority of the Verdant Lotus Sect.

"Word has reached us that a dangerous criminal may be hiding in these mountains. He's posing as a disciple of Narrow Stone Peak, which is likely why he has escaped your notice so far. I ask that you assist us in locating him before more harm is done."

The innkeeper's eyes flickered toward the shadows inside the building. His hand lingered on the doorframe. "I—I don't know who you're talking about," he said, but there was a tremor in his voice that told me otherwise. "My inn wouldn't house any criminals. We're a reputable establishment."

"You're lying," I said softly, stepping closer. Tianyi's wings rustled, her presence adding weight to my words. "If you protect him, you'll be sharing in his crimes. Is that what you want?"

The innkeeper squinted, his skepticism lingering, but he was visibly more unsettled. "What exactly does this fellow look like?"

I nodded, as if expecting the question. "Bushy eyebrows and a scar on his upper lip. He may be visibly injured, walking with a limp."

The innkeeper's eyes widened briefly. Barely a flicker, but enough for me to catch. I pressed on, speaking with a slight edge of urgency. "This man is wanted for murder and robbery. His presence here puts everyone at risk. Please. Tell me what you know."

He blanched and then gulped, his eyes darting toward the shadows within the inn. His voice dropped to a whisper.

"There is . . . someone."

Zhao Wen lay sprawled on the thin mattress, his breathing shallow and uneven as he stared up at the ceiling. His ribs throbbed with a dull ache, each pulse a reminder of the brutal encounter he hadn't been prepared for. The image of her eyes—cold, unblinking, and predatory—lingered in his mind, piercing through the haze of his pain. The woman had been unlike anything he'd ever faced.

The ever-calm, unyielding voice of his Senior Brother played in his memory.

Lie low. Burn everything after you read it. Leave nothing for them to trace back to us.

Zhao Wen scoffed bitterly, his lips curling into a grimace. *Lie low.* As if lying here, half-broken, could be called anything else.

He turned his head, eyes settling on the small brazier in the corner of the room. The faint embers glowed dimly beneath a layer of ash, barely warming the cold air around him. In those ashes lay the remnants of Wei Long's last letter: burnt scraps scattered with meticulous care, just as instructed.

He muttered curses under his breath, the bitter taste of resentment rising unbidden. Wei Long always had the perfect plan, the perfect orders. But why did they always seem to leave Zhao Wen as the one doing the dirty work?

"Why hadn't Senior Brother informed me?"

The orders had been clear and brokered no room for negotiation. Zhao Wen was to wait here, stay hidden, and await further instruction. But waiting was agony. Every creak of the inn's old wood set his nerves on edge.

Suddenly, a sound broke the silence. Soft footsteps up the stairs, drawing closer, echoing in the quiet of the night. Zhao Wen tensed, the hair on his arms prickling. The steps stopped right outside his door.

His pulse quickened. For a moment, he thought of remaining still, hoping they'd leave. But the silence stretched unbearably, each second pressing down on him until his nerves snapped.

The door exploded inward with a deafening crack, splinters flying in every direction. Zhao Wen's eyes widened as his worst fears materialized in the doorway. Her. The woman with those piercing eyes, flanked by the serpent and a boy in maroon robes.

No words were spoken. They didn't need to be.

Zhao Wen threw the blanket forward, a desperate attempt to shield himself as he moved. But before he could take another step, a sharp, tightening pressure coiled around his arm. Serpentine scales glinted in the faint light, wrapping around his wrist like a vise.

Pain blossomed in his side as a fist drove into his ribs, and Zhao Wen's strangled cry filled the air before the world turned dark.

CHAPTER THIRTY-EIGHT

Breaking Point

With Zhao Wen bound and gagged, slumped unconscious against the horse's side, I mounted up and set out back to the village. My thoughts were a steady hum, all fixed on one purpose. Each passing mile stoked the fire inside me.

My fists gripped the reins even tighter, feeling the weight of the impending confrontation. I had sent letters through the Azure Silk Trading Company, informing Huan to be discrete and fast, but there was no guarantee they'd arrive in time—or at all.

"It's been three days since I sent the letters," I mused, gazing at the horizon. "If they received them, they should arrive today."

Still, today was the day Narrow Stone Peak would be exposed. Whether or not they arrived.

Hours later, the sky had lightened, casting a thin morning glow over the village square as I entered, Zhao Wen tied behind me like a heavy, irrefutable truth.

Villagers were already stirring, watching me in confusion, faces peeking out of doorways and windows, some beginning to follow as I made my way toward the center of the square.

I pulled the horse to a stop, hopped down, and with one strong tug, dragged Zhao Wen off the horse, dumping him unceremoniously onto the ground. The villagers gasped, inching closer. Some murmured, recognizing him. Others stared at me, their shock mingling with concern, as they saw the quiet rage on my face.

"Is that my horse?"

I softened my expression. "Sorry, Elder Wen. I had to borrow it for an emergency. I'll make it up to you, I promise. But . . ." I looked at the small crowd that formed. "I need your help now. Please wake everyone else up. I've caught the culprit who attacked my garden last night."

The murmurs grew louder, and within moments, villagers spread the word, hurrying to rouse the rest. Soon enough, familiar faces started arriving in the square. Lan-Yin and Wang Jun pushed through the growing crowd to stand beside me, their faces marked with both worry and curiosity. Elder Ming appeared soon after, his expression pensive as he took in the scene.

Lan-Yin shot me a questioning look, glancing at the woman standing close behind me, her form both familiar and strange. "Kai, what's . . . going on? And who's she?"

I turned, my expression softening as I glanced at Tianyi, who stood calmly, her gaze steady as she regarded the villagers. Her wings remained folded underneath her robe and her hair shimmered in the dawn light with a bluish tint.

"This man," I said, gesturing at the bound Zhao Wen, "is the bandit who attacked my garden."

Gasps and mutters filled the air, but I pressed on, ignoring them. "As for the woman beside me . . . This is Tianyi."

A fresh wave of murmurs rippled through the villagers. Wang Jun's eyes widened, and even Elder Ming's normally composed expression slipped, surprise evident as he took in Tianyi's new form.

I could see Li Wei peeking out from the crowd, his eyes flitting back and forth between the man on the floor and Tianyi.

"She achieved a human form not too long ago," I explained. I couldn't keep the pride out of my voice. "I had to keep it hidden because of the Narrow Stone Peak cultivators. I couldn't risk them finding out, and there was never a right moment to discuss it."

Just then, a stir at the edge of the crowd caught my attention. Someone pushed past the villagers, forcing a path through the throng. Wei Long. His face was a mix of confusion and irritation, but as he reached the front of the crowd, his gaze fell on Zhao Wen, bound on the ground. His expression morphed, disbelief flashing to anger, before quickly being suppressed into a cool mask.

He opened his mouth to speak, but I raised a hand, stopping him before he could get a word out.

"We all need to hear this," I said, my voice ringing clear. "Zhao Wen, this man who attacked my garden, isn't just *any* bandit. He's one of their own—a Narrow Stone Peak disciple, sent here to intimidate this village into asking for their *protection*."

The crowd erupted in angry whispers, disbelief laced with shock. Some faces turned accusingly toward Wei Long, who seemed momentarily caught off guard by the accusation.

He forced a smile, attempting to regain his composure. "This is absurd. You bring an injured man before the village, make wild accusations, and expect everyone to just believe it?"

"Then tell me, Wei Long," I said, my voice steely, "do you truly not know this man? Zhao Wen. Does that name mean nothing to you?"

Wei Long's smile wavered, but he held his composure. "He could be anyone. A bandit with some skill, maybe, but he's no disciple of ours. You can't prove he's connected to us. We are a righteous sect."

I scoffed, gripping Zhao Wen by the hair and forcing his unconscious face into view for the crowd to see. "Is that so? Well, if he's just some regular bandit, then there's no harm in making sure he *never* attacks anyone else, is there?"

I felt the anger twist inside me, something dark, something I hadn't felt before.

"Why don't I just destroy his dantian? Right here. Right now."

The murmurs of the crowd fell into a stunned silence. Everyone's eyes fixed on me. I didn't look away. My gaze remained locked on Wei Long, daring him to challenge me.

His face remained calm, but his jaw tightened. "That's a drastic measure, Kai," he replied, his voice smooth but strained. "Destroying a man's dantian . . . That's as good as sentencing him to death. And we don't even know for sure if this is the man who—"

"I don't need your confirmation," I cut in. I was done with his games, his lies. "I know he's the one. Tianyi and Windy tracked him, and they don't lie." My hand gripped Zhao Wen's hair tighter, a part of me sickened by the act but refusing to let it show. "And are you saying you don't trust their judgment? Or mine?"

I could feel Elder Ming's gaze on me, his eyes shadowed. The silence between us was heavy, but I didn't back down. I had to show them all that I would not be toyed with, that my village and everything I cared about weren't just pawns in someone else's scheme.

Wei Long's expression flickered, a hint of unease betraying his mask of composure. He took a breath, visibly attempting to regain control. "Kai," he began, softer now, attempting a conciliatory tone, "think carefully. This man may not even be the one responsible. There's no obvious proof, and you wouldn't want to harm an innocent person."

"Innocent?" I asked in disbelief. "Don't insult me. I have *nothing* to gain from attacking some random man. But I heard the truth, straight from the mouths of the Five Fists. Green Peak Inn, east of the village. How do you think I got the information?"

The first-class disciple bit his lip, closing his eyes tightly.

I leaned forward, the anger clear in my voice, unfiltered and sharp. "So here's the choice, Wei Long. Either you let me destroy his dantian, ensuring he can't hurt anyone again, or you admit what he really is—a Narrow Stone Peak disciple sent here on your orders."

His eyes darted around, searching for an escape, but there was none.

I'd backed him into a corner, and I wasn't about to let him slip out of it. There was no doubt: Wei Long was a sly man. Savvy, just like Elder Jun. The more time I gave him, the more dangerous it became.

"No answer? Don't worry. I'll make the choice for you."

"Wai—!"

I rolled Zhao Wen onto his back, my fist tightening, letting the rush of qi fill my arm. I located his dantian, marking the spot with a cold certainty. My fist raised high, I prepared to bring it down, and—

BAM!

A deafening crack split the air as flesh met flesh.

The world turned upside down, and I flew backward, crashing into the crowd with a force that jarred every bone in my body. Tianyi had caught me in midair, killing some of my momentum.

Through blurred vision, I saw Wei Long standing tall, his arm still outstretched, the faint hum of qi dissipating from his fist as he stood over Zhao Wen protectively.

I saw Windy, a blur of white and blue wrapped around Wei Long's arm in a vise grip. Wei Long's gaze flicked to Windy, irritation flashing across his face as he flexed his arm, tensing against the snake's crushing grip. His arm bulged, muscles straining as he moved to grab Windy, but the serpent slipped free with a quick twist, retreating with a venomous hiss, his scales flashing under the morning light.

Wei Long stood before me, his face unreadable but for the tight line of his jaw. The speed, the power of his punch—it had all happened in a single breath. And now he was there, unshaken, while I was reeling.

But the damage was done.

By protecting Zhao Wen and attacking me, he confirmed my suspicions.

The man's eyes darkened as he stood there, realizing the implications of his actions, same as I did.

I got up, heart hammering in my chest. "If this isn't proof, what is? Admit it! Admit you tried to use my village as your foothold!" My fists shook as I stared Wei Long down, daring him to deny it again.

A small high-pitched voice pierced the tension like a sharp knife: "Bully!"

All heads turned to the source. Standing near the edge of the crowd, his tiny frame trembling but his voice unwavering, was Xiao Bao. Defiance flushed his face, and he clenched his fists tightly at his sides. "You think you can scare us? My dad says we don't need you!" Xiao Bao shouted. "And—and your hair is stupid!"

The crowd murmured, a ripple of agreement spreading through the villagers. Wei Long's mask of composure cracked for a fraction of a second, his eyes narrowing at the boy.

"Out of the mouths of babes, huh?" Master Qiang's deep, booming voice followed, drawing all eyes to the blacksmith as he stepped forward, his broad shoulders like a wall of iron. "I always knew there was something off about you lot. Too much talk about protection, not enough action when it mattered. If you were really here to help, you wouldn't be standing there trying to worm your way out of this."

The crowd stirred again, louder now.

"That's right!" Jian Wei, Li Wei's father, called out, his voice quivering with anger. He stepped forward, pointing an accusatory finger at Wei Long. "You dare come into our village, into our homes, and try to destroy what we've built with your schemes? How dare you!"

Other voices joined in, growing bolder by the second.

"You think we're weak because we're a small village?"

"This is our home, and we won't let you take it!"

"You call yourselves righteous, but your actions are as rotten as the worst bandits!"

Wei Long's jaw tightened, his eyes darting across the growing crowd, the realization sinking in that the villagers' anger had reached a boiling point.

The crowd closed in behind me, faces hardening with resolve. Lan-Yin and Wang Jun stepped forward, each of them tense and ready, and even Elder Ming took a step closer, his face lined with a grim determination I'd rarely seen.

Wei Long's gaze swept over the crowd, assessing the mounting hostility. His eyes narrowed, and his calm mask cracked, revealing a sneer that twisted his face. He lowered his arm, rubbing his wrist where Windy had coiled, then met my gaze with a cold glint in his eyes.

"Why couldn't you just hand over this village without a fight?" he asked. He sounded different. Rough, biting, a veneer of civility stripped away. "You think you're a hero? All this, all of it, would've been easier if you'd just kept your head down and accepted your place."

"Accepted my place?" I spat, taking a step forward. "My place is here, with the people who trust me. Not under the boot of your sect."

Wei Long's sneer deepened, his expression darkening further.

"Then you've made your choice. All of you have." He cast a scornful glance around at the villagers, who edged back slightly but held firm. "This is where it ends, Kai. I gave you a chance to avoid all this bloodshed. Now it's out of my hands."

His threat was plain, raw with the implication of violence, but I didn't flinch. Behind me, I felt the unwavering presence of my friends and neighbors, the people I'd fought for, protected, and who stood by me now.

Wei Long looked back at me, his voice dropping to a sinister murmur. "You think numbers will help you? You think this is some fairy tale where you all charge me, and I just lie down in defeat? I'm a first-class disciple. None of you stand a chance against me."

"Then why don't you try it?" Lan-Yin challenged.

Wei Long laughed, but it was cold and mirthless. "Go ahead. Raise your fists, your little tricks and your anger." His tone was dripping with scorn, but his eyes darted to the crowd, assessing the faces staring back at him with fierce determination. "Even if you win here, even if you somehow manage to bring me down, nothing changes. Narrow Stone Peak has already taken notice of this place. You've barely begun to grasp what you're up against. Hundreds of disciples—skilled, ruthless, and loyal. They'll descend on this village like a storm, and all your unity will crumble beneath their might. You can't escape the sect's reach."

His words cast a bleak shadow over the square, cooling the fighting spirit we had mustered.

CHAPTER THIRTY-NINE

Roots of Resistance

The crowd was a tense, pulsing mass of fear and determination, everyone holding their breath as we faced down Wei Long. His mocking smile was infuriating, that smug tilt of his head as he scanned the crowd, sneering.

Each second felt like an eternity. Had my messages been in vain? Was I foolish to pin my hopes on a distant possibility?

"What's the matter?" he drawled, eyes sweeping over us with mocking disdain. "Where's all that fighting spirit now? You've come this far. Why don't you take the last step?"

His fingers flexed, and he shifted forward, his intentions clear in every movement.

A sudden gust shot past me as Tianyi launched forward, her foot swinging up with a speed that sliced the air. The impact sent a burst of wind spiraling out, making my hair whip wildly.

But Wei Long caught her kick, his hand clamping down like a vise. "Wrong move."

Without a second thought, I leapt into action, sprinting toward him and swinging my fist. He saw me coming, his lips curling into a smirk as he twisted to block, but then there was a flash of white and blue. Windy sprang from behind, his sleek body twisting through the air, wrapping tightly around Wei Long's eyes like a makeshift blindfold, rapidly tightening around his thick neck.

Wei Long's smirk vanished, replaced by a flash of irritation. He threw Tianyi at me and I caught her midair, setting her carefully down. I turned back to see Wei Long's hands clawing at Windy, trying to pull the snake off his face.

"Stay back!" I shouted to the villagers as they surged forward. Lan-Yin and Wang Jun were ready to join the fight. "It's too dangerous. Just hold on a little longer."

I turned my gaze back to Wei Long, my heart hammering. I'd seen the strength of second-class disciples like Lan Sheng and Feng Wu; I knew what it took to even go toe-to-toe with them. But Wei Long was on another level, a first-class disciple. A sect's most elite force.

This was going to be brutal.

Windy hissed in pain, as the man gripped his body with a force that crushed his scales.

I didn't wait, pressing the advantage. I darted forward with another punch, aiming for his ribs. Infusing my fist with every ounce of qi I could muster, I drove it into his side.

My fist connected, the force rippling outward—only to meet an unyielding wall. It was like striking a boulder. There was no give, no recoil—nothing.

With Windy still latched around his head, Wei Long's hand shot out and clamped down on my shoulder like an iron vise. His grip tightened, fingers digging painfully into my skin as he reared back, making visible eye contact with me through the gap in between Windy's body. I barely had time to brace myself as his forehead came crashing down in a devastating headbutt.

ROOTED BANYAN STANCE!

My stance was imperfect, diminishing the effectiveness of my technique. The impact rattled my skull, sending stars across my vision. My balance wavered, and I stumbled back, disoriented, but I forced myself to stay upright, shaking off the daze as fast as I could.

Windy fell to the side, uncoiling as the damage became too much.

Wei Long laughed, his gaze sharp and mocking. "Is that it?" he sneered, rolling his shoulders as if warming up, his gaze sweeping over the crowd of villagers with a wicked glint. "This is your grand plan? Holding on, waiting for . . . what? Some savior to appear out of thin air?" He tilted his head, letting out a bitter chuckle. "Do you think I'll just *let* you?"

He shot forward, eyes glinting dangerously. He reached for one villager behind him. I saw Lan-Yin stiffen, her fists clenching, and the crowd took a collective step back, but he was too fast for any of them.

I couldn't let him hurt anyone else. The strategy of waiting, drawing him out—it was gone. There was only one choice left. My feet surged forward, and I funneled my qi into my legs, propelling myself with a burst of speed.

"STOP!"

Wei Long's arm halted mid-reach, and his body twisted with an unnatural fluidity. He turned to face me, and I could see the flex of his muscles as he readied a vicious hook aimed straight for my face. His knuckles came close, so close I could feel the rush of air from the punch.

I veered my head just off-center, his knuckles grazing my cheek, missing by a hair. I capitalized on that instant, swinging my fist with every ounce of strength I had. My knuckles connected solidly with his jaw, sending a shock of satisfaction up my arm.

His head tilted from the impact, and he slowly straightened, a mocking smile on his face.

My chest tightened with frustration, but Tianyi darted in before I could think of my next move. She launched herself upward, knee cocked and ready, bringing it down with a brutal force aimed at the side of his head. It connected, sending the first-class disciple tumbling off to the side.

"Go! Go!"

I watched Elder Ming evacuate the villagers. I sighed in relief. That would give us some breathing room.

But against him, we needed every advantage we can get.

My limbs grew heavier with every exchange, breaths turning ragged. As brief as it's been, the mental toll of knowing every blow might be my last was draining.

Time was slipping away, and so was my strength.

Wei Long got up, gingerly touching his temple where Tianyi struck.

A thin line of blood streaked down his fingertips as he inspected them. He lifted his hand, showing the drop of blood to us with a dark expression on his face.

"All that for a single drop of blood."

He surged forward with a renewed fury. We scrambled, weaving around him, keeping our distance as his attacks lashed out.

We formulated a plan—disjointed and desperate, borne from instinct rather than any prepped strategy, but a plan nonetheless.

Tianyi took the lead, her form darting in and out of the fray like a blade of wind. She was untouchable, her movements too fluid, too unpredictable for Wei Long to pin down with us supporting her. Her wings shimmered faintly, qi swirling around her as she launched herself into another attack. Her foot connected with Wei Long's side, a strike aimed to stagger rather than overpower.

I seized the moment, diving in from the opposite side. My fists were slower, my strikes heavier. Each blow was infused with qi, not to cause damage but to draw his attention. I aimed for his arms, his ribs—anywhere I could disrupt his rhythm. I was the distraction, the bait, and I had to play my part perfectly.

Wei Long turned to me, his focus narrowing as he lunged with a sweeping backhand. I braced myself, gritting my teeth as I caught his arm. Pain erupted, but I held my ground, twisting with the impact to minimize the damage. I stayed upright, forcing a grin onto my face.

"Is that all you've got?" I taunted, my voice coming out sharper than I actually felt.

He snarled, his attention fully on me now, and that was all the opening Tianyi needed. She darted behind him, her wings slicing through the air with a faint hum. With a sharp pivot, she drove her knee into the back of his leg, aiming for the joint. His stance faltered, a split-second shift that gave Windy his chance.

The serpent sprang from the side, his coiled body snapping like a whip. He latched onto Wei Long's arm, his muscles constricting with incredible force. Wei Long growled, his free hand reaching for Windy, but before he could grab the serpent, Tianyi was on him again.

Her foot slammed into his ribs with a thunderous crack, the force driving him a step back. Windy released his hold, slithering away just as Wei Long's hand closed on empty air.

"You pests!" Wei Long roared, his aura flaring. His qi erupted in a burst, forcing us all to retreat momentarily. The ground beneath him cracked as his power surged, his gaze burning with fury. "You think this is enough to stop me? I'll show you the difference between us!"

He feinted toward Tianyi, and in a heartbeat, changed direction, reaching for me. I felt the air shift just as his fingers stretched toward me, and my body froze for an instant, realizing I couldn't avoid him in time—

A shout rang out, and then a solid mass collided with Wei Long from behind. Wang Jun had tackled him, wrapping his arms around Wei Long in a fierce bear hug. "Now's your chance!" he yelled, voice straining as he struggled to keep his grip.

Wei Long scoffed, clearly expecting to break free easily. But he stilled, eyes widening in surprise as Wang Jun's feet dug into the earth.

I didn't waste a second.

Tianyi darted in beside me, her fists flying in rapid strikes. I went for Wei Long's vital points, driving my fists into every soft spot I could find.

Amid the clash, a faint rumble reached my ears—hoofbeats? Or was it just the pounding of my heart?

Windy slithered down and struck at Wei Long's ankle, his fangs sinking in to deliver a potent dose of venom.

Wei Long growled, his face twisting with irritation as he fought to shake us off. "Enough of this!" With a powerful surge, he wrenched his arms free, breaking Wang Jun's hold and sending him crashing into the earth with a vicious backhand. He stomped the ground with enough force to send cracks racing outward, the earth beneath us shuddering and sending us off-balance.

My instincts screamed to move, but before I could fully react, his hand darted forward and clamped onto my arm. With a savage twist, he yanked me closer, trapping my forearm in the vise-like grip of his armpit.

It felt as though Windy himself had coiled around my arm. Pain lanced through my bones, and I grit my teeth to keep from crying out. The pressure was suffocating, as though my entire arm was being ground to dust.

Wei Long didn't stop there. His fist shot forward, connecting with my ribs in a blow that felt like a boulder smashing into me. The air left my lungs in a choked gasp, my vision flashing white. Before I could recover, another punch followed, this one slamming into my shoulder and sending me reeling. My knees buckled, and I struggled to stay upright, the world spinning from the force of his strikes.

"You should've stayed in your garden, boy," Wei Long growled, a low rumbling of menace.

From the corner of my eye, I saw Tianyi streaking toward him, her wings shimmering with concentrated qi. She aimed her strike at his side, but Wei Long anticipated her move. He released my arm and pivoted, snatching her midair with a precision that defied his size.

Despite the pain, I scrounged up every ounce of willpower within me to raise up once more.

"LET HER—"

I felt his fingers clamp around my neck, cutting off my air in an instant. We thrashed, resisting his hold, but the pressure on my throat only grew stronger. My vision blurred, the world narrowing to the iron grip around my neck.

Is this where I die?

HISS!

Windy struck again, this time wrapping around his arm, constricting fiercely. Wang Jun came in from the side, attempting to wrestle his other arm free, his face contorted with effort.

"Let go of him! You bastard!"

In my struggle, I could see Lan-Yin leaping in, her hands reaching out to jab at his eyes, hoping to force him to release us. But Wei Long's hold only tightened, his strength monstrous.

My lungs screamed for air as I felt the bruising pain spread across my neck. Black spots danced across my vision. Sounds muffled.

A distant roar—or was it speech?—pierced the fog encasing my mind. Just as I thought I couldn't hold on any longer, something struck the first-class disciple's wrist, forcing him to let me go.

A green bladed fan contrasted to the white, muted background.

I fell to the ground, gasping for breath, Tianyi collapsing beside me.

Through the haze of my dimming consciousness, I saw a silhouette dart in, retrieving the bladed fan, forcing Wei Long back.

Support had arrived.

"Feng Wu . . . !" I said hoarsely.

I tried to speak, to thank him, but the pain in my throat flared as I struggled to catch my breath.

I looked around, seeing a shape approaching in the distance, a shadowed figure atop a horse-drawn wagon. The morning light made it difficult to see, but there was something unmistakable in the posture, the silent confidence of the person guiding it closer.

The Verdant Lotus Sect had sent support! They got my message!

Wei Long's gaze shifted, his mouth curving into a cold sneer as he released Tianyi. Irritation laced his voice. "And why exactly is the Verdant Lotus Sect interfering here?"

"Because there's a matter of injustice to resolve." Feng Wu's face remained impassive, his eyes steady and sharp. But for a brief second, his gaze flickered toward me, a reassuring smile on his lips.

Despite the chaos, his presence steadied me.

"One concerning a friend."

Wei Long let out a humorless laugh, the sound grating in the tense silence of the square.

"This"—he gestured around at the village—"this is what you're risking your necks for? A backwater village and an uppity alchemist? The Verdant Lotus is more arrogant than I thought, to assume they can waste resources here instead of fighting the Silent Moon."

The second-class disciple's expression didn't waver. He took another step forward, despite the hostility radiating off Narrow Stone Peak's elite. "It's not a matter of resources. We're resolving this today."

Wei Long's smirk grew. "Brave words. But do you really believe you can stand against me?"

Another voice cut in. "Maybe not. But I can."

Before Feng Wu could respond, the wagon creaked closer, coming to a stop beside us. I turned, struggling to focus through my pain, and saw the figure lift his hood.

The man stepped down from the wagon, his eagle-like eyes surveying the scene with a piercing gaze, his silver-gray hair gleaming in the early light. The figure, now clear, was unmistakable. My breath caught as I recognized him. I sent the message as a last resort, as a backup. But to think *he* would come himself.

"Tian Zhan . . ." Wei Long's voice wavered, his eyes widening in surprise and, for the first time I'd seen, genuine fear. He snapped his face toward me in genuine disbelief. But my expression mirrored his.

I never imagined he would personally answer the favor he owed me.

The air seemed to change, as the brute of a man stepped backward for the first time since battle began.

"It seems you have quite the situation here, Kai Liu," Tian Zhan said with a smile. "Perhaps a first-class disciple would prefer facing someone of equal standing."

Wei Long's posture tensed, his bravado faltering as he met Tian Zhan's sharp gaze.

CHAPTER FORTY

Hope on the Horizon

Tian Zhan strolled forward, each step calculated, like a storm gathering strength. I could feel the tension tightening as Wei Long stood frozen, torn between anger and confusion.

"What are you doing here?"

But Tian Zhan only gave him a disdainful glance, dismissive, as if he were an inconvenience rather than an adversary.

"You don't deserve an answer from me," he said coolly. The blatant disregard, dripping with disdain, visibly rattled the Narrow Stone Peak disciple, his face slowly flushing red. And as much as I hated the man, it was almost comical to see him shrink, his rage barely contained in the face of Tian Zhan's utter confidence. It was a remarkable contrast: Wei Long, built like a bull, fists ready to crush, but visibly holding himself back in front of a man no taller than I was.

I felt the briefest opening and turned to Tianyi. "Are you all right?" I whispered urgently, reaching out to steady her. My heart twisted at the sight of her, even in the pale morning light.

There were faint, spiderwebbed cracks along her neck, each line a reminder of Wei Long's brutal strength. And all over, those raised lines on her skin now held darkened edges from the blows she'd taken.

She gave me a small nod, trying to brush it off, but I couldn't help it. I pulled her close, arms wrapping tightly around her.

"I'm sorry. This is my fault," I murmured, the words breaking in my throat. She was tougher than I could ever be, but seeing her like this, almost shattered, brought every hidden fear to the surface. She said nothing, only leaned into the hug, and for a moment, the chaos around us dimmed, replaced by the quiet relief of knowing she was still here.

Windy let out a soft hiss, giving me a soft smack on the arm, clearly affronted.

"And you as well, Windy. Come here."

A loud slap cracked through the air, snapping me from the moment. My head whipped back to the scene in front of us, my eyes widening as I took in the sight. Tian Zhan stood with his palm still outstretched, and there, frozen, was Wei Long, a bright red handprint seared onto his face, his expression blank with shock. His disbelief turned quickly to rage, his face contorting.

"How dare you!" he snarled, every muscle in his body tense and poised to strike.

But Tian Zhan just raised an eyebrow. "Oh? Are you resisting me?" He took a single step, pressing his head forward as though daring the ox-like man to hit him back. "I think someone like you would understand the implications of that."

The threat hung heavy, so raw that it left the entire crowd silent. Even Wei Long, prideful as he was, seemed to waver, his fists twitching with suppressed fury. "Is this how the Whispering Wind Sect operates?" he asked through gritted teeth.

"This is the authority I wield as a sect leader candidate," Tian Zhan replied coolly. "What sect would sit idly by when another threatens their rising star?"

Wei Long's face twisted with indignation, his cheeks flushing a deep red. "Ridiculous!" he spat. "You're the one who barged in here unprovoked, and now you accuse me of aggression? You started this!"

The gray-haired man glanced leisurely around the village square, his gaze settling on the scene; the cracked earth, and the villagers who still watched warily from a distance. "Did I?" he mused, his tone almost casual. "From where I'm standing, it seems you initiated hostilities by attempting to seize control of Gentle Wind Village."

Wei Long's eyes flickered, a brief hesitation betraying his uncertainty. "I was merely carrying out the interests of Narrow Stone Peak," he retorted. "This village lies within our sphere of influence. You have no say on what we can't do."

"Ah, so you admit to overstepping your bounds," Tian Zhan said smoothly. "Tell me, does your sect endorse the destruction of property and the endangerment of innocent lives to expand its influence?"

Wei Long's jaw tightened. "Don't twist my words."

"I'm not twisting anything," Tian Zhan replied, his gaze piercing. "I'm simply observing the situation. You attacked this village, harmed its people, and now feign innocence when confronted. It's unbecoming of a first-class disciple."

As I watched their exchange, it settled over me. Tian Zhan was deftly turning the tables, using his authority and eloquence to paint Wei Long as the aggressor. I realized how easily power controls the narrative. Despite only relaying a fraction of the details in my plea for help, Tian Zhan had taken command of the situation effortlessly.

Now this . . . this was power.

Wei Long's fists clenched at his sides, his knuckles white. "You have no right to interfere in our affairs," he bit out.

Tian Zhan cocked his head. "Interfere? When a fellow sect threatens the peace and well-being of innocents, it's not interference—it's responsibility. Unless, of course, you'd prefer we involve the sect elders to mediate this . . . misunderstanding. Or we could bring this case to the magistrate if you so desire."

A flicker of doubt crossed Wei Long's face. "You think your status allows you to meddle without consequence?"

"My status grants me the duty to act when others abuse their power," Tian Zhan countered. "And judging by the state of this village and the testimonies of its people, it's clear who the abuser is."

The silence stretched out, punctuated by the faint rustling of movement. The Five Fists staggered into the square, rubbing their eyes as they took in the scene, confusion quickly shifting to loyalty as they recognized their leader's battered form.

"Senior Brother! We'll save you!"

Wei Long's jaw tightened as they moved forward. "No!" he bellowed in warning, but it was too late; they were advancing, ready to defend him at any cost.

Feng Wu took a quick step forward, but Tian Zhan moved first. A fierce gust of wind exploded outward, knocking Wei Long back as it swept across the square. The Five Fists found themselves caught in the tempest, barely able to steady themselves before Tian Zhan struck. His movements were nothing like the elaborate techniques I'd grown used to seeing; no flashy moves or overt displays of qi. A simple punch, a clean kick, a sharp chop—Each motion flowed like water, yet with such brutal speed and power that every disciple fell with a single strike.

One by one, they dropped, too stunned to defend themselves, their shock mirroring my own as we all watched in awe.

Wei Long stumbled back to his feet, his face twisted in rage, but he froze midstep as Tian Zhan held up a single hand, the unspoken command clear.

"I'll forgive your disciples' insolence," Tian Zhan said, voice cold, his gaze unwavering on Wei Long. "They're young, immature, third-class at best. But you . . ." His words hung in the air, dripping with finality. "You remember what I said, Wei Long. Make one more move, and I will consider it an act of war against the Whispering Wind Sect."

A long silence stretched out. Wei Long's face hardened, his eyes smoldering with humiliation and hatred, but he knew he was outmatched. Slowly, he lowered his fists, his jaw set, every line of his body radiating defeat.

I watched him, my heart thudding in my chest, disbelief and relief warring within me. The man who had terrorized our village, who had dared to bring ruin to everything we held dear, was finally brought to his knees. Here I witnessed the end of Wei Long's arrogance, brought forth by a towering wall named Tian Zhan.

Wei Long's shoulders sagged, his gaze fixed on the ground as he finally accepted the inevitable. The arrogant fire in his eyes had dimmed, replaced by something else. Something hollow.

He opened his mouth, perhaps to mutter some last threat, but before he could, Tian Zhan stepped closer, the air around him chilling. His hand snapped forward in a brutal slap that echoed across the square. Wei Long staggered back, his hand instinctively lifting to his reddened cheek. My breath hitched in my chest.

He's already won! Why keep pushing? This is only going to make things worse!

He took another step forward, his voice slicing through the silence. "You should be thanking me for this correction, Wei Long. For the mercy I'm showing you—and your sect—by letting you walk away."

Wei Long's face contorted, his eyes blazing with a hatred he barely kept restrained. Through clenched teeth, he forced out the words, each one dripping with resentment. "Thank you . . . for your correction."

Before I could speak up, Feng Wu glanced sharply at me, shaking his head. As though warning me not to interfere. The sound of painful, cracking slaps continued as Tian Zhan humiliated Narrow Stone Peak.

The sight made something inside me twist. Seeing the once-mighty Wei Long, humiliated and subdued, was a satisfaction I hadn't expected. But there was a deeper layer, an uncomfortable truth that struck me as I watched the power dynamics at play. Here was a man, a terror to our village, reduced to this state not by the justice of right and wrong, but by the authority Tian Zhan wielded with ease.

If Wei Long had been the one to hold that power, would we have fared as well?

"Senior, I think that's enough. I believe he's learned his lesson," Feng Wu said diplomatically, coming forward to stop Tian Zhan.

The man's sharp eyes analyzed Wei Long critically. The ox-like man had his head down, trembling, either from rage or fear. Though shadowed, I could see veins popping up on his head as he silently endured everything.

"Is this enough, Kai Liu? Do you think Wei Long has repented enough?"

My gaze snapped to Tian Zhan, and we made eye contact.

I nodded, heart pounding. Despite the pain in my throat and chest, I forced myself to speak. "Yes, senior. I believe he's learned his lesson."

Tian Zhan's expression softened a fraction. "Good." He turned back to Wei Long, his voice icy and unforgiving. "Then thank Kai Liu and the Verdant Lotus Sect for this leniency, Narrow Stone Peak disciple. Consider this your final warning."

The man clenched his jaw, the words practically wrenched from his throat as he turned to face us, hands clasped together with his head bowed. "Thank you . . . Kai Liu, and to the Verdant Lotus Sect for their mercy."

The humiliation dripped from his voice. It felt like both a victory and something else entirely, something heavier. As Tian Zhan dismissed him with a flick of his hand, Wei Long dropped to his knees, his spirit subdued, moving stiffly as he unbound Zhao Wen and lifted the groaning members of the Five Fists from the dirt. I watched as he carefully avoided meeting anyone's gaze, his defeat absolute and devastating.

The square was silent, the weight of everything pressing down like a storm after the battle, thick and laden with unspoken truths. And in that quiet, a realization struck me—one that ran deep and cold.

I'd thought calling in a favor was straightforward. I'd thought power worked in simple exchanges, that justice would feel clean. But today, as I watched Wei Long's spirit crushed under Tian Zhan's heel, I saw something more. My stomach twisted with understanding. The world Elder Ming had warned me about. About how the Jianghu was filled with dangerous people with ill intentions.

I was just lucky to stand beside someone who could turn the tables in my favor.

He'd tried to warn me, to guide me, and I'd thought I understood. But as Tian Zhan commanded Wei Long to never so much as look in our direction again, as Wei Long nodded, defeated, I realized that I was just beginning to understand what true power meant in the Jianghu.

CHAPTER FORTY-ONE

Allies and Ambitions

I sat cross-legged on the worn floor of my shop, sorting through the last remnants of my medicinal herbs. Most of them were bruised, like the people they were meant to heal, and barely enough to cover the worst of our wounds. My fingers trembled slightly as I worked, but I willed them steady, ignoring the dull throb radiating from my chest. Each breath came with a faint hitch, a reminder of the punches Wei Long had delivered, but I refused to let it slow me down.

I sighed, shaking my head at the limitations, but there was no point in complaining. With gentle fingers, I crushed the dried leaves into powder, applying it over Windy's bruised scales. My arms protested the motion, but I pushed through, forcing myself to focus on the task at hand.

Using the last of my extracted chamomile essence, I poured it over the powder and watched him coil, a faint hiss slipping out as the medicine stung.

"It's all right, Windy," I murmured, patting his small head. "You're a tough one."

Windy gave a reluctant nod, his usually sharp eyes softened, if only slightly, by pain. Lan-Yin, the least injured among us, tended to the rest of the villagers. Beside me, Wang Jun sat with two massive bruises along his forearms and a broken nose from his contest of strength against Wei Long. He shot me a look that was half grimace, half smile.

"Didn't expect a beating like that today," he said.

"I'm sorry for getting you all pulled into it," I replied quietly, casting a glance toward Tianyi. She sat a little apart from us, leaning against the wall, her face as serene as ever. However, her eyes seemed calmer, the only tell from her expressionless face to determine what she was feeling. Her human form was still unfamiliar to me, but the patches of spiderweb-like cracks running along her neck and shoulders reminded me all too much of the damage we'd endured.

The rhythmic ache in my chest surged again, sharper this time, as if my body were chastising me for ignoring it. I resisted the urge to probe the bruising around my sternum. I could already guess the extent of the damage; probably cracked, if not broken ribs. But those could wait. There were more pressing matters at hand.

As I worked, I noticed a thin thread, shimmering faintly, stretched across Tianyi's shoulder.

The source was apparent: that shadowy spider, Yin Si, hiding just within the shadows, her delicate legs weaving intricate strands that formed a makeshift bandage across Tianyi's worst injuries.

It wasn't just a patch job, either. There was something almost . . . purposeful about her weaving, as if she understood what each thread needed to do.

Tianyi noticed my stare and gently extended two thin strands of her own hair toward the spider. There was a quiet moment of concentration on her face as she closed her eyes, her fingers brushing over the threads. When she pulled her hand away, the strands glowed briefly, as if infused with a spark of her qi. Yin Si paused, her mandibles twitching before she nodded, looking like she'd gained a sudden burst of energy. With one last look of—was that derision?— toward me, she disappeared back into the shadows.

I blinked, surprised. "Tianyi . . . did you just . . . give her some of your qi?"

Tianyi tilted her head slightly, her lips curving into a faint smile. "She needed it," she replied gently. "She used up much of her silk to fix me."

Before I could think on it further, footsteps echoed from outside, and a knock sounded at the doorframe. I straightened, biting back a wince as the motion pulled at my bruised neck. Feng Wu and Tian Zhan entered, their forms casting long shadows into the room. Both looked composed, though faint lines of weariness touched their faces.

"It's over," Feng Wu said. "Narrow Stone Peak has departed. Your village won't have to worry about them anymore."

A wave of relief washed over me, though it didn't entirely erase the unease coiling in my chest. "Thank you," I managed, my voice hoarse. "Both of you . . . you really didn't have to go that far for us."

Tian Zhan stepped farther inside, glancing around at the simplicity of my home with a slight nod of approval. "It was necessary. To prevent any misunderstandings in the future."

"Prevent misunderstandings," I repeated, trying to wrap my head around how his "necessary measures" had resulted in slapping a first-class disciple into submission. Still, it was difficult to argue with the results.

Feng Wu crossed the room, his hand resting lightly on my shoulder as he inspected the bruises across my arms. "You handled yourself well," he said. "But you should recover. There's no need to push yourself beyond what you already endured."

I let out a laugh, rubbing at the back of my neck. "Didn't feel like I handled much of anything, if I'm honest. But thank you."

I turned to Tian Zhan, struggling to find the right words. "I . . . don't know what we would've done without your help."

Tian Zhan nodded, though his eyes held a keen, assessing glint. "It's no trouble. You've earned a favor for helping my Junior Sister, and I keep my promises."

The statement, though simple, held a power that left me quiet.

Feng Wu and Tian Zhan exchanged glances as they stepped further into the room, their expressions softening as they took in the sight of us nursing our wounds. Tian Zhan seemed at ease. It was strange seeing him so relaxed, like a different person from the one who'd commanded Wei Long to heel.

Tian Zhan shifted a large weathered bundle off his shoulder and held it out to me. The rough cloth had been knotted hastily, its threads sticking out at odd angles. He set it down carefully, and as he untied it, I could see several vibrant herbs and delicate stalks spilling over the edges, their fragrances mingling in the air. The bulb of a Jadeleaf Lily, the Sunfire Blade Grass, and other rare, high-end ingredients peeked out from the wrinkled cloth.

"These are from Jingyu Lian and Zhi Ruo," Tian Zhan explained. "They heard about what happened and sent what they could. Quickly, as you can see."

I took in the bundle, surprised not just by the quality but by the obvious rush in its packing. The herbs and ingredients seemed like they'd been snatched off shelves and bundled together without thought, leaves twisted and stalks bent, as though they'd thrown in whatever valuable ingredients they could find in their haste to help.

"Thank you," I said, overwhelmed. "Please . . . thank them for me. I don't think I deserve all this."

Tian Zhan gave a smile, one that softened his otherwise intense expression. "They'll be glad to hear it. Though my Junior Sister would probably remind you she's still the better alchemist."

Before I could respond, Feng Wu stepped forward, setting down a polished wooden box, wide and deep with a sturdy latch. He opened it, revealing an orderly array of seeds, bulbs, and small rhizomes, all carefully stored in sections. Unlike the vibrant colors of Tian Zhan's gift, this looked humble, each herb variety carefully labeled.

"I thought these might be useful," Feng Wu said, gesturing to the neatly arranged box. "It's not as . . . dramatic as Tian Zhan's gift, but we wanted to help you get your garden back on its feet. These are sourced from Tranquil Breeze Farm, so there's no doubt about their quality."

Over a dozen types of seeds, bulbs, and rhizomes; everything I'd need to start fresh and fill my garden with a complete range of practical herbs. It was a gardener's dream, a perfect foundation to restore everything I'd lost.

"Thank you, Feng Wu. Both of you. I owe you a debt."

Tian Zhan shrugged, crossing his arms and leaning against the wall, his posture casual, almost unguarded. "We did what was necessary, Kai. Leaving a talent like yours to suffer would be a disservice."

Still, I glanced between them, unable to hold back a hint of confusion. "Even after everything? Jingyu Lian . . . she didn't have to go this far. We're not that close, either."

"Although I'm repaying my debt by being here, I suppose this is her way of repaying you for the Gauntlet," Tian Zhan replied.

As I carefully arranged the herbs and seeds, I noticed him watching me, a faint amusement in his eyes. His earlier harshness with Wei Long felt worlds away, replaced with something softer, like he was a completely different person. He must have noticed my lingering contemplative look, because he inclined his head, meeting my gaze.

"If my methods seemed . . . harsh," he began, his voice measured, "I apologize. Sometimes extreme measures are necessary to prevent retaliation. Humiliating Wei Long publicly was the best way to ensure Narrow Stone Peak wouldn't think of returning here."

I nodded slowly, the pieces falling into place. Tian Zhan's harsh actions weren't just displays of power. He'd calculated those moves to secure peace for us. Where I'd focused only on avoiding conflict, he had seen the longer game, one where deterrence mattered more than appeasement.

"Thank you for explaining," I said thoughtfully. "I hadn't thought of it that way. I was only worried about provoking them further."

Feng Wu offered a nod of approval. "It's a fine line to walk, Kai. Compassion is important, but sometimes strength alone ensures peace."

I took a deep breath, feeling both grateful and a touch unsettled by the moral complexity of it all. But as I looked between the two of them, their gifts spread before me, I knew that whatever our differences, they were allies who'd risked themselves for us.

And I was fortunate to have such friends.

As the weight of their words settled between us, Feng Wu's gaze shifted over to Tianyi, who sat quietly in her corner, the segmented lines on her skin highlighted in the dim light. His eyes widened ever so slightly as he took in her human form.

"Tianyi?" Feng Wu wondered. "Has she truly achieved a human form?" He seemed lost in thought.

Tian Zhan, meanwhile, stared with open curiosity. His eyes scanned her intricate, segmented skin and the silk of Yin Si still woven around her neck. "I've never seen a Spirit Beast take a human form before," he admitted. "And certainly not one with such unique . . . qualities."

Tianyi met their gazes with her usual impassive calm, but when her eyes lingered on Tian Zhan, I caught a faint flicker of interest. It wasn't admiration or curiosity; it was more an intense assessment, like she was trying to discern something fundamental about him. Then, without a word, she looked away, folding her hands in her lap.

Feeling the need to break the silence, I turned to Feng Wu. "How rare is it for a Spirit Beast to achieve a human form?" I asked. "The Heavenly Interface said something about it being possible only at the Essence Awakening Stage, but . . ." I glanced at Tianyi, unsure of the specifics.

Feng Wu tilted his head thoughtfully. "It's certainly rare. The Heavenly Interface isn't incorrect, but it doesn't account for the individuality of each Spirit Beast. Some never find the need to take human form. Take Ma Xi of Tranquil Breeze Farm; I've never seen him as anything other than his true form. And if rumors are correct, he doesn't even know how to shift, though his strength is unquestionable. For most, human forms aren't necessary for their survival or goals, so they rarely pursue them."

Tian Zhan nodded in agreement, still eyeing Tianyi appreciatively. "From what I understand, it's a matter of will and need. Some Spirit Beasts that could transform choose not to, while others keep it hidden if they do. That makes it noteworthy that she decided it was necessary."

I glanced at Tianyi, who continued to observe our conversation with that serene, unreadable expression. It was strange to imagine that she'd chosen this form deliberately, with a purpose of her own.

"Feng Wu . . . I remember you," Tianyi said as gently as a whispering wind. Her gaze softened ever so slightly, a trace of warmth that rarely broke through her neutral demeanor. "It is good to see you. Thank you for saving Kai."

"Likewise, Tianyi," Feng Wu replied with a modest smile. "I'm glad we arrived in time."

But when her eyes fell on Tian Zhan again, they narrowed slightly, as if she was scrutinizing him. She held his gaze a moment longer than necessary, then looked away without a word, dismissing him. Tian Zhan raised an eyebrow, perhaps a bit amused, perhaps a bit surprised, but he didn't press her for acknowledgment.

"Quite the companion you have, Kai," he said, his voice light. "It seems Gentle Wind Village is full of surprises."

"She's . . . unique, to say the least," I replied, glancing at Tianyi, who met my gaze for a fleeting second before turning away. Was she mad at me?

The conversation drifted on, but my focus waned. I nodded absently as Tian Zhan and Feng Wu discussed the logistics of rebuilding the village's defenses, their voices low but steady. My thoughts pulled me in another direction—one I couldn't shake, no matter how hard I tried.

The truth was stark. Without the Verdant Lotus and Whispering Wind Sects' intervention, Narrow Stone Peak would have crushed Gentle Wind Village. All my efforts—Tianyi, Windy, the hours spent cultivating, foraging, and learning—felt small compared to the centuries of power and influence wielded by these sects.

I glanced at Feng Wu and Tian Zhan. Each a distinct, incredibly capable individual, only a few years older than me.

What did I have? A garden in ruins, a few Spirit Beasts, and a budding talent in alchemy. It wasn't enough to protect anything. Not yet.

Zhi Ruo had warned me against standing out, against drawing attention that could invite danger. But wasn't the village already a target? Avoiding conflict hadn't protected us. If anything, it had only delayed the inevitable. If I didn't grow stronger, if I didn't elevate Gentle Wind Village beyond its current state, this reprieve would be temporary. The next time, there might not be allies to intervene.

My gaze fell on the gifts spread before me: the vibrant herbs and meticulously labeled seeds, symbols of the connections I'd forged. They weren't just gifts. They were lifelines, reminders that standing alone was no longer an option.

Tianyi shifted slightly, her segmented lines catching the light as she adjusted her position. Even she, with her newfound strength and human form, wasn't enough to change the balance of power. Not yet. I clenched my fists, a quiet resolve settling into my chest.

I looked up, cutting through the soft murmur of conversation. "Tian Zhan, Feng Wu," I said, my voice firmer than I'd expected. Both turned to face me, their expressions curious. "I wanted to thank you again for everything you've done. But . . . I think we need to discuss something more."

Tian Zhan raised an eyebrow, his posture shifting slightly, as if preparing for a heavier topic. "Go on."

I took a steadying breath. "The truth is Gentle Wind Village can't stand on its own. Today proved that. And while I'll do everything in my power to strengthen it, I don't think I can do it alone." My voice wavered slightly, but I pressed on. "What would it take to form a partnership between the village and your sects? Something that ensures the safety of the people here in the long run?"

Standing out might not be a choice, but a necessity. If the village was to survive, if I was to fulfill the potential others seemed to see in me, I had to take the first step.

CHAPTER FORTY-TWO

The First Planting

I clenched my fists against my knees, the pounding in my chest a reminder of how audacious this was. Still, I couldn't afford to back down now.

Feng Wu finally opened his mouth, but I raised a hand, cutting him off. "I know what you're going to say," I began, my voice firm but steady. "And I know that you won't—and shouldn't—do this for free."

I glanced at Tianyi, who sat quietly in the corner. "The reason Narrow Stone Peak was so determined to take this village is because of the ambient qi here. It's stronger than anywhere else in the region. Haven't you noticed it since you arrived?"

Feng Wu's brow furrowed. "I did notice the abundance of qi. It's unusual, to say the least."

"It's not natural," I admitted. "It's because of Tianyi. She has a skill called Qi Haven. It passively enhances the ambient qi in the area around her. She's the reason cultivation has been easier here, for me and everyone else in the village."

Tian Zhan's posture shifted, his expression sharpening. "A passive skill with that much influence? That's rare."

"Rare enough to draw attention," I agreed. "And I understand that alone might not be enough to justify your sect deploying a squad here. But there's more."

I stood and moved toward one of the shelves, scanning the neatly labeled vials until I found the one I was looking for. Holding it up to the faint light, the liquid shimmered like sunlight caught in a jar. Sage essence.

Turning back to face them, I took the ginseng-sage hybrid, one of my more successful experiments. Its leaves glistening, the result of its unique composition.

Feng Wu's eyes widened slightly as recognition dawned. "Is that . . . ?"

"A hybrid," I confirmed. "Using Essence Extraction and spiritual infusion, I've developed a technique to combine plants, creating entirely new species with unique properties. It's why I asked you if Master Li Tao had ever done the same."

I carefully uncorked the vial and let a single drop fall onto the plant. The reaction was immediate: the flickering leaves pulsed, their glow intensifying as the essence fused with the plant. Within moments, fresh shoots sprouted, curling upward like they were reaching for the heavens.

"This," I said, gesturing to the plant, "is only one example. By experimenting with hybrids, I can create pills that circumvent resistance. You know how cultivators build resistance to repeated use of the same ingredients, right?"

Tian Zhan nodded slowly, his sharp eyes fixed on the plant. "You're saying you can bypass that entirely?"

"In theory, yes," I replied. "By using hybrids, I can create pills with unique combinations that don't trigger resistance. It's not perfect yet, but the potential is there."

"This village," I continued, "could become more than just a training ground. It could be a resource hub, producing pills and herbs that even your sects can't replicate. With Tianyi's Qi Haven enhancing cultivation and my hybrids providing unique alchemical products, it's a mutually beneficial arrangement."

The room was silent again, but this time, it was the kind of silence that held the weight of consideration. I observed their expressions shift and their minds at work as they processed my proposal.

To steady myself, I took a deep breath. "I'm not asking for charity. I'm offering an alliance—one that benefits us all."

Tian Zhan exchanged a glance with Feng Wu, his lips curling into a faint, almost-imperceptible smile. "You're more ambitious than I gave you credit for, Kai."

Feng Wu nodded slowly, his thoughtful gaze lingering on the hybrid plant. "This . . . could work. But it's not a decision we can make lightly. I'm sure the elders would agree, and I'll advocate on your behalf."

The first-class disciple of the Whispering Wind Sect barked out a laugh. "We? I'll take that deal right now. The sect can deal with the headache of it all later. But I'll discuss the specifics here with you right now."

I nodded, relief flooding my body. "Of course. The sooner, the better."

While the specifics of the agreement with Feng Wu and Tian Zhan remained tentative, one thing was clear: The Gentle Wind Village had gained a lifeline. Now it was up to me to show the potential I had promised them.

It began in the garden, or what was left of it.

With the seeds and bulbs Feng Wu had brought and the rare ingredients gifted by Jingyu Lian and Zhi Ruo, I had everything I needed to start anew. Even if it was winter, even if it wasn't ideal, I had to start now. My village depended on it.

I knelt in the dirt, crumbling soil between my fingers as I prepared the first row of planters. Tianyi hovered nearby, her presence calm yet attentive. Occasionally, Windy slithered over, his compact form coiling around my leg.

As I pressed the first bulb into the soil, a sharp pain flared in my chest, stealing my breath for a moment. I froze, my fingers tightening around the fragile stem as I clenched my jaw. The bruises from Wei Long's blows pulsed dully, a deep ache that reminded me of every strike. My herbalist instincts screamed at me to stop, to tend to the damage before it worsened, but I shoved the thought aside.

"No time for that now," I muttered, forcing myself to steady my breathing and continue. "Let's start with the basics. We need a sound foundation before we can experiment."

Tianyi tilted her head, watching silently as I pressed the bulbs into the soil. With everyone returning to their respective spaces, it was nice to have some peace. Without the weight of Narrow Stone Peak on my shoulders . . . I felt free.

As I worked, my thoughts drifted to the challenges ahead. Creating hybrids had been an experiment born out of curiosity, but now it would define the village's survival. I'd have to refine my techniques, scale up production, and ensure the quality remained consistent; all while maintaining my training.

The newly built greenhouse became my next priority. With the ambient qi enhanced by Tianyi's Qi Haven, this space would be the heart of my work. I carefully arranged the Sunfire Blade Grass and Jadeleaf Lily into separate compartments, their vibrant colors adding a sense of life to the otherwise barren structure.

As I moved to the sunlit inner curve of the greenhouse, my ribs protested with a deep, throbbing ache. I paused, leaning on the edge of a planter to catch my breath. The motion sent a sharp twinge through my side, but I quickly masked it, straightening and brushing soil from my hands.

I eyed the inner curve of the greenhouse. After consulting Li Wei, I realized that this would be the area where sunlight would hit most, year-round.

And that made it the optimal spot to place the Golden Bamboo.

Even if the immediate danger had passed, it didn't mean the work was done. In fact, I felt like the fight with Wei Long was a prologue, a warning of what could come if I wasn't prepared. My hands pressed into the dirt, firm but careful, as I planted a single seed of Golden Bamboo near the inner curve of the greenhouse.

I stepped back, brushing the soil off my hands, and surveyed the garden. The rows of newly planted seeds and bulbs looked sparse and small, a far cry from the lush, thriving sanctuary I'd worked so hard to build. My heart ached at the loss, but as I planted seeds, I couldn't help but feel a spark of hope.

Every seed was a promise, a tiny capsule of hope carrying the potential for a new beginning.

Tianyi's presence was a comforting constant. She stepped closer, her human form silent but steady as her gaze swept over the garden.

"It will grow," she said simply, her voice carrying a quiet certainty that soothed my lingering doubts.

"Yes," I murmured with a smile. "It will."

Hours passed, and the sun hung low in the sky as I walked to the village with Tianyi and Windy in tow. They were reluctant to leave me alone, and I wasn't keen on being far apart from them, either.

As I made my way back through the square, the atmosphere was a mix of weariness and determination. Though the weight of the incident still lingered, the village was stirring with activity, a quiet resilience in every movement.

Lan-Yin stood near the entrance to the teahouse, her sleeves rolled up as she handed out bowls of warm soup to the villagers hard at work. The rich aroma of her cooking filled the air, mingling with the faint scent of earth and ash. A group of children clustered around her, Xiao Bao among them, carrying trays of bread and water to the able-bodied men repairing the floor after Wei Long's attack.

"Kai!" Lan-Yin called out, catching sight of me. She waved me over, her expression a mix of exhaustion and relief. "You've been at it all day. Sit down and eat something before you collapse."

I hesitated, my eyes darting to the villagers still working tirelessly. "I'm fine, Lan-Yin. Save it for the others."

She planted her hands on her hips, giving me a look that brooked no argument. "Don't make me chase you down, Kowtow Kai. You've done enough for one day."

Xiao Bao tugged at my sleeve, his round face streaked with dirt, but his eyes bright with determination. "Big Brother Kai, you need to eat too! You're always helping everyone else, so let us help you this time."

I couldn't help but smile at his earnestness. "All right, all right. You win."

Lowering myself onto the bench, I suppressed a wince as my bruised ribs and neck flared in protest. I adjusted my posture slightly, leaning forward to ease the strain, and forced a faint smile as Lan-Yin handed me a steaming bowl of soup.

The warmth spread through my hands as I sat. The first sip soothed and grounded me like a balm; for a moment, I simply breathed. Around me, the children darted back and forth, delivering food and drink with a zeal that lightened the somber mood. Their laughter, though subdued, was a reminder that life continued, even after chaos.

Tianyi took an offered bowl from Mei-Li, looking around for a moment, before carefully sipping it bit by bit. She offered a spoonful to Windy, but the serpent turned its head in disinterest.

Lan-Yin sat down beside me, her usual sharp wit tempered by quiet concern. "How are you holding up?" she asked softly.

I stared into the bowl, the steam curling upward like wisps of thought. "I don't know," I admitted. "It feels like we've been given a second chance, but it's hard not to think about what could've happened if things went differently."

She nodded, her gaze distant for a moment before she looked back at me. "That's the way of it, isn't it? We take the hits, pick up the pieces, and move forward. You've done more than anyone could ask, Kai."

Her words settled over me, comforting but not quite dispelling the weight in my chest. "Thanks. I'll try to remember that."

She stood, brushing off her apron. "Good. Now finish that soup before it gets cold. We're going to be up all night, by the looks of it."

As she moved to join the others, I finished the last of the soup and stood, feeling a renewed sense of purpose.

I passed the forge, the rhythmic clanging of a hammer on metal drew my attention. Wang Jun stood by the anvil, his face set in a look of fierce determination as he shaped a blade. Sweat dripped down his brow, but his movements were steady, purposeful. It was clear he'd thrown himself into his work with renewed vigor.

"Wang Jun," I called out, stepping closer.

He paused, looking up with a faint grin that didn't quite reach his eyes. "Kai," he said. He sounded tired. "Done with your garden?"

"Yeah, I was just passing by," I replied. "Wanted to check in. How are you holding up?"

He glanced at the blade in his hands, then back at me. "Better now that I've got something to focus on. After everything that happened . . . I can't just sit around. If another fight comes, I want to be ready. And if I can't fight, I'll make sure everyone has the tools to defend themselves."

I nodded, my chest tightening with a mix of pride and guilt. Wang Jun's resolve mirrored my own, but I couldn't shake the feeling that my failure to stand against Wei Long had pushed him to this point.

"Thanks," I whispered. "For everything. You didn't have to stand with me, but you did."

He shrugged, his gaze turning back to the blade. "We're in this together. You have our back, and we have yours."

I left him to his work, his words echoing in my mind as I continued toward the village square.

Li Wei was crouched near the center of the square, his hands moving deftly as he worked to fill the cracks and gouges left behind by Wei Long's attacks. His usual quiet demeanor was unchanged, but there was a certain urgency to his movements.

"Li Wei," I greeted, stopping a few paces away.

He looked up briefly, his eyes flitting toward Tianyi and Windy before returning to me, offering a small nod before returning to his task. "Kai."

I watched him work for a moment, clearing debris and soil with the other able-bodied villagers. "You're making quick work of this. Do you need help?"

"No, you rest. You've done enough," he replied simply. "The square is the heart of the village. If it's broken, everything feels . . . off. Just trying to help coordinate the cleanup."

I crouched beside him, watching as he prepared baskets of loose dirt. Likely to fill in the loose gaps made by his foot-stomp. "It's amazing, what you can do."

Li Wei paused, his eyes flickering to mine. "You think so? I think you're the amazing one, considering you went toe-to-toe with Narrow Stone Peak."

His words caused my face to burn with embarrassment. I scratched the back of my neck, unable to meet his eyes directly. "Toe-to-toe? That's not exactly how I'd describe it. I couldn't even scratch him. I was just trying to hold on, hoping someone would show up to stop him before it was too late. Windy and Tianyi did most of the work."

Li Wei stopped what he was doing and turned to face me fully, his expression calm but firm. "From where I was standing, it sure looked like toe-to-toe. You didn't back down, Kai. Against someone like that, just standing your ground was more than most would've done. And it wasn't just about the fight."

I frowned slightly, unsure what he meant. "What do you mean?"

He gestured around the square with a small wave of his hand. "You gave us the courage to stand, too. When someone that strong shows up, most people run. But you didn't, and because of that, none of us did either. That matters more than whether or not you landed a good hit."

His words left me momentarily speechless. Distracted by my failures and feelings of powerlessness, I'd neglected to consider any outside perspective.

"I . . . I guess I never thought about it that way," I admitted, stunned.

Li Wei offered a faint smile, his hands resuming their work. "That's because you're too busy being hard on yourself. But trust me, Kai. What you did today mattered. For all of us who were watching."

I nodded, the weight in my chest easing just a little. "Thanks, Li Wei," I said. I found myself thanking a lot of people. And I'm glad I did. There were many things to be thankful for.

"Anytime," he replied, and it was genuine. "Now go on. I've got this. You've earned a break, even if you don't think you have."

I stood, brushing off my hands as I prepared to leave. "All right. But let me know if you need anything. Tianyi, Windy—let's go."

I left him to his work, my heart a little lighter as we resumed our walk to Elder Ming's house.

CHAPTER FORTY-THREE

Carrying the Flame

As we walked in silence toward Elder Ming's house, Tianyi's gaze lingered on me. Her presence, usually a quiet comfort, felt unusually intent. Finally, she spoke, her voice soft but firm. "You're hurt."

I stiffened, shaking my head without looking at her. "I'm fine."

"You are not," she said, stepping in front of me and stopping my stride. Her sharp eyes scanned me, seeing through the facade I'd worked so hard to maintain. "Why do you ignore it?"

"There's too much to do," I replied, sidestepping her. "The village needs me right now."

"The village needs you whole."

Before I could argue, she stepped behind me, her arms wrapping gently around my torso. I froze, startled by the gesture. Warmth bloomed where her hands rested, spreading through my chest and ribs in a soothing wave. The lingering ache in my side eased, and the tightness in my throat relaxed. It wasn't a complete cure, but the relief was enough to steal my breath.

"Tianyi . . ."

She leaned her chin lightly on my shoulder. It seemed the act had taken a lot out of her. "You don't need to do everything alone, Kai. Let us help."

I nodded, my voice caught in my throat. "Thank you," I managed after a moment.

Her lips curved into a faint smile as she turned, motioning for Windy to follow. As I watched her walk ahead, the warmth of her qi still lingering in my chest, I found myself standing a little straighter, the weight on my shoulders feeling just a little lighter.

The stone path leading to Elder Ming's courtyard was quiet, the air heavy with the chill of dusk. The faint scent of jasmine lingered from the garden lining the entrance, though many of the plants were dormant in the cold season.

I paused briefly at the threshold, gathering my thoughts. Inside, I could hear the murmur of conversation—Elder Ming and Feng Wu.

I stepped inside cautiously, not wanting to interrupt. Elder Ming sat straight-backed, his gray hair illuminated faintly by the lantern hanging nearby. Feng Wu stood beside him, his expression calm but focused.

"I'll speak to Tian Zhan," Feng Wu was saying as I entered. His gaze flicked to me, and he gave a small nod. "Kai."

"Feng Wu," I replied, bowing slightly. "I hope I'm not interrupting."

"Not at all," he said smoothly, stepping back. "We can wrap this up here. I'll discuss the details with Tian Zhan and see what the Whispering Wind Sect is prepared to do. Rest assured, we'll help the village."

I nodded, grateful but feeling the weight of the unspoken implications. "Thank you. Truly."

Feng Wu offered a faint smile, then turned to Elder Ming. "I'll take my leave, Village Head." He strode past me, his movements unhurried but purposeful.

Now it was just Elder Ming and me, and the air grew noticeably heavier. The silence stretched, and for a moment, I wondered if he was upset with me. After all, I had acted without consulting him; hiding my plans, threatening Zhao Wen, and risking more than just my life.

"Sit," Elder Ming said finally, gesturing to the chair across from him. His voice was calm, but it incensed me even more.

I obeyed, settling into the chair. Tianyi, who had been quietly following me, hesitated before moving to stand nearby. Windy slithered in without a care.

Elder Ming's gaze shifted to her, his expression softening ever so slightly. "Would you care for some tea as well?" he asked.

She tilted her head, but noticed the steaming teapot and recognition dawned on her face. She gave a small bow, her movements graceful and com-posed despite her fledgling human form. "I would. Thank you."

Elder Ming poured the tea with steady hands, sliding a cup toward her before offering one to me. I took it with a murmured thanks, my eyes flicking between the two of them as the atmosphere subtly shifted. There was no hostil-ity here, no reprimand.

Just a quiet, measured calm.

"You've grown strong, Tianyi," Elder Ming said after a moment. The way he looked at her was as though he could see something beyond the surface. "Though I must admit, I hardly expected to see you like this."

"It is . . . different," she admitted. "But necessary."

"You've chosen to walk alongside Kai, then," he said, more of a statement than a question.

"I have," she answered. "He is kind. And determined. It is not an easy path, but it is one I wish to take."

I felt a warmth rise in my chest at her words, but before I could respond, Tianyi turned her attention fully to Elder Ming, her eyes narrowing slightly as though inspecting him. "You are still not well."

Elder Ming raised an eyebrow, a flicker of surprise crossing his face. "Oh?"

Tianyi's voice softened. "Your pain. I felt it, even before this form. You hide it well, but it lingers."

Her words struck me, pulling a memory to the surface. Tianyi, in her butterfly form, often circling Elder Ming when we stayed here. I had thought it was curiosity, or perhaps her way of showing affection. But now I realized it had been something more. She had sensed his pain, even then.

And there was only one injury that could be this persistent, unhealed by Tianyi's potent aura.

Elder Ming's hand hovered over his teacup for a moment before he chuckled softly, the sound dry but not unkind. "You're perceptive," he said, glancing at me briefly. "It's true that the injury to my dantian has long since healed in the physical sense, but it never truly heals. You grow used to it."

Tianyi's gaze was steady, her voice a mere whisper. "I see."

Elder Ming sipped his tea, his expression contemplative. "It is not an easy thing, to lose one's dantian. Losing strength is only part of it. The greater wound lies in the loss of connection—to qi, to the world, to oneself. But it is a lesson as much as it is a burden."

The weight of his words pressed on me, bringing back the memory of my own threat to destroy Zhao Wen's dantian. Then, it had felt like the only way to protect the village, but now . . . I couldn't help but question the choice.

"I—" I began, but Elder Ming raised a hand to stop me.

"You did what you thought was necessary," he said, neither approving nor condemning me. "But remember, Kai, that such actions leave marks. On others, yes, but also on yourself."

His words lingered in the air, heavy with meaning. Tianyi's eyes flicked to me briefly, and I could feel her quiet support, unspoken but steady.

Elder Ming turned back to her, his expression softening once more. "You are different now, but I can still see the spirit that fluttered through this village. And I thank you, Tianyi, for what you have done for our people."

Tianyi bowed her head slightly, her voice soft but firm. "It is my home as much as it is Kai's. I will protect it."

Elder Ming nodded, his gaze distant as he turned his attention back to his tea. For a moment, the room fell into a contemplative silence, the weight of unspoken thoughts settling over us. Then he let out a quiet sigh and looked at me with a small, tired smile.

"Do you remember what I told you about my dantian?"

I nodded. "You said it was destroyed by your Senior Brother. He betrayed you, and your friend helped you escape after killing them in revenge."

He inclined his head, his fingers absently tracing the rim of his teacup. "Indeed. But there's more to that story than what I've shared before."

I leaned forward slightly. Tianyi, too, seemed to focus her attention fully on Elder Ming, her expression showing a flicker of curiosity.

"When I lost my dantian," he began, "I was left with nothing. My cultivation, my place in the sect, my purpose. It all vanished in an instant. At first, I thought I could recover, rebuild what was broken. But the reality was cruel. No sect wants a crippled disciple. No city wants to harbor a fugitive."

His eyes grew distant, his gaze fixed on something unseen. "For months, I wandered from place to place, trying to find work, food, shelter. Anything that would give me a semblance of normalcy. But no one would take me in. My dantian was gone, and with it, any worth I might have had in their eyes. To them, I was a failure."

"And then," he continued, "there was my sworn brother. The one who saved me, who fought against all odds to get me out of that place. I held on to hope that he was alive, that we would reunite. But after months of silence . . . of searching . . . I realized the truth. He was gone. Either he was captured, or . . . worse."

Elder Ming closed his eyes briefly, as if to collect himself. "I knew I couldn't stay. I had to move on, to go somewhere so far from the sects and the mainland that no one would think to look for me. And so, I fled to Tranquil Breeze Province, never looking back."

The words hung heavy in the air, each one a fragment of a life shattered and painstakingly pieced back together. I struggled to find something to say, but Elder Ming's voice cut through my hesitation.

"When I arrived here, I was nothing more than a wanderer. I didn't plan to stay. This village was just another stop on a journey to nowhere." He gave a faint smile, his gaze flicking to the garden visible through the window. "But then a week passed. Then a month. Then a year. And before I knew it, decades had gone by. The people here—they gave me a place, even when I thought I no longer had one. And so, I found purpose again."

"Elder Ming . . . I can't imagine how hard that must have been."

He chuckled softly, shaking his head. "You don't have to. Kai, you've encountered your share of difficulties. You've felt the sting of powerlessness, the burden of responsibility. I see it in your eyes, the way you carry yourself. You think you're weak because you couldn't defeat Wei Long, because you had to rely on others. But let me tell you this: Victories alone do not measure strength."

I frowned, his words stirring something deep within me. "Then . . . how do you measure it?"

Elder Ming set his cup down, his gaze steady as he met mine. "By the choices you make when all seems lost. By the people you protect, even at significant cost to yourself."

"I . . . I want to be stronger," I admitted. "Fighting Wei Long . . . I realized just how I underestimated him. If Feng Wu and Tian Zhan had been a minute late, then I would've died. I want to become strong, strong enough to stand with my own feet. Not just for me, but for the village. For everyone who stood with me today."

Elder Ming's smile grew faintly, a flicker of approval shining through his otherwise tired features. He nodded slowly, as if weighing my words against some unseen scale. "And I feel I've failed you by not sharing all that I could. Let's change that together."

I tilted my head questioningly.

"I've held back these teachings out of fear—fear of revisiting old wounds, fear of what might happen if I let the past resurface. But perhaps it's time I let go of that fear for the sake of your future."

I straightened, his words catching me off guard. "Elder Ming, you've done more than anyone could ask. I wouldn't even be where I am without your guidance."

He raised a hand, silencing me gently. "And yet, it hasn't been enough. Your fight against Wei Long made something clear to me. You're ready. Ready for more than just cultivation exercises and simple techniques. You need a foundation strong enough to stand against the world."

"What do you mean?"

Elder Ming leaned forward, his expression contemplative. "I'm going to teach you everything I know. My martial arts, my techniques, the principles of my former sect. Including the Heavenly Flame Mantra."

The name struck like a spark igniting dry tinder. I stared at him, my breath catching. "Really?"

He nodded, his gaze turning distant, as if he were looking back through time. "Yes. The Heavenly Flame Mantra was the core style of our sect. I want to teach you what I know of it. Understand, Kai, that my knowledge is incomplete. I was still a third-class disciple when my dantian was destroyed. I never reached the later stages of the art myself. But I can give you the principles, the foundation upon which you can build your own path. My sworn brother gave everything to save me. He believed in a future I could no longer see. Passing on this mantra, incomplete as it is, is my way of ensuring that his spirit endures."

The idea of learning the Heavenly Flame Mantra ignited a flicker of hope in me.

This might be the answer—the missing piece I'd been searching for. Against Wei Long, I could defend, evade, and endure, but I couldn't strike back with enough force to make a difference. My techniques were solid defensively, but offense? I had nothing that could tip the scales.

If Elder Ming's martial art could bridge that gap, it might be exactly what I needed.

I clenched my fists, the warmth of Tianyi's earlier healing still faintly lingering in my chest. "I don't want to just endure anymore, I want to stand on my own, to fight for this village and everyone who believes in me. If the Heavenly Flame Mantra can help me do that—help me protect them—then I'll do whatever it takes."

Then Tianyi, who had been sitting quietly for the entirety of the conversation, spoke up.

"Can I learn too?"

CHAPTER FORTY-FOUR

The Butterfly and the Snow

The days that followed were a whirlwind of training, though not in the way I'd anticipated. Elder Ming's lessons were rigorous, his sharp eyes catching every flaw in my stances and every hesitation in my strikes. He corrected me tirelessly, his words precise, his movements deliberate. For the first time, I felt the edges of the Heavenly Flame Mantra take shape in my hands.

Not just a technique, but a principle, a rhythm.

Tianyi, however, was another story.

At first, she had tried to follow along with Elder Ming's instructions. She mimicked the stances and movements with her usual grace, but it quickly became clear that something was off.

Elder Ming's style, born from years of human cultivation and training, clashed with Tianyi's very nature. Where I stumbled through footwork drills, Tianyi glided effortlessly, her steps so light they barely disturbed the ground beneath her. Her strikes, though precise, lacked the deliberate structure Elder Ming wanted.

"She's . . . not learning," I admitted one evening, my voice hesitant as I watched her move through another set of drills. Her movements were elegant, beautiful even, but there was something almost too instinctive about them. Like she wasn't truly learning but simply doing.

Elder Ming nodded thoughtfully, his arms crossed as he observed. "She's not like you, Kai. Her body, her mind, even her instincts . . . they're shaped by her nature as a butterfly Spirit Beast. Her movement and combat style are inherently optimized, honed not through training but through her very existence."

"So . . . what do we do?" I asked, glancing at Tianyi. She stood off to the side, her expression as unreadable as ever, though I caught a faint tilt of her head as if she knew we were discussing her.

"We adapt," Elder Ming said plainly. "Tianyi's strength doesn't lie in following human methods. Teaching her in the same way as you would be a waste of her talents. Instead, we'll make her your sparring partner."

I blinked. "Sparring partner?"

"She's faster than you," Elder Ming pointed out, his tone matter-of-fact. "Stronger, too. And her instincts are sharp. By fighting her, you'll learn to adapt, to overcome an opponent who is naturally superior in many ways. And for her, the challenge will force her to think creatively. She'll learn by doing."

And thus, led me to today.

I narrowly dodged, Tianyi's outstretched leg brushing past my shoulder as I twisted to evade her strike. The motion sent a sharp jolt through my ribs, a grim reminder of Wei Long's attack. My balance wavered for a split second, just long enough for her to capitalize on my hesitation.

My hands came up instinctively, open palms glowing faintly red—the early manifestation of the Heavenly Flame Mantra. The technique was still far from complete in my hands. Where the flames should have seared with blistering intensity, my palms merely radiated a feeble warmth. Barely enough to stave off the cold. Compared to my established fighting style, it felt like I was a step behind, trying to incorporate offense into my usually defensive style.

Still, it was progress. And sometimes, things have to be worse before they can be better.

I thrust my palm forward in a counterstrike, aiming for her center. The broad surface of my hand was designed to deliver maximum impact, a key principle of the Heavenly Flame Mantra. But Tianyi was already gone, her movements impossibly quick. She twisted midair, her foot snapping out in a vicious kick that caught me square in the jaw.

The force launched me backward, and the world spun as I skidded to a stop near the edge of the courtyard. Stars danced in my vision as I groaned, rubbing my jaw.

"Too slow," Tianyi said, almost bored. With careful slits added to the back of her robe, courtesy of Lan-Yin, she was able to unfold her wings freely.

The butterfly-human hovered where she'd landed, her stance relaxed yet poised, as if ready to strike again at a moment's notice.

Laughter erupted from the sidelines. I turned my head, still dazed, to see Wang Jun and Lan-Yin sitting cross-legged nearby, clearly enjoying the show.

"You'll never land a hit at this rate!" Wang Jun called out, grinning. With his arms folded, the bruises from his last sparring match with Elder Ming were visible. "You need to keep her grounded, Kai. Try dragging her back down to our level."

Lan-Yin snorted, adjusting the linen wraps around her wrists. "Good luck with that. I've seen feathers fall faster than her."

I shot them both a glare, which only made them laugh harder. It wasn't unusual to see them here these days. Since the incident with Wei Long, they'd thrown themselves into training with a fervor that rivaled my own. Elder Ming's courtyard had become something of a hub, with Wang Jun hammering away at physical techniques while Lan-Yin honed her precision and footwork late into the night.

"I don't see either of you jumping in to help!" I shot back, dragging myself to my feet.

"Someone has to keep morale up!" Wang Jun retorted, gesturing grandly to himself and Lan-Yin. "Think of us as your cheering section."

"We'll jump in when you're done," Lan-Yin said. "You're not the only one who needs to be ready next time."

Her words struck a chord, and I felt a flicker of determination reignite. I squared my stance, raising my glowing palms again.

Tianyi's expression didn't change, but I caught the faintest tilt of her head, like she was curious about what I'd do next.

"All right," I muttered, mostly to myself. "Let's try this again."

Tianyi didn't wait. She blurred into motion, darting toward me like a shadow. But this time, I was ready. Or as ready as I could be. As she closed in, I focused not on her form but on her rhythm, the slight shifts in her movements that hinted at her next strike.

She lashed out with a sweeping kick aimed at my ribs, but this time I was prepared. I pivoted on my back foot, twisting just enough to avoid the full force of her strike. My open palm shot out instinctively, catching her ankle in midair. The faint red glow of the Heavenly Flame Mantra shimmered against her pale skin, and though the heat wasn't enough to burn, it was enough to make contact meaningful.

The moment I caught her, her momentum shifted. Tianyi, ever the opportunist, used the leverage of her caught leg to swing herself upward. Her other leg snapped around my shoulders, locking me into a straddle as her weight bore down.

I staggered slightly, trying to keep my balance, but she clung to me like a stubborn vine.

"It's warm," she said, her voice carrying a rare note of delight as she adjusted her position on my shoulders. Her arms wrapped around my head, pulling me into what felt more like a hug than a sparring maneuver. "I like it."

The courtyard fell silent for a beat, the only sound my labored breathing as I tried to process what had just happened.

Then Wang Jun's laughter shattered the quiet.

"Is that it? Is that the big finishing move?" he howled, clutching his sides. "Kai's ultimate technique: the warm hug!"

Lan-Yin doubled over, laughing so hard she nearly fell off her seat. "I don't think that's how sparring works!"

I scowled, shifting awkwardly in the position. She was extremely light, but it made moving difficult with her blocking my vision. "This still counts as a win, right?" I said, looking to Elder Ming for some form of validation.

The old man's lips twitched, though he masked it quickly. "Technically, she stopped attacking," he said, his tone deliberately neutral. "But I wouldn't call it a victory."

Tianyi, still perched on my shoulders, rested her chin on my head. "A win is a win," she said, completely unbothered. "This disciple has learned well."

I sighed. Perhaps she'd been reading too many of Liang Feng's novels.

The garden was quiet under the soft glow of moonlight, save for the rustling of leaves in the breeze and the occasional chirp of crickets. Tianyi stood just outside the greenhouse, her wings faintly twitching as her sharp eyes scanned the area. A faint hum of energy from the plants soothed the night's chill.

Windy coiled around her shoulders, his body a reassuring weight. His scales brushed against her neck as he shifted closer, his intent clear: warmth.

"Cold?" she murmured, her voice barely audible. Reaching up, she ran a hand over his smooth, shimmering form. He hissed softly in confirmation.

A sudden movement caught her attention. A bird was pecking at the glass of the greenhouse, its beak tapping insistently against the surface. Tianyi narrowed her eyes, irritation flickering to life. With a flick of her wrist, a sharp gust of wind spiraled out, scattering the creature. It squawked in alarm before taking off into the dark, its wings beating hurriedly.

"Stay away," she muttered, her gaze lingering on the spot where it had been.

She sighed, pulling her thoughts back from the distraction. But her attention wandered again as faint voices drifted from the shop, carried on the stillness of the night. She didn't intend to eavesdrop, but the clarity of the sound made it impossible not to hear.

"Are you leaving so soon, Tian Zhan?" Kai's voice, familiar and earnest, reached her ears.

Tianyi tilted her head slightly. Something about him lingered in her memory, though the details were vague. Leader? No, not quite. There was an air of authority about him, but it wasn't a title she understood. But she knew one thing.

The man was strong. Indescribably so.

"Yes," Tian Zhan replied, his voice calm and even. "There's much to do, and this partnership hinges on results. If your pills prove effective, the Whispering Wind Sect will provide the support you need. Until then, it's a matter of trust."

"I understand," Kai said. "I'll make sure they're the best I can produce."

"That," Tian Zhan said with a trace of approval, "is the attitude you should have. Focus your efforts there."

Another voice entered the conversation, one Tianyi recognized as Feng Wu. "I'll remain here for now. The Verdant Lotus Sect will need a full report, and I'll await their instructions. In the meantime, I'll oversee things here."

The conversation dissolved into the background of Tianyi's thoughts. Whatever arrangements the immortals were making, they didn't concern her directly. At least, not yet.

She trusted Kai would handle things well.

Turning away from the courtyard, she drifted closer to the greenhouse. The faint warmth radiating from within drew her, a stark contrast to the night's chill. The light, the energy, the hum of life . . . it all felt familiar, almost comforting. Windy adjusted his coil again, squeezing gently as if sensing her unease.

Stronger. The thought resonated within her, unspoken but insistent. She had to be stronger.

The sparring sessions with Kai were something, but they weren't enough. The memory of Wei Long's attack lingered in her mind, a vivid, visceral thing. She could still feel the pressure of his hands around her neck, the sharp edge of his intent to kill. The faint, hairline fractures on her skin were a reminder, fragile and stubborn.

She had survived, yes, but survival wasn't enough.

Tianyi perched on the wooden fence, her knees bent and heels raised, balanced effortlessly on the balls of her feet. Frost had begun to edge the wooden posts beneath her, sparkling faintly in the moonlight. Around her, the garden lay still, blanketed in the quiet of the season.

Windy stirred on her shoulders, coiling tighter for warmth. She could feel his scales against her neck, cool but reassuring, and absentmindedly ran her fingers along his back. Her breath left faint wisps of vapor in the air, vanishing almost as quickly as they formed. The stillness of the night was comforting, but her thoughts were restless.

The soft creak of wood broke the silence, and her gaze shifted toward the shop. Tian Zhan emerged, his steps steady and unhurried. The pale light of the lanterns cast long shadows across his form, highlighting the sharp lines of his face.

Her indifferent eyes met his as he passed. They held each other's gaze for a moment, hers calm and unblinking, his sharp and measuring. His own gaze was sharp, piercing even, like a bird of prey surveying its surroundings. Not like the small, bothersome birds that pecked at the greenhouse, but the kind she remembered from her time as a butterfly, hunters that stalked creatures far larger than herself.

Then, as suddenly as it began, the moment broke. Tian Zhan inclined his head slightly in acknowledgment and turned away, the faint crunch of frost beneath his boots the only sound as he moved to leave.

Something about his presence, however, tugged at her thoughts. Almost on instinct, she called out, her voice cutting through the stillness.

"What makes you so strong?" The question escaped her before she fully realized she'd spoken. Her voice cut cleanly through the stillness of the garden.

Tian Zhan paused midstep, clearly caught off guard. Slowly, he turned back, one brow raised, his expression a mixture of amusement and curiosity.

"You know," he began, his voice carrying an easy nonchalance, "I thought you didn't like me. You've been staring at me every time I've been here, and not once did you say a word. Honestly, I figured you were plotting something."

"I don't dislike you," Tianyi replied evenly. Her wings shifted slightly, catching the faint glow of moonlight. "You're . . . interesting."

Tian Zhan blinked, then chuckled, his breath fogging in the cold air. "Fair enough. All right, then. You want to know what makes me strong?"

She nodded, her gaze steady, but her wings stilled, as if mirroring her focus.

He crossed his arms, leaning back slightly as he mulled over her question. "It's individuality," he said at last. "The overwhelming belief in being my own person. If you spend your life chasing others, trying to mimic their paths, you'll never be more than a shadow of what they are. You'll never become more than that."

Tianyi tilted her head slightly, her fingers brushing Windy's coiled form as she considered his words. "Do you think I can do it too?"

Tian Zhan's surprise was evident for a moment before it gave way to a wide grin. "You? I'd say you don't have much of a choice. Look at yourself. There's no one else like you. Probably never will be. You're already one of a kind. That means your path has to be your own, whether you like it or not."

Tianyi's gaze lowered briefly, her fingers trailing over the faint marks on her neck. The memory of Wei Long's strangling grip lingered there, a reminder of her near defeat.

"Good luck, butterfly," Tian Zhan said with a casual wave as he turned away. "I'll be looking forward to seeing what you do with it."

His figure disappeared down the path, his silhouette swallowed by the growing shadows of the trees. Tianyi remained perched on the fence, her gaze lingering on the empty space where he had stood.

Above, the first flakes of snow drifted down, light and soft, blanketing the garden in pristine white. Snow soon covered the path before her in a smooth, unbroken sheet. It stretched endlessly into the night, pale and shimmering in the faint moonlight.

Her lips curved into the faintest smile as she murmured to herself, "Stronger." Then, with Windy still coiled around her neck, she skipped from the fence, her form blending into the quiet snowfall as she walked her path.

CHAPTER FORTY-FIVE

One Step Back, Two Steps Forward

Sweat dripped down my temple as I lunged forward, my palm alight with the faint red glow of the Heavenly Flame Mantra. The heat wasn't intense enough to burn, but it was enough to make the air shimmer faintly around my hand. I poured everything I had into the strike, aiming squarely for Feng Wu's chest.

And just like the first time we sparred, he sidestepped effortlessly.

Before I could recover, he pivoted and delivered a light tap to my back with his palm. A reminder that he could have ended the match there if he wanted to. I stumbled forward, catching myself before hitting the ground, and spun around to face him again. My frustration bubbled to the surface.

"You're kidding me," I muttered, breathing hard. "This is just like last time. Are you even trying?"

Feng Wu smiled, his posture relaxed as if this was all just a warm-up for him. "Oh, I'm trying, Kai. It's impressive you're even standing, let alone sparring, Kai. Few people could take the kind of beating you did from Wei Long and be back to training days later. It's all right to be a step behind."

His words stung, not because they were untrue, but because they were entirely accurate. I could feel it in every exchange. But it wasn't just that.

During our first spar, if it could really be called that—the gap between us had been insurmountable; his speed and finesse had made my every move feel clumsy and telegraphed. But now, even though my power, speed, and technique had undeniably improved, something else had changed.

Something I couldn't put my finger on.

I lunged again, this time feinting left before spinning into a sweeping strike with my glowing palm. Feng Wu leaned back effortlessly, evading the arc of my attack with a movement so smooth it was almost insulting. As I pressed forward, trying to follow up, I noticed it.

He wasn't reacting to me.

He's moving before I attack.

"That's not possible," I said. He wasn't clairvoyant.

I briefly wondered if it was the growing pains of learning a new martial art style. Initiating the offense, channeling my qi into my palms—it was difficult. Especially when Elder Ming forbade me from using my main techniques until I digested the Heavenly Flame Mantra. Even with my added options for offense, using a new martial art would have its drawbacks.

But to test this, I threw another punch, this time aiming low. He stepped aside again, his body already positioned to counter with a swift kick that stopped just short of my knee.

Frustration boiled over as I dropped to the ground, my back hitting the packed dirt with a soft thud. My chest heaved as I stared up at the cloudy sky, trying to swallow my irritation. "All right, I give. How? How are you doing this? You weren't this strong last time we fought, but somehow, you've gotten even stronger, faster than I did. Did you take a pill? Found enlightenment? Achieved mind-body unification?"

Feng Wu crouched beside me, his expression contemplative. "That would be nice, but no. I've just been working on something new,"

"Something new?"

He nodded. "You're not the only one who's been training hard, Kai. While you've been here in Gentle Wind Village, I've taken a break from missions to hone my Memory Palace."

I sat up, intrigued despite my irritation. "Memory Palace? What does that have to do with dodging my attacks like you're reading my mind?"

"It's not mind-reading," he corrected, crossing his arms. "But I've adapted the Memory Palace into something . . . more practical for combat. I completed a quest recently, which granted me a skill: Combat Anticipation Array."

"Combat . . . Anticipation Array?" I repeated, the name rolling awkwardly off my tongue.

He nodded again, his expression turning serious. "The skill uses the principles of the Memory Palace. By visualizing combat scenarios and storing them in my mind, I've built a library of movements and counterattacks. During a fight, my mind reflexively draws on that library to predict the most likely attack based on my opponent's stance, rhythm, and intent. It's not clairvoyance," he added quickly, seeing my skepticism. "It's just experience, applied faster than I could consciously process."

I stared at him, trying to wrap my head around the implications. "So, you're saying it's like . . . simulating the fight in your head while it's happening?"

"Exactly," Feng Wu said, his lips quirking into a faint smile. "It's not perfect, of course. It's limited by my knowledge and how much I've trained. But it's sped up my reaction time immensely. I've gotten ahead of Lan Sheng in our spars, and he can't figure it out. It's been frustrating him to no end."

The way he described it reminded me of my Refinement Simulation Technique, which allowed me to visualize alchemical processes in real time and adjust on the fly. The concept was different, but the core idea was the same: using mental visualization as a tool to anticipate and adapt.

And before this, I already took his advice, learning how to visualize opponents and using them to practice within the confines of my mind. But what he was describing was combining those two together.

"The Memory Palace . . ." I murmured, more to myself than to him. "It's not just a storage method. It's the foundation for so much more."

Feng Wu raised an eyebrow. "Figured that out, did you? The Memory Palace isn't the end goal. It's what you can do with it that matters. For me, it's Combat Anticipation. For you . . . Well, who knows? But I wouldn't be surprised if there are dozens of techniques that can stem from it."

My mind raced with possibilities. If Feng Wu could develop something like Combat Anticipation Array from the Memory Palace, what else could I create? Could I adapt the Refinement Simulation Technique into something that applied to combat? Or even further refine my alchemical processes with new insights?

The familiar hum of the Heavenly Interface echoed faintly in my mind, and a notification blinked in the corner of my vision.

Quest: Beyond the Memory Palace
—Successfully evade or counter ten different attacks by predicting
their trajectories using a simulated visual map in real time. (0/10)
—Land five precise hits on a moving opponent using openings
simulated beforehand. (0/5)
—Use the Refinement Simulation Technique on an alchemical
reaction mid-combat to create an advantage. (0/1)

A grin spread across my face as I stood, brushing the dirt off my robes. "Looks like I've got my next challenge."

Feng Wu's smirk mirrored my own. "Good. Because if you don't close this gap soon, Han Wei and Li Na will leave you in the dust. They're training just as hard as you are."

We made our way back to the shop, the chilly air cooling the sweat on my skin as we passed through the snow-laden clearing. My eyes drifted toward the distant hill where Tianyi and Windy were sparring—or at least, something resembling sparring. Windy coiled and darted like a striking whip, his white scales gleaming against the snowy backdrop, while Tianyi flitted with an almost playful air, her movements fluid and precise. A strange, mesmerizing dance unfolded between them, as if they were testing each other's limits without actual intent to harm.

I shook my head, a smirk tugging at my lips. Even my Spirit Beasts were training harder than I was. Perhaps I'd enlist their help to complete this quest.

Inside the shop, the warmth of the hearth greeted us, its gentle crackle a welcome contrast to the biting cold outside. I busied myself with the teapot, setting it on the counter as Feng Wu shrugged off his outer cloak and leaned casually against the wall.

Placing the finished leaves into the teapot, I poured the boiling water over them and brought the tea to the table. Feng Wu took a cup without hesitation, sipping thoughtfully as he sank into the chair across from me.

"So," I said, leaning back in my seat, "what's the word from the Verdant Lotus Sect?"

Feng Wu set his cup down, his expression shifting to something more serious. "They've agreed to the partnership. The sect will send resources and personnel to reinforce the village and set up accommodations for cultivators. It's a big step forward."

I smirked, already picturing the reactions when the sect members arrived. "They're going to be in for a surprise. Li Wei's been working on the expansion since yesterday. He's already laid out the foundation for it."

Feng Wu raised an eyebrow. "Li Wei? You mean the boy who made your greenhouse?"

"The master carpenter," I corrected, my tone exaggerated and mock haughty. "Kid's a genius. Second only to myself, of course."

Feng Wu chuckled. "Second only to you? I didn't realize carpentry was part of your skill set."

I waved him off. "That's not the point. The point is this village is full of talent. Take Wang Jun, for example. He's probably the second-best blacksmith our age in the province!"

"Second best? Out of how many?" Feng Wu was amused. "Let me guess: You know exactly two blacksmiths, and the other is better."

"Don't nitpick the details!" I shot back, though I couldn't stop the grin creeping across my face. I wondered how Tao Ren was doing. "The Verdant Lotus Sect is lucky to invest in Gentle Wind Village. We've got talent, ambition, and drive. They won't regret it."

Feng Wu lifted his cup in a mock toast. "Here's hoping you're right. But regardless, we won't let your village bear all the costs associated with expansion. The Azure Silk Trading Company has many connections. And I'll be helping to escort them here."

As he drained the last of his tea, setting the cup down with a satisfied sigh. He leaned back in his chair, his relaxed demeanor a stark contrast to the thoughts swirling in my mind.

As I watched him, something unspoken pressed against the back of my throat. It was easy to joke with Feng Wu, to trade jabs and talk about training like it was just another part of life. But the truth was I owed him more than I could ever repay.

"I just realized," I said, disrupting the companionable silence, "I haven't properly thanked you, one to one."

Feng Wu raised an eyebrow. "For what?"

I shifted in my seat, glancing at the teapot as if it could help me organize my thoughts. "For everything," I said at last. "Coming here when the village was in danger. Standing by my side when Wei Long attacked. Staying here, training with me, teaching me. I wouldn't have made it through any of this without you. Or if you hadn't recruited me for the Gauntlet."

He tilted his head, studying me like I was an odd puzzle he hadn't quite solved yet. "You don't owe me anything, Kai."

"I do," I insisted. "You've done so much for me, for this village. It's a debt I'll probably never be able to pay back in my lifetime."

Feng Wu stood slowly, slinging his cloak over one shoulder. His expression softened, a rare flicker of seriousness crossing his usually laid-back face. "Kai, if you spend your life trying to repay everyone who's ever helped you, you'll never have time to walk your own path."

I blinked, surprised.

"It's not about paying it back," he continued, pulling the cloak around his shoulders. "It's about paying it forward. Take what you've gained and use it to help someone else. Build something that lasts. That's how you honor the people who've stood by you."

For a moment, his words hung in the air, settling over me like the gentle warmth of the shop's hearth. I opened my mouth to respond, but nothing came out. Instead, I just nodded.

"Pay it forward," I commented. I chuckled despite myself, standing to follow him to the door. The cold air nipped at my skin as he stepped out into the snow-covered clearing, his figure sharp against the white landscape. He glanced back, his face softening into something almost contemplative.

"You've got good people here, Kai. Don't forget to lean on them when you need to. And don't let me hear you're slacking off."

"I won't," I said, one corner of my mouth quirking upward. "And, Feng Wu?"

"Yeah?"

"Have a safe trip."

He smiled and raised a hand in farewell, his steps crunching through the snow as he walked away. I watched him disappear into the horizon, his figure fading into the quiet expanse of white.

I felt the cold bite into my skin as the snow fell softly around me, and I stood there for a moment.

As I entered the garden, the sun's warmth softened the morning chill, filtering through the clouds. Before me stood the greenhouse, its structure finally restored to its former glory. Inside, the plants were thriving once more, their vibrant energy filling the air with a subtle hum of life.

And just near the edge of the garden, a tiny golden shoot poked through the soil—a bamboo sprout, its delicate form almost imperceptible but unmistakably there.

I smiled, letting out a breath I hadn't realized I'd been holding. Progress. Small but real.

Off in the distance, Tianyi and Windy's sparring continued, their figures darting and weaving in the snow-covered hills. Everyone was growing stronger. Recovering. Moving forward.

"Kai?" Lan-Yin's voice broke through my thoughts, pulling my attention back to the house. She stood in the doorway, her expression faintly troubled. "I . . . I think something's wrong."

"What is it? What's wrong?"

She waved me off, brushing a hand through her hair. "It's nothing serious. I've just been feeling . . . nauseous. A little dizzy. It's probably nothing. But it's getting hard to ignore."

Still, I ushered her inside, sitting her down at the table and brewing a fresh pot of tea. As she listed her symptoms, I couldn't help but fall into diagnostic mode, mentally running through the possibilities.

Dizziness. Fatigue. Nausea.

"All right," I said, pulling a chair up to her. "Let's break this down. When did it start?"

She furrowed her brow, resting her chin on her hand. "A few days ago, maybe? I thought little of it at first. Just figured I was tired."

"And the nausea?" I pressed, leaning forward slightly. "Does it come and go, or is it constant?"

"It's not constant," she replied. "Mostly in the mornings. Sometimes it fades by midday, but other times it sticks around. It's annoying, but not unbearable."

Morning nausea. I filed that away. "Any other symptoms? Dizziness, you said. What about appetite? Any changes?"

Lan-Yin shrugged, looking faintly embarrassed. "I've been hungrier than usual, but I thought it was just from training harder. Wang Jun keeps saying I need to eat more anyway, so I didn't think it was strange."

I nodded, suppressing a small smile at the mention of Wang Jun. "What about fatigue? Do you feel more tired than usual?"

She tilted her head, considering. "I guess? But again, I thought that was just training. Elder Ming has been working me harder lately, and I've been pushing myself to catch up."

Fatigue. Hunger. Dizziness. Nausea. My mind sifted through possibilities, but something about her symptoms pulled at a distant memory. When was it? It was years ago, when Xiao Bao's mom had . . .

"Lan-Yin," I began cautiously, setting the pot down with deliberate care. "Have you noticed any other changes lately? Anything different in the past few months?"

She looked at me, her brow furrowing as she tried to make sense of the question. "What kind of changes?" she asked.

I rubbed the back of my neck, choosing my words carefully. "You mentioned feeling hungrier and more tired, but . . . have you had any other symptoms? Anything unusual?"

Lan-Yin's eyes narrowed, her tone sharpening. "Kai, if you have something to say, just say it."

I hesitated, my thoughts spinning. Could I really say it out loud? What if I was wrong? But the more I considered her symptoms, the clearer the answer became.

My voice dropped to a murmur, almost as if I were speaking to myself. "This reminds me of Xiao Bao's mom . . . when she was—" I stopped myself short, glancing at her uncertainly.

Her eyes widened, her expression shifting rapidly from confusion to realization, then disbelief. "Kai Liu," she said, her voice dangerously calm. "What. Are. You. Suggesting?"

I swallowed hard, my hands raised defensively. "I—I'm not saying anything for sure, it's just . . . your symptoms—they're common for . . . pregnancy."

Her jaw dropped, and for a moment, she just stared at me, utterly speechless. Then her voice shot up an octave. "You think I'm *what*?!"

The teapot rattled slightly on the table as I winced. "It's just a theory!" I said quickly, trying to backpedal. "I mean, I could be wrong, but—"

I started to respond but stopped, realizing this was a no-win situation. Meanwhile, she buried her face in her hands, letting out a muffled sound of disbelief.

The silence that followed was thick and awkward. I sat frozen, my mind running through the consequences of this revelation. And one thought loomed above the rest.

How am I going to tell Wang Jun?

CHAPTER FORTY-SIX

Calm Waters, Hidden Dragons

The chamber was dimly lit, the flickering light of a solitary candle casting elongated shadows along the rough stone walls. Elder Cheng moved silently to the first corner, his fingers deftly placing a talisman etched with complex symbols. The parchment fluttered briefly before adhering to the wall as if drawn by an unseen force.

"No chances," Elder Wei muttered. "Not with ears everywhere."

The other two elders mirrored the action in the remaining corners, each positioning their talismans with practiced precision. A subtle hum resonated through the room as the enchantments activated, sealing their conversation from any prying senses.

Elder Fang adjusted his robes, the fabric rustling softly, the sound precise and deliberate. "The barriers are secure," he confirmed, his eyes sweeping the room. He lingered briefly on each talisman, as if testing their strength with his gaze alone. "For now."

Elder Cheng took his seat at the low table in the center, the others following suit. He sighed heavily, the lines on his face deepening. "The barriers may hold, but our plans do not."

"Our search remains fruitless," Cheng continued, his voice a low rasp carrying years of tempered authority.

Elder Fang leaned forward, his eyes narrowing. "We're too close to losing momentum," he said. "Each day, the forces around us grow bolder. The western forests already reek of corruption. A Bloodsoul Bloom . . . Their arrogance knows no bounds."

Elder Xun scoffed, settling heavily into his seat, his thick arms crossed over a broad chest. His skin bore the faint, crisscrossed scars of someone well acquainted with physical conflict, and his gaze carried a perpetual challenge, dismissive and piercing. He barked out a laugh, his scarred face twisting with disdain. "Demonic cultivators? Overgrown brats playing at power. A single fist would remind them why their kind rarely survives past infancy. If they want to reveal themselves, let them. I'll crush them myself."

"Perhaps," Elder Cheng mused, stroking his beard thoughtfully. "But even a cornered rat can bite. It's best we avoid unnecessary entanglements. We can't afford distractions."

Xun smirked, leaning back with a dismissive wave of his hand. "Let them bite. We'll crush their jaws while they try."

Elder Wei leaned forward, resting his forearms on the table as his sharp eyes flicked between his peers. "Grandstanding won't fix our problems. The Phoenix Tears remain inert without balance. We wouldn't even be in this wasteland if we'd secured the Lunar Essence Yin Lotus before our departure."

Elder Fang's lips pressed into a thin line, his tone measured but cold. "And if we had stayed longer, we'd be corpses. The Azure Sky Sect was already circling. We were lucky to escape with our lives."

A heavy silence settled in the room, broken only by the faint crackle of the candle. Each elder sat with their thoughts, the weight of past failure casting a shadow over the dimly lit space.

Elder Xun clenched his fists, his knuckles whitening. "So here we are," he growled. "Scrambling for Beast Cores like beggars."

The other elders turned their attention to the basket of Beast Cores provided by the Silent Moon. The glimmering pile, rich with latent power, should have been a treasure beyond measure. But to them, it was a reminder of their dependency, a crude patchwork solution to a greater problem.

Wei sneered, his tone dripping with disdain. "This region is a wasteland of mediocrity. What they call treasures wouldn't earn a second glance in the mainland. The ambient qi is weak, and resources are scarce. Our qi stagnates, and without proper cultivation, our progress halts."

Elder Fang shot him a sharp look. "You would waste the Phoenix Tears, then? They are for resurrection, for rebuilding from ruin—not for avoiding discomfort. Use it too soon, and what would we have risked our lives for to steal them?"

"Patience isn't merely a virtue; it's survival," Cheng said sharply, commanding attention. "Recklessness invites ruin. Have we forgotten Li Peng's end so quickly? His haste cost him more than his cultivation. It shattered our momentum. We cannot afford another failure like his."

The mention of their fallen comrade lingered, the room momentarily still.

"He thought consuming a fraction would bolster his strength," he recalled bitterly. "Instead, the unbridled yang qi tore him apart from within. And he was the most well-versed to handle yang qi among us, with his Nine Sun Flame technique."

Elder Fang's eyes narrowed. "A harsh lesson. The Phoenix Tears are potent beyond measure. Without an equally powerful yin component, they are uncontrollable."

Elder Xun sighed heavily. "We keep gnashing our teeth over what we don't have. It's pathetic. This province may be a wasteland, but no land is truly barren. Somewhere, there's a herb, a beast, a technique that can tip the scales. Weak qi or not, we'll tear this place apart to find it."

Elder Cheng shifted to commanding again. "The Silent Moon Sect has proven useful. Their offerings keep us afloat, and their sect leader, Jun, is pliable. So long as he believes we are his greatest benefactors, their resources are ours."

"But dependency is not a strategy. Control is. And control requires more than strength. We'll hollow them out, and by the time they realize their mistake, the Silent Moon Sect will belong to us in all but name." Wei said.

Elder Fang raised an eyebrow. "Jun is ambitious. Ambition breeds betrayal."

"Then let him betray us. We'll break him when the time comes."

Elder Fang drummed his fingers lightly on the table, his expression contemplative. "It's a waiting game, then. We lie low, strengthen ourselves as best we can, and continue the search for the yin component we need."

Elder Xun leaned forward, his scarred hands flattening against the table, his voice cutting through Fang's calm suggestion. "Waiting? That's your grand plan? We're already at the mercy of the Silent Moon's scraps. If their sect leader stops playing nice, where does that leave us?"

His eyes flicked toward the basket of Beast Cores as though the sight disgusted him. "They call this generosity. I call it leverage. Dependency makes my skin crawl."

Elder Cheng raised a hand. "And what would you propose, Xun? Charging blindly into the wilderness in search of a solution? Picking fights with demonic cultivators until one of them coughs up a miracle herb? Patience isn't complacency—it's strategy."

The burly man's jaw tightened, but he leaned back with a begrudging grunt. "Strategy or not, this place is a wasteland. We'd better find something worthwhile soon, or we might as well pack up and leave."

Elder Wei's lips curved into a thin smile, his words calculated and precise. "Leave? And miss the opportunity to turn this backwater into the foundation of our resurgence? No, Xun. The Silent Moon Sect may think they've gained powerful allies, but they've made a mistake." He steepled his fingers, his eyes glinting with cold satisfaction. "With Jun as our puppet, we won't just use their resources—we'll hollow them out from within."

Elder Fang resumed. "Still, we cannot rely on the Silent Moon alone. If we were to orchestrate attacks on other sects, perhaps uncover the treasures they hoard, we might find the component we need. This province cannot be entirely destitute.”

“Other sects? You mean the Whispering Wind Sect, don’t you? They’re supposedly the strongest in this region.” Xun leaned forward, a dangerous glint in his eyes. “I’d love to see their so-called elders stand against us. If their strength is anything like their disciples, it won’t take much more than two of us to knock them down.”

Wei chuckled darkly, his tone dripping with scorn. “Strength is relative, after all. Here, our skills are enough to send tremors through their foundations. They’ll never see us coming.”

The others laughed softly, their confidence palpable, each of them reveling in their perceived superiority.

Here, they were giants among insects.

Elder Fang raised an eyebrow. “An intriguing proposition, but such actions could unite the sects against us. We’d need a proper justification to avoid inciting an all-out war.”

“Agreed,” Cheng said, steepling his fingers. “One false move, and we’ll find ourselves hunted across this province like cornered rats. Fabrication isn’t enough; it must be flawless, irrefutable. If we falter, we’ll have united the sects against us for nothing.”

A slow smile spread across Elder Wei’s face. “A clever strategy. We eliminate potential threats, acquire valuable resources, and solidify our control.”

Xun let his fingers trace the surface of the jade-inlaid table, his disdain barely concealed. “Look at this,” he said, gesturing to the lavish furnishings around them. “Gold-plated walls, carved beams, incense burning like they’re kings. No wonder this sect needed us. They’re so busy polishing their treasures, they’ve forgotten how to sharpen their blades.”

Fang nodded, his tone colder now. “And that forgetfulness is exactly what makes them useful. But don’t underestimate them. Ambition makes even dull blades dangerous when desperation sharpens them.”

Cheng waved a hand dismissively. “Jun and his ilk will never have the strength or vision to challenge us. Without us, they’ll remain minor players in this province. Let them think they’re in control.”

A murmur of satisfaction swept through the chamber, their expressions smug and at ease, every word thick with confidence bred from long years of survival and conquest. To them, these locals were little more than pawns in a much larger game, and the elders played it masterfully.

“Let them scramble,” Elder Xun said, smirking. “We have nothing to fear in this backwater.”

The elders shared a final glance, their smirks and knowing looks confirming an unspoken truth: They were untouchable.

As they plotted, their influence seeped outward, unnoticed by most. But not all eyes were blind to their ambition.

In a forgotten corner of the province, another force stirred, aware of the Silent Moon's growing shadow.

The man moved with measured precision, his polished boots clicking softly against the uneven cobblestones of Old Pine District. His back was straight, his chin raised just enough to suggest authority without arrogance, but the faint sheen of sweat on his temple betrayed the weight of the task ahead. Only the rustling leaves in the occasional breeze disturbed the deserted street's quiet.

This area of Crescent Bay City had a stillness that didn't belong to its bustling heart. Old Pine was a refuge for retirees, for the forgotten or for those content to let the world pass them by. He passed modest homes with neatly swept porches and weathered shutters, their gardens wild with overgrown herbs and flowers.

At the end of the lane stood his destination: a small unassuming building, its wooden facade worn by years of salty air and neglect. The paint peeled at the edges, exposing the graying wood beneath. Above the door hung a swaying signboard.

The Wandering Wind Press.

The door creaked open, and the esteemed man stepped inside, cutting through the silence. A bookkeeper's head turned, a smile spreading across his weathered face.

The musty scent of ancient pages filled the bookstore, curling around the shelves and winding up to the dusty beams above. At the counter, the old man, hunched and quiet, traced a finger over an open ledger, his eyes closed, yet aware.

"Welcome," he greeted warmly. "How can I assist you?"

The figure paused, glancing over the dim shelves, before stepping forward. "I'm not here for books," he said. "I come on behalf of the magistrate with a request."

Request. The word held an unusual weight, a marked humility. In this province, the magistrate was second only to the sects, his power vast and unquestioned. He was not known for making requests. Orders, yes. Demands, perhaps. But a request was rare, a gesture that suggested both respect and necessity.

The old man, still hunched over the ledger, lifted his head ever so slightly, the faintest flicker of amusement in the lines of his expression. He gave a nod as though to himself, his smile faint but perceptive.

"Request, is it?" he asked. "The magistrate is indeed a courteous man."

The man's throat tightened inexplicably, his mouth going dry as he continued, "It . . . it's a matter of great importance. I wouldn't be here otherwise." He swallowed, his pulse a dull thud in his ears. "The magistrate . . . asks for your assistance. Regarding the Silent Moon Sect."

For a moment, the air in the room seemed to thicken, the sounds from the busy streets outside fading into silence. Though the old bookkeeper did nothing overt, it was as if the very atmosphere had shifted, pulled taut with a quiet, undeniable gravity.

The messenger, struggling to continue, felt his chest constrict, and his words tangled. "The . . . the sect has grown increasingly active, and the magistrate . . . he believes your expertise might . . ."

The bookkeeper's eyes, clouded yet seeming to perceive something beyond sight, opened slowly. A flicker of something ancient, vast, and hidden sparked within them. The faint tremor of a breeze stirred the dust motes in the air, and for an instant, it was as though the world itself held its breath.

"So." The old man's voice was soft, each word precise and deliberate, laced with a gentle edge of amusement. "He seeks my counsel. What does he fear, exactly? That the Silent Moon's ambitions have grown too . . . bold?"

The man nodded, feeling as though some invisible weight pressed upon him. "Yes. They've amassed influence, seemingly unchecked, and the magistrate fears they'll soon reach beyond their bounds. We suspect the elders they recruited originate from the mainland."

The old man nodded thoughtfully, his fingers resuming their quiet, rhythmic tracing over the spine of the ledger. "Very well," he said, as if to himself. "A request from the magistrate is no small thing. Tell the magistrate I shall consider it. But also remind him that I am no tool to be summoned when convenient."

The air lightened then, and the messenger's breath returned to him. He nodded, almost too eagerly, feeling as though he'd been dismissed from an unseen trial.

"Thank you," he managed, bowing slightly. "I will convey your words."

With a final nod, the messenger turned, eager to escape the oppressive stillness of the bookstore.

As the door creaked shut, the old man sat back, his fingers still tracing the edge of the ledger. The faint hum of the room's silence returned, broken only by the soft flutter of a page turning, though no hand touched it. The single candle on the counter flickered, the flame twisting unnaturally, as though caught in an unseen wind.

His lips quirked into a faint smile. "From the mainland, you say?" he said, voice barely audible, though no one remained to hear. The flame steadied, its light pooling in his clouded eyes, reflecting something vast and tempestuous within. "Interesting. I wonder . . . who's truly bold here?"

The faintest stir of wind brushed through the bookstore, despite the windows and door being tightly shut. Then, as quickly as it had come, the air stilled, leaving silence in its wake.

Acknowledgments

The third volume marks yet another milestone on this journey, and truthfully, this one felt like a trial straight out of a xianxia story. Life came at me like Ping Hai vs Kai this time around, juggling new projects, career pursuits, academic demands, and social obligations.

And even when I knew my back was pressed against the wall, I'd find a way to sneak off and procrastinate (i.e., rereading the entirety of *Hunter × Hunter*, getting addicted to crappy mobile games, watching my favorite basketball team, etc.).

Did I mention I run a social media account completely unrelated to writing? And I post every day there as well?

In other words, I got the hell beaten out of me the entirety of writing this book. It was a balancing act, but somehow, through all the chaos, we made it.

This volume took longer than it should have, but every delay came with its own lessons, and I can only hope those lessons seep into the story you're now reading. Writing this series has never been easy, but the support I've received has been nothing short of inspiring.

To my wonderful girlfriend, Amanda, who didn't let me lose focus, even when life tried its best to scatter my attention. Thank you for being there during late-night brainstorms and for your unending patience.

To my family, for continuing to cheer me on and reminding me that I have a home base no matter where life takes me.

To my friends and my community on RoyalRoad and Patreon; you've been my rock, my critics, and my greatest source of motivation. Every comment, critique, and shared laugh keeps the fire burning.

Last, to all the dreamers trying to balance the chaos of life while chasing their passions: This one's for you. May you find your own path, no matter how thorny or twisted it may seem.

Here's to volume three, and here's to keeping the balance.

About the Author

Carlos Calma is a Canadian author who has been captivated by LitRPG and progression fantasy since he was young. He began reading these genres as a child and started writing his own stories while in high school. This passion has continued into his adult life. Calma resides in Toronto, Ontario.

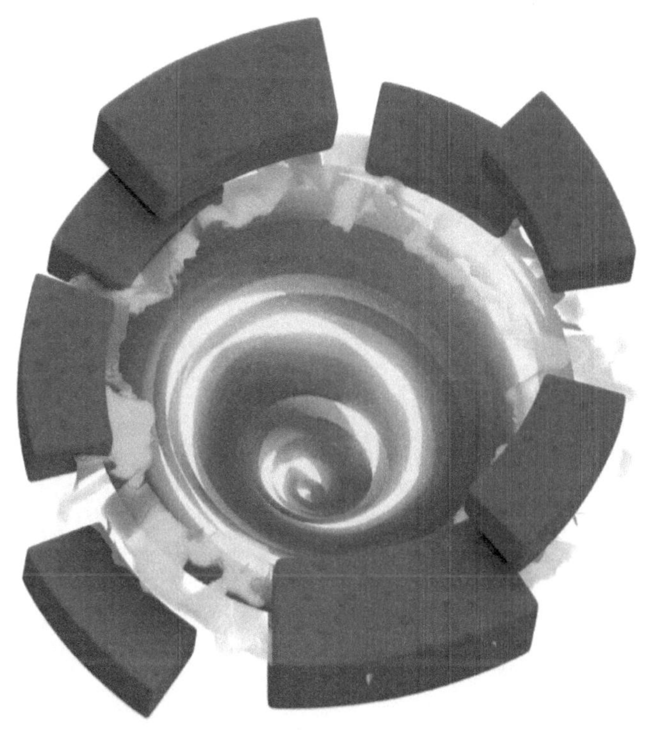

RESPAWN YOUR CURIOSITY

follow us on our socials

podiumentertainment.com

@podiumentertainment

/podiumentertainment

@podium_ent

@podiumentertainment